RESTLESS SEASONS

RESTLESS SEASONS

David Matson Hooper

iUniverse, Inc.
Bloomington

Restless Seasons

iUniverse books may be ordered through booksellers or by contacting:

iUniverse
1663 Liberty Drive
Bloomington, IN 47403
www.iuniverse.com
1-800-Authors (1-800-288-4677)

ISBN: 978-1-4759-8447-7 (sc)
ISBN: 978-1-4759-8448-4 (ebk)

Library of Congress Control Number: 2013906355

Printed in the United States of America

iUniverse rev. date: 04/17/2013

Cover Art: Robert Schmid. Back photo: Karen Atha.

AUTHOR ACKNOWLEDGEMENTS

The author would like to thank the following people involved in this project:

Steve Brooks for editorial assistance, and Mike Mullin and Jans Frankena for research assistance.

This book is dedicated to Janneke (The Muse), and to Rodney Bryce Jonk (1946-2012).

CHAPTER ONE

Between Two Worlds

"Ladies and gentlemen . . . please return to your seats and fasten your seatbelts!"

The high-pitched woman's voice crackled over the public address speakers, rising in intensity, while the overhead lights at the end of the narrow corridor flashed—FASTEN SEAT BELTS, in lurid red, and my stomach tightened reflexively.

"We are experiencing some turbulence . . .," The agitated voice was cut off in mid-sentence as the aircraft suddenly lurched, rocked, and buffeted somewhere over the North Atlantic, storm-surrounded blackness punctuated with lightning flashes.

My hands gripped the armrests of the jetliner seat as if they were the only things holding me aloft six miles above the Earth's surface and safety. I felt fear raise the hackles on my neck as I contemplated that only the thin metal skin of this heavier-than-air machine kept me protected from the storm and a plunge to certain violent death.

I had been plagued all day with an unsettling feeling, almost a premonition of impending disaster, and now those feelings were being amplified like the voice over the PA. Oh, how I wished I were still on the ground in Amsterdam, preferably in the warmth and safety of Monika's arms. How long ago was that? I was afraid to open my eyes to look at my watch. However, the morning's events came back to me in clarity of detail.

The day had started off all wrong, as if the fates were conspiring against my leaving.The alarm had failed to go off on the wind-up clock in Paddy and Annie's cramped flat above the Haarlemmerstraat.

I awoke on the hard floor, and crawled out of my sleeping bag, glanced at the clock, and realizing that I was already behind schedule, I quickly dressed, rolled up my sleeping bag, strapped my back pack over my shoulders, and said goodbye to my friends and former bandmates, one American and one Irishman. I rushed down the steep winding stairs, into the narrow street in Amsterdam's Jordaan district, and hurried by foot and by tram to the Central Station, from where my train was about to depart. I looked around for Monika, whom I'd planned to meet an hour earlier for coffee, and there she was on the platform, waving, her lithe figure hurrying toward me, her long blond hair brushing across her shoulders.

"Steve," she said with her cute feminine Dutch accent, "I thought you would miss your train."

"I almost did," I said. "I just have enough time to get a ticket and get onboard."

"I brought you some breakfast," she said, handing me a bag that contained coffee and a pastry. "Maybe you should have stayed with me last night," she continued, "then you wouldn't be running late."

"Maybe so," I replied. But I hadn't wanted to reopen old wounds.

"I have to go."

"I know," she said sadly.

"It's been great seeing you again," I said. "I'll miss you, and I'll miss Amsterdam."

"I'll see you in America," she said hopefully.

"Goodbye," I said, and hugged her.

"*Tot ziens*," she smiled, and gave me a final, tender kiss.

And then I was off to get a ticket, hurrying onto the train. I took a seat by the window, facing the platform, and waved to her. She waved back. The train gave a shudder, lurched forward, and rolled down the track and out of the city and into the flat, green countryside of late summer, 1974. I watched the tiny farms and distant windmills roll by, and felt a quiet sadness as the train left Holland and clicked and clacked across Belgium.

Disembarking in Brussels, and knowing I was on a tight schedule to catch a flight back to the States, I asked around for transportation to the airport, and was directed to a bus about to leave the station. I paid my fare and climbed aboard, lugging the backpack, and settled back impatiently for the twenty-kilometer ride. Arriving at Brussels South Airport, close to departure time, I searched around in vain for my airline. At an information booth, I found to my sudden horror that I was at the wrong airport. No one had told me there were two airports, and now I panicked.

I hailed a taxi and told the driver to take me to Brussels International, and to step on it. The cab seemed to move at a snail's pace as I glanced constantly at my watch, knowing I couldn't slow the sweep of the second hand, but praying for a miracle. When we finally pulled up to the correct airline in the correct airport, I was certain that I had missed the flight. According to the departure time printed on the one-way ticket in my shirt pocket, the plane was already in the air, without me.

But my prayer for a miracle had been answered. The chartered airliner, which flew between New York and Brussels, had been delayed, and was at this moment still somewhere over the Atlantic. And I was about to spend eight long hours cooling my heels in a Belgian airport. Except that I didn't cool my heels. I sat for for a while, drinking coffee and figeting impatiently.Then I paced and I fretted, and tried to read the *Herald American*, but tossed it away when I spotted an article about an airplane crash.

When I finally boarded the aircraft, I noticed the crew seemed exhausted, especially the pilot, whose shirt was wrinkled, his face strained, and his eyes a bleary red. Knowing we weren't going to get a fresh crew made me feel uneasy.

And then we were flying out over the Atlantic Ocean. I'd had had plenty of time while hanging out at the airport, to reflect upon my years of vagabonding around Europe, and on the group I'd been with, "Uncle Zeke's Band." I thought about Paddy and Annie, and about Star, and "Uncle Zeke" himself—Victor Power. Vic had been the reason I'd gone to Europe in the first place, the guy who'd lured me into the music business years ago. He had been my friend, role model, and mentor. In fact, he'd seemed more like a brother than a friend. We had hit the highs and the lows of life on the road together, and for a while it had cemented the bond between us. But there is a certain fragility to relationships, and if they aren't tended to with love and respect, and a certain amount of patience, they run their course and die, like everything else in life.

Now I was returning to California, land of my birth, to bid goodbye to my familial brother Mark, who had recently committed suicide. And although Vic and I had parted ways more than a year ago, it seemed he'd always be a part of my life, for he had shaped the person I had become, for better or worse.

California, Europe, and the band seemed a lifetime away, as I sat suspended between the past and the future, Europe and America, miles above the Earth's surface in a fragile flying machine currently at the mercy of wind and storm, with the laws of gravity defied only by powerful jet engines I prayed wouldn't fail.

The plane lurched again—bucking, rolling, dropping through the blackness and back up again like a rollercoaster. I hung on tight with closed eyes for what seemed to be eternity, as the thought of eternity becoming our next destination crossed my mind.

As it turned out, however, our next destination was a refueling stop in Newfoundland. We dropped down through the clouds, buffeted by turbulence, and got under the worst of the weather. The pilot announced our approach, and I tensed as the wheels came down and locked into place. We made a hard landing, bounced, braked noisily and rolled slowly up to a terminal. The passengers disembarked during the refueling, and I ducked inside a restroom, where I seriously contemplated hiding out till after the plane had once again become airborne. Then I would find another way to New York. But after splashing water on my face, and staring at the frightened eyes in the mirror for a long moment, I decided that I was over-reacting. I gathered my courage and reboarded.

My decision was met by approval of sorts, when the storm abated once we became airborne again. The winds and the buffeting dissipated, the rain became lighter, and I relaxed by degrees. At some point I quit gripping the armrests, the muscles in my body untensed, and I sank back into the seat.

With eyes closed, I began to take in the sounds of the passenger cabin, the sighs and breathings of sleep and gentle snoring. And then another sound crept into my consciousness—that of jet engines outside on the wing. As I drifted off to a fitful sleep, the sound seemed to change and morph into another sound, one of long ago. It became the sound of surf on a Southern California beach.

CHAPTER TWO

California Dreaming

"Surf City here we come . . ."

The sets of waves rolled in, one after another, in an unbroken pattern, and washed up in foam on the sun-kissed white gold Southern California sand. A salty mist blew off the tops of waves, carried by the offshore breeze, and hung like a protective blanket between the bright overhead sun and the bronze beach blanket bodies laying along the shore. Flimsy scattered clouds sailed along overhead while long board surfers lined up outside the breakers, each awaiting his turn to catch a wave.

I stood in the parking lot that overlooked the beach next to the Huntington pier, surveying the scene, while a nearby transistor radio blared out a familiar song—Jan and Dean's "Surf City". It was the number one hit on KFWB's Top 40 survey on this Saturday in July of 1963, and everyone said that Surf City was in fact Huntington Beach. So there I was, smack dab in the vortex of the surfing capital of the world during the Summer of Surf, dressed not in baggies and huarache sandals, but in street clothes which showed that I was not a surfer, but in fact a "hodad". A sudden shout in my direction wrenched my attention away from a curvaceous young surf bunny strolling along the sidewalk toward the pier.

"Hey, Dupree—get your ass over here and give me a hand with this equipment!"

"Okay, Vic", I said to our bandleader, who was standing next to drummer John Logan's beat up station wagon.

There was a reason Vic was the guy in charge, for even though only average in height and stature, he had a certain charisma about him that commanded attention. His facial features were as if chiseled; sharp, with no rounded edges. He had a Roman nose, and his jaw was rough cut. He had a prominent forehead, sharp cheekbones, and his firm straight mouth was usually set in seriousness. There seemed to be nothing soft about Vic Power, save his brown puppy dog eyes. But even they burned in intensity when passion or anger flared. Nor was there anything subtle about his movements. He strutted rather than walked, his head jerked rather than swiveled, and his hands stiffly punctuated a point he was making, or an argument he was pushing.

I found out early on that it was best not to argue with Vic, because he was usually right, even when he wasn't. So when he commanded, I hurried to his side and helped to lift the Fender Twin Reverb amplifier out of the back of the wagon and set it on the ground. Vic had named the band after his amp. "Hey," he'd said at the time, "if Eddie and the Showmen can name themselves after the Showman amp, I can name my band after the Twin Reverb."

Vic handed me his Fender Stratocaster guitar, in its tweed rectangular case, and a microphone stand. "Get all the equipment together while I go find a place to set up."

"Got a place in mind?" I asked.

"Yeah, that snack bar," he said, pointing toward a nearby shack at the edge of the beach. "Those places always have power. Watch this stuff for me, I'll be right back." Then he swaggered off to give the Power sales pitch to the snack bar manager. I hauled out my pawnshop bass guitar and amp, placed them next to Vic's gear, and gave John a hand with the drums.

At eighteen, John Logan was a year older than Vic and I, out of high school now, and had a regular full time job to support himself with. He was wiry but muscular, smiled easily, had a hawk-like nose and hawk eyes. And like a hawk, he seemed to be always on the edge, ready to swoop. So pounding on the drums came easily to him, a way to dissipate some of his pent-up energy. He liked to roll his pack of Marlboros up in his tee shirt sleeve. He tapped one out and stuck it between his lips, then snapped open a silver Zippo lighter, struck it, and cupped his hand against the breeze as he lit up and took a drag. He fished sunglasses out of his tee shirt pocket, snapped them on, and took a long look around.

"Leave it to Vic to not have this deal set up in advance," he said. Then he added with a slight grin, cigarette dangling from his mouth, "Wanna bet they tell him no?"

"You're on," I said. "Don't underestimate the Power power of persuasion."

"Yeah," John agreed with a laugh, "no lie. I think he's missed his true calling in life. The boy's a born salesman."

From the far end of the parking lot came the rest of the band, making their way toward us: Scott, alto sax case in hand, and Patrick O'Brien, guitar in one hand and amplifier in the other. Stocky, blond haired, sad eyed Patrick (or Paddy, as we all called him) was Irish and had come to surf music by way of country-western and Irish folk songs. He'd taught himself guitar, and played exclusively in G tuning. His chunka-chunka style of rhythm guitar playing was so unique to us we called it the "Paddy rhythm." Paddy worked in a bakery and lived with his sister and her husband. He was so poor he couldn't afford a case for his beat-up cheapo guitar.

Trailing him was our own answer to Bobby Vinton—our erstwhile singer, Jackie Dallas. Jackie was skinny, curly-haired, and not much of a stage presence. We all agreed that he wasn't much of a singer either, so we only used him on a handful of songs. But Jackie had other attributes that Vic found indispensable. He had a car, a recording studio, and at twenty-one was old enough to buy us beer. So Vic let him have pretensions of being a singer.

"On your knees, Dupree, or I'll give yez a bash wit me shillelagh." Paddy held his guitar aloft like a club, but his face wore a wide grin that betrayed crooked teeth. He was the only one of us who had a crew cut. Having immigrated to the States a few short years ago, he was clueless as to current teenage styles.

"Aw, leave Steve alone," said black haired, brown-eyed Scott, who was the same age as me. "We need him to lure away all the fat and ugly chicks." John and Paddy laughed, but I didn't see the humor. I may have been shy, and no ladies' man, but I didn't consider myself bad looking. I was at least above average. I looked a little bit like Vic, though without the sharp features. My hair was dark (his was lighter, with a reddish tint), and it was thick and wavy. But in emulation, I wore it in a jellyroll like Vic, and kept it in place with a liberal amount of Brylcreem. My eyes were blue, and they didn't have the intensity of Vic's. Girls usually referred to me as "cute", but they called Vic "mysterious." Their parents thought of Vic as dangerous.

Momentarily, while we were clowning around, up strode Vic, smiling like the cat that had gotten the cream.

"Okay, guys," he said, "it's all set. Get your gear and follow me."

I turned to John and said, "You lose, pal."

We all followed Vic out of the lot onto an asphalt access road that ran the length of the beach, and over to the snack bar, which sold hot dogs, hamburgers, french-fries, soft drinks, and all other manner of summer snacks. We plugged our amps into extension cords and ran them to an outside outlet. Jackie helped John set up his drums on the access road just behind the snack bar, while the rest of us set up on the sand, facing the Pacific Ocean. Vic ran the microphone through one of the two channels on his amp, making it a poor man's PA. Within minutes we were up and running. Vic tested the mike, and after it made a screeching feedback sound, turned down the volume knob. Now we were ready to go. He faced the crowd and made an announcement.

"Hey, everybody, I'm Vic Power and we're The Reverbs. We're playing at The Pier tonight, opening for the Lively Ones. Come on down. In the meantime, here's a preview of what you'll hear." He stepped away from the mike, guitar at the ready, and nodded to Scott. Scott leaned in and screamed out, "Ahahahahahaha! WIPE OUT!"

Then Vic kicked his amp to get some reverb, and we were off and running. Heads began bobbing up from towels along the beach and turned toward us. Kids walking along the sand, heading for the water or the pier, stopped in their tracks and began heading our way. By the time we kicked off the second tune, one of Vic's original instrumentals titled "Walkin' the Board," we were gathering a crowd, some of whom began dancing right there on the beach. It was like a scene out of a recently released movie, *Beach Party*, where Dick Dale and the Deltones hold a makeshift concert on the beach while everyone dances around a campfire. Only this was no movie, it was real life, and we were getting away with it.

Jackie Dallas, who seemed to have been born with a permanent case of stage fright, stood off to the side, looking tense and pale, his eyes darting about. But now it was his big moment to shine. Vic introduced him with, "And now direct from Hollywood, Jackie Dallas. Step on up here, Jackie." Jackie did just that, and stood ramrod straight in front of the mike, arms stiffly at his side, looking nervously around, waiting for his cue. We launched into another of Vic's songs, one that showed his disdain of surfers.

> "*Well, I'm a summertime surfer, summertime surfer*
> *Call me a kook, but I don't care*
> *I gotta go home and get my huaraches, and pour some bleach on my hair.*"

Jackie was butchering the song, his stage fright causing him to sing flat and behind the beat. But just then a black and white patrol car pulled up, its lights flashing, and stopped short of crashing into the drums. Two tall burly cops climbed out, decked out in summer uniforms, sunglasses, nightsticks, and side arms. One of them headed straight for the power cords, yanking them out of the wall. "Summertime Surfer," which had been dying by degrees, was now suddenly and mercifully put out of its misery. The other cop stomped over to us and demanded, "Who's in charge here?"

"I am," said Vic. "Is something the matter, officer?"

"You're damn right there is," said the cop, standing over Vic, while Vic stared at his own reflection in the sunglasses. "Let's see your permit."

"What permit?"

"I thought so. Okay, wise guy—here's the deal. You got two choices. Either I run you all in on a variety of charges, including blocking a fire lane, trespassing, unlawful assembly, and disturbing the peace, or you get your asses off my beach right now. What's it going be?"

Vic set his jaw and clenched his guitar, and in that moment I thought there would be trouble, with him challenging authority. Instead he weighed his options and decided to comply.

"I'll take the second choice."

"Good answer, punk. Now git."

As we started to pack it in, the crowd turned ugly, booing, yelling, swearing. Both cops now stood in front of us, facing the mob, hands menacingly on their nightsticks.

"Okay, break it up, all of you, the party's over!" said one cop.

"Move along or I'll declare this an unlawful assembly," said the other.

The crowd grumbled and moaned, but in the end they all shuffled off and went back to their sunbathing, surfing, and girl watching. We returned to the parking lot and the cars. This had just been another one of Vic's great promotional ideas that had ultimately fizzled out. But I had to admire his moxie. Although we'd only been together a few months, Vic had already set his sights on what he referred to as the "Big Time."

"I don't believe in starting at the bottom," he'd once said. "That's for the chumps. There's more room at the top."

Victor Power had entered my life in my freshman year at La Mirada High School. He'd just blown in from the Midwest like a young James Dean, hungry for fame and fortune. He even resembled Dean physically, and some of that was calculated (like the way he dressed and wore his hair), as Dean was his hero. And like Dean, he loved to play the rebel, cause or no cause.

"I'm going to be a star someday," he said matter-of-factly one day in drama class. "Everyone is going to know my name." I didn't know Vic well then, but he spoke with such assurance that I believed him. And why not? He not only looked the part, he even had a name like a matinee idol—VICTOR POWER. And he also had the attitude. He was proud and cocky, and if his acting was a little over the top, well, that was okay with him. At least he got people's attention.

Vic was everything I wasn't, so he became my role model and we began hanging out together. Vic taught me how to smoke cigarettes, dress cool, and when we were sixteen taught me to play guitar. I'd already been taking guitar lessons for a couple of years, but Vic gave me practical knowledge. We were working in a summer play together, when he invited me over to his house to jam. We only had acoustic guitars then, but Vic was no folkie. He knew the lead parts to all the popular guitar instrumentals, like "Walk Don't Run," and the chords too. He not only showed me which chords to use, but how to use them as a rhythm guitarist, and immediately I was hooked into Vic's world.

A few months later, surf music invaded the Southern California airwaves. It was a musical revolution led by local bands Dick Dale and the Deltones, the Beach Boys, and the Marketts, among others. Soon, other groups were popping up all around L.A. and Orange Counties. They had names like the Belaires, the Chantays, the Challengers, and the Lively Ones. Vic, never one to put the horse before the cart, saw an opportunity to pursue stardom from another direction. He acquired a Fender Stratocaster guitar and a Princeton amplifier, and then booked himself a gig as The Vibratos. Never mind that he didn't have a band yet. He had set it up with the drama teacher to play at the cast party of the play we were about to wrap up near the end of 1962. He approached me next.

"Hey, Steve, want to join my band?"

"Sure," I said.

"You'll need to get an electric guitar and amp right away."

"I don't know if I've got enough savings. Maybe after Christmas."

"I can't wait that long. I'm going places and I need an answer now."

"Okay," I said after a moment. "I'll see what I can do."

I had saved enough money from my paper route to buy a Silvertone guitar from Sears, but I had to borrow the amp from a friend. Then Vic corralled a guy named Gary from the school concert band to be our drummer. Vic couldn't find a bass player in time, but we went on anyway as a trio. Trouble was, we were only able to learn half a dozen songs together before the gig, so we just played them, and then we repeated the same six songs. No one seemed to mind, and that may have been because the punch bowl got spiked. After we'd packed up, Vic motioned me outside to sneak a cigarette.

"So what did you think?" he said, turning his collar up against the December chill and lighting a Marlboro.

"About what?"

"The band, Dupree, that's what. I thought we sounded great. I see some possibilities here. All we need now is a sax player and a bass man. You with me?"

"Yeah, okay," I answered as he passed me the cig.

"Good. I'll print up some business cards and start looking for some players and some places to play."

Not surprisingly, Vic found a sax player right away, a little Hispanic kid named Rudy. But instead of a bass player, he next brought in another guitarist from our school, Dixon L. Gayer. Dixon was a piece of work. A real surfer was Dixon. The rest of us were just lame middle class kids who had neither the means nor the inclination to get down to the beach. But Dixon was the genuine article, from his long wavy bleach blond hair to his Pendleton shirt and wingtip shoes. His family was well off, so he drove a Woodie, and had an expensive Gibson guitar and amplifier. He knew all the latest songs, and he could play rings around Vic. And Dixon was smugly arrogant about his own abilities. So naturally, Vic made him rhythm guitarist, while keeping the lead spot for himself. That left us with three guitarists and no bassist. Vic took me aside and said, "We need a bass player, Dupree. I nominate you."

"I don't know how to play bass," I complained.

"You don't need to. It's tuned like the bottom four strings on the guitar. Just play notes inside the scale, follow the chords, and keep time with the drummer."

"What about my brand new guitar?" I asked. Fortunately, I hadn't bought an amp yet.

"Dump it. I'll go down to the pawnshop with you and we'll trade it in on a bass. Maybe we can find an amp there, too."

And that's just what we did. I borrowed money for a used bass amp, and Vic set about converting his family's garage into a practice room, and in no time at all we were a bona fide garage band. We had learned only a handful of songs before we got our first money making gig, a rowdy beer party in La Habra. I don't remember much about that night, other than us being little more than background music to some raucous drinking and carryings on in someone's garage and back yard. But I do remember clearly the bouncer, a bear of a man with a limited vocabulary. He passed the hat for us and had a great way of grabbing someone by the arm and shaking him down.

"Hey—money for the band!"

Another thing I remember about that gig was how Vic took charge and showed some real leadership qualities.

"Rudy—make that sax honk! Get more of a gravelly sound. Gary—lay back on the cymbals, give me more hi-hat. Steve—you're dragging the beat. Follow the drums!"

We somehow survived our first job and made some pocket money, so Vic got busy lining up more work. We played teen dances and parties, and then went after the public schools for sock hops and after-game dances. The business cards Vic had printed up read like this:

> *THE VIBRATOS*
> *Versatile Entertainment*
> *With Modern Sounds.*
> Contact Vic Power. 521-4855

A few months later, Vic booked an hour's worth of time at a little recording studio in Bellflower so we could make a demo tape. And that was how we came to meet Jackie Dallas. That was the name he went by, and I don't think we ever knew his real name. He had built the studio mainly to record himself, and became a recording engineer in the process. We may have been his first paying clients. And it so happened that Jackie knew a guy who was an aspiring radio announcer and was willing to do the voice-overs for a six-pack of beer. The finished tape sounded something like this:

> "*PRESENTING THE VIBRATOS!*"
> (sample of music)
> *"The Vibratos are available for your dance, party, or organizational event."*
> (sample of music)
> *"Contact Vic Power at 521-4855. THE VIBRATOS!"*
> (final sample of music and fade out).

Vic was real proud of that tape—used to carry it around with him everywhere, in case he spotted a potential place to play. He and I were on foot in those days, so Vic's hustling involved a lot of walking and hitchhiking. For a time, Dixon was the only one of us with wheels. But that changed when Jackie joined up. He needed a band to sing with, and we needed another car and driver. We also got some free studio time out of the arrangement, so we spent whatever time we could making demo tapes of Vic's songs. Right away, Vic showed a talent for songwriting, mostly instrumentals. Later on he became an accomplished wordsmith as well.

Vic's hustling brought us to the attention of the Spartans Car Club, and we became the house band for their monthly beer parties. They liked us, and especially liked Vic, because he was a greaser like them. Dixon was the only surfer among us, but he soon split to form his own band. As a matter of fact, he staged a coup and took most of the Vibratos with him, leaving only Vic and I to carry on. He felt his talent was wasted playing second fiddle as it were to Vic. He also took exception to Vic's constant barbs about surfers. Soon, Dixon had added a bassist and pianist—both surfers—and was playing around town as the Vibratos. That did not sit well with Vic, but when he found out the new Vibratos were playing the next Spartans Car Club party, he blew a fuse.

"C'mon, Dupree," he said. "We're gonna go have a talk with the head car club guy." The conversation with the club president, as I remember, went like this:

"Hey, Cliff, this is a bunch of shit. I'm the Vibratos, not that surfer jerk Gayer."

"What do you want from me? We already hired them. Besides, you don't have a band anymore."

"Yeah, I do," Vic lied. "I got Dupree here, and some new guys."

"What do you call yourselves?"

"The Vibratos."

"Vic, you can't both be the Vibratos."

Vic had just recently traded up to a Twin Reverb amp, so he came up with the new name on the spot. "Okay, we're the Reverbs."

"So you're the Reverbs. Like I said, we already got a band this month."

Thinking fast, Vic said, "Okay, how about this—we have a battle of the bands. The winner gets the door and future parties."

Clifford thought about this for a moment and then said, “Okay, why not? We’ll be getting two bands for the price of one. I’ll set it up with the guys.”

Now, we just needed a band.

I found the new sax player, Scott Duncan, at the music studio where I took guitar lessons. Vic dug up drummer John Logan from a notice he posted on the bulletin board of the local music store, and we got Paddy through word of mouth. Steve looked him up at the bakery, introduced himself, and hired him without even an audition. He figured if Paddy could play country music, he could play surf music. Besides, we didn’t have much time to get a band together. As Vic liked to say, we were going places. This car club gig was important to Vic, because it was a matter of personal pride. He wasn’t going to let Dixon steal his thunder. That in mind, he decided to take no chances. He brought in a ringer, John Rill—front man for Johnny Rill and the Thrillers, to play lead guitar for this one night only. John was older, a professional musician, and could play anything from rock to blues and jazz. Surf music should be a piece of cake for him. Vic would take the rhythm guitar slot, and Jackie and Paddy would sit the gig out.

The big night came, and we arrived at the Spartans’ clubhouse in two vehicles. John Rill had already arrived in his own ’56 Chevy. The Battle of the Bands was about to begin. The Reverbs set up on one side of the room, while Dixon and the Vibratos set up on the other. We would each play a set, and may the best band win. It was like a Madison Square Garden setup.

“In this corner, looking cocky and professional, the current champions: THE VIBRATOS! And in this corner, looking greasy, nervous, and ragged, the challengers: THE REVERBS! Go to your corners and come out rocking!”

The Vibratos not only looked like a surf band, they sounded like one. They played all the surf hits from “Pipeline” to “Surf Rider” to “Miserlou,” sounding as good as the records played on the radio. They retired from their corner to gloat.

We came out swinging with less known surf songs (“Caterpillar Crawl”), oldies (Bill Dogget’s “Honky Tonk)”, and Vic’s originals (“Aqua Mania”). Even with the ringer, we sucked. John Rill sounded like Barney Kessel trying to do the Lawrence Welk Show.

Vic kept hitting the wrong chords, and I was completely lost. Dixon's band had played circles around us, walked all over us, stomped us. It wasn't pretty. In a fair contest, we would have been banished forever from the monthly beer party, left to slink home in disgrace. But this was not a fair contest. With their chopped and lowered and souped-up hot rods, the Spartans were at heart, if not in fact, all greasers. And so was Vic. And if the rest of us weren't exactly greasers, at least we weren't surfers. So after the votes were tallied, we walked off with the door money, future gigs, and all the beer we could drink. The Vibratos slunk off without fanfare. We stuck around and drank beer, except for Jackie, who was a teetotaler. Vic felt vindicated.

In September, Vic and I began our senior year at La Mirada High. Over the previous summer, the Reverbs had done a lot of playing and recording and had begun to coalesce as a band, enough so that we were starting to get steady gigs. And it was at this point that Vic's uncle began to take notice of us. Uncle Stan, as we called him, was a car salesman, but he needed a hobby, so he decided he would become our manager. At Vic's insistence, he had shown up at a couple of our gigs, and liked what he saw. He took copious notes on our performances, and checked out some of the other surf bands playing around the area. In particular, he liked what he saw down at the Harmony Park Ballroom in Anaheim, where Dick Dale and his band packed them in tightly every weekend. Stan found out that Dick's father, Jim Monsour, managed the band. He was the guy that printed up the handbills, sold the tickets, and kept track of the box office receipts, among other things. Stan Power had a look at some of those receipts, and so in October, he approached Vic about managing The Reverbs. We found out he was to become our manager at a band rehearsal in Vic's garage, where it was announced that Jackie Dallas was out of the band, and Vic's cousin Marty (Stan's son) was in, playing keyboards.

Under Uncle Stan's supervision, we began pulling in bigger and better gigs. We looked more professional on stage with our matching black collarless "preacher coats" (like the Righteous Brothers wore), our white shirts and black ties, black pegged slacks, and Italian boots. And Uncle Stan bought us new equipment. He asked Vic, what did we need, and Vic gave him a shopping list. Paddy inherited Vic's Stratocaster and Twin Reverb amp, while Vic stepped up to a new Fender Jaguar guitar and Showman amp. I stepped up to a Fender Precision Bass and Bassman amp, and we were treated to a good vocal mike. Marty was given a Fender Rhodes electric piano. The new equipment was to be owned by Uncle Stan, but sort of leased to the band. We had "THE REVERBS" stenciled onto John's bass drum head.

Although our bread and butter gigs were still teen dances and parties, we began appearing at shopping center functions and opening act and off-night gigs at some of the bigger venues, like the Retail Clerks Union Hall and the Rendezvous Ballroom. Then there were the lame gigs, like the VFW hall and the Rotary Club. But at least they paid well, and outside of Paddy and John, none of us had to work after-school or weekend jobs to have a little spending cash. We also had a fan club, courtesy of Stan, who put it together. The Reverbs Fan Club was made up of mostly teen and pre-teen girls, but there were some guys in it too, who liked our music and had the same idea that Vic did that we were going places. Stan also saw to it that we got lots of press, with write-ups in the local papers, and flyers posted around town. We all started to believe in Vic and Stan's Big Time dreams, almost as much as they did.

The next item on Stan's agenda for the band was a recording contract. But even before that could be accomplished, we needed a good demo. Downey Records, a small recording studio set up in the back of Wenzel's Music in Downey, was chosen because the Chantays had recorded their hit "Pipeline" there. Bill Wenzel, the owner, had released the song on his own label, and later peddled it to Dot, where it had become a national hit. The Rumblers and The Pastel Six had also recorded at Downey, and had had modest hits. Uncle Stan was hoping for the same results for us.

The moment we walked into the studio, Vic's usual bluster and swagger deserted him. He froze up in the studio, standing stiff as a rail, with anxiety written on his face, and it took a number of false starts to get each of his two songs recorded. He became short-tempered as well, and got into a row with the engineer after the session, accusing him of trying to steal his songs by secretly making copies for himself. The engineer tried to explain that it was standard industry practice to make a backup safety master as insurance in case the other acetate is lost or damaged, but Vic would have none of it. He had the safety master destroyed and cast aspersions on the ethics of the label.

After that, Bill Wenzel wanted nothing to do with us and told us to take our business elsewhere in the future. We were all kind of bummed out by the experience, but John Logan simmered. I don't know why Uncle Stan hadn't tried to smooth things over. Instead he had allowed Vic to run off at the mouth, and shrugged it off. John, however, did not shrug it off, and it all came to a head at the next band practice.

Vic and John began arguing about a drum arrangement. John wanted it done one way, and Vic another.

"Hey, who's the drummer here anyway?" said John confrontationally.

"Who's the leader?" snapped Vic.

"Oh, yeah?" countered John, standing and clenching his drumsticks in his hand like a weapon, "Is that what you call yourself? Nice job of fucking up our recording deal at the Downey studio. I'm getting sick of your bullshit, Power!" He stepped away from the drum kit towards Vic. "Someday you're going to get your ass kicked."

"You want to try?" said Vic, putting down his guitar and cocking his chin.

"I just might," answered John.

"Let's go outside," said Vic.

We all followed them out to the backyard, where they had it out. John was muscular and quick on his feet, but Vic was on the Varsity wrestling team, so it was a fair match. When we finally broke them up after they had rolled around on the ground for a while, it seemed like a draw. But it didn't matter—John was out of the band. Vic told him he was fired, but John shot back, "Fuck you, asshole, I QUIT!" Then he packed up his drums and left, and we never saw him again.

"We'll get another drummer," Vic said when we complained about John's exit. "Drummers are easy to come by. They're all just gunsels anyway." We didn't know what that word meant, and doubted Vic did either. But it sounded cool.

Vic didn't waste any time finding a new drummer. At our next band practice we were introduced to tall, long-haired, sleepy-eyed surfer Lee Andrews. And Lee not only had a good drum kit, but access to his parents' station wagon. He was just the kind of drummer Vic liked—quiet, steady, compliant, easy going. He kept a steady beat, and he knew his place, which was in being subservient to Vic.

Outside of the band, Vic and I both stayed involved in high school drama and community theatre, often competing for the same parts. I'd beat him out for the lead in the fall high school play. Opening night was to have been November 22, but President Kennedy's assassination postponed it for a week. The next weekend was league football playoffs for our school team, so there wasn't much of a turnout for the play. Football beat theatre any time. However, our team won the championship the following weekend and the Reverbs played the after-game dance, and we felt like stars with the room filled to capacity, and everyone in a celebratory mood. Outside of a private party, it was our last gig of the year. But Vic and Stan had big plans for our future..

We began 1964 with high hopes. Uncle Stan had managed to wrangle a recording contract for a one-off single with Invicta Records, a small label out of Hollywood. We would be doing two of Vic's songs, "Aqua Mania" b/w "Kickin' Out." One day in January, in the middle of the week, we cut school to caravan down to the Sunset Strip in Hollywood in two cars. Scott and I joined Lee in his family's station wagon, with all the equipment crammed in the back. Stan drove the other car with Vic, Paddy and Vic's girl Cheryl. We pulled into the parking lot of Sunset Sound Recorders, next to the Ventures' equipment van, and then we all piled out. We were to record in Studio A, while the Ventures were recording in Studio B. It was Vic's idea to have us all wear our stage clothes to the session. He thought it might make us look more professional. But I felt quite the amateur when we entered the cavernous studio, with mikes and cords and headphones scattered all about. It looked as if a complete orchestra could fit in the main room, which in fact was the case. There was an isolation booth for the drummer and another for the singer, which we wouldn't need, as our songs were instrumentals. Separated off the main room was a glassed-in control booth where two recording engineers sat. The producer and the lead engineer set me up in there, running my bass directly into the board. Uncle Stan and Cheryl sat with me. They set Lee up in the drum room, and the other three guys in the main room in a circle facing each other. We all wore headphones, but I could still hear enough of the banter between the engineers to know they thought we were pretty green.

Vic was intimidated by the surroundings, and you could tell he was nervous by the stiff way he stood, and his jerky movements and the false starts. It looked to be a repeat of the Downey sessions, and I hoped Stan would keep him from flipping out again. As it turned out, though, he didn't need to. Vic was duly impressed by the size and scope of the place, and he wasn't about to blow it this time. He knew what we all knew—this was what the Big Time looked like.

After the initial jitters wore off, we settled into a groove and laid down both songs. There were no overdubs—we played live. We packed up the gear while our manager and producer had a little pow-wow, and we schlepped everything back out to the cars. Stan took group photos in front of the Ventures' van to document the occasion, and then we made the homeward trek on the smoggy Hollywood Freeway in heavy afternoon traffic. Most of us would be back in school the next day, but for now we felt like stars. In just a few weeks the record would be released, get lots of airplay, become a hit, and we'd be surfing a wave of fame. Only it didn't pan out that way.

Dick Dale and the Deltones had by this time moved out of the Harmony Park Ballroom and into the larger Hollywood Palladium. Uncle Stan saw a golden opportunity and rented out the ballroom in Anaheim to be our new venue. He would now be realizing his own dream of being the kind of manager Jim Monsour was. He would be the guy putting up the handbills, selling the tickets, and counting the receipts. Except that in the end, the receipts didn't cover the expenses. The first night at Harmony Park, we looked out from the big stage onto a mostly empty dance floor. There were maybe two-dozen kids, mostly the Reverbs Fan Club, hanging around in front of the stage. It was kind of embarrassing.

"Don't worry, boys," Stan assured us, "things will pick up."

But things did not pick up. By the third weekend, we decided to call Harmony Park quits, before we lost any more money. But Stan still believed in us, and Vic still had stars in his eyes, and we continued to book whatever gigs we could scrounge up. Then one Sunday night in February, I sat in front of the T.V. with my parents, watching the Ed Sullivan Show when the Beatles made their debut. In that moment I knew I was witnessing the future of rock and roll, and the subsequent demise of surf music, folk music and the pop music the songwriters in the Brill Building in New York had been cranking out for years.

Next day in school, Vic told me the Beatles were just a flash in the pan, and if I stuck with him, we'd be on the Ed Sullivan show ourselves some day. I didn't believe him, but I gamely soldiered on with the band. We continued playing concerts, dances, and parties, but never got to hear our record on the radio. It was released soon, but too late for anyone to care. By then, The Beatles held the top five slots in the Top 40, and the old order was quickly being swept aside by the wave of the British Invasion. We were redundant, and our music was about to become extinct. Kids all over the area were starting up Beatle copy bands and growing their hair long. But the Reverbs weren't ready to lie down and die just yet.

Uncle Stan booked us into the Teenage Fair in March. It was held at the Hollywood Palladium, where Dick Dale had been headlining. We also entered the Battle of the Bands there, and finished fourth, not enough to win big. We were given a consolation prize, though. The Capitol Records booth let us each pick out an album to take. They had two choices: a Beach Boys LP or *Meet The Beatles*. Like everyone else, I chose the latter. It was a sign of the times. In the future, the Beach Boys would steer away from surf songs, singing instead about cars and girls, and then make a complete musical transformation with the brilliant "Good Vibrations."

Meanwhile, Vic and I carried on our friendship. We hung out sometimes after school and on weekends, going out cruising and drinking beer, and planning out our futures. Vic still craved fame and fortune. A couple of times, we got into minor scrapes with the law (Vic loved to play the rebel), but nothing too serious, mostly for having beer in our possession or being out after curfew. On campus, Vic usually hung out with his girl Cheryl, or some of the bad crowd, the guys we called hoods. You know the type—black leather jackets, greasy hair, motorcycle boots, bad attitudes. Guys who were in and out of Juvenile Hall and whose own idea of the Big Time was prison. But somehow, Vic moved freely among them. I guess he thought it was good for his James Dean persona. Toward the end of the school year, Vic realized his fantasy of being James Dean when he was cast in the role of Jim Stark in our community theater production of *Rebel Without A Cause*.

In May, Uncle Stan set us up with a three-week tour of the Midwest to take place in July. He also gave us formal contracts to sign, which Vic handed out at band practice. Everyone but me signed that night. There was a clause about a portion of our pay being withheld for Uncle Stan's fees, and another portion to be withheld to pay for the band instruments. It looked to me as if we'd be working for free from now on, so I told Vic I wanted to think about it.

"Okay," he said, "but don't think about it too long. I'm going places with or without you, Dupree."

A few days later at school, Vic asked if I was ready to sign yet.

"I'm still thinking about it."

"I need an answer now. You gonna sign or not?"

"Well, if you put it that way, Vic, then I'll have to say no, at this moment I'm not going to sign."

"Okay, then you're out of the band."

"What do you mean?"

"You're fired, Dupree, that's what I mean."

"Who will you get to take my place?"

"My cousin Marty."

"But he's the keyboard player."

"Well now he's the bass player. I taught you how to play, I can teach him. Besides, the equipment belongs to the band, and you're no longer in it."

"Okay, Vic, if that's how you want it. See you around."

And I did see him around, for we still had drama class together, and I also wound up at the band's next gig, a music store opening at a shopping center. By now they had changed the band name to Vic and The Reverbs. I didn't mind the new name. I wouldn't have opposed it if I were still in the band, but I felt very out of place in the audience, and regretted not signing the contract. I missed being up on stage with them.

Graduation day came in June, and Vic and I hung out together at the all-night party afterward. In July, Vic and Reverbs headed out on the road for their first and last tour. The trip became a complete disaster, everyone had issues with Vic, and before the tour was finished, the band was finished—broke, busted, and disgusted.

Uncle Stan gave up on his show business dreams and contented himself with selling cars, something that had a proven formula for success. Lee went back to high school and surfing. Scott and I went off to community college in the fall. Marty graduated from the eighth grade and went on to high school. Paddy went back to the bakery, and later put down his guitar, picked up a rifle, and joined the army. It was part of his plan to gain citizenship. And Vic? Well, Vic went to work for his uncle, selling cars. He married Cheryl, and they settled into a small apartment in Bellflower. For the time being, he put down his guitar.

But he wasn't done with it yet, not by a long shot. He soon put together a rock band he named Powerglide, and went back to square one.

With money from my part-time job bagging groceries I bought a nice acoustic guitar. When I wasn't busy with my classes, my studies, or my job, I learned folk songs and became something of a singer.

In the fall, Lyndon Johnson was officially elected President of the United States. Throughout the next year, I would read in the newspapers about sweeping Civil Rights legislation, and also more and more about America's involvement in a war over in Southeast Asia, in a little country that used to be called French Indochina. Now it was called Vietnam. As time went by the war escalated, and became a regular feature on the nightly news, like a bad TV series that should be cancelled, but instead lives on in perpetual reruns. And as the war continued to ramp up, Uncle Sam's draft boards needed to find fresh bodies to ship overseas, preferably young men of college age. And since I fit into that catagory, my future was about to be put on hold.

CHAPTER THREE

Door Number Three

The summer after high school, I found my life becoming like a bad television game show. "Here are your choices Steve Dupree, and remember the clock is ticking. Behind door number one we have a job waiting for you—a crummy, low paying mind-numbing job. Behind door number two—the Army, and an all expenses paid vacation in the tropical paradise of South Vietnam. And behind door number three—community college, with the option of postponing real life for awhile."

"Hmm—let me think this over. I'll go for door number three."

"Congratulations Mister Dupree! You've just won yourself two years of education at an institution of higher learning, and as an added bonus, a deferment from the draft."

Vic Power also enrolled, as a part time student majoring in journalism. He didn't do it for the draft deferment, for as a married man, he already had one. He just wanted to develop his writing skills by studying journalism. He also worked fulltime in sales and led a band, playing a couple of nights a week wherever he could. He had a lot on his plate. I had enough on mine just going to school and holding down a part time job.

With the British Invasion sound dominating the Top 40 airwaves, Vic jumped on that bandwagon, growing his hair Beatle style, dressing accordingly, and filling the band's set list with Fifties rock, Beatles cover tunes, and original songs in those styles. But when he discovered Bob Dylan in the summer of 1965, he found a new role model—one to replace the James Dean of his high school years. He copied Dylan's hair and clothing styles, and also his song writing style, trying his hand at protest rock and wordy abstract lyrics. But Vic didn't emulate his new hero strictly to make money and be current. He honestly dug the music, and found he had a knack for writing songs of social protest. And since he had always worn an anti-establishment chip on his shoulder, he found a new musical niche for himself. Unfortunately, he couldn't seem to keep a regular lineup, as musicians came and went like a revolving door. Most of them found Vic too demanding.

It was during his Dylan phase that Vic started experimenting with drugs. It began with uppers (Benzedrine) to keep him going for his late night gigs, knowing he had a job and classes to go to during the day. Then he tried pot, and he dug smoking it so much, he began turning his friends on to it, myself included.

At first, I was apprehensive about smoking a joint with him. After all, parents, teachers, and authority figures had been warning me for years not to get hooked on that stuff, as it was the devil's own weed. But Vic had great powers of persuasion, which is why he worked in sales, and he sold me on smoking a joint with him. I loved it right off the bat, and not only became a pothead myself, but went around converting my own friends as well. After awhile, Vic found that being married, working, going to school, and staying up late playing gigs, popping pills and smoking pot, was just too much for one person to handle. Something had to give, so he dropped out of school. After the first year, I dropped out too.

In my case, it wasn't that I had too much on my plate, but that school bored me. I had no ambition, no direction, no career plan, and no imagination. I lost my deferment, and the draft board re-classified me 1-A. That meant I was Army bait, and with the draft board now breathing down my neck, my future was looking bleak. What to do? I enlisted in the Navy. Vic laughed and told me I was a chump.

"They'll never draft me," he said. "I'm too slippery to get caught."

I didn't think it was such a bad idea at the time. After all, I'd beaten the draft, and maybe I'd get to see the world. As it turned out, though, the only parts of the world I saw were San Diego, brief glimpses of Hawaii and the Philippines, and more than I wanted of the South China Sea. And while I languished in sweltering tropical heat off the coast of Vietnam on Yankee Station, Vic soldiered on with Powerglide until it ran out of steam and self-destructed.

I'll say this about Vic Power—he was tenacious and resilient, and he never missed a trend. By 1967 the San Francisco Sound was happening, and groups like the Grateful Dead, Jefferson Airplane, and Big Brother and the Holding Company (with Janis Joplin) were hitting the radio airwaves, especially the new FM underground stations, and were selling a lot of albums and filling a lot of concert halls. Vic got hip to the sound, grew his hair even longer, and with the help of Paul Curtis, formed his own psychedelic band.

Vic had met Paul at a party and jam session, and liked the way he played the sax. Paul also played flute, guitar and piano; sang, and wrote songs. Paul Curtis was long and lean and had blond hair that reached past his shoulders. He and Vic decided they had a similar vision for a band, and with the agreement that they would be co-leaders of the group, they set about to put one together. Vic brought in Marty Power on bass, and a drummer named Sticks. Paul added his friend Tom "Huck" Finn on piano, and a chick singer named Mary on vocals. They began calling her Micro Mary because of the mini skirts she wore. She could belt out songs like a cross between Janis Joplin and Grace Slick, and she oozed sex appeal. They christened the band Morning Glory, after the hallucinogenic morning glory seeds, and had business cards printed up that read:

MORNING GLORY
"Head Music For Heads"
Contact Vic Power or Paul Curtis

With Vic and Paul both writing songs, and working together, the band coalesced. Vic ran the rehearsals and hustled up the gigs, while Paul, who had some formal musical training, worked out the arrangements and helped create the band's sound. Everything seemed to be falling into place for Vic's climb to the Big Time. Although they were starting from the bottom, Vic didn't plan to stay there for long. Morning Glory began gigging all over the local area, then expanding outward. No seedy bar or teenage hangout was too humble for them, and after a while they began moving up the rungs, playing bigger venues, and attracting the attention of Dick Desmond, who became their manager. He set them up in high profile venues, opening for groups like Iron Butterfly, The Seeds, and Canned Heat.

It didn't take long before Huck Finn, basically a laid-back guy, began to feel the pressure of success, and the intensity of Vic's drive for it. He had clashes with Vic and then with Paul, and one day he just left. However, with the Irish luck of good timing, Paddy O'Brien, recently discharged from the Army, stepped into replace him in the rhythm section, albeit on guitar, not piano. With Marty also in the band, Vic had half of the old Reverbs under his command again. And none too soon, for Morning Glory was on a roll, and going places, as Vic was fond of saying.

Around this time, my ship finished its West Pac cruise, and returned to its homeport of San Diego, and I got a weekend pass just in time to catch Morning Glory headline a gig at our old community college. I watched from the audience as they played from the stage set up in the gym, and I was spellbound, both by their sound, and the audience's reaction to it. As I watched, I imagined myself up there with them, playing the bass again. Later on, backstage, I told Vic how much I dug the band, and how much I wished I could be a part of it.

"You probably could've been," said Vic, "if you hadn't been such a chump and joined the Navy."

"Yeah, I know," I said sheepishly. "Maybe you were right."

"Ah, fuck it," said Vic. "That's water under the bridge. Give me a call when you get out. Maybe we can use you then. You never know in this business."

"I got a year and a half to do," I said glumly.

"We'll be in the Big Time well before that," said Vic. "We're talking record deal with a major label, and Dick's putting a summer tour together."

"Well, good luck," I said.

"Same to you, Dupree."

I didn't see Vic for a long time afterward, but I'd get news of him from his sister Sandy, who had married a sailor and was living in San Diego. Through Sandy, I followed Morning Glory's successes secondhand, and then I heard of its demise. First the record deal fell through, after Vic got into a tiff with the label's A&R man. Then out on the road, Vic and Paul began fighting, splitting the band into two warring factions. It all blew up in Colorado, when Paul stormed offstage in the middle of a set, after Vic had purposely upstaged him. After the show, Paul had told Vic to fuck off, he was quitting, and he and Micro Mary (now his girlfriend) were going back to L.A. Sticks was fed up with all the bickering and the bullshit, and decided he was going to go live in the woods of Oregon for a while. Suddenly the band was down to just the former members of the Reverbs. Paddy decided he'd had enough as well. The whole thing reminded him of the band breakup of 1964, and he wanted no part of it. He'd already decided earlier on the tour that he wanted to go back to Ireland, for which he was homesick. Now the band was a duo. Vic confronted Marty.

"I suppose you're going to walk out on me now?" he said accusingly.

Marty looked away from him as he packed up his bass and said quietly, "Yeah, I guess so. I know we're family and all that, but I don't dig all the bad vibes that have been going down."

"So you're going to run back home too?"

Marty turned to face him now. "No. As a matter of fact, I'm thinking of going to the East Coast. I'd like to check out New York, and since we're already halfway there, this seems as good a time as any. So if you want to buy out my share of the band and pay me off, I'll just get in the wind."

Vic's face tightened and his eyes flashed anger.

"I shouldn't give you anything," he said. "But since you're family, I guess I have to. I'll see that Dick gets you some bread."

Dick Desmond had other bands to manage and decided he'd invested enough time and energy into Vic Power's dreams, so that was the end of Morning Glory. That was also the end of Vic's rock and roll dreams, at least for now.

My ship went back out to sea, and I lost touch with Vic and his sister for a good nine months. After the tour of duty, we returned to San Diego, I snagged a weekend pass, and decided to look Vic up. I stopped by his apartment in Bellflower, only to find that he'd moved and left no forwarding address. I thought to check at his parents' house, and that's where I found him. It was a surprise to us both when he answered the knock on the door.

"Dupree," he said, "what are you doing here?"

"I was about to ask you the same thing."

"Well, I'm living here again, temporarily. Come on in, and I'll give you the lowdown. It's a long story."

He led me to the converted garage, where the Reverbs used to practice.

"This is my temporary pad now," he said, a little embarrassed. "Make yourself at home."

I looked around, and there wasn't much to see—a couch to sleep on, some clothing strewn around, his Fender guitar and amp in a corner. Not much else to imply that it was anyone's abode.

"How long you been here?" I asked

"Not long. Just since I got out of the joint."

"You were in jail?" I asked incredulously.

"Yeah, after I got drafted. Oh, and I got divorced too. And how've you been, Dupree? Still have a home in the Navy?" he said sarcastically.

"Never mind that," I said. "What's been going on with you?"

"Like I said, it's a long story. I guess the draft board was running out of fresh meat to ship off to Vietnam, so they started calling up the married men. First I got reclassified to 1-A. Then I got my draft notice, which I tore up. Next day I went and checked myself into a mental hospital for observation. They kept me a week and let me go. Then I got my second notice. This one made a lot of threats, so I figured I'd better report. When I showed up for my physical, they wanted to know why I didn't report the first time. I told them I was in the looney bin. So now they send me to see the Army shrink. I pull out my drama chops and start acting paranoid and delusional, so the shrink sends me home."

"That was it?" I asked.

"Not exactly," he continued. "I told you it's a long story. Next thing I know I come home from a gig one night and Cheryl tells me the FBI had been by earlier with an arrest warrant—draft evasion. So I take it on the lam. I hide out here for a few days, but they got the place staked out and they nab me. Next thing I know, I'm in the slammer. But I keep up the crazy act. Lucky for me one, of the hoods I knew back at La Mirada High, Kenny Price, he's in the joint too, for armed robbery. He puts out the word I'm a partner of his, and if anybody fucks with me, they fuck with him. So that's cool. I go before the judge, the PD pleads insanity and shows my funny-farm papers, and the next thing I know, I'm back out on the street, and I get reclassified 4-F. But when I get back home, Cheryl's gone, she's filed for divorce, I've lost my job, and I'm evicted for not paying my rent. That's why I'm back here with the folks."

"What are you going to do now?"

"Well, there's nothing going on for me around here. I've been thinking about selling the PA and the electric guitar and amp, and going acoustic. Hit the road, like Woody Guthrie. Maybe head up to Frisco—see what's going on up there. I had a lot of time to think about things while I was in the joint," he said philosophically. "Of course, I had to keep up the crazy act, but I did some meditating and a little soul-searching as well. I came to the conclusion that it's okay to stand up for your beliefs. Most people probably think I'm just trying to dodge the draft because I'm a pussy. But the truth is, I'm actually against the war. I can't see that sending Americans to fight a civil war in Vietnam is going to solve anything. War isn't the answer. I'm thinking Martin Luther King and Gandhi had it right, man."

He paused a moment to collect his thoughts before continuing. "After I got out of the joint, and found out Cheryl had left me, I dropped some acid, and it was a real trip. It was beautiful. I saw the connection of all living things, and it blew my mind. I have an idea about what those hippies up in Frisco are into. It's not just a bullshit pose. They really are into love and peace, and I think I want to get on that trip too."

"That's far out," I didn't know what else to say.

"The only thing that really bums me out is Cheryl leaving me. I wouldn't have done that to her. Didn't she believe in me?"

The hurt look in his eyes was real, and was one of the few times I'd ever seen Vic let down his guard and be vulnerable.

"I'm sorry, Vic.".

"Ah, I'll get over it. I trust everything will turn out alright."

We visited for a little while longer, and then said our goodbyes and wished each other luck. I went back to my ship, and true to his word, Vic hit the road with just a backpack, a sleeping bag, and an acoustic Fender guitar.

I had a few more months to do in the Navy, pulling shore duty in San Diego. I kept in touch with Vic's sister, who would hear from him occasionally. That's how I found out he was up in Monterey, had met a girl, was living in her parents' garage, and was busking—playing for change, on Fisherman's Wharf. He also played at a coffeehouse in the area. Sandy showed me a handbill. It was a pen and ink sketch of Vic with an Abe Lincoln beard announcing that he would be performing on Saturday night. The flyer was a recent one.

"Good for Vic," I said. "He's really doing it, he's following his dream."

"You could be doing it too," said Sandy.

"Yeah, but I'm in the Navy," I protested.

"But not for long," she pointed out, which got me to thinking that since I had no plans past my discharge, maybe I could.

My enlistment came to an end, but before trying to pick up the thread of my life again, I wanted to make a trip up to San Francisco, just out of curiosity, since I'd never been there. Not yet owning a car, I talked my best Navy buddy Lenny into taking a week's leave and driving up with me. His father and stepmother owned a resort in the Sierras near Yosemite, so the plan was to camp out in the mountains, then visit his folks, continue on to San Francisco, and spend a couple days there before we'd head back. He would drop me at my folks' place on the way back to San Diego.

The first part of the trip went according to plan. We camped out at Mammoth Lakes, sleeping under an immense canopy of star-studded sky. We brewed coffee over an open fire in the morning, drove through Yosemite Park, and stopped off in the afternoon at Whispering Pines Resort; a cluster of cabins in the woods, ringed around a main office and a modest swimming pool. As Lenny's guest, I was invited to dinner and a happy family reunion. We were offered the use of a cabin for the night, free of charge.

We lounged around the next morning; swimming, reading, relaxing, and then Lenny announced a change of plans. He'd decided he wanted to stay right here until the week was up, and I was welcome to join him. San Francisco, it seemed, had nothing to offer him.

But I was restless with wanderlust, and was itching to see San Francisco, and whatever other mysteries were over the next horizon. So we parted ways with a handshake and good wishes, and I walked across the road with my sleeping bag tied to my backpack, and stuck out my thumb.

Soon I was looking out the windshield of a stranger's car onto a big blue-sky day, winding down out of the Sierras and the foothills, watching scenery fly by, and an occasional redtail hawk that would swoop overhead. Tall pines turned to grey oaks and scrub brush, the rolling hills colored a summer gold. Then we were out of the hills and on to the valley floor, where the great San Joaquin Valley spread out before us like a long carpet woven in the colors of many different crops. We rolled along between the foothills we'd left and the coastal range to the west. The driver dropped me off in the parking lot of a Merced supermarket. I thanked him and hefted my gear on over to the northbound on-ramp of Highway 99.

The air was hot, dry, and still, punctuated with the sounds of cars and long-haul trucks rushing along the traffic artery. Tractor-trailers bursting at the seams with recently picked produce headed for the markets and the packing plants. Pickups and station wagons rolled by with their loads of farmers, field hands, traveling salesmen, and vacationing families while I stood in the heat and dust of the August afternoon, waiting with little patience. I lit a cigarette and began reading the graffiti inscribed on the on ramp sign.

I spent two days at this miserable spot. Corky 6/5/69
T.C. was here
This place sucks. Bear

I felt like adding my two cents worth, but I had nothing to write with, and anyway, I had no sad tale of woe, for it was a beautiful day and I was footloose and free. By the time I'd finished my cigarette, a beat-up pickup inching onto the highway had pulled over in front of me, and the driver had reached over and opened the passenger door. I tossed my backpack into the bed and climbed on up into the front seat, beside the driver. The floorboards were worn and bare, and seemed to match the driver's appearance. He was grizzled and dressed in dirty torn overalls and a faded blue work shirt. I took him to be a workingman, maybe a farmer. His dark, leathery skin bore the mark of many seasons of sun and wind, dust and rain, and deep lines of laughter and sorrow were engraved upon his face. A ball cap was screwed down on dark, greasy hair. He put his rough, calloused hand in mine and pumped it once, firmly.

"I'm Jake," he said plainly. "Where ya headed, son?"

"San Francisco, sir. Thanks for stopping."

"Don't mention it. San Francisco's a mighty ways off, but I'll get you down the road apiece. Whatcha gonna do there? Ya live there?"

"No, sir. I'm just taking a little vacation. Thought I'd like to see the sights up there, but I don't have a car."

"Well, I'll take ya far as I can."

And he did so. We headed north on 99, then cut over west through the hills on a smaller road that intersected with Highway 101, and I got dropped off just south of San Jose. The next ride took me through that city, and I found myself humming "Do You Know The Way To San Jose" as we rolled on through its sprawl. Not as pretty as the song made it out to be, maybe, but I knew we were getting close to San Francisco now and I just had to hum happily along.

I had but a short wait on the other side of San Jose, my shirt sleeves rolled up to reveal sunburned arms, when a blue Ford sedan slowed to a halt and its driver beckoned me. He asked my destination and invited me to hop on in, which I did gladly. He said he was a salesman headed to San Francisco for a convention, and it was clear he was yearning for company on the trip, for he talked incessantly as we drove on chasing the setting sun. He mentioned he'd been on the road most of the day, and it struck me that I had been as well. We raced along the highway, as if trying to beat the sun to the horizon, and before long we were racing through the hills of Oakland.

Cresting a hill, we saw San Francisco loom into sight, white and grey against a paling sky and surrounded by the deep blue bay. My face broke into a big grin and my heart beat faster. Frisco! We rolled across the Bay Bridge in the gathering twilight and parted at a traffic light atop a steep hill. I stepped out onto the sidewalk and hefted my backpack onto my shoulders, startled as a sudden punch from a cold breeze hit me, as it blew its way inland from the Pacific Ocean toward the great Central Valley from which I had just come.

Pulling out a jacket from my backpack and zipping myself up inside it, I loped down the hill, towards the glitter and bustle of The City. I walked through a canyon of tall buildings, along crowded sidewalks flanking busy streets lined with cable car and bus tracks. At the bottom of the hill, a signpost told me I'd reached Market Street, which, unbeknownst to me, lay just off the Tenderloin District. Across from the Greyhound station was a seedy hotel, where I plunked down three dollars for a room for the night. I climbed the rickety stairs to a sad bare bones room that smelled of decay. I emptied the contents of my backpack, washed up in the sink, changed my clothes, and rushed out into the night to discover what I might of the sights, sounds, and flavors of this great old Gold Rush city.

I found a cable car stop and as the car approached I jumped aboard, grabbing on to the same pole that an attractive young lady was draped around. We greeted each other and she told me her name was Stephanie and that she was a stewardess for American Airlines on a layover. I told her excitedly that this was my first visit to the city, and she offered to be my tour guide.

"Then you'll have to let me show you around," she said. "I come here often."

"Lead on," I replied.

The car stopped at a turnaround near Ghiradelli Square.

"Let's walk over to Fisherman's Wharf," she said. "I'll treat you to dinner at Alioto's."

"You don't have to do that," I protested. "I have a little money."

"Yes," she said, taking my arm, "but I have an expense account, and I insist you be my guest."

Knowing full well the state of my finances, I decided not to argue. "Thanks," I said. "I do appreciate it."

After a great candlelight dinner at Alioto's, complete with glasses of wine, we walked around Fisherman's Wharf, talking and sightseeing and smelling the cool summer night air that was mixed with aromas of the bay: of raw and cooked shellfish from outdoor stalls, and Italian food wafting from a restaurant. We wound up back at the cable car turnaround, and queued up for the next car to arrive. At the turnaround, a jug band was playing music for the crowd that gathered there and the tourists and night trippers that passed by. Three young hippies in long hair and colorful clothing banged away on guitar, banjo, and washtub bass, while the fourth guy sang and played harmonica. The guitarist had his case open to catch spare change, which people would toss in from time to time. I watched them closely as we waited, and couldn't help but notice that they seemed to be having a great time, and I pictured myself standing among them, playing and singing my heart out. I didn't know it then, but I was catching a glimpse of my future life.

A clattering of steel wheels on steel tracks and the clanging of a bell signaled the cable car's arrival, and we hopped aboard, finding seats this time, and as the car worked its way up the steep hill to North Beach, I craned my neck to try and keep the jug band in sight as long as possible. We arrived at Stephanie's stop, and I walked her to her hotel. I thanked her for the evening, and she thanked me for my company as she gave me a hug. I watched her as she walked through the front door, and noted that her hotel was much classier than mine. But that didn't bother me as I bounded on down another long steep hill toward Market Street and 7th, where my wino hotel stood in all its shabbiness. Fearing bedbugs, I rolled out my sleeping bag on the bed, crawled inside it, and fell asleep in the light of a neon sign winking through the battered window shade with the sounds of the street below for company.

Next afternoon, after checking out of the fleabag, and tramping around the heart of The City on foot, I decided to split on down to Monterey and try to hook up with Vic Power. I bought a ticket and boarded a Greyhound bus. The Old Grey Dog rolled out of the depot into bumper-to-bumper traffic, crawled along onto Highway 101, and headed south. It pulled into the Monterey station around sunset. I asked directions, and discovered it was walking distance to Fisherman's Wharf, so I hoofed on over. I strolled out onto the pier, looking for the café that Vic busked in front of, and found it closed for the day. So I walked on down to the end of the pier and had a good look around at the bay, watching fishing boats at anchor and one as it entered the harbor, its work done for the day, while I pondered what to do next.

I couldn't remember the name of the coffeehouse where Vic played, had no idea where it might be or whether he'd be there that night, and wished I'd gotten an address or phone number from Sandy before I'd left San Diego. I turned my gaze away from the harbor and toward the fog shrouded hills to the east, and wondered if I should find a place for the night, and look for Vic the next day. Then I decided against it. I wanted to sleep out under the stars again, and I'd heard that Big Sur, just south of Monterey, was the place. I tramped on down to Highway One—the Coast Highway—dropped my backpack by the side of the road, and stuck out my thumb. I waited in the darkness and silence and smoked a cigarette.

In a little while, an old pickup that had seen better days—its faded coat of paint worn down to primer in places, and rusted around the edges—pulled over. I tossed my pack in the bed and climbed in. The aging hippie behind the wheel smiled a crinkly smile. His long hair hung down around his shoulders, and his salt and pepper beard was thick and curly. He was dressed in a Pendleton lumberjack shirt, khakis, hiking boots, and a blue denim jacket worn over the Pendleton.

"So you're headin' down to Big Sur, huh?" he said in a friendly casual way. "Gonna do some campin'? Well, I'm goin' right past there so I can drop ya off at the state park. Nice place. Might not be able to see the stars tonight, but you'll sure hear the ocean. My place is just a little south of there. God's country."

We told each other little bits about ourselves, and then settled back to listen to the night close in, as gears shifted, tires hummed, and worn metal parts rattled on the truck along the winding road. We crept along next to cliffs overhanging the ocean, the fog gathering around us like a blanket muffling the sound of waves crashing against rocks, narrowing our world down to headlights probing out a few narrow feet of asphalt as we wound up and down and around hairpin turns and switchbacks and along straight stretches of fog shrouded road. Next thing I knew I was standing outside the entrance to the Big Sur State Park campground, listening to the old pickup rumble off through the fog, and squinting at a sign that said No Vacancy. What to do now?

I looked around and saw a yellow light glowing dimly through the mist, and wandered on over to it. As I got closer I saw that the light illuminated a little general store that was still open. Suddenly I felt hungry, and I realized I hadn't eaten since breakfast in a coffee shop in San Francisco. After counting out my meager funds—ten bucks—I followed my hunger inside, grabbed a can of pork and beans off a shelf, paid for it, and parked my body on the steps of the wooden porch. I pulled an Army surplus can opener and spoon out of the backpack, and set upon the cold beans with gusto.

I was finishing up the contents of the can when a thin young hippie appeared out of the fog and hit me up for spare change. I handed him a quarter, while examining him with interest. He looked to be still in his teens, with stringy blond hair, barefoot, and kept from the cold only by tattered blue jeans, a dirty tee shirt, and an unbuttoned Levis jacket.

"Thanks, brother," he said. "You wouldn't happen to have a smoke too, would you?"

I pulled a pack of cigarettes from my shirt pocket and offered him one. When he made no attempt to light it, I whipped out my lighter and fired it up.

"You just get in?" he asked, taking a drag.

"Yeah."

"Where from?"

"Monterrey and San Francisco."

"The City, huh? I spent some time in the Haight. Where you headed now?"

"Well, I was going to camp out, but it's full, so now I don't know."

"You mean the campgrounds? Don't worry about that. It costs money anyway. I just crash in the woods over there." He pointed off across the road. "A bunch of us do. There's plenty of room. Just be careful, and stay away from the road. The Rangers come around at night, checking. But they don't find you if you're in far enough."

I thanked him for that piece of advice, and then asked him about himself. He told me he was from the Midwest and had been hitchhiking around the country all spring and summer. He'd been in the Haight-Ashbury before landing here a few days ago. He was going to L.A. next, or maybe Eugene, Oregon—hadn't made up his mind. He told of how he'd pick up odd jobs as needed. It sounded to me like descriptions of hobos during the Great Depression, only in his case, he had chosen this way of life. He continued his tale, all about how he'd worked on a farm in Kansas and had bedded the proverbial farmer's daughter. She had been enthralled with his long hair, his sense of freedom, and lack of convention. When he'd left, she made promises to meet him in San Francisco, but he hadn't seen her since.

I finished scooping out beans from the can, he finished the cigarette, and I gave him one for the road in parting. I made my way off into the woods in the direction he'd indicated, far from the road. I found a large tree, hollowed out at the base, and laid my sleeping bag out inside. It made a nice fit, so I crawled in, and listened to the sounds of the night. After a while, I could hear Rangers stomping about in the woods, and could make out flashlight beams off in the distance, searching out illegal campers. It sounded like they'd found one and were rousting him. But they didn't find me. I burrowed deeper into my nest and fell peacefully asleep.

In the morning I was up and about early and back on the road, hitching a ride to the next town, where I splurged on a breakfast in a coffee shop, spending most of what little money I had left. A succession of rides throughout the day took me south and onto Highway 101. In passenger seats and beds of pickups, I watched the scenery change from the golden, rolling hills of the central coast to blue Pacific Ocean and white beaches around San Luis Obispo, Santa Barbara, and Ventura, and finally into the urban sprawl of Los Angeles County. At last, I stood at the front door of my parents' house, the place I had called home before I'd joined the Navy, and hesitated before opening it.

I sensed I was at a crossroads in my life. Part of me wanted to pick up the pieces of my life where I'd left it years before, to try and fit the past with the present, like pieces of a puzzle. Another part of me longed to get on the road again, seek out Vic, and follow in his footsteps, chasing the music muse. Family and home and security and the trappings of the middle class lifestyle I'd grown up with had a strong pull—very strong. After a night in my old bed in my old room, I went shopping first for a car, and then for a job. 1969 soon slipped into 1970, and I began to forget about Vic and the siren song of the road.

CHAPTER FOUR

On The Road, At Last

It was a weekday in the summer of 1970. I'd slept in late, and when I awoke groggy and thick-headed, the morning had already become hot, the air still, the way it did in Carbon Canyon. Today was my day off, so I didn't have to make the long trek to La Habra to punch a time clock. Instead, I could devote some time to what I liked to call my stalled music career, by sitting in a straight-backed chair in my tiny stucco cottage, and playing some blues riffs on my guitar. I kept reminding myself that I was in a band again, even though we hadn't played any gigs yet. We rehearsed though, a couple nights a week in Jerry's garage, and he tried to keep us fired up with pep talks about the contacts he had, and the great gigs he planned to book for us. While Jerry filled his life with these dreams, I filled my time with distractions—like the wine I'd had too much of the night before, or the records I'd spend hours listening to over at Bummer's. Bummer rented the only cottage in our enclave in Sleepy Hollow that had more than one room, so it was something of a hangout. We all shared a communal kitchen, a building in the center of the cottages. Bummer was a talented artist, but he had monthly payments to make on his sports car, so he held down a job at the same record store I worked at, and despised the working life more than I did.

My low-rent lifestyle in Sleepy Hollow seemed to suit me just fine. Life here was quiet simplicity. No televisions or telephones, no fast-paced rat race, no middle-class expectations of acquiring material possessions and keeping up appearances. Most of us in this little community were young dropouts existing on unemployment, welfare, food stamps, and odd jobs. Bummer and I were the only ones who still kept an air of respectability through our regular jobs, which were slightly less than full time. I felt a sense of belonging and of community here, and a special kinship with Bummer and with Ed and Sue, a likeable young bohemian couple.

"Don't call us hippies, man," Ed had said when we first met. "That's just media hype. Call us freaks instead. That's what society thinks we are." He said this with an open, infectious smile.

Ed was a slender five foot eleven, with long flaxen hair, a small soft mouth, and eyes that reminded Sue of the clear blue skies of Iowa, where they'd grown up. Ed had worked briefly in a slaughterhouse there, and become a vegetarian soon after. Sue was a brunette, small of stature, possessed of a natural earthy beauty and a radiant smile. Both were soft-spoken and unassuming. The third member of their family was a black Labrador named Coal. They were planning to move up to Northern California at some point, and live in the woods. Ed liked the idea of being in a place where he could drop acid and commune with nature. He said he was on a spiritual quest. To pay the bills, he made crafts and sold them at street fairs and in consignment shops. He said they didn't need much to get by on. The material life, he explained to me, was filled with traps and pitfalls to distract you from the spiritual path. I liked Ed, but he made me feel guilty for my life somehow.

I put down my guitar, and gazed out the window at the concrete artificial mountain that marked the outside boundary of our group of cottages, and the reason for them being here in the first place. Some time in the past, no one knew for sure when, a misguided visionary had planned a ski resort on this spot. Problem was, it never snowed here in Southern California. But that fact didn't stop our entrepreneur. He would build a mountain and cover it with plastic cones to act as artificial snow. A ski lift would take people to the top, and they would ski happily downhill, no doubt yodeling all the way. He then built an enclave of cottages near the ski slope, like a little Alpine village, and prepared for the money to roll in. The ski resort opened to great fanfare and closed soon after to a flurry of lawsuits. Plastic cones and concrete, it seemed, just couldn't replace real snow, especially for hard landings. The failed dream had languished before becoming its current incarnation of low-rent, off-the-beaten-path housing for folks living on the fringe of society.

As I looked at one man's folly, I took stock of my own dreams, and fretted about my future. I was about to hit the ripe old age of twenty-four, no longer a teenager, and thirty wasn't far off. It wasn't just that I had nothing to show for my life to date, I didn't really have a vision, not even a crazy one like the founder of this place. I had only an unfulfilled longing to become a musician, like Vic Power. But other than rehearsing with Jerry's blues band, and hoping he had the energy and talent to take us somewhere (which by now I doubted), I had no idea how to make the transition from record store clerk to working musician. Not a clue. I wished I could be like Vic, but it seemed I lacked his resoluteness and focus.

I hadn't seen Vic since just before he'd hit the road, when I was still in the Navy. His cousin Marty was back from New York, living in Whittier, married and with a baby. He worked the midnight shift at some factory, but sometimes I would visit him before he'd have to go off to work, and he'd keep me updated on Vic's whereabouts and doings. Last I'd heard, Vic and his girlfriend had hitched up to San Francisco and were crashing with Huck Finn. Vic was playing in some coffeehouses and doing a bit of busking in the streets. Marty had heard that Paul Curtis and Micro Mary were up in The City as well.

Now while I sat in the chair, looking out the window and feeling sorry for my pathetic little life, I was startled by a knock at the door. Who could it be? Bummer was working today, Must be Little John, I concluded, come to borrow some coffee or a smoke. I walked to the door, flung it open, and blinked. Two figures stood there framed by sunlight, a man and a woman. The man stood facing me wearing rumpled clothing, a headband holding his long hair out of his eyes. He had sharp angular features and sported an Abe Lincoln beard. I blinked again as his face cracked into a smile.

"Hey, Dupree," he said. "Aren't you gonna invite us in?"

"Vic," I said, "what the hell? What are you doing here?"

He slapped me on the back good-naturedly as he brushed on by me and through the doorway. I stood aside to let the woman follow him in.

"Just came down for a visit, man. Wanted to look you up, By the way, this is Star. Star, meet my old partner Steve."

She held her hand out to me. "Nice to meet you," she said. "I've heard a lot about you."

I took a good look at her now, She had a closed-mouth smile that she couldn't quite contain, and when it broke briefly into a full smile, she seemed embarrassed, possibly because she was self-conscious of her overbite. But she needn't have been, for her face was radiant with a simple, natural beauty, even with a lack of makeup. The clothes she wore were simple, homespun and charming. Her light brown eyes had an innocent youthful sparkle. She stood about five foot four and had long, fine, sandy-colored hair. Her form was slender, yet with the proper curves.

"I'd offer you a chair," I said apologetically, "but all I have is this." I pointed to the straight-back chair. Vic picked up my guitar from the bed, and sat down. Star sat beside him. Vic cradled the guitar on his knee.

"Me and Star hitched down yesterday," he said, "then borrowed the Old Man's car to get out here."

"How the hell did you find me?"

"Marty said you were working at the Licorice Pizza in La Habra, so I stopped by there. You buddy Bummer told me how to find you. Since you don't have a phone out here, he drew me a map. Said you'd probably be home." He glanced around the room and then added, "Nice pad you got here. Simple but rustic." He began strumming on the guitar absent-mindedly.

"How long are you down for?" I asked, still trying to adjust to the notion that Vic was actually here.

"Oh, just a few days. Wanted to see the folks, and Marty and his new baby. And Star wanted to take a trip—see someplace new. We live in Sebastopol now, you know."

"No, I didn't know. Where's Sebastopol?"

"Up in Sonoma County, about fifty or sixty miles north of Frisco. We're crashing with Huck Finn and his old lady. Paul and Mary from Morning Glory are living with us too. We're out in the country. It's really nice man, peaceful. You should get up there sometime. So what've you been up to, Dupree, besides selling records? Doing any music?"

"Not much," I admitted. "Playing rhythm guitar in a blues band with Jerry Spitz, but we're just in the rehearsal stage. He's married now, working full time. He asked about you."

"That's cool, man, you're hooked up with Jerry. He was always a good head."

"Yeah, trouble is we haven't gotten any gigs yet and I'm getting discouraged. I really wish I could be doing music for a living—like you." I felt embarrassed for saying that, but there it was—my confession.

Vic gave me a long look and then said, "Well, Steve, if you're serious about it and want it bad enough, you should do it. Leave everything else behind, like I did, and get out of here, split up to Sonoma County. There's a lot of good musicians up there, and places to play. Paul and Mary have a rock band together, and Huck's got a jazz trio. Sonoma County's a nice place to live. No smog or traffic like down here, nobody's in a big rush. There's some beautiful country up there, redwoods, apple orchards, the Russian River. You'd dig it."

"Yeah, I'd like to," I protested weakly. "But I've got a job, rent to pay, other expenses, not to mention a girlfriend I've been seeing kinda steady."

"Bring her with you, man. Star came along with me." He looked at her and she blushed with a closed mouth smile.

"Yeah, okay," I said meekly. "I'll have to think about that."

"If you change you mind, stop by and see me. I'll give you my address. Got anything to write on?"

I gave him a pen and a notebook and he jotted it down. After handing it back to me, he began strumming on my guitar.

"Want to hear a song I wrote when I was living in Monterey?"

"Sure."

"This is about a girl I met when I was down and out. Her name was Marianne." He began singing a tale about a girl in Monterey who could cheer him up when he was feeling low, with just a smile. It wasn't a love song, exactly, but it was a story that drew me in, and made me marvel at his craft of songwriting.

"Great, Vic!" I enthused. "Play another one."

"Okay. One time in Monterey, when I was really starving, I decided to go out and pick strawberries with the braceros. That's when I discovered how exploited they are by the big landowners and straw bosses. This is a song about a straw boss named Montegro. It's called 'The Search For The Great Montegro.'"

What followed was a story song in the tradition of Woody Guthrie all about the straw boss lording it over the workers, and how the big landowner overworked and underpaid them. Maybe Vic had just latched onto someone else to copy and emulate, in this case Woody Guthrie, but I marveled at how his songwriting had improved and matured. It seemed to me that he'd finally found his voice, and I was impressed. I knew I wanted to follow in his footsteps, and become a folksinger like him, and a sense of urgency began eating at me that the time to do it was now. I felt I was being shown the way, given a chance to get out of my rut. I sensed I was at another crossroads. And yet, as I watched Vic and Star drive off that day, I didn't think I had it in me to make that radical a break with the life I was getting used to.

But life is like a movie, with sudden plot twists and turns, and I was about to experience kismet, in the form of Ray Harris. Ray was from the neighborhood I'd grown up in, and a friend of my brother Mark. Less than a week after I'd seen Vic, Ray showed up at the record store, strolled up to me with a laconic grin on his face and said, "Hey Steve, you got time to talk?"

"Sure," I said. "It's about time for my morning break, anyway. Let's go outside."

As we headed for the door, I asked Ray what was up, and that brought another grin from him.

"I'm heading back up to Oregon and looking for someone to go with me. I was living there for a while on the coast till my money ran out. So I came back here, got a job at the Shell station pumping gas, and now I've got some bucks saved up again." He paused, looked at me closely and said, "You interested in getting out of this place? Your brother said you might be."

"Maybe", I said cautiously. "Tell me more."

"Okay," he said, smiling again, "dig this—it's a real paradise up there, quiet and laid back, and the people are real friendly. The whole area is practically all forest—no urban sprawl like here. Nobody's rushing around to get someplace.. And it's cheap to live there too. I was renting a little house for fifty bucks a month. While

I was there I watched a film crew shoot some stuff for a movie starring Paul Newman called *Sometimes A Great Notion.* Pretty cool, huh?"

I had to agree with him.

"Anyway," he continued, "I've got some bread saved up but no wheels. I'm looking for someone to do the driving, and I'll share expenses. Are you interested? I think you'd love it up there, Steve."

"Yeah, Ray, it sounds good. I do want to get out of this place. I don't know if I can live out on the coast though. If I'm going to be a musician, I need to be in a populated area, where there are places to play."

"How about Eugene?" he offered. "It's a college town. I passed through there, and it's really a cool little place. They got a coffee house there."

"I know a guy there," I said. "How far is it from where you're going?"

"Not far. Maybe a hundred miles."

I thought about that for a few seconds and said, "Okay, count me in. I guess I've just been waiting for an opportunity like this, and for someone to give me a little kick in the ass. When do we leave?"

"I'm ready now," he said. "When can you go?"

"I don't know. This is all so sudden. I should give at least a week's notice with my job, and with my landlord too. And I'll need that long to get ready, get my shit together. How about leaving a week from now?"

Ray broke out into another big grin. "Great, Steve. I'm really glad I asked you."

"I'm glad too," I agreed. We shook hands on the deal, and I gave my notice as soon as I returned from my break.

In the days that followed, I busied myself with preparations for leaving, and with saying my goodbyes. It didn't bother me too much cutting ties with family and friends, and Jerry's blues band, but it surely hurt to take leave of my girlfriend Vicki.

We had met in the early spring when she had walked into the store and into my life by asking if we had the latest Van Morrison album. I checked and found we were out of stock, but I invited her over to my place to listen to my copy. She'd laughed and asked me if I was hitting on her, and I said yes. I took her out that weekend, not to my place, but to dinner and a movie. It was the following week that I showed her my little cottage. But we hadn't listened to Van Morrison that night, for by then she'd found her own copy at another record store. Soon, we were seeing each other on a regular basis, and I thought it was a good relationship—we liked each other's company and always had a good time together. I knew I wasn't in love with her, and doubted that she was in love with me either. Still, now that I was getting ready to pull up stakes, I realized how attached I was to her, and how hard it was going to be to leave her.

Vicki was nineteen, and still living at home. She took classes at the community college and worked part time at a department store. My last night in town, I picked her up at her parents' house, we went out to the drive-in, and missed most of the movie. I got lost in her sparkling dark eyes, ran my fingers through her long, silky black hair, caressed her soft cheek, and decided we should skip the ending of the flick. We made love for the first time that night in my cottage, and our farewell scene on the porch of her house just after midnight was heartbreaking for me. I felt as if I were going off to war, never to return, rather than just to another state.

"God, I'll miss you so much," she sobbed into my shoulder as I held on to her, not wanting to let go.

"I'll write," I promised. "And I'll get down here to see you again as soon as possible." But my words sounded hollow.

Back at the cottage, I tossed and turned, seeing Vicki's face in my mind, and feeling a heaviness of heart. Maybe I was making a mistake, I thought, rushing off like this into the great unknown, when there was someone right here, right now, who cared for me.

When I awoke mid-morning the sun was already high in the sky, heating up the August day, and I was already behind schedule. I glanced around the room and found it mostly bare now, a heap of clothes on the floor, my acoustic guitar sitting in the corner. The rest of my belongings were stacked up in a pile, ready to be loaded into my 1957 Buick. I wasted no time in getting dressed and packed and on the road. I wound down through Carbon Canyon for the last time, and into La Mirada to pick up Ray, who'd been waiting for hours, with only his sleeping bag and backpack to carry along. We stopped at Denny's for a breakfast just before the lunchtime rush, and got into heavy freeway traffic, headed north toward L.A. As soon as we could, we switched onto Highway 101, and continued north.

It was early afternoon when we finally climbed out of the urban sprawl of Los Angeles County. Heading downhill now, and into Ventura County, we watched as the smog dissipated into clear blue skies, and it felt as if we'd stepped out of a dark, crowded smoky bar into the fresh air and sunlight. We both let out a whoop, because now we were really on our way.

As the smog disappeared, so did my anxieties and apprehensions about this big change in my life. I settled back into the rhythm of the road as we rolled on through Santa Barbara, and inland to the gentle rolling hills and wide-open spaces of the central California coastal plateau. Around San Luis Obispo, Ray suggested we slow down and take the coastal route. "Hey, we've got all our lives to be in a hurry," he said laconically. So we intersected Highway One, a slow and winding but scenic route, at Morro Bay, and the afternoon spun leisurely along, like the gulls that circled offshore.

South of Big Sur, in the fading light, we found a little campground alongside the road overlooking the ocean. It was nothing more than a picnic table and a fire ring in a space just large enough to park the Buick. Across the road, a little artesian well bubbled out of a pipe in the side of the bluff, where we drew water to drink and wash up with. When the sun dipped below the horizon, we made a little fire in the ring with firewood that someone had kindly left behind. I pulled out my guitar and sang a few songs around the fire, we watched the stars come out, and then with bags laid out on the ground next to my car, we turned in early. I lay awake for a long time, thinking about Vicki, missing her, and struggling with the fear that I was making a big mistake.

We were up soon after the sun, and in the clear, bright morning we had a breakfast over the campfire of bacon and eggs and coffee, and washed up and brushed our teeth. I gazed out at the ocean while I smoked the first cigarette of the day, and took stock of my life. Let's see—I had no job, no home, very little cash, and no prospects for the future. I began to panic. Just then, though, Ray brought me out of my funk.

"Man," he grinned, "this has been a great trip so far! Isn't it a beautiful day? Just think—we're actually on our way to Oregon. Hey—you want to stop in Monterey on the way, and look the place over? We got time?"

"Sure," said. "We've got plenty of time. Maybe I'll make a phone call when we get there." I was thinking of calling Vicki.

We took a wrong turn somewhere, and wound up in the town of Carmel instead of Monterey, but that was fine with Ray. It was someplace new for both of us. We drove around until we found a market, and while Ray went inside to buy a few things, I used the phone booth outside to call Vicki.

This being Saturday, I knew she didn't have classes, and I was hoping she wasn't at work. I lucked out—she was at home, and answered the phone right off. Hearing her voice again thrilled me and bolstered my spirits. It was a lifeline to the past, my old life of routine and security, and I wished I could reach through the phone line and hold on to her. But we didn't have much to say. It seemed we'd said it all the night before, when we kissed goodbye. The operator signaled my three minutes were up before I could say anything meaningful, so I just said goodbye again. Ray returned with a bag of snacks, we got the Buick back onto Highway One, then over to 101, and we were back on the road, headed for San Francisco.

We gassed up before we hit The City, and just drove on through without stopping until we were on the other side of the Golden Gate Bridge. There, we pulled into the scenic overlook and took in the view of the city and the bay, and it was impressive. I couldn't help but think that the bridge held a special significance to me. The south side of the bridge was as far north as I had yet ventured. What lay ahead of me now would be the unknown, and it gave me a little thrill of anticipation. I got the idea that Ray and I should drive up to Sebastapol and find Vic, and spend the night. I ran the plan by Ray and he agreed.

"Hey," he said, "it sounds good to me. I'm in no hurry. Maybe we can get a shower there."

We pushed on through the hills of Marin County, and into Sonoma County, and I reveled in the sight of open spaces with pastures and trees between Novato and Petaluma. At Cotati, we took the Highway 116 turnoff that led to Sebastopol, and when we blew into the small agricultural town, we asked directions at a gas station, which pointed us west on the Bodega Highway heading toward Bodega Bay. The two-lane road meandered a few miles out into the country, past apple orchards ripe with fruit. We passed a small roadside café whose sign said:

Spring Hill Café
Gas Groceries Cold Beer

Then we found our turn at West Sexton Road, and followed the little country road that wound up into the hills surrounding a little valley filled with apple orchards and pastures. We found the address Vic had given me on a mailbox at the front of a little gravel road, which led to a small two story farmhouse painted a bright yellow. I turned into the driveway, parked, and killed the engine. For a moment there was silence. Then over the sound of the engine ticking as it cooled down, was the sound of a bird chirping on this summer late afternoon. After another moment, I heard myself say, "Guess I'll go to the door." As I stepped up onto the weather beaten wood porch, the door opened and a tall, longhaired brunette appeared through the screen door, eyeing me curiously.

"Hi," she said in a friendly way, "can we help you?"

"Yes," I said, "I hope so." I'm Steve Dupree, an old friend of Vic Power, and I've just come up from L.A. for a visit."

"Oh, Vic," she said, a light of recognition on her face. "I'm Kathy. Vic's not here right now, but come on in."

She opened the screen door and led me through the doorway and into a small living room. "Would you like to talk to Star? Yes? I'll go get her."

She walked out of the room and called to Star, who soon entered the room. Her eyes lit up in surprise. "Why Steve Dupree! When did you get here?"

"Just now rolled in. I've got a friend with me too, out in the car. Where's Vic?"

"Oh, he's just down the road at Spring Hill Café. He hangs out there to write songs. You want to go down there? I'll show you where it is."

"I saw it as we drove in. But I wouldn't mind if you'd like to ride along. Then we could all visit."

"Vic will be so surprised to see you. What brings you up here anyway?"

"Well, I've sorta dropped out. Come on, I'll tell you all about it."

I gave her the short version on the way to the café. We parked in front, and I was the first one through the rusty screen door that tripped off a little old fashioned bell hanging over it as I opened it. Inside, it was only a shade darker than the twilight outside. Vic, hunched over a cup of coffee and a notebook at the short counter, half turned in his stool with a mildly interested expression, as if wondering who would now be joining the proprietor and himself in the little place. A pipe sat in the ashtray next to the coffee cup, and Vic nearly knocked it over as he now spun fully around, a look of surprise on his face. 'Dupree!" he said, as if he'd just seen a ghost.

The woman behind the counter, wiping her hands on an apron, stared curiously at me as I plopped down on the stool next to Vic and shook his hand, grinning widely. By now Star and Ray had followed me in, and the woman smiled in anticipation of having some real paying customers. But our business was strictly with Vic, who was dressed in work boots, faded baggy jeans, and a loose fitting long sleeved minstrel shirt that looked homemade.

"Vic," I blurted out, "it's good to see you, man. How's life in the country?"

"Steve Dupree," he said again in disbelief. "I never expected to see you up here. How'd you get here? What are you doing?"

"Remember when I saw you a couple weeks ago, and you said I should come up here? Well I took your advice, quit my job, and here I am."

"I don't believe it," he said.

"It's true. Only I'm not staying here. Ray and I are heading up to Oregon, and we wanted to visit you on the way. By the way, meet Ray." The two shook hands. "Ray's from La Mirada too. This trip was his idea."

"What are you going to do in Oregon?"

"I don't know yet. Live, I guess, and play music. I had to get out of L.A."

"I don't blame you. That place is a madhouse. Hey, I'm really glad to see you and to see you got out of there and on the road. Star and I have been talking about going up to Oregon sometime to scout out gigs. I'd like to get a traveling circuit going from here up to Canada of gigs to tour on. How long are you going to be around before you head out again?"

"Just overnight. Why?"

"Maybe we could ride along. Would you mind? Is there room?"

"I'd love to have you come along. What do you think, Ray?"

Ray just grinned his usual grin and agreed to the plan.

"We can make space," I said, "if I leave some of my stuff behind. If you'll share the gas, I can bring you back here and pick up everything then. That gives me a chance to look around and figure out where I want to land. It'll be great!"

"Your timing is right on," said Vic. "Hey, let's all go back to the house and have a party or something. Paul will be home soon and we can have a big dinner. We're all vegetarians, Paul and Mary and us, and also Huck and his old lady Kathy. They've been renting a room out to Paul and Mary and letting me and Star crash there till we find our own place. Actually, we might go in on something together with Paul and Mary, because Kathy's pregnant, and they're going to need some privacy soon. But what are we all sitting around here for? Let's go back to the pad and eat and drink and sing, and you can spend the night. And in the morning, we'll all take off for Oh-ree-gone."

We stuffed Vic and Star into the back seat and drove to the house, where Ray and I took showers, changed clothes, and laid our sleeping bags out on the floor of a small back room. Soon Paul and Mary showed up, and while I still recognized her, I had to look hard to recognize Paul. Since I'd last seen him, he'd put on weight, and had grown a beard and his hair was even longer—halfway down his back. To my surprise, he remembered me and was happy to see me again. "Finally out of the Navy, huh?" he said. "Welcome to Sonoma County." I asked him about himself and he told me about his new band, Phoenix Rising, and how he made ends meet by studying music on the G.I. Bill (he'd spent six months in the Navy before he'd met up with Vic). During the summer, when he was between semesters, he supplemented his income doing odd jobs, a few paying gigs, and collected food stamps.

"It's tough to make a living up here," he explained. "There's not much of an economy. But there's a lot of good music happening and it's a great place to live, man."

Huck showed up and we all sat down to a simple but tasty vegetarian meal, accompanied by warm conversation. Vic mentioned our plans to everyone, and said he and Star might be gone a couple of weeks, and that they would look for a new place to live when they got back. After dinner, we all sat around drinking beer, smoking joints, playing guitars and singing. I got to hear a couple more new songs by Vic, and I thought they were just great.

When I finally crawled into my sleeping bag for the night, I no longer had doubts about my decision to hit the road. I felt that as long as Vic was coming along with me everything would be all right. I looked forward to the next day and getting on the road again, and was filled with a sense of adventure. I nodded out feeling grateful to be alive, and the hard floor beneath me felt as comfortable as a feather bed

CHAPTER FIVE

Northwestern Odyssey

Sunlight streaming softly through the window and across my face lifted me back into consciousness. In the quiet of the morning I heard the song of a bird outside, and the sound of Ray's breathing as he slept, and I smelled the summer sweetness of fruit ripening on trees. For a split second I didn't know where I was, but then I remembered I was in the country and all was peaceful. I lay there reflecting quietly for a few minutes, and then Ray stirred and awoke as well. He greeted me with a big grin, "Hey, Steve, how'd you sleep? Man, what a beautiful morning."

Soon we were up and dressed and freshly shaved, sleeping bags rolled up and packed away, and we all had a breakfast of coffee and what Star liked to call "crunchy granola," homemade by Kathy. We piled into the crowded Buick and headed back down Bodega Highway toward Sebastopol. I had left a whole backseat and more of my belongings behind in the back room where we had slept.

Ray, a guy never in a hurry, suggested we take the slow but scenic coast route to Oregon, and we all concurred. Vic wanted to stop off outside Forestville to pick up a demo tape at a coffeehouse called "The Brothers." He would need it for booking gigs. We headed out of Sebastopol on Highway 116, a two-lane road that wound through apple orchards and small houses set at odd intervals alongside. When we hit the tiny town of Forestville, Vic had me stop the car in front of a restaurant.

"I know this place," he explained. "It's close to lunch time, and maybe we can busk here. Wait for me—I'll go talk to the owner."

He came back to the car with a smug smile and said, "Okay, Dupree, get out your axe and come on in."

He grabbed his own guitar, and we all piled out and went inside the small Mexican restaurant. Ray and Star took a table and Vic and I set up in a corner, and I tried to follow him on guitar as he sang a half dozen songs. Then Star passed the hat, smiling and thanking the diners, and we retired outside to count the money, which Vic handed over to me. "Here's some gas money," he said, and we were on our way again.

Outside of Forestville, the road began threading its way through a forest of redwood and fir, and after a couple of miles Vic pointed to a large cabin set off beside the road in the forest and said, "There it is." The sign on the cabin said "The Brothers." We pulled up and walked up to the porch and through the unlocked door, Vic in the lead.

The light was dim inside, but I could make out a small stage and a bar, and between them tables and chairs. "Hello! Anybody home?" said Vic, whereupon a tall bearded man dressed in jeans and a denim shirt emerged from a back room.

"Hi Vic!" he said amiably. "What brings you here?"

"Hi Slim! These are a couple partners of mine from L.A." He nodded toward Ray and me, and we said, "Hi."

"We're headin' up to Oregon to scout out some gigs," Vic continued, "and I wanted to pick up that demo tape I left here."

"Sure thing, Vic. I'll go grab it. It's in the office I think." He disappeared back into the room and when he emerged, he had a box containing a reel-to reel-tape, and a booking calendar. He handed Vic the tape and set the calendar on the bar. "How about booking something for next month while you're here?" he said.

"Sounds good to me," said Vic. "What've you got?"

"How about the first Saturday?"

"What's the date?"

Slim told him, and he wrote it down in a little notebook he carried in his pocket.

"Thanks, man," he said.

"Have a good trip," said Slim. "Nice meeting you guys," he added.

"Take it easy, brother."

The two-lane winding road now took us across a bridge that spanned the lazily flowing Russian River and into the town of Guerneville, which looked like something out of the Wild West, with it's crowded single story buildings, many built of redwood, that lined a two block stretch of the highway. We turned west and followed the river as it flowed to the ocean, through old-growth redwood so tall and thick that sunlight and shadow played out a little dance as we threaded our way past Duncans Mills, windows rolled down to feel the warmth of the sun until we hit the coast at Jenner and turned north on Highway One. A strong offshore breeze brought with it enough of a chill for us to roll the windows back up.

The Buick crawled northward on the winding road, up and down grades, and around little switchbacks, the golden rolling hills of Sonoma County on one side, the blue Pacific Ocean on the other.

Sonoma County became Mendocino County, and the coast highway turned inland. Heading north through Garberville, we came into groves of giant redwoods at the Avenue of the Giants, and we felt dwarfed by the massive trees. Some of them were hundreds, even thousands of years old. They reached for the heavens and grew close together, thick and stately, shutting out the afternoon sun, except in places where it filtered through like butterscotch, and we once again rolled down the windows to smell the sweetness of the conifers. We passed company lumber towns and caught the sickly sweet scent of redwood chips smoldering in giant burners.

The afternoon had dimmed into evening when Vic suggested we stop at a little market in Eureka for supplies. We bought food and drink, firewood and coffee, and back on the road we began looking for a place to camp for the night. As the sun was setting, we found a state beach outside of Arcata, pulled into the parking lot near the bathrooms, and all piled out. We saw a notice saying that it was a day-use park only, but decided to camp here anyway. The sun had now dipped below the horizon, and the wind blew even harder, kicking up sand and blowing spray off the breakers. Logs and driftwood of all size and shape had washed up on the beach. I laid my sleeping bag behind one huge log, Ray put his next to mine, and Vic and Star rolled theirs out behind a tall sand dune. In the last of the fading light, we built a fire on the sand behind a protective dune, pulled up a log to sit on, had a meal of sandwiches and fruit, and then brought out the guitars to sing under the stars that shone in spots through the thin overcast. When we had all climbed into our bags that night, it was the perfect ending to a perfect day, like frosting on a cake, and the sound of mighty breakers rolling ceaselessly against the sandy beach lulled me to sleep.

The morning came on cold and grey, with wind and mist blowing off the high surf. I wrapped myself more tightly in my cocoon, feeling the dampness that had settled into my bag, and tried to get some more sleep. But after a short while, I could hear Ray stirring, and then getting up, and the sound of Vic and Star talking quietly, so I crawled out of my sack, rolled it up and brushed it off, and packed it away. Then while Ray got a fire going, I rummaged around in the car for the coffee, the pot, and some cups, and began boiling water over the fire. Star fixed us some granola and bananas, and after using the restrooms and cleaning up, we headed out, gassing up at Crescent City.

The road forked off at Crescent City, with Highway 199 running up through forests to Grants Pass in Oregon. But our route ran straight and true and ever northward along the coast. We crossed over the Smith River, and the state line and let out a big whoop when we saw the sign that announced we were entering Oregon. We took a roadside break to gaze at wildflowers and the beauty of a rocky, windswept beach. The Buick hummed along as we passed through a string of tiny towns and many roadside campgrounds, and nowhere to be seen was the kind of hustle and bustle clutter of the Southern California sprawl I'd so recently escaped from. We were now in territory familiar to Ray, who became excited and animated, telling stories, and pointing out places of interest.

"This is Reedsport coming up," he said with a grin. "It's got a small harbor. Good place for salmon and crabbing."

We had noticed a lot of sand dunes south of Florence, but now the coastline became steeper and rockier, with big waves beating against log-strewn beaches, before turning inland again through thick forest. All up the coast, we had passed cars going the other direction plastered with bumper stickers saying "Sea Lion Caves". Now we came upon the tourist trap, and while we vowed to avoid it, we nevertheless took a break in the parking lot to stretch, smoke, and try to spot seals. The next place we hit was Yachats, where Ray had lived before, and was now his final destination.

"Waldport's the next town," he said, pulling on a sweater. "That's where you'll be turning off to get to Eugene. But this here's my stop. Hope I can find work on a fishing boat." Yachats was a small unassuming hamlet of cottages and a main street of mom and pop businesses, bordered by a coastal bluff at the end of town. We dropped Ray off in the center of town in front of a café.

"Thanks a lot for the ride," he said, shaking my hand. "It's been a great trip. It was nice to meet you, Vic and Star. I hope you find lots of gigs. And I hope you enjoy Eugene, Steve, and can get your music thing together. Now just turn right at Waldport before you go across the bridge, and that road will take you into Corvallis, and from there you turn south to Eugene. Just follow the signs, you can't miss it."

And then he was off. We watched as he slipped his backpack onto his shoulders, crossed the road, and strode into the town. At least he knows where he's going and what he plans to do, I thought. And in my heart I wished him well.

Highway 34, a small winding road actually, cut a swath through the Siuslaw National Forest as it followed the contours of the Alsea River. We gazed out the windows in awe of the great vastness of forest, and hills covered in fir and evergreen, tamarack and fern, green and thick and seemingly endless. Rolling out of the forest and into the long and wide Willamette Valley at Corvallis, we turned due south toward Eugene. The valley was rich with farms and fields, green and golden in the sun, the day was bright and warm and cheerful, and I felt anticipation as we neared our destination. Interstate 5 runs straight through the Willamette Valley on its way to Canada, but we were west of the interstate on Highway 99, poking along and sharing the road with pickups, farm tractors, and logging trucks.

For no reason at all, it occurred to me that I had an aunt in Portland I'd like to visit sometime, and when I mentioned this to Vic, he said, "Hey, let's all drive up there this week. We'll scare up some money for the gas tank. I'll bet there's a booking agent there I could talk to about gigs in the Pacific Northwest and maybe Canada too." Sounded good to me. My life right now was a clean slate, and my appointment calendar was empty.

Soon Eugene came into view, like an oasis for weary travelers, in a valley ringed by forested hills, and the Willamette River running through it. As we drove into town, it was a scene even better than I had imagined. There was a small-town charm about Eugene. We drove down quiet streets of unpretentious wood frame houses, Dairy Queens, college kids on bicycles, and I felt as if I belonged in this setting. I had the address and phone number of one person in Eugene, a guy I'd known in the Boy Scouts of my youth. He'd long ago moved to Oregon, but I'd kept in touch through Christmas cards, and now I decided to call on him. I found a phone booth and gave him a jingle, and he said to come on over, he was nearby, and then he gave directions. We soon found the small tan-colored frame house at 1677 Pearl Street, and parked out front. Mike came to the door to meet us, give us handshakes, and welcome us inside.

"Good to see you again, Steve. God—how many years has it been? But you still kinda look the same, only grown up now."

I introduced him to Vic and Star, and he graciously offered me the couch to sleep on for the night. Then he said he'd call the Hotline, an information service for travelers like us, to find the others a free place to crash. I asked Mike if he knew how we could get work, picking crops for some gas money. He told us of a place where we could pick beans in the morning, and drew a map. Then after a phone call to the Hotline, I gave Vic and Star a ride over to the house where they would be spending the night. When I returned, Mike offered me a beer, and we sat out on the front porch catching up with our lives.

Mike still had the blond hair and blue eyes I'd remembered from our Boy Scout days, but now he had a little mustache as well. He had grown to my height and build, only thinner, and still had the same direct and sincere manner I'd remembered. He'd developed some muscles as well, probably from the hard work of lumberjacking that he did in the summer months. During the other nine months of the year, he attended Lane Community College.

"I'm happy to see you again," he said, "and glad for you that you got out of L.A. Oregon's a great place to live, even if it is hard to find work. The economy pretty much revolves around the lumber industry. I'm studying to be a welder. I figure that'll give me a useful trade. What about you? What are your plans?"

I told him I wasn't sure. I wanted to be a musician, maybe a folksinger, but that I realized I'd have to have some kind of a job for a while to support myself. The short-term plan was to drive to Portland and look around, drive Vic and Star back to California, then pick up my belongings and return to Eugene.

"You're welcome to stay here for a while and sleep on the couch," he offered. "I'll help you find work too, if I can. I should turn in pretty soon, as I have to get up before dawn and head out to the woods. My roommate Chuck should be home soon, so just introduce yourself, and tell him you're an old buddy of mine. I'll show you where the bathroom is. You probably want to take a shower."

Mike turned in, I took my shower, unpacked some clothes, and spread out my bag on the couch in the small living room, and stretched out. It felt blessedly comfortable. I lay there for a while, taking in the cool fresh night air that rustled through the curtain in the open window next to my head, smelling of pine trees and freshly cut and watered lawns. In the quiet of my surroundings, I listened to the sounds of the night: a dog barking, a television on next door, a motorcycle cruising down the street. I had only arrived here, and yet it already felt like home. I pondered the future, and what it might bring. Then I thought about Vicki. In my mind's eye I could see her plainly, smiling at me, I could remember the touch of her hand holding mine, and the music of her voice. I slept comfortably and soundly.

Mike and Chuck left quietly in the early dawn, trying not to wake me, but still I heard them rustling around. Then I closed my eyes again and overslept. So of course we got a late start to the bean fields out of town, took some wrong turns, and by the time we reached the place, they already had enough hands, and told us to come back another day.

"No big deal," said Vic philosophically. "It wasn't in the cards, and I'm glad we're not going to pick beans, because it's hard work."

"What about gas money?" I said.

"No problem. This is a college town, right? So there's probably some place to busk in town. Let's cruise around and look."

So we drove back to town, found the University of Oregon, and cruised the nearby streets. "There's a place," Vic pointed to a building on the corner with a sign hanging above the door that read "Old World Café". I pulled over to the curb.

"Grab your axe, Dupree, and we'll check it out."

The Old World Café was a cross between a café and a coffeehouse, the room crowded with tables and students having coffee, snacks, or lunch. Vic spoke to the woman behind the counter, thanked her, and told me we had the okay. So just as we'd done in Forestville, we set up in a corner, sang some songs, and Star passed the hat. We picked up enough change to gas up the car, and head up to Portland, a mere hundred miles away. I called my aunt from the phone in the café and asked her if we could drop on by later, and she said by all means come on up. I hadn't seen her in years. We stopped by Mike's, where I picked up my sleeping bag and backpack, and left a note thanking him and saying how we'd be back through in a couple of days. Then we headed out.

The great Willamette Valley unfolded before us, as the sun arced westward and we drove north. The panorama that rushed by us was that of blue sky with puffy white clouds, green and golden fields and farms, and forested hills. The windows were rolled down, the wind came rushing in, and Vic and Star sat beside me in the front seat, the way it seemed it should be, for now we three were a unit, a family whose destinies were intertwined.

"Hey, let's go all the way to Canada," said Vic. "We'll see British Columbia, and Vancouver, and find some places to play. We can always busk, too."

"It's okay with me," I said, "provided the car holds up. Right now it's over heating, and I want to get it checked out in Portland."

Though the sun steadily advanced toward the horizon, there was a sense of time standing still, as if we were always in the moment, right here and now. As if we had always been on the road like this, and ever would be, and so there was no sense of urgency to arrive somewhere, only the car and the road and the three of us. We passed right through Junction City, Albany, Salem, and kept moving. But then, because Star had to use a restroom, we took a little break just outside Portland.

"Aren't you glad you quit your job, Steve?" said Vic. "You don't have to go back to that grind anymore. You can be like us—gypsies, living in the moment, playing music, living life to the fullest."

Then we rolled into Portland, a big city by Oregon standards, but not nearly as big or sprawling as L.A. It was a port city, sitting between the Willamette and Columbia Rivers. We crossed over one of the many bridges on the Willamette, found a phone booth, and I called my aunt for directions. We found her house near the top of a hill in the Belmont district, and she welcomed me with a hug, and offered to put us all up for the night. After dinner, she fixed up the guest room for Vic and Star and the couch for me. After my friends turned in, I had a chat with my aunt about my plans for the future, and she nodded dumbly, but I could tell she didn't understand. She advised me to find a nice safe job and to stick with it. She'd grown up in the Great Depression of the 1930s, and nothing I had to say made any sense to her. She did say though that she thought Star was sweet and would "make somebody a fine wife." It was apparent she didn't mean Vic.

In the morning, my aunt left for her job, and we headed downtown to find a garage to have my cooling system checked. While the mechanic was flushing out the radiator, and telling me I probably could use a new one, Vic found a booking agent in the phone book, and jotted down the address. He didn't call for an appointment, however, figuring he probably wouldn't get one. It would be better just to show up and take our chances.

We drove on over to the agent's office in the heart of the city, and barged in on him. He was actually on the phone when we showed up, and he shot us a look of annoyance as we stood waiting for him to hang up while Star waited in the car. After he set down the receiver, Vic gave him the old Power sales pitch and handed the balding middle aged man the demo tape, which he threaded through a tape machine, punched a button, and sat back to listen to. Vic's guitar and voice came out clearly through the speaker, as he sang a John Lee Hooker blues tune. The booking agent, whose ashtray already held a burning cigarette, lit a fresh one and squirmed uncomfortably in the swivel chair behind his cluttered desk. He wore a cheap looking rumpled suit, and his tie was loosened. I noticed a bottle of Maalox tablets on the desk as he cleared his throat in the stuffy room. Before he could say anything though, Vic continued the sales pitch.

"Yes sir, I do blues and folk songs, mostly original, and they really love me down around the San Francisco area. I'm trying to expand my territory, though. I'm hoping to get some gigs in the Pacific Northwest and Canada. I travel light."

The phone rang as the man got up to turn off the tape. He answered the call and talked enthusiastically with the client on the line about a tour he was working on, while he unscrewed the cap on the Maalox bottle and tossed a couple tablets in his mouth. He finished the call cheerfully, set the receiver down, walked over to the tape machine, took the tape off, and handed it back to Vic. He remained standing, unsmiling, and said, "I'm sorry. I'm sure you're quite talented, but I don't think I can do anything for you. Your music isn't very, uh, marketable. Thank you for coming by." Then he walked over to the door and held it open for us.

"But you haven't heard the whole tape," said Vic. "I've got other songs."

"I've heard enough. I'm sorry, but I'm a busy man. Thank you for stopping by."

We walked slowly back to the Buick. Vic was sullen. I tried to cheer him up.

"Aw, don't worry about it man. He was just a jerk. Probably couldn't do anything for you, like he said. He looked pretty small time."

"Yeah, maybe so. But we can still go to Canada, can't we, and find our own gigs?"

"I don't think so," I said. "The mechanic says I need a new radiator, and I can't afford one. I'm running out of money fast."

"Okay, then," Vic said cheerfully. "Let's go see Sticks, my old drummer from Morning Glory. He married a woman with a couple of kids, and they live on a farm a few miles west of here. We can go there tomorrow. Tonight we can find some coffeehouses to play in where we can pass the hat."

Like Eugene, Portland was a college town, and where there's a college, said Vic, there's a coffeehouse. We found two of them that night. The first one had more folk singers in the audience than listeners. Nonetheless, Vic sang at both places, Star passed the hat, and we made enough to fill up the tank again. Next morning, we said goodbye to my aunt, thanked her, and hit the road. I was filled with contentment as we headed out of Portland. This traveling life seemed to suit me.

We took Highway 26, a little country road really, that headed toward the ocean, but long before reaching it, we found the old farmhouse where Sticks had settled, old and weather beaten and in need of paint. It stood two stories tall, weeds over grew the porch, and berry bushes rambled as they pleased around the property. But the house had a certain charm to it, as if it had withstood decades of change and was now feeling comfortably broken in. Vic hadn't seen Sticks since Morning Glory had broken up, and I had only met him once before. But no matter, we were welcomed as if long lost cousins by Sticks, his wife, and two children. Sticks looked the perfect country bumpkin in his overalls, work shirt, boots, and scruffy beard. He invited us into his high-ceilinged living room, and we sat down on a well-worn couch. Sticks looked like the farmer in the dell, but he explained that he made the house payments through his job with the phone company. Farming, for now, was just a hobby.

They had a little vegetable garden and some chickens, and to prove it, he gave us a tour of the property. After leading us back to the house, he rolled up a fat joint, handed it to Vic, and invited him to fire it up, and then said, "So how the hell are ya, brother, and what brings ya up this way?"

Vic lit the joint, took a hit, and passed it on. He gave Sticks and Bonnie the short version of our trip, then pulled out his guitar, and began singing a song he'd been working on since morning.

On a northern odyssey
Me and Star and Steve Dupree
Played and sang in Eugene town
In a coffeehouse we hung around.
Is anyone going to Canada,

Vancouver or Victoria?
We've got room for just one more,
Gonna sing a song and walk out the door.
Car broke down in Portland town,
But that's okay, we'll hitch our way.
With our sleeping bags and our guitars
We're bound to ride in other cars.
Is anyone going to Canada,
Vancouver or Victoria?
We've got room for just one more,
Gonna sing a song and walk out the door.

Soon the gathering became a party, an evening filled with song, home-cooked dinner with vegetables from the garden; beer, wine, and pot, and plenty of stories and reminiscing. We spent the night, of course, and I rolled out my bag on the floor, found it to my liking, and thought how this gypsy life seemed to be one big adventure.

Sticks had the following day off from his job, but he wasn't one to just hang around the house doing nothing. He owed a favor to his neighbor, and was about to repay by helping stack bales of hay. He enlisted the help of Vic and I, and so we drove over to the neighbor's farm in Sticks' old pickup, bumping over unpaved roads and kicking up dust. Other neighbors were already there, loading up bales, and stacking them in the barn, before the rain came. Sticks pointed to ominous clouds in the sky that seemed to grow darker and thicker by the minute. "Gotta make hay while the sun shines," he said with an ironic smile.

The farm was situated in a valley, surrounded by green rolling hills, and as far as I was concerned, we could be anywhere, so far were we from the tell tale marks of modern civilization: malls, freeways, housing tracks, road signs and billboards. It felt good to be sweating outdoors under a brooding sky in rural Oregon. Being a stranger to manual labor, Vic soon wore out and had to rest. I wasn't in much better shape myself, but I didn't want to appear soft, so I willed myself to keep lifting and heaving, until the job was done, and I felt sore all over. It crossed my mind that it would be nice to stay in this area for a while and just unwind, but we had to get back on the road.

Back in Eugene, we pondered various ways of making gas money for the southbound trip. We discussed the merits of busking versus crop picking until Mike hit upon a better option. There was another coffeehouse in town, The Odyssey, at 161 Willamette Street. Inside the Odyssey was the Switchboard, an information service that, in addition to finding crash pads for travelers, hooked up drivers with riders. We had room in the car for a couple of riders who could share the gas with us. We split on over to The Odyssey, and after putting in a request for riders, Vic played a set onstage, and Star passed the hat. The Switchboard provided us with the names of two college girls who needed a ride to Berkeley, so we gave them a call. They agreed to go with us, and said they'd be ready to leave in the morning. We said our goodbyes to Mike that night before he turned in, and thanked him for everything. He said he'd see me when I returned from down south.

The girls were not in any rush to get to Berkeley, so we took off late in the morning. They were traveling light, so we put them in the back seat, and Vic and Star and I all squeezed into the front. We headed south on Interstate 5, which ran through the Willamette Valley and then alongside the Cascade mountain range. Many of the hills we passed in southern Oregon had been logged out, but were still green with grasses and brush.

We pulled into the sleepy college town of Ashland to gas up, and when Vic noticed a poster advertising the Shakespearean Festival, he decided Ashland held some good busking potential. "There must be a coffeehouse in this town," he said. There was and we found it, but it was closed and wouldn't open up until the evening. So we cruised around until Vic spotted a little store that sold crafts and souvenirs, and such. He spoke to the owner, a laid-back hippie type, who agreed to let us set up on his wooden porch and play for change. We didn't make much, so the old guy kicked in a couple of bucks and thanked us. Vic asked the girls if they'd mind sticking around town a little while longer, at least until the coffeehouse opened, and they said okay.

As soon as the place opened its doors, Vic was inside trying to sell the manager on us singing there, but he said he already had an act booked for the night. Maybe we'd like to book something for a future date? No, we said, we didn't know when we'd be back this way. How about sticking around for the show, he offered. We could get in free as his guests. Okay, we said, and by the way, did he know of any good places to camp for the night? He told us about nearby Crater Lake, and how to get there, but later that night, after we'd seen the show, I took a wrong turn and we ended up out in the middle of nowhere; nothing around us but a gravel road, rocky barren hills, and the blackness of a moonless night, the Milky Way our only light. By now I had had enough of driving. We would camp right here, and find our way back to the interstate in the morning. We scattered our sleeping bags out on the hard ground and tried to get some shut-eye.

In the morning, we stumbled out into a hot bright sunlight day with a cloudless blue sky. Star fixed us all some breakfast, and we retraced our path back to the highway that led to I-5. We were close to the border with California, and soon after crossing it we were herded into an agricultural check station.

"Where are you coming from?" asked the stone faced customs man in a green uniform and Smokey The Bear hat as he stuck his head in the open window and looked around.

"Oregon," I said.

"Where are you headed?"

"California."

"Are you carrying any fruits or vegetables?"

"No."

There was an uneasy silence and for a moment I thought he was going to ask to search the car for contraband, but instead he said, "You may proceed," and waved us by.

After hours of barreling down the interstate, we took a cutoff north of Sacramento that pointed us to the San Francisco Bay. We crossed over a bridge and were soon taking the Berkeley exit. The girls got off near the university, and we helped them with their bags into the old Victorian house with bay windows, and a nice view from the second story. We took our leave, drove across the Bay Bridge, through The City, over the Golden Gate Bridge, and north to Sebastopol. We stopped at a little fruit stand on Highway 116 to buy apple juice and veggies, and Star said with a full toothy smile, "Doesn't it feel good to be home, Vic?"

"It sure does," he said, lighting his pipe and puffing on it. "There's no place like home."

But as it turned out, they'd both spoken too soon, for when we arrived at the farmhouse on West Sexton Road, we found out it was no longer their home. While we'd been gone, Paul and Mary had rented another place for themselves, and Huck and Kathy took in the welcome mat for Vic and Star. It seems they'd already overstayed their visit before we'd even left on our journey, and the place that the others had rented was too small to accommodate another couple. We would all have to spend the night somewhere else.

Vic knew a guy up the road, at the end of West Sexton, where we might be able to crash. His name was Sean, an older guy, but a free spirit. He lived in a cabin surrounded by redwoods, and he invited us all in. We all sat around in his small living room with a fire going in the wood stove, swapping stories, singing songs and smoking a joint. Sean played the banjo, frailing style, and we jammed into the night. He said it was getting too crowded here in Sonoma County, so he was thinking of splitting to Alaska. That night I slept on the living room floor, while Vic and Star took their sleeping bags to the tree house out back. They were still hanging out in the tree house when I left that morning, the stuff I'd left before all crammed into my back seat.

"We'll be okay here for a while," said Vic. "We'll make out all right. In fact, it's going to be kinda fun living in a tree house, just like being a kid again. But I'm bummed out that Paul and Mary didn't find a place big enough for all of us."

"Well, honey," said Star, "maybe they found a real good deal and had to move on it immediately."

"Yeah, maybe," grumbled Vic. Then he turned to me.

"Well, Steve, thanks for the ride and the adventures," he said, shaking my hand. "I hope you get your music thing together up in Eugene. It looks like a great place to live."

As I pulled out of Sebastopol and headed for Interstate 5, I keenly felt the absence of Vic and Star. I was alone now in the front seat with all my possessions in the back. But I looked forward to getting back to Eugene and Mike, and so I pushed the Buick onward. Before long it began overheating, the temperature gauge pegged on red.

I would pull over every now and then to let the engine cool down, but the constant climbing through the foothills of the Cascades kept it running hot. Late into the night I stopped at a gas station to fill up and to check the water and oil. An ominous rattling sound had been coming from the engine. When I looked at the dipstick, there appeared to be water mixed in with the oil.

"Doesn't look good," warned the mechanic. "Might be a blown head gasket. I wouldn't drive it any further if I were you."

"I've got to," I said. "I haven't got the money to fix it, and I need to get to Eugene."

"I wouldn't recommend it. You're still over a hundred miles away. But if you insist on driving, go slow, don't push it, and don't let it overheat."

I nosed the Buick back on the road for the last time, and pointed it north. The gauge pegged red again, and just as I was coming into the little logging town of Myrtle Creek, the engine blew with a loud bang and a cloud of steam. It had thrown a rod. The engine seized up and died, losing all power. I gripped the wheel hard, steering toward an off ramp, and coasted down into a bean field. Now there was complete silence as I sat there, frozen in fear and heartsick. I turned the key one last time, but nothing happened. No sound, except for the beating of my heart and heavy breathing.

Then I surrendered to my fate. I got out the sleeping bag, wandered further into the bean patch, rolled it out, and crawled inside. I would make plans in the morning. Now I would sleep. But sleep wouldn't come. The ground was cold and hard and I was filled with anxiety. How would I get to Eugene now? How would I live without a job? I was nearly broke. And now I was alone, and I shivered in the bag until the sun appeared in the eastern sky.

There was an auto wrecking yard nearby that I walked to in the morning. I traded in my car keys and pink slip for a tow out of the bean field and a promise from the owner to hold my belongings for me for a couple of days. I lugged my pack, my sleeping bag and my acoustic guitar over to the Greyhound station, where I bought a one-way ticket to Eugene.

CHAPTER SIX

Down and Out

I walked from the Eugene Greyhound station the few blocks to Mike's and sat on the porch until he and Chuck returned from a hard day in the woods, all grimy, sweaty, and beat. But as soon as Mike heard my tale of woe, he insisted on driving the hundred miles to Myrtle Creek immediately to retrieve my belongings, which included an electric guitar. We raced down in his Porsche, and he wouldn't even accept gas money from me. All the way there and back he reassured me that things would work out. I could sleep on the couch as long as I needed to, and he would do his best to help me find work, which he did try, driving me around to lumber mills and the like to fill out applications. He also helped me apply for government surplus food commodities. That's when I learned the true meaning of friendship, and a truer friend than Mike Grafton would be hard to find.

Now that I was down and out and without wheels, life really slowed down. I got to know and love downtown Eugene as I walked its streets daily, searching in vain for work. I found myself hanging out at The Odyssey a lot. Eventually, I got up enough nerve to sing a few songs on the stage, but didn't have enough confidence (or, I might add, talent) to pass the hat. If Vic had been with me, though, with Star to pass the hat, we would have made some walking around money.

As a way of filling up some of my time, I began volunteering at the Switchboard, the space inside the Odyssey that acted as a referral service for wanderers passing through town. Eugene seemed to be a way station for hippies that summer, who were coming and going to San Francisco, Seattle, L.A., and all points of the compass. It seemed everyone was on the move. I'd answer the phone and direct someone to the free clinic, or hook up riders with drivers, or find someone a crash pad for the night. Through my unpaid job at the Switchboard, I heard about Vortex.

Vortex was to be a three-day rock festival, patterned after Woodstock, to be held at Milo McIver State Park, outside of Portland, for which the state of Oregon would pick up the tab. It was scheduled to take place the same weekend as an American Legion convention in Portland, where anti-war demonstrators were planning to take to the streets. Fearing a repeat of the Democratic Convention in Chicago two years before, Governor McCall weighed his options. He could call out the National Guard, or he could create a diversion to draw the young people out of town.

There was a rock festival planned for that weekend in neighboring Washington State, so why not have another one outside of Portland? It would probably be easier on the state budget than calling out the National Guard, it would draw attention away from Portland, and no heads would get busted in the process.

The fact that the festival was free piqued my interest, and using my position at the Switchboard to score a ride, I headed out of town that weekend for, hopefully, three days of peace, love, and music.

Milo McIver State Park turned out to be a paradise of tall stands of fir and other trees, and meadows with campsites. The shallow and swift moving Clackamas River ran along its border, shining silver and cool in the sun. I found a nice spot beneath a tree and near the river, and stashed my sleeping bag and canteen to stake my claim. Then I went exploring. Hippies were abundant everywhere; skinny-dipping, playing guitars, beating on drums, smoking pot, romping with dogs. There was a large stage set up in a meadow, a first aid tent, and a kitchen area to feed the thousands that were still pouring in. I headed on over to a hillside overlooking the stage, where a band was just setting up, On the way there, someone offered me a tab of LSD, and without pausing to think twice, I popped it into my mouth. I found a nice spot on the hill, under a pine tree, and began tripping on the acid while listening to the music, as the sun disappeared and the stars took its place in the ink colored night sky. By now I was tripping heavily, and when I'd look at the stars, they would spin crazily, as if out of control. The trees began to move before my eyes, emitting vibrations, the stage pulsated in crazy color patterns, and my body began going into spasms. The trip had turned ugly, and I became filled with anxiety, feeling alone and insignificant, detached from reality and my surroundings. I began to panic.

A sandal clad, smiling hippie strolled up the hill, and sat down beside me, then pulled a blanket around his shoulders. I turned and began talking to him, to make sure I wasn't going crazy.

"Hey, man," I said shakily, "I don't feel so good. I dropped some acid a while back, and now I'm freaking out."

"Was it some of that bad acid that was going around?"

"I don't know. Some guy handed it to me and I took it."

"Well, brother," he said "it was probably the grey acid they were warning about over the PA system. They were saying to stay away from it. People are having bad trips. There's a first aid tent around here somewhere. If you need to go there to come down, I'll help you find it."

"I don't think so, thanks. I just feel very weird."

"Well, here, brother, I'll share my blanket with you. You'll be okay."

"Yeah—thanks. This is nice of you, man, to look out for me."

"We're our brother's keeper, right?" he said.

I was still tripping badly, but now I felt like I could hang on. The next thing I knew, the emcee was bringing up the next act, and my ears pricked up.

"And now from Sonoma County, California, please welcome Phoenix Rising!"

"Hey," I said to my blanket brother, "that's Paul's band, I know him! I need to get down to the stage. I've got to see him and talk to him."

I felt that seeing someone familiar would restore my fragile hold on reality, and help bring me back down. But when I tried to stand up, I found I couldn't move. I was just too stoned. So I just sat there paralyzed while Phoenix Rising played a set and left the stage. Another band came on followed by yet another. The guy beside me fell asleep, but I was still wide-awake and shivering when the dawn came and the sun began warming the air again. The effects of the acid had worn off enough now that I could move, so I came down off the hill, found my campsite, and tried to sleep. But by mid-morning, it was too warm and too bright to stay in the sleeping bag, so I visited a portable toilet, and then the soup kitchen. I lined up for breakfast and was ladled out some simple but filling vegetarian food. After I ate, I took a dip in the river, and tried to sleep again. But it was no use. I was beat, and drained from no sleep and bad acid. I wanted to go back to Eugene. I walked out of the park to the road and began hitching.

The first ride took me down a country road through farmlands and forests. After standing there for a while, tired and lonely, I saw a guy walking toward me along the side of the road. He was tall, thin, taking long strides, and carrying a walking stick. As he got nearer, I could see that he was older than me, with a mustache and long dark hair tied in a ponytail, and sporting a dark tan. He smiled and flashed me the peace sign.

"Good day, brother," he said pleasantly. "Where you headin' to?"

"Eugene. You live around here?"

"Nope. As a matter of fact, I'm heading to Eugene myself. I just like to walk while I hitch. It makes the time go faster, and if I walk I'm just that much closer to where I'm going. Been here long?"

"About an hour, I guess. There hasn't been much traffic. Hope I don't get stuck here."

Well," he said, "when you get impatient, just start walking. One time down in California I walked all night. But when I finally did get a ride, it was from a guy named Neal Cassady, and he took me down to La Honda to Ken Kesey's place, where there was always something groovy going on. So it was worth the wait. Kesey lives outside of Eugene now, in Springfield. I've been there too, but nothing was happening. Guess everybody settles down sooner or later. By the way, where you coming from?"

"Vortex," I said. "I just left there. I had a bad acid trip."

"Well, maybe it's a good idea you're leaving. People are pouring in there like rats, too many it seems to me. With bad acid going around, you never know what might happen." After a pause, he added, "Don't worry, sooner or later we'll get a lift. After you've done this a while, you learn to trust."

He was right, of course. We got a ride sooner than later, and it was a great one at that. We climbed into an old Metro step van that had been outfitted to live out of, sort of a hippie RV, and off we went in a cloud of pot smoke and music blaring from an eight-track tape player, through speakers strategically placed in the front and back of the van. I moved to the rear and sat on a Persian rug, my back against the paneling that had been installed to give it a more homey feel.

We had a smooth ride all the way to Eugene, where my new friend and I were dropped off downtown. We parted there with a handshake, since we were going different directions now, and I began walking toward Pearl Street. Dark clouds gathered in the sky, and I walked faster now to stay ahead of the oncoming rain, all the while enjoying the smell of the clean pine scented air of an Oregon summer afternoon. As I hit Pearl Street and could see the tan house about a block away, drops began falling slowly, feeling cool against my face. I was glad to be back, because now I realized that this was my home as well as Mike and Chuck's. The sky opened up with pellets of rain just as I opened the door and stepped inside.

The next night, as I was sitting in the living room, playing my folk guitar, there came a knock at the door. Mike was over at his girlfriend's and Chuck was off somewhere else, so I figured I'd just tell whoever was knocking to come back later. So it came as a complete surprise to find Marty Power standing there on the porch, looking a little beat, with an attractive young woman by his side.

"Well, howdy Steve," he said with a grin. "I wasn't sure if this was the place or not, but I guess it is, seeing as how you're here."

I was too startled to say anything, other than to invite them in. They took the couch.

"I got your address from Vic," Marty began. "I saw him down in Santa Rosa. He and Star are living in a motel there. Oh, hey, let me introduce you to someone. This is April. We've been traveling together."

I said hello, and let my eyes fully explore her. She had striking features: silky black hair, smoldering dark eyes, a large full bust, and a sultry voice. I wondered what had become of Marty's wife and baby.

"April and I were just up by Seattle at the Sky River Festival. We met up on the road, and headed there. We didn't have any money, so we tried to sneak in. We got caught in this huge undergrowth of blackberry bushes and tried to fight our way through for what seemed like hours. Finally, when we thought we were through it, we found that we were right in front of the entrance, and they wanted us to pay. So we just gave up, told them we didn't have any money, and they just waved us in."

"That's far out," I said. "I just got back from a rock festival myself—Vortex, near Portland."

"Oh yeah, I heard about that. How was it?"

"It was nice, other than some bad acid. I left early, though. Paul Curtis' band, Phoenix Rising, was there."

"Oh yeah? Did you get to talk to him?"

"No, unfortunately." I decided not to go into detail about it. "What brings you all the way up here?"

"Well, Steve, I just had to get away for a while. Clear my head out, you know? So I'm on the bum for now. Guess I'll hitch to Frisco next. April's going that way too. She's hoping to find a ride here in town."

"I might be able to help you there," I offered. "I'll make some calls."

"What are you doing up here, Steve? Vic told me about your trip, but I'm kind of amazed. You've never hit the road like this before. I figured you'd spend the rest of your life in La Habra, selling records, or become a banker like your old man." He laughed, but I could hear a tone of respect in his voice.

"I don't know. Just had to break out I guess, seeing as how Vic did it. I guess I'm trying to follow in his footsteps, make a new life for myself with music." I handed him my guitar. "Why don't we jam a little bit?"

I got out my electric guitar and played it acoustically, without an amp. We sang, told stories, and hung out. Mike came home accompanied by a friend of his, who just happened to be riding his motorcycle down to San Francisco in the morning. He took one look at April and happily agreed to take her along. In fact, he said, she could even spend the night at his place. Marty spent the night on the floor, and in the morning, after breakfast, I walked with him down to the onramp for the interstate, and waited with him until he got a ride. He waved goodbye, and headed south.

During the time I spent in Eugene, Mike and I rekindled our friendship, and hung out a lot together. He introduced me around to his other friends, and I was getting more used to the idea of settling down here. I did miss Vicki, though, and wrote to her often. Mike and I took a trip out to the coast one day, to see the wild rugged beauty of a windswept beach. Another time he showed me around town, we hit a couple of night spots, and drove up to Skinner's Butte with its great view of the city and its lights. He told me stories and anecdotes about Eugene's history to make me feel more at home here, and reassured me about how I'd made the right choice to get out of Southern California. Now if I could only find a job, I could stop worrying about being broke.

September arrived, and while Mike was enrolled for the fall semester at Lane Community College, I was running out of money, hope, and patience. I tried to pawn my electric guitar, but the guy behind the counter wouldn't even give me ten bucks for it. I began feeling like I was dead weight, and had nothing to contribute to Mike or anybody else. And I'd made no more headway at becoming a musician than when I'd been living in California. I got homesick for my old life of routine and security, and longed to be with Vicki again. The day came when I was down to my last dollar, and I decided it was time to throw in the towel. I walked down to the Greyhound station, electric guitar in hand, and shipped it off COD in care of myself to the nearest depot from La Mirada. Then I bummed ten bucks off Mike, promising to pay him back when I could, and the next morning after he left for his classes, I rolled up my bag, packed my pack, picked up my guitar, and headed out the door. Before I split, though, I left a note thanking him for everything, and saying how I hoped to return some day.

With my pack on my back and guitar in hand, I walked on down past the Greyhound station to the end of Pearl Street, and hoofed it down Franklin to the onramp. I dropped my pack, stuck out my thumb, and began obsessing about Vicki.

It was a good day to be on the road, all things considered. The sky was clear, and the air was warm, and I had a nice spot to start out from, a quiet little entrance by the side of a bluff near downtown. It didn't take long for the first car to stop, although it wasn't the type of car I'd been hoping for. This car had a rack of colored lights on top, and was carrying the markings of the Highway Patrol. The officer motioned me over. Putting down my thumb and leaving my gear where it was, I walked on up to the officer's rolled down window.

"Where ya headed, boy?" he said behind sunglasses.

"California," I answered with a polite smile.

"Well, that's good, that's real good. But you'd better find another way to get there. Hitchhiking is illegal in this state, so you'd better move along."

"Look, sir," I explained, "I've got ten bucks to my name and I'm trying to get back home. What if I just stand by the side of the road, but don't stick out my thumb. Then if someone offered me a ride, it wouldn't be hitching would it?"

He gave me a good looking over before answering. "The law states that you cannot solicit a ride. It doesn't say anything about waiting by the side of the road. Just don't stick out your thumb. And good luck."

With that, he drove off, looking for bigger fish, I supposed.

I rummaged around in the pack and dug out a pen, some notebook paper, and a piece of tape and made a sign that said "L.A." in bold letters and taped it to the back of my guitar, then held it up as a sign. If the cop came back, I could just turn the guitar around and start playing it. But he didn't return, and soon I scored a ride. As Eugene disappeared around a bend, I silently said goodbye to a place I'd grown to love, but at the same time I looked forward to seeing family and friends, and especially Vicki

We rolled south past Myrtle Creek, where my Buick Roadmaster now sat in a junkyard, the graveyard of automobiles. We continued through the hills of southern Oregon to Grant's Pass, where the Rogue River wends, and roads intersect and travelers change direction, as did the car's driver. I thanked him and hopped out at the station he'd pulled into to gas up. I walked up the hill to the southbound onramp of I-5. A sunburned kid stood there, with backpack, and looking beat in the noonday sun.

"Hey, man, how's it goin'?" he said listlessly. He was young, tall, and blond, and looked like a surfer on the bum, which is exactly what he turned out to be. I discovered later he was only seventeen, but for now I just got his name—Chip.

"I'm Steve," I said. "Where you headed to?"

"L.A."

"So am I. What part?"

"Orange County."

"I'm going to La Mirada."

"Anaheim," he replied.

"Far out! That's just south of me. You want to team up? It might be easier for both of us that way."

"Sure, why not," he said with indifference.

We passed the next hour sitting and standing in heat and road dust. I told him a little about my time in Eugene and he gave me a sketchy version of his travels. We talked mostly to break the boredom of waiting.

"I hope we get a long ride," he said. "I'd like to see a trucker pull over and take us a few hundred miles."

As if in answer to his wish, a double flatbed tractor trailer pulled over, air brakes screeching, wheels kicking up rocks and dust, and came to a stop about fifty feet ahead of us. The trailers had ropes lashed across them to hold bales of hay, but on the first trailer, they held eight hitchhikers. This must be the hippie version of a Greyhound bus, I thought to myself. Chip and I grabbed our gear and ran over to the rig and up to the cab. The young driver opened the door and stepped down to the ground, grinning.

"Where you guys headed?" he asked.

"California," said Chip.

"L.A." I added.

"Well, I can take you as far as Stockton, about four hundred miles from here. Go ahead and climb up, secure your gear, and hang on—you're in for a ride."

He wasn't kidding. It was a hell of a ride. We climbed onto the second trailer, nodded to the others on the first trailer, and lashed ourselves on tight. The driver released the brake, dropped into gear, got back on the road, and roared off. And then like hoboes on boxcars, with a ribbon of asphalt instead of steel tracks, we sat back and watched the world fly by. We rolled along between two great mountain ranges, the Cascades and the Siskiyous, the countryside green and wild and beautiful. Wind whipped around us, and I fished my fringed leather jacket out of the pack, put it on, and buttoned it up. It wasn't an easy thing to do, for the pack was lashed under a rope. With the jacket now in place, I gripped my guitar with one hand, and a rope with the other.

In Weed, California, the driver pulled over to a small convenience store, where he bought soft drinks and chips for all of us. After a short break, we started out again, but not before picking up more hitchhikers. As a matter of fact, he kept right on picking up more hippies until we numbered eighteen in all, and all of us hanging on for dear life. We passed Mount Shasta and Lake Shasta as the sun was setting, turning the snow capped volcanic peak different shades of red and pink and lavender.

With the sunset, darkness came on quickly, and with it the cold. Stars began winking on one by one, until the black sky was filled with them. The truck's headlights lit the road, running lights lit the two trailers, and the moon appeared to light the heavens. I shivered with the cold and fatigue, my eyes stung from the wind but my senses were sharpened and I never felt so alive. I thought about Vicki, and about Vic and Star, about Mike, and about what the hell I would do when I got back home. Then I shut off the incessant flow of thoughts and worries, and just watched the scenery flash by as the night closed in tighter and we headed farther south into the Golden State.

Down in California's Central Valley, where the air was warmer, the driver took a cutoff to Highway 99, and reached his destination at Stockton. Our hippie bus depot was the warehouse where the trucker would pick up his load of hay in the morning. Those of us who wanted to bed down for the night could sleep on a bale. But Chip and I wanted to get back on the road, so we hoofed it on down to a southbound onramp of 99 and dropped our gear. It was well past midnight, so traffic was light. The night air of the San Joaquin Valley was warm and sticky with humidity. We were both exhausted, and passed the time in silence.

The first ride came with a glare of headlights, the sound of a transmission downshifting, rubber tires on gravel, and a car door opening. We were dropped off on the outskirts of Modesto, where we found an open coffee shop and ordered coffee, then refills, and were shown the door when they closed at two in the morning. But the night cook was nice enough to give us a lift down the road.

After hearing the car door slam, and the car's engine fade out into the distance, it became completely quiet and still, and I felt as if the night had swallowed us. I looked up and down the highway. It was empty. Chip sat down, put his head on his pack, and dozed. Wound up by coffee, I paced restlessly, sat down, got back up and paced some more, all the while chain smoking cigarettes until the pack was empty. Then I lay on my back, hands locked under my head, and gazed at the sky. I fretted about my future until the sky became lighter in the east, and I could hear birds waking up. Soon, the rest of the world began stirring as well, as a new day dawned. All over the valley people were now, or would soon be, leaving their safe, orderly homes and going off to work or to school, fulfilling purposeful lives, while I just stood by a highway, hoping to get a ride to someplace else.

But even with a new day underway, the spot we were stranded at wasn't exactly a hotbed of activity. In an hour's time, I counted only six vehicles pass us by at the onramp. Then a 1954 Ford crept cautiously toward us, the driver giving us a hard stare before pulling over in front of us. Chip came to life, jumping up and throwing his pack onto one shoulder. I picked up my gear and walked slowly up to the driver's door, and said through the open window, "Thanks for stopping!"

The driver sat slouched in the seat with one hand over the steering wheel. He wore a faded denim jacket over a tee shirt, and jeans. His hair was dark and greasy, and hung across his forehead. A cigarette dangled from his lips. He was wiry, with a hard looking face, and said through tight lips, "We're headin' south. Hop in."

I caught a glimpse of the guy in the passenger seat. He looked to be in the same age range as the driver, mid to late twenties, and was dressed similarly, only his tee shirt was black, with a pocket that held a pack of Camels. He was stocky, muscular, and had a tattoo of a black panther on his arm. He had medium length black hair, combed into a waterfall, giving him a 1950s delinquent look.

Chip and I got into the back seat, happy just to be moving again. The guy with the tattoo leaned his elbow on top of the seat and turned to us with a snarl of a smile.

"How far you goin'?"

"L.A."

"Yeah?" he said, with a sideways glance at the driver. "We might be going that far, huh Buck?"

Buck laughed slyly. "Yeah—maybe. We haven't decided yet. Me and Reno are just out for a drive. Wherever we end up's where we end up. Depends on how much dough we can scare up for the tank."

Reno, leaning over the seat at us, and looking menacing, said, "You got any bread you can contribute to the cause, boys?"

"Not me," said Chip. "I'm stone broke."

Reno eyed me coldly. "I got a couple bucks," I said, pulling two bills from my wallet and forking it over.

"Thanks, that'll help. That'll get us down the road apiece. We'll just drive for a while, then plan the next move. Let's blow, Buck."

"Right," he said, tossing the cigarette out the window and gunning the engine. We roared off down 99, and I watched as farms and fields blew past. But I felt uneasy. There was a tension in the air, something didn't seem right, something I just couldn't quite figure. I decided to let the feeling pass. After all, we were on the road again, and I was getting closer to home. Buck and Reno talked among themselves like they were both in on a private secret as they made some nebulous plans about looking up someone in L.A., or maybe someone else in San Diego. After a while, Reno said, "Hey Buck, why don't you open her up and see what this jalopy will do."

"Good idea," he said, a cigarette glued to his lower lip. We began accelerating and I looked over the seat at the speedometer and watched the needle move over to the right. Sixty. Sixty-five. Seventy. Seventy-five. Eighty. Then I looked below the speedometer and noticed there was no key in the ignition, and that there were wires hanging down from the steering column.

"OOO-WEEEE! She really moves, boy!" said Reno, slapping his knee and baring his teeth. His eyes burned with intensity and

I thought he looked a little deranged. I decided we'd better get out of this car first chance we got. I glanced over at Chip, and he was dozing contentedly. Suddenly, Buck said, "Man, I'd better slow down. We don't want to get pulled over."

"No, we don't want that," agreed Reno, his smile suddenly gone. The Ford slowed back down to sixty, and I let go of the grip I had had on my backpack.

Everyone was silent now. As we came into the Fresno city limits, Buck said to Reno, "Hey—I know where we can pick up some dough in this town. We'll pay a little visit to Sharon."

"Good idea," said Reno, who then turned in his seat to face us with his evil little smile. "We got a friend in Fresno, a gal we know who'll probably . . . loan us some bread. Then maybe we'll head down to L.A. and give you guys a ride that far."

"Gosh, thanks," said Chip. I said nothing.

We took the second Fresno exit.

"You know how to get there, man?" asked Reno.

"Yeah," said Buck. He pulled the car over to the curb and parked.

"We're gonna drop you guys off here, visit our friend, and then come back for you. You can just leave your stuff in the car if you want."

"Uh, sure,' said Chip, opening the door.

"That's okay," I said. "We'll just take it with us. Thanks anyway."

When we got out, Reno said, "We'll pick you up in about an hour."

"Okay," I said with a forced smile. "Thanks. We'll see you later."

The Ford crept down the street, around a corner, and out of sight.

"Let's get going," I said. "The onramp is just down the street."

"Why? Those guys will be back for us."

"No they won't. And if by chance they do show up, it'll only be to rip us off. That was a stolen car they were driving. Good thing we got our stuff back."

"Wow, yeah," said Chip, his eyes wide open. "Let's get out of this place."

We spent four hours in the hot summer sun, and never saw Buck or Reno again. Finally a pickup stopped for us, and we both collapsed in the bed, exhausted. The sun was setting as we rolled into Los Angeles County, the evening heat mixing with smog, giving the twilight a sick, brownish glow.

I was hot, tired, sweaty, dirty, yet relieved to be back in Southern California, and almost home. But I also felt sadness and a sense of shame for having failed in my grand plans of being another Vic. I felt like a failure, and I knew it was going to hurt my pride to be showing up back home like this—broke, hungry, and beaten, looking like a bum and feeling like the prodigal son. I laid my arm on my sleeping bag, put my head in the crook of my arm, and wept silently. I was spent. I wiped my tears on my shirt, and watched from the truck bed as we entered the sprawling mass of the big city.

The week after I got back home, a smog alert was declared for Los Angeles County, and a thick brown fog settled in over La Mirada, stinging eyes, burning lungs, cutting down visibility. I wanted to escape back to Oregon, but my chance had passed. I was stuck at home again, sleeping in my old bed, feeling humbled. I had no wheels, so I found a job in a men's clothing store, walking distance from home. Every morning, five days a week, I'd get up, have breakfast, and walk to work. In the evenings I'd walk home in time for supper. Then I would get on the phone with Vicki. When we went out on weekends, either she would pick me up, or I'd borrow the family car. It was like being back in high school.

The nice thing about my life, though, was seeing her, for by now I was in love with her, and my priorities all got rearranged. Being in love, and under the roof of my parents' house, the music thing to me now seemed like a foolish dream. The current plan was to return to college in the spring and take business courses. Maybe I could end up managing a record store somewhere. And maybe I would settle down and marry this woman I was in love with.

Having given up my dream, for the time being anyway, the only passion in my life seemed to be this current relationship. I certainly had no passion for my safe, secure, boring job. Nor was the idea of returning to school very exciting. But for now, I was working at least, and I was saving up money to buy a car.

Vicki must have sensed that I'd changed, become more ordinary, a person with no big dreams, and nothing much to offer her. And so in a few short months our relationship went from desire and burning love, to dying embers to ashes. Before the year was out, she'd found someone else—a fraternity guy with a sports car and a future as an engineer.

The new year of 1971 hadn't even arrived when the old one died ingloriously for me. There were months ahead of me for mourning lost love, but in the meantime I knew I needed a change of plan. With a relationship no longer holding me back, and a growing restlessness inside me, I bought a Ford Econoline van and fixed it up for traveling. The new plan was to save up a little nest egg, move up to Sonoma County, and hook up with Vic Power. But first, I needed to move out of my parents' house.

A few days before I'd left for Oregon, I noticed a police helicopter flying low over our little community in Sleepy Hollow, as if it was doing reconnaissance. When I got back from Oregon I found out from Bummer that a drug raid had come right after I'd left. Seems the Sheriff's Department had decided that since there were a bunch of hippies all living in the same place, it must be a commune, and therefore it must also be a drug haven of illicit activity. One morning a task force of Sheriff's Deputies and Federal Agents swarmed all over the peaceful little enclave, search warrants in hand, and proceeded to round everyone up at gunpoint. In the end, all they found was a small stash of pot, and a couple of hits of LSD. But it was enough to make a couple of arrests and to have the place shut down as a public nuisance, and have everyone evicted. So everyone scattered. Ed and Sue and their dog Coal went to live in the woods of Mendocino County. Bummer got an apartment in La Habra with a fellow artist named Worm. They placed a colorful sign over their door that read:

Bummer and Worm
Artists At Large

In mid-January, I moved in with them, sleeping on the couch as I'd done in Oregon, and living like a nomad. I was still going off to work every day and socking away money, but I took a little out of the savings to buy a new guitar, a Guild acoustic with an electric pickup, and played it every day. I even made a poor attempt at songwriting, in emulation of Vic.

Winter slipped into spring without much fanfare, as it is wont to do in Southern California. But with the subtle changing of the seasons, and the smell of orange blossoms from nearby orchards, an uneasy feeling came over me. I recognized it for what it was, wanderlust, the call of the road. I had to get away for a few days and see Vic and Star again.

In April, when schools shut down for Easter break week, I begged a few days off from my job, and headed north in my Ford van. Climbing over the grade and into Ventura County again, I rolled down the window, smelled the clean fresh spring air, and rejoiced in the turning of the seasons.

CHAPTER SEVEN

Bodega to Boonville

I had kept track of Vic through his cousin Marty, and had stayed in touch. He and Star were currently living in the little town of Bodega, west of Sebastopol, and near the coast. All I had to go on was a post office box number, but if Bodega was really that small, I should be able to find them.

Once again I drove across the Golden Gate Bridge, through Marin County, and into Sonoma County. I took the turnoff for Petaluma, and wended my way on sleepy streets lined with Victorian houses out of a Norman Rockwell painting, and on out of town through farmlands and hills still green from the spring rains. The country road led west, intersecting with Highway One at the coast, where offshore breezes pushed puffy clouds along in the deep blue sky. Driver's window down, I drove north to the turnoff at Bodega Highway, a small country road really, past an old graveyard guarded by tall Eucalyptus stands, and then behind a sudden curve, Bodega popped into view.

Bucolic and somehow familiar looking. Bodega was a modest couple of blocks of old windswept, white painted wooden houses and buildings from a previous century, signs rusting from salty ocean air, sitting quietly in the noonday sun. A study in simplicity, the town boasted an old one-truck fire station, a saloon, a general store that doubled as post office, a lumber mill down the road that led off to the left, and smack dab in the middle of town, standing like a sentinel on a hill, the old schoolhouse from Alfred Hitchcock's *The Birds.*

I pulled over in front of the little general store, stretched, and went inside. In the dimly lit cramped room were shelves and counters containing all manner of goods, from groceries to fishing bait and tackle, hardware, beer and soft drinks, and a rack of dusty postcards. I found the small counter and window that contained the post office, now closed (this was Saturday, after all). As I was about to turn away, a voice called out from the other counter.

"Hello! May I help you?" said the plain dressed grocery clerk looking to be in his fifties.

"I hope so. I'm looking for a friend of mine, Vic Power. I know his post office box number, but not his street address."

The man placed his hand to his forehead and narrowed his eyes in concentration.

"Vic Power, you say. Hmmmm—I'm sorry, I know most everyone in town, but that name doesn't ring any bells."

"He's about my size and build, a bit taller, has long brown hair and a beard. Plays guitar. Lives with a pretty young woman named Star."

Suddenly, his eyes sparked in recognition, and a smile appeared on his face.

"Oh, yes. Now I know who you mean. Yes, they live just down the road with the Dugans. It's a big Victorian farmhouse, about a quarter of a mile down on the left. Got a barn in back and a picket fence around the place. Can't miss it."

I thanked him for the information, and took off down the road, found the farmhouse, and pulled into the gravel driveway. I mounted the large wooden porch and knocked at the door, where a woman appeared, with Madonna-like face. She was thirty something, dark, with attractive Italian features, and wearing a long flowing homespun dress. She had a self-assured self-possessed demeanor, and a question mark in her eyes.

"Hi, I'm Steve Dupree. I'm looking for Vic and Star. I was told they live here."

"Oh, yes, they mentioned that you might show up. I'm Angela." We shook hands. "I'm sorry," she continued, "but you just missed them. They're playing at a music festival out at the fairgrounds. Do you know where that is?"

I said I didn't, so she gave me directions. Basically, I would just get back on Bodega Highway until I got to Santa Rosa, and the fairgrounds would be right there. "You can't miss it," she added.

I pointed the Econoline van in the right direction, and off I went, out of the valley that cradled Bodega, surrounded by green, bald hillsides long ago logged out, and past cattle pastures and open fields. Just on the other side of Highway 101, the Sonoma County Fairgrounds sat in the shadow of green rolling hills. The sky was a brilliant azure, looking swept clean by recent rain, and white clouds drifted lazily across it, west to east. Quite a contrast to the dull gritty brown of L.A. skies, I noted.

I parked the van in the lot and walked into the fairgrounds, made my way to where a crowd gathered near a large stage, and began scanning the faces in the crowd. I spotted Vic backstage, looking colorful in a home made minstrel shirt and his leather headband. I gave a great shout, and then we were shaking hands and grinning, while Star looked on approvingly.

"Hey, Steve, great to see you, man! Did you catch our set?"

"No, I just got here. Sorry I missed it."

"Too bad. We were pretty good. Afterwards some crazy redneck came up to me and started yelling that we were devil worshipers. I said what the hell are you talking about, buddy? And he said, 'you were singing we got demons, we got demons. I heard you—WE GOT DEMONS.' I tried to tell him the song went 'Nicodemus, please redeem us, Nicodemus,' but he just kept screaming 'we got demons, we got demons—I heard you.' So I told him to fuck off. And how was your trip, Dupree?"

"Nice," I said. "Took my time and camped out last night."

Vic turned to Star. "Hey Star, say hello to Steve."

Star greeted me with a shy smile. "Hi Steve," And then Vic said, "Hey, I gotta have you meet my partners, Annie and Matthew. I call him Brother Matthew, because he used to be a minister in some mail order church. Had a congregation and everything down in The City. But then he started smoking dope and getting tempted by the desires of the flesh—teenage girls and all that." He gave a wink and a leer. "So now he's not Brother Matthew anymore, except to me. He plays bass with us and is quite a character. Star and I rent the shed out from him and Angela, and Annie rents a room. Annie is our fiddler. I met her through Paul Curtis. They were both studying music at Santa Rosa J.C. When I went down there one day to see Paul about something, I met her and we started jamming, and before you knew it, we had a band together. Annie is really good. She's classically trained. This is the first time she's played country and folk music."

Vic then introduced me to Brother Matthew, who was leaning on his standup bass and smoking a pipe. He was about a decade older than us, stocky with reddish hair, and a beard streaked with grey. He wore glasses, was jovial, and if he were a little heavier and a little older, would have made a good department store Santa. He shook my hand, and with a twinkle in his eye said, "Hi, Steve! It's good to meet you. Vic's told me a great deal about you. Says you two grew up together. Come on by the house and we'll feed you and put you up, and do a little dope smokin' and jammin' later."

Annie, by contrast, was more reserved, although friendly. She was slightly shorter than Star, with a fuller figure, not chubby, but womanly. Her umber brown hair hung long and straight and was covered with a red kerchief that, along with her white peasant blouse and long red skirt, gave her the appearance of a Gypsy. She was attractive in an understated, natural way, with freckles, granny glasses, and an open toothy smile and quick little laugh. I liked her right away. I found out later she had turned twenty a few months back.

"So you're friends with Vic, huh?" she said in a friendly way. "Do you play music too?"

I told her that I did, or at least was trying to, and planned to follow in Vic's footsteps.

"Well," she said, "I've only been playing with Vic for a few months, but it's been fun. Did you get to hear us today?"

"Sorry, I got here too late."

"If you're coming over to the house, maybe we can all jam later."

"I'd like that."

"Well, nice meeting you," she said, and I said the same. Then I visited with Star, and it was wonderful to see her again. With Vic standing there, his arm around her, she radiated happiness. As for Vic, I'd never seen him so centered and peaceful looking, at ease with himself and the world. His self-confidence no longer seemed driven by boast and bluster, and his demeanor was more down to earth and sincere. Star seemed to have rounded out his edges and softened him.

We all headed back to Bodega, Vic and Star riding with me, the others in Matthew's old Dodge pickup. Vic gave me a sightseeing tour on the way, pointing out places of interest, and then telling me the story of how they'd wound up living so far from town.

"We love it out in Bodega. It's mellow. Only drawback is having to hitchhike around when you're so far out. So far I've always been able to hitch to a gig, or ride with Matthew. So I guess it's really just a matter of faith."

When we got back to "The Spread", as Vic called it, he gave me a tour of the shed they rented for thirty dollars a month. There wasn't much to see. It looked like my idea of a migrant farm worker's shack. It was tiny, with one door and one window, but somehow looked like a home, mainly due to the touches Star had added, like handmade curtains for the window, and hand drawn pictures on the walls. Their sleeping bags lay on the floor, a kerosene lantern provided light, and a woodstove gave warmth. There was an outhouse in back, and they showered in the main house. "It don't look like much," offered Vic. "But it's nicer than the dump we had in Santa Rosa. It's been our happy home, but we'll be moving on soon."

"Where to?" I asked. "You moving back to town?"

"Oh, I guess I didn't tell you," said Vic with a self-satisfied smile. "We're going to Europe. Gonna be traveling gypsies, me and Star and Annie. Gonna have us a little traveling band. We're leaving in June. We'll hitch across Canada, and then fly out of Montreal."

I was stunned. "How can you afford to go to Europe?" I asked, looking around at their meager surroundings and possessions.

"We've already got our plane tickets. The city of Santa Rosa paid for them. You see, we were living in this old run down motel, and they were tearing it down, along with several blocks of buildings. Urban renewal, they call it. They're gonna knock down the past and put up some fancy dancy new high priced buildings. Make the town look respectable, I suppose. Anyway, they gave us some money for displacing us, so we decided to go to You-ropey. Of course Star's dad thinks I'm crazy. He says this is the twentieth century, and you can't do that kind of thing anymore. But I say gamblers and musicians make it anywhere."

"Tell Steve about Paddy," said Star.

"Oh, yeah. We're going to Ireland first, after we fly to England. We're going to stay with Paddy O'Brien for a while. I've been in touch with him. He's playing the banjo now, and he says there's lots of pubs in Drogheda and Dublin we could play in. After that we might go to Amsterdam, in Holland. I hear it's a real cool little place."

"That's great, Vic," I said, still stunned.

"So what are your plans, Steve? Still planning to get out of L.A. and back to Oregon?"

"Sort of," I said. "Actually, I had planned on coming up to Sonoma County and joining up with you."

"Looks like you're a little late on that deal," said Vic thoughtfully. "But you could still move up here and play my old turf. This is a good place to get it together. If you get up by the end of May, you can make our going away party."

"I don't know if I can make the move that soon," I said, "but I'll sure try to make the party. Let me know when it is."

"I will," promised Vic. "And if you come, bring my cousin Marty. I haven't seen him in a coon's age."

We ambled up to the main house where we all gathered in the living room and smoked a joint, and then broke out instruments and began playing. Brother Matthew leaned in on his bass, pipe in mouth, and thumped the strings with great animation, all the while tapping his toe. Annie held her violin close to her chin, lost in concentration, tenderly making love to the strings. Vic stood in the middle, head erect, eyes sometimes closed, strumming his 12-string guitar forcefully, and singing out with passion. One song in particular caught my attention. It was a story about Bodega in the nineteenth century, and about a stagecoach and a bandit who robbed from the rich and gave to the poor. I wondered how Vic had the imagination to write songs seemingly about anything that came to his mind. After he finished, he explained.

"You see, there used to be a stage line that went right through Bodega to Santa Rosa. So I just thought up a story to go with that bit of historical information."

Vic played a couple more new songs, and then asked me if I had anything to share. I had only written one song that I wasn't ashamed to play in public, so I sang it self consciously, and when I was finished, Vic nodded his approval. "Not bad, Steve," he said. "Keep it up, you might become a songwriter yet." That seemed to me a great compliment, coming as it was from Vic. When we had finished our little jam, we sat down to a vegetarian meal that Angela and Star had prepared, and the atmosphere was so familial, so cozy, that I wanted the evening to go on like this forever. When we had finished the meal, and the table was cleared, Vic said, "Let's go cruise the town. We'll do it on foot, like the teenagers here do on Saturday nights. They walk up one end of town, turn around, and walk up the other end. Not much else for them to do around here."

"They're kind of cute to watch," added Star.

So we walked out the door and into the quiet star-studded night, and headed for town. Vic pointed out the schoolhouse and another building that had been used in *The Birds*, and when we ended up down at the general store, he said, "I wish this place was open so I could buy a beer. They roll up the streets way too early on Saturday night."

"Don't you think you've had enough beer?" scolded Star.

"Aw, you wouldn't begrudge me a little beer now, would you, Star?" said Vic in the manner of a henpecked husband.

Star laughed at this and said, "No, honey, I won't begrudge you your beer."

"Good," said Vic boisterously, slapping her on the ass. "Let's go in the saloon and get a cool one."

In the saloon across the street, we sat at a table and had our beers, while the regulars ignored us. Annie's name came up in conversation, and Star said, "She's a regular trooper. When we started this band and moved out here to Bodega, she left her parents' house in Santa Rosa and joined us. Now she's going along to Europe. And you know, she's never even played in a band before."

"Yeah," added Vic, "she was innocent and naïve till she met me. Now I got her smokin' dope and runnin' off with gypsies."

We finished our beers and wandered down to the farmhouse, and when it was time to turn in I said I'd go sleep in the van. But Angela wouldn't allow it. "You're our guest, and you'll sleep on the couch. I insist." Then she was off to fetch me some bedding and a pillow.

As I lay awake on the couch, I thought about what had been said of Annie, how she had the gumption to just pack up and follow Vic off to Europe, chasing gypsy dreams. Maybe there was something about Vic that inspired that in a person. Whatever it was, he had that spell over me. Soon I would move up to Sonoma County and follow the trails he'd blazed and maybe have my own band in time. It was something to ponder on. The moon rose late and I watched its light peek through the thin curtains in the Victorian windows of the darkened living room, where not even the sound of the grandfather clock's ticking disturbed the slumber of the stately old house. I found the moonlight and the room itself to be comforting, much like the blanket that covered me. The ticking of the old clock soothed me to sleep.

Then it was back to Southern California and my job, and the house in the suburbs that Bummer and Worm and I had relocated to, that the neighbors called "that damned hippie house." I made the commute to work in the morning, came home in the evening, played my guitar at night, and marked the days off on my calendar. Near the end of May, I took a long weekend, picked up Marty Power, his wife Meg and their two year old son, and we made the trek up Highway 101 to Sonoma County, where Vic was having his great, going-away-to-Europe farewell party.

And one hell of a party it turned out to be. It lasted three days and two nights. People drove in from all over. Besides Marty and his family and myself, Vic's younger brother Pat, just back from Vietnam, was there with his wife. Scott Duncan from our old surf band, The Reverbs, showed up as well, six months out of the Army and hair halfway to his shoulders. He was living in a communal house in Berkeley, and had gotten the invitation when he'd run across Vic singing at a local coffeehouse. Annie showed up with her fiddle and her new boyfriend, who was the reason she had decided not to go to Europe after all. Brother Matthew was there, of course, with his bass and his homegrown pot. And other sundry friends came and went as well during the three-day blowout.

The official celebration was to take place in Bodega Bay, five miles north of Bodega. We caravanned in cars and VW microbuses, stopping along the way to buy a half dozen gallon jugs of Sonoma Red wine, Vic's favorite brand. He and Annie had a friend in Bodega Bay, R.J., who had offered to host the big shindig at his little fisherman's cottage on Bay Flat Road, which ran along the inside of the bay, and stropped at Bodega Head, where the land ended and ocean waves crashed against the cliffs.

The party carried on both inside and outside the little cottage, not much more than a shack, really. There was no shortage of food or drink, pot or music. When we weren't playing live music, records were blasting away over the stereo speakers, and there was singing, dancing, and even a little fighting (Vic and Pat wrestling around on the ground outside, both drunk, and both laughing afterwards). R.J. had erected a four-man tent in his front yard, a strip of sand between the cottage and the road, for folks to sleep in. In addition, people crashed in cars and vans, and on the floor. Except for a few quiet hours in the pre-dawn, the party continued around the clock.

R.J., of medium height, slight and slender, had long stringy sandy colored hair that hung past his shoulders, a hawk nose, and a droopy mustache above a narrow mouth that wore a permanent smile of amusement, much like the Buddha. His blue-grey eyes behind wire-rimmed glasses had the kind of directness, accompanied by a twinkle, that expressed both guilelessness and sincerity. He was the perfect host, moving freely through the throng like the quiet through the storm, making sure everyone was happy and well taken care of. He didn't seem to mind it when we tracked sand into the house or spilled beer on the floor, to him it was just part of the experience. The neighbors didn't seem to mind, either, since they not only joined in, they provided fresh salmon for the barbeque, some of the beer, and corn on the cob.

Then the last song had been sung, the last beer drained, the debris cleared away, and people began saying their goodbyes and drifting back from whence they'd come. I said my goodbye to Vic and he said, "Keep in touch, Dupree. And don't forget to check out those gigging spots I told you about when you get back up here." Marty and Meg and I headed back down south, and when I returned to work at the men's clothing store, I gave my two week's notice.

In mid-June, on my next to last day on the job, Ed and Sue showed up at my door. They had hitched down from Boonville for a few days to visit friends and take care of some business that involved a marijuana deal, and now here they were, with a borrowed car Ed needed to return soon, after which they would hitch back home.

I said, "Hey, Ed, you're timing's perfect. I was about to move up to Sonoma County, in two or three days. If you can hold off a little while, you can ride as far as Santa Rosa with me." Ed made me a better proposition.

"I tell you what," he said, "if you'll take us all the way to Boonville, I'll show you the cabin, and you can stay there with us for a while. It's a good place to come down from the bad vibes of L.A." Serendipity! Of course I said yes, and in a few days we were packed and on the road.

We drove all day and all through the night, and just before dawn we were at the Mendocino County line. Highway 128 wound down through the beautiful Anderson Valley and about twenty miles on, as the sun was rising, we reached the sleepy hamlet of Boonville, a place so isolated, it had its own secret language called "Boont", that some of the old timers still spoke. Half a mile past the end of town, we turned off at the narrow mountain road that led to the cabin, seven miles up through a dense Redwood forest. The road turned and twisted until we finally came to a little wooden bridge on the left that led up to the cabin itself.

It was small and unimposing, its dark natural wood blending into the forest that surrounded it. It sat perched on a small hillside, a spring-fed creek running alongside at the bottom of the hill, and an outhouse above and behind the cabin. This is the place Ed and Sue had been renting for next to nothing, and for good reason, for there was no electricity or running water. Also, the cabin was un-insulated, and even in June, at this altitude it could still get down to freezing at night. The creek served all their water needs, from drinking to cooking to washing. They bathed in a nearby pool of the creek. For heat they had a woodstove in the center of the room, which was stoked every night. For light, there was a kerosene lantern, and a Coleman stove was used for cooking. Life at the cabin was about as basic as you could get. Ed and Sue subsisted partly on government surplus food. This they picked up once a month in Boonville and stuffed into a couple of backpacks for the seven-mile hike back up the mountain road. To supplement this meager handout, they'd been making the fourteen-mile roundtrip down the mountain on foot once a week to buy fresh fruit, vegetables, eggs, and whatever else they needed. But now that I was going to be staying a while, we could all just drive into town instead.

Ed was right about it being a good place to come down from the city vibes, and it took about a week for me to work the hustle and bustle and wound up energy and distraction out of my consciousness, and to settle in to their life of simplicity and harmony with nature. Yerba Buena grew at the base of Redwood trees, and one of the things Ed liked to do was rummage through the woods gathering it. He would dry it and brew tea from it. He also liked to wander upstream and find a quiet pool to sit by while he read from books like *Autobiography of a Yogi* and *The Aquarian Gospel of Jesus The Christ.* Sometimes he'd drop LSD while he meditated by the creek, and one time he included me in his trip, sharing a tab and keeping me from freaking out by handing me a book of meditations to study. For an indeterminate time that day, listening to the murmur of the creek and feeling the sun warm on my face and smelling the sweetness of the forest, I felt at one with the universe.

Ed seemed more at home in the forest than he had at our enclave in Sleepy Hollow. His eyes shone and he radiated peace. He and Sue were both sweet and quiet spoken and in love. Their closest neighbors lived about a half mile down the road. Bill and Nikki were much the same in temperament as Ed and Sue, but mirror opposites in appearance. Nikki was tall and thin, blond and shy, while Bill was dark haired and bearded and more talkative, but in a quiet way. They had a log cabin that had been built more than hundred years earlier, with an earthen floor, a stone fireplace, and devoid of the modern conveniences of running water and electricity, relying on oil lamps for lighting the two rooms. They were supplied with water from the same creek that flowed past Ed and Sue's, and down the mountainside. It was a cozy little place, simple and comfortable.

Occasionally we'd walk down for a visit, to hang out and maybe smoke some pot. And then we'd walk back up the hill at night in total darkness with only the moon and stars to light the way, and the only sounds were of the creek, crickets, and bullfrogs. I would usually join Ed and Sue in the cabin for supper of evenings, then we'd get the fire going, and later I'd go off to my van to sleep. It was so cold at night I'd have to climb into my sleeping bag warmly dressed, including a sweater, and then still wake up in the pre-dawn darkness shivering. Eventually, I got acclimated to the cold nights and slept fine on the floor of the van.

Since I had wheels, we would sometimes make excursions into civilization. As I drove lazily down the road one day on our way to a fruit stand that sold cold homemade apple cider, a car came up from behind and began riding my tailpipe. I kept glancing in the rear view mirror and then at the speedometer and finally said out loud, "Well, looks like I either need to speed up or pull over."

I pulled over and Sue said, "Good, Steve. Now I know you really want to be like us and live life in the slow lane."

One weekend, we went to the wedding of their friend David, a folksinger who had once played in a band with Paul Curtis. The wedding ceremony took place in a meadow inside a campground, by the Navarro River, and was performed by a mail order minister. Hippies had come from all over, though most of them had never even met the bride and groom. It turns out that David had placed flyers all around the Haight-Ashbury and other parts of San Francisco announcing the wedding and inviting, "Come One Come All." The kicker was the photo on the flyer. It was of David and his girlfriend, stark naked, wrapped in each other's arms.

The ceremony went off well, and the party afterwards also went nicely and peacefully, up to a point. That was the point at which, in the middle of the night, a contingent of Hell's Angels in full regalia came roaring into the campground, in a single file, colors flying, kicking up dust, and scaring the shit out of everyone around. They then set up their own little arena of fun next to us. It seems they'd seen the flyers too. The foul, greasy, menacing horde broke out their stash of beer and pot and amphetamines and got their own party going, and it soon got very loud. In a while, there came ringing through the tall redwoods the sharp sounds of shouts and threats, and heads getting busted and faces getting stomped. I didn't know if they were stomping hippies or each other, but I wasn't about to wait around and find out. I bundled Ed and Sue into the van, and out of the campground, and back down Highway 128 toward the safety of the cabin.

At the end of three weeks of living in the forest, I noticed some changes in myself. My hair was getting longer, my beard was starting to grow, and I had given up cigarettes. I had, as Ed put it, come down from the city vibes somewhat, but now I was getting restless again. I wanted to go back into the world and begin my journey as a folksinger. It was time to head on down to Sonoma County. I thanked Ed and Sue for everything, and as I backed out across the little bridge and onto the asphalt, I took a long look at them standing on the porch, leaning against the railing, beaming, smiling, and waving goodbye. I realized as I drove down the hill, alone for the first time in weeks, that I had already begun to miss their company.

CHAPTER EIGHT

Footprints in the Sand

The only people I knew in Sonoma County were all Vic's friends. I decided to pay a visit to R.J., partly because I knew where he lived, and partly to thank him again for hosting the going-away party. Maybe he could help me find a place to live as well.

I pulled off Bay Flat Road and around to the front of his cottage, which faced away from the bay, and parked next to his VW microbus. My timing was good—he was at home, just hanging out. The reason for this, I soon found out, was that he was a professional college student, living off grants and student loans, and school was out for the summer. He invited me in and put on a pot of coffee. He said he was glad to see me. We talked for a while, and he told me he'd moved out from Minnesota two or three years earlier. He also mentioned that his dad (a writer of children's books and inventor of games) lived just down the road. We talked of Vic and Star and Annie and of ourselves, and then R.J. said, "Let's take a walk down to the beach."

"What beach?" I said.

"Oh, I know a secret beach nobody goes to. There are no roads leading there and to get there you have to cut across private property, so not many people know about it."

"Great," I said, "let's go."

"Bring a jacket," he said. "It's windy there."

We set out across the little road behind the cottage, cut between two neighbors' houses, and up a hill covered in Eucalyptus trees; and then by secret trails we reached tall sand dunes where just beyond them was a long white unspoiled beach, littered with driftwood from winter storms. It stretched all the way from the bluffs at Bodega Head northward to Salmon Creek. We were the only ones there, and R.J. was right—it was windy, but the fresh salty air felt good. Clean and bracing. The waves rolled in set after set with a powerful surge, and all that could be seen between the waves and the horizon were seagulls, whitecaps, and an occasional far-off fishing boat. We walked along the beach, not saying much, for what was there to say? It was a moment for just taking in the surroundings of the breathtaking beauty of the north coast. We walked back by the same trails, leaving footprints in the dunes that the wild winds would soon erase, and gathered again at the cottage.

I scanned the simple fisherman's shack, which had made a complete recovery from the big party. The main room, whose south-facing wall was framed by a long un-curtained window, also doubled as kitchen. There was a large deep sink and counter and an old gas stove. The bathroom was accessed through a narrow door, behind which were a toilet and shower stall. A woodstove sat in the kitchen area, and R.J. kept it stocked with scavenged redwood kindling from the Bodega lumber mill. The refrigerator stood in an adjoining utility room, which also held a table and chair against a small window that faced the bay. Back in the living room, in addition to an easy chair, a rattan chair, and standing lamp, there was a table and chairs by the window. Shelves held a stereo and records, books and magazines. Another room that had a curtain for a door was R.J.'s bedroom. The large bed took up most of its space.

We talked some more, and I mentioned I was looking for a place to stay and R.J. offered to put me up.

"We can split the rent," he said. "Your share would come to thirty dollars a month."

This was a deal I couldn't refuse, for in addition to being dirt cheap, I'd realized that R.J. was a kindred spirit. He told me there was a small mattress in the utility room and I should drag it into the living room, and roll out my sleeping bag. We took a drive into town to get some beer at Diekman's Market. On the way, we passed the Tides Wharf and Restaurant, which I recognized from scenes in *The Birds*. Back at the cottage after a simple meal of rice and beans and tortillas, we waxed philosophically over beers, pondering the meaning of life and love, and sharing our own personal plans and dreams. That night, as I lay in my bag on the mattress on the floor, fire in the woodstove burned down to glowing embers, moonlight streaming through the window, I felt gratitude for my great fortune, and felt like I'd really be starting a new life.

Fogbanks along the coast were the norm in the summer months, and Bodega Bay was often socked in, which made for cool days, good weather for walks to the beach or to Bodega Head. Whether it was sunny or foggy, I spent many an hour that summer sitting at the table by the big window, looking out into the harbor or the hills, playing my guitar, learning songs, or trying to write them. The apple orchards of Sebastopol were now heavy with fruit, and in a few weeks they would ripen enough to be picked, and when we drove into town for supplies, we could smell the budding sweetness of the fruit in the air.

R.J. gave me tours of the area, and showed me where the coffee houses were, and the other places where I might be able to find gigs as a folk singer. It had all the makings of an idyllic summer, but as the days became weeks, I began to feel restless for the road again. Vic had wanted to drive all the way to Canada the previous summer, and this year he and Star had finally hitched there. I wanted to follow his path.

One day I got back out on the road, and picked up three hitchhikers in Willits. They sat by the side of Highway 101 on the outskirts of town, two men and a woman, all young hippies. They wore smiles of relief on their faces when I pulled over and asked them where they were going and they said Seattle. I said I'm going right through there—hop in. The girl, part Native American by her features, sat up front with me, while the two guys flopped down in the back against their packs, and got comfortable. A little ways past Leggett where the river ran alongside the highway, I pulled off the road; we walked down the hill, and found a spot to skinny dip, out of sight of the highway. The girl kept her panties on, but back in the van she left her bra off for a while to let the cool breeze caress her skin. I had to smile when startled drivers, suddenly spotting her, would gape open mouthed and nearly run off the road. I put a tape into the eight-track and cranked up the volume. David Crosby began singing "Everybody's saying that music is love . . ." Amen, brother.

Once the darkness closed in, I just found a suitable spot to pull over at Humboldt Lagoons, out of sight of the road, and we made camp there. I took the van for myself, and left the others to fend for themselves on the ground somewhere. I could hear the ocean, but I couldn't see it. It was kind of like my plans. I was going to Canada, but I really couldn't explain why.

I dropped the hitchhikers off on Vashon Island, off the coast of Seattle. We took the ferry across the sound, and I spent the night on the floor of a cabin in the woods where the two guys were staying. Then I rode the ferry back to Seattle, and headed north again, toward the Canadian border. After a sojourn in Vancouver, and then in Victoria on Vancouver Island, I headed south into Oregon, and caught the exit into Eugene. Where the swift Willamette River runs through the center of town, and trees line the banks and the surrounding hills, I cruised happily along quiet streets to Mike Grafton's house and pulled up in front.

"Hi Steve," said Mike, greatly surprised to find me at the door. "What are you doing here?"

"Invite me in, and I'll tell you all about it."

"Of course," he laughed. "Let's go in the kitchen." I sat at the table while he got a couple of beers from the fridge and joined me.

"Ah, Blitz Weinhard," I said, taking a swig of the cold brew. "I haven't had one of these since I left Eugene last summer."

"Are you back for good now?" asked Mike. "If you are, you're welcome to stay here, you know."

"No," I said. "I've moved to Sonoma County. I'm just passing through town right now from a trip to Canada."

"I ought to get out of town myself," said Mike gloomily, rubbing the stubble on his chin. "A change of scenery might do me good."

"How so?"

Then he opened up and told me how his girlfriend had recently left him, and he just couldn't seem to shake the blues. "I know how you feel," I said. "I'm still getting over my breakup, which happened quite a while back."

"How long are you going to be in town?"

"Just overnight. Then I might drive down to San Francisco and see if there's any places for me to play music."

"Really? Mind if I tag along? I have a cousin who lives in Berkeley. I haven't seen her in a while, but I bet she'd put us up for a couple of days."

In a few days, we were pulling off at the University Avenue exit and driving down Berkeley streets, looking for Becca's apartment. Becca, a twenty-one year old chestnut haired beauty, offered to put us both up, but I begged off, preferring to sleep in the van overnight. Now that that was settled, we all sat around visiting over a bottle of wine, and then after a great dinner, I took off on foot with my guitar, looking for a place to busk. I wandered up and down Telegraph Avenue, imagining how Vic had done it. Did he just pop into a place unannounced, like he'd done when we were on the road? I tried it, without success, until I finally came across a little pizza parlor on a side street. The owner wasn't around, so the manager let me sing a few songs. I passed the hat afterwards, and made a little change. A diner offered to buy me a glass of wine, and as I sat at his table and sipped it, I felt like folk singer royalty. I had made money that night from singing, and I felt like I'd just climbed the first rung of success. Unlike Vic, I was willing to start at the bottom.

Mike and I stayed with Becca two days and nights. After she'd heard his tale of woe and heartbreak, she'd arranged to set him up with one of her single friends, a free spirited young lady named Amy, with whom Mike was about to embark on a brief but passionate fling. The three of us took off to explore The City, and I showed them around North Beach and Fisherman's Wharf in much the same way as a flight attendant named Stephanie had taken me around those areas two years previously. We caught the ferry to Sausalito, and tripped around the streets at night like tourists, laughing and joking and having fun. Then Mike decided he'd better get back home to Oregon, so we all said our farewells, and the next day we headed up towards R.J.'s place in Bodega. I dropped Mike by a northbound onramp in Santa Rosa, and I split back to the coast.

The experience of busking in Berkeley had given me confidence, and now I began seeking out open mike nights around the county. Besides The Brothers, there was one at the Rosewood Forest and another at Uncle Sam's. Everyone had a chance to do two or three songs at the open mikes, and they also served as audition nights. The host was usually someone local who had a following, thus guaranteeing at least some attendance. The host would do a long set in the middle of the evening, and introduce acts the rest of the time. Open mikes were held on off-nights, usually on Sundays. Norman Greenbaum regularly hosted the open mike at the Rosewood Forest on 4th Street in Santa Rosa, but since he'd had a number one hit with "Spirit in the Sky" some months back, he was often out of town to do a gig. On the nights he was gone, Ron Warden took over the duties. Warden was the host the night I made my debut there.

"We have a newcomer tonight. Let's welcome Steve Dupree to the stage!"

I nervously sang one of my original blues songs. I watched the audience's reaction. Stone faces, numbing silence. No applause. I tried a second song, one of Vic's. Again, the crowd sat silently, no reaction. I clapped my hands together, providing my own applause. Warden hustled me offstage. The following Sunday night I showed up again, and Ron told me, "Sorry, we've already heard your stuff."

"But this is an open stage," I protested. "Anyone is welcome."

"Not you."

Another singer, an older more seasoned performer named Elliot Gould ("I'm the real Elliot Gould," he was fond of saying), stuck up for me. "Give him a break, Ron. Everyone's got to start somewhere." Warden relented, and I did better that night, getting at least a smattering of applause.

Uncle Sam's, a rowdy beer bar outside of Sebastopol, also held a Sunday night open mike. It was there I met the Mississippi Moaner, a young blond bearded blue-eyed blues singer. I dug his style and asked him to show me a few of his cool blues licks.

"Sure, I'll be glad to," he said with a bright smile. "I usually busk in Sproul Plaza at U.C. Berkeley during the week. Come down some afternoon and I'll teach you a few licks."

He was surprised when I actually showed up a few days later, but took a break from his singing to show me a few riffs, which I practiced and began using with my songs.

"Music's been good to me," he said. "I can always trust it. Women leave, but my music always remains. Right now I'm supporting my old lady, a dog, and a Volkswagen Beetle with it. I play over in The City on Fisherman's Wharf, and do some coffeehouses and bars around the area."

I never saw the Moaner again, but I did try my hand at busking in Sproul Plaza. I had better luck with a couple of coffee houses in Berkeley. One of them, a small wood and brick room on the second floor of a building off Telegraph, named "The Seventh Seal", had an open mike night that advertised a "featured performer" each week to do a 45-minute set. The idea was that the best talents from the open mikes would be given a chance to show off a little more. It only paid ten bucks, but that was at least gas money and bridge toll for me. That summer of 1971, the women in the coffee houses were singing mostly Joni Mitchell songs, and all the guys were doing James Taylor, but that was not for me. In addition to my own songs and those of Vic Power, I did some by John Lee Hooker and Fred Neil. I sounded different from the rest of the folkies, and maybe that's why I landed a featured performer slot.

August was a succession of lazy days that revolved around open mikes and trips to Berkeley and The City to busk and play in coffee houses. In Bodega Bay, I watched the fog roll in and the boats sail out, through the big window in the cottage while reading, writing, or working on songs. But as summer faded and autumn loomed, my savings had dried up. I'd blown through them in three months' time, and now to pay the rent, I took out the eight-track player from the van and sold it.

It was obvious that I wouldn't be making a living from music any time soon, so rather than look for a job, I decided to take the lead of Paul Curtis and go to school on the G.I. Bill. I filled out the necessary paper work with the V.A., and R.J. drove me down to Santa Rosa Junior College to help me sign up for classes. Since I'd already had a year of college, I would be entering as a sophomore, and only needed to transfer transcripts. I would be getting free music lessons as a music major, and receiving a check for three hundred dollars from the government every month. It seemed like a good deal. I took a shine to the college campus with its old ivy-covered brick buildings and laid-back vibes.

The government checks wouldn't start rolling in for several weeks, and in the meantime, I still needed an income. So I took a job working in a pizza parlor Friday and Saturday nights. One Saturday night on my way back to Bodega Bay from my job in Santa Rosa, I fell asleep at the wheel and totaled the van. Now I was on foot. I answered a "Roommate Wanted" ad on the bulletin board at school, and moved into an apartment above a beauty salon across the street from campus.

I began making new friends. One of them, Gary Pihl, was lead guitarist in a rock band named Crossfire. He loaned me his P.A. to do a gig I'd booked for myself on campus, playing for the lunch hour crowd on an outdoor stage under stately old oak trees. I got paid twenty-five bucks. I was moving up in the world. The student body president approached me after my set and offered me a gig singing at the new coffee house that was opening up on campus. I said, sure, I'll be happy to play. I was feeling great about getting these gigs, not because they were anything special in or of themselves, but because I was getting experience playing in front of audiences, and that was good for my self confidence.

I made another friend at the J.C., a woman named Jane, who was also majoring in music. She played guitar and flute and sang, and we hung out a lot together that fall. She was an earthy, sweet person, a hippie with similar views on life and music as myself. Her boyfriend, a conscientious objector, was doing alternative service for two years in lieu of the Army, working at a mental hospital in Ventura County. He would come up on occasional weekends for a quick visit. I kept her company the rest of the time. She was from Southern California, and when Christmas rolled around, and with it the semester break, she planned to drive her VW bus down to visit family. I wanted to visit mine as well, so we rode down together.

It was nice to see my parents and my brother again, but the person I really wanted to see was Vicki. I hadn't been able to shake her memory, and still held out hope that maybe we could get back together. So I called her at home. Her mother answered, and reluctantly put Vicki on. Our conversation was strained, to say the least. She told me she was engaged, and suggested I find someone new for myself. After a long silence, I wished her well, and said goodbye. I felt empty inside, but finally realized that the nails were in the coffin of this relationship. So I spent the rest of my time visiting old friends and hanging out with my younger brother Mark.

Mark still lived at home, and worked at a nearby Shell station, pumping gas and sometimes working on cars. But he wanted more out of life. He wanted to find a career, meet a nice woman, get married, have kids, and buy a house in the suburbs. In short, he wanted the American Dream. And he didn't understand my lifestyle.

"So why are you studying music in college?" he asked me one night as we were cruising around town in his car.

"I want to be a musician."

"There's no money or stability in that," he said. "Mom and dad worry about you. They don't understand why you live the way you do, and neither do I."

"It's just something I feel compelled to do. I feel like this is my calling in life."

"I think you ought to be more realistic," he said.

I changed the subject by asking him about himself. He confided that he'd met a girl he really liked, but was shy around her, and was hesitant to ask her out. I knew that he had low self esteem, and also had bouts of depression, which also affected his self-image.

"Go ahead and ask her," I said. "What's the worst that can happen? She might actually say yes. It's worth a try."

My last night in town, he did ask her out, and she accepted. He thanked me.

After a week visiting family and friends, I was itching to return to Sonoma County. I'd outgrown my former life and neighborhood like an old set of clothes. Finally, Jane called me up and said she was ready to head out, so we got back on the road in her VW. While we drove, she told me she needed to make some changes in her life, mainly her living situation.

She'd been renting a room in a house in Windsor, but was having issues with a roommate. I told her I needed a change as well. Although living just across the street from campus was convenient, my roommate like to party excessively, and I liked to study and practice. Shortly after we returned to Santa Rosa, and before the spring semester began, Jane located a little place for us to share about three miles from the J.C. It was a stucco cottage set behind a fortuneteller's place. Madame Rachel was to become our landlady. The cottage had one long room with a hardwood floor and fireplace, a tiny kitchen, and tinier bathroom with a curtain for a door. It was meant for one person to live in, but it could accommodate a couple. Jane and I placed our beds on opposite sides of the room, and she hung a muslin drape around hers for privacy. The cottage also had a nice little porch, where we would hang out with our guitars, smoke a joint, and do some jamming together. Or we'd hang out inside and do the same.

I was still in touch with Vic and Star, and the last letter I'd received had come from Spain. They were living in Barcelona, and his letter boasted of the band he had put together, and of all the gigs and studio work they'd been getting. He painted a grandiose picture of his prospects. He even hinted around about making it to the Big Time again. He seemed to think that his big break was just around the bend. I sat on the porch one night, listening to the rain patter against the roof and watching rivulets run down the gravel driveway toward Madame Rachel's, whose neon red sign blinked in the window that faced Sebastopol Road. I imagined Vic banging away on his 12-string guitar and belting out a song at the Red Lion club in Barcelona, and then imagined myself with him. If he had a band, could he use another player? I began making plans to hook up with him, which included buying a one-way plane ticket to London. I'd start saving up money now, and I could take off at the end of the semester.

That became my new dream—to head off to Europe, like Vic had done, with just a backpack, sleeping bag, and guitar. The dream lasted for about forty-eight hours, and then something completely unexpected happened to change it. It came in the form of a knock at the door, just after Jane and I had finished a home cooked meal of lentil soup, salad, and chapatis. I stood up, walked to the door, and opened it. There in front of me stood Marty Power dressed in jeans, tee shirt, and Levis jacket. He appeared cold, ragged, and beat.

CHAPTER NINE

Uncle Zeke's Band

"Hi Steve," said Marty, one hand in his jeans pocket, and his jacket collar turned up against the cold. "Mind if I come on in?"

He stepped inside, and after shaking my hand, wandered over to the fireplace to get warm. He turned down our offer of soup and salad, but welcomed a cup of tea. Jane put the kettle on.

"Mind if I smoke?" he asked, lighting a cigarette.

"What a surprise," I said, after introducing Marty to Jane. "This is like Eugene all over again. What brings you up here, and where's your car?"

"Meg and I just can't get along," he began. "We had one fight too many, so I split. Slammed the door and stuck out my thumb."

"How'd you find me?" I asked.

"Hitched up One-O-One. Caught a long ride out of Santa Barbara, and another in San Jose. Ended up at R.J.'s in Bodega Bay. I remembered the place from the party. Spent the night there. Would've called you, but you don't have a phone."

"We don't have much of anything," I added.

"R.J. gave me your address and dropped me off in Santa Rosa. He was running late to a night class. I walked here from the freeway. It wasn't far. But it sure is cold out." He shivered as I handed him a hot cup of tea.

"Is that the warmest jacket you've got?" I asked.

"It's the only one. Hell, I left without nothin' but the clothes on my back. Spur of the moment thing. I had to get away."

"So what now?" I asked.

"I don't know," he said. "Think I'll stay out at the bay for a while and get my head together. R.J. said I could crash in the living room. He's got an extra sleeping bag."

"Well, that's where I got started. It's nice out there. Sorry about you and Meg. I hope it all works out. But it's great to see you."

Marty was warming up now, and the stiffness went out of his body and the tautness out of his face as he relaxed and even managed a little smile. But his eyes betrayed his smile in their sadness. He flicked an ash from his cigarette into the fire, took a sip of tea, and placed the cup on the mantle. "It's real good to see you Steve," he said. "Kinda like old times."

"Well, now that you're here, let's play some tunes," I suggested.

Jane loaned Marty her guitar, while she broke out her flute, and I unpacked my guitar from its case. Soon the cottage was filled with the sound of music, warmth from the fire, and a glow from oil lamps. Marty's spirits began to improve with each new song we played.

"*Travellin' light, I'm travellin' light,*" he sang, "*and I just can't wait to be with my baby tonight.*" It was a song that we'd both learned from Paddy O'Brien back in La Mirada days. I kicked off another song we'd picked up from Paddy, "The Jolly Tinker," and we tried out some folk songs we all knew. Jane and I forgot about our studies for the time being, while we all jammed and joked, and reminisced. Marty spent the night on the floor in my sleeping bag, and hitchhiked back out to Bodega Bay in the morning. He took with him my banjo and an instruction book, and chord chart. We figured since he had a lot of time on his hands and no guitar, he might as well learn a new instrument.

R.J. and Marty began dropping around our place on a regular basis. Marty had been spending all his free time, which was considerable, learning to play the banjo, and was soon proficient enough to play some tunes with us. R.J. just sat around and watched at first, but we decided to get him in on the action too. I put together a washtub bass (or gutbucket as it was also called) from a galvanized washtub, a broom handle, and a length of clothesline. I showed R.J. the basics of how to thump the string and move the pole to change pitch, and soon he was jamming right along with us. I began to live for the jams, and couldn't wait for my classes to end for the day so I could walk the three miles home, get out my guitar, and wait for Marty and R.J. to come rolling into the driveway in the VW bus. We began developing a repertoire, and soon had enough songs together to fill up the better part of an hour.

One day R.J. mentioned that Chinese New Year was coming up, and that we should all go down to The City and see what was going on. So that Saturday night he and Marty picked up Jane and me, and we all headed off to Chinatown. On the way, we passed a jug of wine around and discussed the possibilities of having a real performing band together. "Let's start coming down to The City on weekends and do a bit of busking," said Marty. "I could sure stand to make some dough. I'm so poor the wolf's scratchin' at the door." We agreed that might be a good idea.

R.J. parked the bus at the bottom of a steep hill and we hiked up to Chinatown, watching for fireworks and parades, then wandered the streets of North Beach. Marty had been holding in a lot of pain since coming up to Sonoma County, and he quietly brooded a lot. Music was a good outlet for him; it kept his thoughts at bay and put him in that zone that all musicians who have been there know about. But tonight he'd been brooding again, and had had too much of the wine we'd passed around in the VW. He was stumbling around on Columbus, in his cups, so we decided to sober him up with some coffee. But when he passed out by the window seat inside a coffee shop in North Beach, we helped him back to the VW, and drove back over the Golden Gate Bridge to Santa Rosa.

The following Saturday we returned to San Francisco, in the morning, and set up in front of the ferry building on Fisherman's Wharf. Whenever the sightseeing boat would head out into the bay, or return from its trip, the sound of Tony Bennett would come over loudspeakers singing "I Left My Heart in San Francisco." The rest of the time, Jane and I, and Marty and R.J. would be playing our instruments, singing, and smiling for the Japanese tourists. They carried cameras around their necks as if they were an extension of their bodies, and as if it were a requirement when visiting America to record every little event on 35 mm film. My guitar case sat open on the street before us, catching coins the tourists would toss. We spent the better part of the day there, singing our hearts out until our throats were so parched we couldn't sing another song. So we packed up, divided up the money, and walked over to a pub for a beer to quench our thirsts. The consensus among us was that we'd all had a good time, and wanted to do it again. Marty was the happiest of us, though. He finally had some money in his pocket. "Now I can keep that damned wolf at bay for a while," he said.

At our next practice session, Marty said that if we were going to be a band, we'd need a name to call ourselves. Jane didn't have anything to suggest, and my ideas were pretty lame. But then Marty's face lit up and a wide smile crossed it.

"How about Uncle Zeke and His Silver String Band?" he said.

"Uncle Zeke's Silver String Band," sounds better," I countered.

"I like it," said R.J.

"I hate it," said Jane with a laugh. "It's a terrible name."

"Looks like you're out voted," I said.

"Guess like it's all settled then," said Marty as he looked around at our faces. Then he added, "Say, Steve, do you ever see Annie Greenwood around? You know, the girl who used to play fiddle with Vic?"

"Yeah, as a matter of fact, I run into her on campus now and again."

"What's she up to? Is she playing with anyone?"

"I think she's just going to school."

"Maybe she'd like to play with us. Why don't you ask her to come over and jam the next time you see her?"

"Okay," I agreed. And by chance, I ran into her at school the very next day, and gave her the invitation. She said she'd love to, but didn't have a car. She lived with her parents and walked to school, so R.J. arranged to pick her up and bring her over to our next session. She and R.J. were already friends, which is how he came to know Vic in the first place. She played some tunes with us, and picked them up so quickly, we invited her to come busking with us on Saturday. Someone had beaten us to the spot on Fisherman's Wharf, so we set up by the cable car turn around across from Ghiradelli Square. I couldn't help but remember when I'd seen the jug band playing here in 1969, and how I'd visualized myself on this very spot, playing this kind of music.

The mild Sonoma County winter ran its course, and it had been a rainy one. As spring quietly arrived, the hills became lush with green grasses, and the apple orchards blossomed pink and white and fragrant in the warm sun. On a pleasant sunny Friday afternoon, Uncle Zeke's Silver String Band made an appearance on the outdoor stage of Santa Rosa Junior College. It was a benefit concert, and included other bands and solo acts, so we didn't get paid. But it was our first real gig, and we were excited about it, and the idea of having an audience of our peers. Our set was a mix of Irish tunes we'd learned from Paddy, some folk songs, a couple of tunes we'd picked up from Jim Kweskin's Jug Band, some songs Marty had done when he was with Morning Glory, and a couple of my originals. It was a mish mash of styles, but the crowd seemed to like both the variety, and our enthusiasm. After we got offstage, I met a guy named Randy Bleu, who took classes at the J.C. and mentioned he also played guitar and sang. He was lanky, six feet tall, with long hair, and a friendly face. "We ought to get together sometime and jam," he said, and gave me his phone number.

The following night we played the open mike at Uncle Sam's beer bar, and while we didn't get a gig out of it, we had fun, and so did the audience.

"You know," I said to Marty, "I'm beginning to feel right at home on a stage. It's like I this is what I'm supposed to be doing."

"I know what you mean, Steve. I feel the same way."

Uncle Sam's turned out to be Jane's swan song with us, though. She decided the band was cutting too much into her study time. Also, her boyfriend had come up for a visit recently, and was uncomfortable with knowing that she was living in such close quarters with me. So Jane quit the band and moved out. A few days later, Annie moved in with me. She had recently broken up with her boyfriend, and reckoned that if she were living in the cottage behind the fortuneteller's house, she wouldn't have to bum rides to rehearsals. Also, she would have more time and opportunity to work on songs with me. We began spending a lot of time together, jamming, rehearsing, and learning new songs. The result was the band became tighter, and soon we were ready to expand our territory beyond just playing in the streets of San Francisco.

We busked a couple of coffeehouses I knew in Berkeley, and then turned our attention to Santa Rosa, and the Russian River resort area. Weeknights we'd drive all over the county, looking for places to play. We'd pop into a pizza parlor or a bar, and ask if we could set up and do a few songs, and we'd usually get the okay. We'd pass the hat, and go on to the next place. We did so well at some of these places, they'd invite us back, and soon we had some regular gigs going on in Forestville and up and down the Russian River: bars, restaurants, places that were live music venues, and other places that up till now hadn't considered having music. Whatever we lacked in musicianship, we made up for in drive and enthusiasm. Marty was especially hungry for gigs because he was—well, hungry. He had no other source of income.

Visually, we commanded attention. R.J. stood with one foot up on the gutbucket, plunking it madly. Marty stood tall and proud in a fringed buckskin jacket, long hair and beard, looking a little like a mountain man, and picking the banjo. I had long hair and a beard, and had also acquired a colorful minstrel shirt, in imitation of Vic. It was made of velour, with blue and red and gold vertical stripes, and laced up with a rawhide drawstring. And Annie was a sight, with her long flowing hair, gypsy blouse and skirt and kerchief. When she wasn't singing, she would close her eyes and become one with the violin. With our look and our sound, we drew crowds of tourists, and the guitar case overflowed with currency.

I was still corresponding with Vic, and updating him on news of the band. He mailed me some lyrics he'd written to a tune Paul Curtis had composed back in the Morning Glory days, and encouraged me to do something with it. Marty would know the song and could show it to me, he added. So one night Marty taught me the melody and chords, and I tried to marry the words to it, but came out a couple of lines short. Then I wrote some lyrics to fill in the missing spot, and we had our own original Uncle Zeke song—"The Rain Came Down." We worked out an arrangement where Marty and I sung the verses together in harmony, and then Annie came in with a third harmony part for the chorus. Later, she added a great violin solo, and "The Rain Came Down" became our signature song. One night when we played at a rowdy bar called The Saloon in Forestville, I recorded one of our sets with a portable cassette recorder, and sent the tape to Vic, who was now living in the German Alps. He wrote back saying he thought we should all come to Europe, that a little group like ours could clean up over there. He even hinted about joining our band.

I gave his idea serious consideration. I'd already bought my one-way plane ticket to London. Because I was a full-time student, I'd paid a cheap student fare, and would be flying out in June on a charter carrier. Now I began to believe that the entire Uncle Zeke group should go to Europe. R.J. said he'd better stick around, finish school, and pay off his student loans. Annie was all for it, she was willing to drop everything and head off to Europe with me any time. Marty said he'd like to, but didn't have any money. Annie stepped in and bought a ticket for herself and another for Marty. He could pay her later, she said.

Annie and I discovered a little vegetarian restaurant just down the road from us, walking distance, so we began playing there once a week as a duo. We'd get a free meal and tips. One night Norman Greenbaum was there with his wife. He dropped a five-dollar bill in the hat, big money in those days, and if he remembered me from my pathetic first days at the Rosewood Forest open mikes, he was kind enough not to mention it.

The band was now playing out several times a week; at benefits, art festivals, parties, just about any place they'd have us. Gary Pihl set us up as the opening act for a concert his rock band was doing with another group at the Phoenix Theater in Petaluma. It was to be a showcase for some record label people from L.A. We would be on a big stage in front of the curtained movie screen playing to a thousand kids, and we were excited about it. However, when we saw one of the flyers that had been put up around the area, we noticed they'd misspelled our name. We were billed as just Uncle Zeke's Band, without the other business about silver strings. "Hell," said Marty, "I like it better this way. Fewer words, easier to remember." We were now Uncle Zeke's Band.

The night of the big concert, we wandered into the cavernous old theater, built in the 1920s, before show time to do the sound check. Someone called out, "Hey Zeke!" I turned around to look, and when I did Marty and Annie broke out in laughter. The young soundman addressing me asked, "How many guys in your band?"

"Just the four of us."

"What kind of amplification do you need?"

"Just mikes for three voices and four instruments," I said.

"Okay, then. Just go up on the stage, and we'll set you up and do a sound check."

"Hey Zeke," said Marty, mimicking the roadie. "Looks like you got a new name."

"Very funny," I said.

"I like it," said Annie, with a teasing smile. "I'll call you Zeke from now on."

The show was a big success. The place was packed, we got a great reponse, and afterwards kids came up to us, patted us on our backs, shook our hands, and said things like, "Hey, man, great band you got! Loved the music. It was fun! Where ya playin' next?"

Where we were playing next was a restaurant in Monte Rio, out on the Russian River, and it was our last official gig before we all headed over to Europe. I'd bought my ticket first, so I'd be leaving first, right after the spring semester ended. Marty and Annie would be following one week behind, on a separate flight. This night, as usual, R.J. drove the VW bus as we wended our way down through Forestville redwood stands, past Guerneville, and along the Russian River to the Village Inn in Monte Rio. The food was great, the atmosphere charming, and we made an effort to give our best performance, toned down to pass as dinner music. We drove home that night knowing that this had been the last gig for the group in this lineup and in this area. The next time we'd perform together would be in Europe. What we didn't know then was that things were about to change even more dramatically

On Monday next, Marty received a summons in the mail He had to appear in a Los Angeles County court.

"It's about child support," said Marty through tight lips. "I guess Meg turned me in. I have to go down to La Mirada and take care of it. I'm hitchin' out today. R.J. is dropping me off by the freeway. I should be back in a few days, hopefully in time for the send off."

The send off he'd referred to would be our big going away bash that R.J. had arranged for the coming weekend. It was supposed to be a carbon copy of Vic and Star's farewell blowout. Invitations went out, and again, people showed up from all over. Annie's sisters showed up; and two old friends of mine from La Mirada, Jack and Ken drove up. My new friend from Santa Rosa J.C., Randy Bleu, turned up with his girlfriend, his guitar, and a couple of joints he said were for smoking on the plane. Scott Duncan drove up from Berkeley. Bummer came down from the commune he was living on near Mendocino. There were other friends and neighbors who came and went, and some who spent the night in sleeping bags. Like the previous party, there was much eating and drinking and smoking of pot; singing and dancing, and trips up to Diekman's store for more beer or hot dog buns.

But there was one thing missing, and everyone noticed it. Marty hadn't shown up, and no one had heard from him. So when the weekend was over, people had scattered to the four corners, and the debris was swept up, I bummed a ride down to La Mirada with my old buddy Jack, and set out to look for Marty. I told Annie and R.J. I'd return as soon as I could, hopefully with Marty in tow.

Finding Marty Power, however, turned out no so easy a task. I called Uncle Stan's house, but Marty's parents hadn't seen him or heard from him. I looked up Meg's parents in the phone book, and dropped by their house. Her dad took one look at my long hair and beard and patched-over jeans, and shut the door in my face. I was beginning to think maybe Marty had been arrested, so I checked to local and county jails. The good news was he wasn't locked up. The bad news was I had hit a dead end. Then, while walking along a La Mirada street, on my way back from another futile search, I was spotted by one of Marty's friends as he was driving by, and he offered me a lift. I told him I'd been looking for Marty. Had he seen him? As a matter of fact, he had.

"Where is he?"

"He's staying with Meg at her new apartment. Would you like me to take you there?"

I said yes, the friend pulled a U-turn, and we drove over to the apartment complex, less than a mile away. He was in a hurry to get to someplace else, so he dropped me off and I thanked him as he sped away. Meg answered the door.

"Steve Dupree! We haven't seen you in a long time. Are you looking for Marty?"

"Yes, I am."

"He's right here. Come on in," she said, opening the door. I stepped inside the compact little living room and spotted Marty sitting on the couch, his son in his lap, looking the picture of domestic bliss.

"Hello, Steve," he said sheepishly. "How are you?"

"Fine. How about yourself? We were worried about you. We missed you at the party. It was a real orgy of excess."

"Yeah . . . well, Meg and I have been patching things up. And I still have to take care of some child support business."

"Are you still planning to go to Europe with us?"

"Yeah, I still want to do that, but I've got some things to take care of here first. I want us to be a family again. Maybe I can get some bread together, and we can all go. Vic took Star, and that's working out okay. I'll just be over later. In a few weeks or a couple of months—as soon as I can. Keep me posted with your address over there, and I'll catch up with you."

Well, that was that. I had a final night with my family. We sat down to a home cooked meal in the old house, my mom and dad, my younger brother Mark, and my older brother Reed, who had an apartment in another town. It was the first time we'd all been together and visited like this in quite a while. And I didn't know it then, but it would be the last time we'd all get together. I had planned to hitch back to Santa Rosa, but my dad, in an expansive mood, sprung for a plane ticket to San Francisco, and drove me to the airport. I took the bus from SFO to Santa Rosa and walked back to the little cottage behind Madame Rachel's. I had one more final to take at school the following morning, and then nothing to do for a few days but to pack my belongings and send off a postcard to Bad Kohlgrub, in Germany, letting Vic and Star know I was on my way. And then, just for the hell of it, I shaved off my beard, but left my mustache. Annie said she thought it was an improvement to my appearance.

It didn't take long for me to pack, because as the song went, I was traveling light. I stuffed clothing into my backpack, tied the sleeping bag to the bottom of the frame, and draped my fringed leather jacket over the back. A cowboy hat fit snug on my head, my harmonica was stowed away in my guitar case, and the harness for it fit over the outside of the case. R.J. and his friend, Derek, who had just moved out from Minnesota, pulled up to the cottage in the VW bus, and Annie and I climbed in. Then we were off to the airport in Oakland, from which my British Caledonian airliner would be flying. On the way we smoked one of the joints Randy had given me, while I saved the other one for the flight over. We pulled into the airport, and they dropped me at the curb, and there was only time for handshakes from Derek and R.J., and a hug from Annie. "See you in Germany, Zeke," she said in parting.

There was the usual checking of baggage and waiting to board the plane, but late in the afternoon I was finally aboard the Boeing 707, and strapped into my seat. I closed my eyes during the takeoff, and when I opened them and looked out the little porthole window on the left side of the plane, we were banking and I caught a good glimpse of the Golden Gate Bridge below. Often obscured by fog this time of year, today it gleamed in the sunlight as little cars drove across it's length, commuters mostly, heading home for the day, as well as travelers passing through. Little white sails on boats breezing around the San Francisco Bay mixed with whitecaps on the water, while the sunlight winked and gleamed off its rippled surface. Then the bridge was gone from sight, and with it the Waldo Tunnel on the Marin County side. But I could make out Angel Island and Tiburon and Sausalito as we passed over them. Then we were climbing, and I no longer recognized any landmarks below as we flew into and above clouds on our northeasterly course.

I stepped inside the tiny lavatory in the rear of the plane, shut and locked the door, and fired up the joint. I only smoked half of it, planning to finish it off before we landed. Then I returned to my seat, and tried to read from a paperback copy of Hermann Hesse's *Journey to The East,* but my mind just couldn't concentrate. My thoughts raced between memories of times with Uncle Zeke's Band, and imaginings about my future in Europe. The airliner hummed along as night descended and I knew we must be somewhere over Canada now, but I had no idea where. I got up and stretched, walking the length of the aisle and back again, and tried to nap. A flight attendant with a British accent came around offering pillows and blankets, and I took one of each, put the seat back, and got comfortable. At some point in the flight while we were over the North Atlantic, I dozed off into a fitful sleep, and dreamt about Vic and Star, and about my old love in California, Vicki. My dreams were all jumbled up, not making any sense. But outside of my slumber, in the darkened passenger cabin that night, a real life dream was coming true.

CHAPTER TEN

Across The Big Pond

I awoke with a start as the aircraft lurched, pitched and banked. Then it seemed to be descending. I opened the shutter on the porthole window and squinted as morning sunlight flooded in. I removed the blanket and pillow, and stored them in the overhead. Soon, the flight attendants were serving breakfast on trays; bangers and eggs, cereal, and toast with butter and jam, and tea with milk. An announcement came over the speakers: "Ladies and gentlemen, if you look below, you will notice we are now passing over the Faroe Islands." I craned my neck to look down out of the window, and could see surf breaking against a green, granite, and rocky isle below. We were definitely descending now, following an unseen line that led to England and *terra firma*. I thought about Lindbergh and his solo flight across the Atlantic in the fragile silver monoplane *The Spirit of St. Louis*. That had been a mere forty-five years before, and it had been less than seventy years since the Wright Brothers had first flown in a gasoline powered flying machine. Now I was making the leap across the big pond in a modern jet aircraft, and what amazed me even more was that I was actually about to hook up with Vic Power again, this time on another continent.

I pulled out his letter from Bad Kohlgrub and read it again. He told of how he'd been run out of Spain, with the *Guardia Civil* on his heels. It seems he'd made quite a nuisance of himself in Barcelona, especially with the busking. He'd been consciously conspicuous in his grey top hat and blue military coat with its brass buttons and epaulets. His long hair and Abe Lincoln beard, and his swagger also drew attention. The *Guardia Civil* took notice and gave him the nickname, "Uncle Sam." Eventually, they became fed up with his ubiquitous presence, and figuring his visa must be expired, planned to arrest and deport him. But a Spanish friend tipped Vic off to the planned bust, and he and Star lit out in the middle of the night, and crossed the border into France.

Vic had met a couple of Americans in Barcelona who were also on the lam, and were heading for a small village in the German Alps to hide out. Albert and Fred were both from Southern California. Albert had been involved with the SDS—Students For A Democratic Society. After staging a campus anti-war protest, he had drawn the attention of the FBI, whose agents were planted in the crowd. With a warrant out for his arrest, Albert had packed his bag, and one jump ahead of the law, caught the next flight to Europe, and landed in Spain. His brother Fred joined him a few days later. The two decided to lay low in Bad Kohlgrub until the heat blew over, and had given Vic their address there. "If you're ever up our way, drop by and visit. We'll hoist a few beers together," said Fred. Vic decided to take advantage of the offer.

After landing in the little village in the German Alps, near the Austrian border, Star had found work as a *zimmermachin*, or maid, in a hotel. Vic found work there as well, doing some basic janitorial work and odd jobs. They got their room free, and a little wage as well. So they had been cooling their heels there, and then a friend of Fred and Albert, a guy they called "Hubcap", showed up for an extended visit. Bad Kohlgrub was becoming quite a little hangout for American expatriates. Vic had sent me a postcard from Bad Kohlgrub of the hotel where they were staying. Two stories tall, it had the appearance of an Alpine ski lodge, quaint and cozy.

The 707 continued its descent, and soon we were over England, below us a countryside of green and brown, of small farms separated by stone fences, cattle and sheep grazing in the fields, little whitewashed farmhouses. We wove through a wispy cloud layer, and the farms and fields and roads were now only seen through breaks in the clouds. Then we were under the clouds and passing over London, which we overflew, landing on the tarmac at Gatwick Airport, twenty-five miles to the south.

Going through Customs, a uniformed official took my passport, examined it, and then gave me the stink eye.

"What is your business here?" he asked officiously.

"I'm on my way to Germany."

"How much money are you carrying?"

"A hundred and fifty dollars, more or less."

He sized me up again. "And how long did you plan to stay in England?"

"I'm just passing through."

"You'd better be," he said sternly. "I'll give you a visa for forty-eight hours. You'll need to be out of the country by then. Do you understand?"

"Yes, sir, forty-eight hours."

He brought his fist down and stamped the passport perfunctorily, then returned it without looking at me. He was focused on the next person in line. It's a good thing he hadn't asked whether I had a return ticket, I thought to myself. Otherwise, I might not have even gotten the forty-eight hour grace period.

Finished with Customs, I went off to change a traveler's check for some British currency. As I stood examining the bills and coins, a Brit stopped, and began pointing to each article in my palm. "That's a quid, 'ere's a shilling, that's a fiver," and so on. I thanked the old bloke, stuffed the currency into a pants pocket, and found the train bound for London.

As the train entered the outskirts of London, I began to get an idea of the enormity of the place, for it seemed to go on for miles; dense industrial sections of soot and smokestack and sad dirty brick buildings squeezing out the sunlight and greenery. I thought about Dickens and Sherlock Holmes and Jack The Ripper. But when we reached the heart of London, although the density was the same, the buildings were cleaner and newer and better kept. We came to the end of the line at Victoria Station, the central gathering of all the trains, and in the very hub of the city, where the River Thames flows through its center. I alighted from the car, and into the cavernous station, a marvel in Queen Victoria's time, and still a marvel to behold in Steve Dupree's time. I gathered my belongings and strolled out of the station, and into the crisp London morning air.

Once on the sidewalk, I looked all around, and not knowing which way to go, just took off walking, away from Victoria Station. I saw a young hippie waiting at a light and approached him.

"Hi," I said. "I wonder if you can help me."

"Hey, man," he answered with a smile, "where are you from?'

"California," I said.

"I'm from The States myself," he said. "You just get in?"

"Yeah, just got off the plane and now I'm jet lagged. I'm looking for a cheap place to crash for the night. Know of any place around here?"

"Yeah, I reckon I do. I've been here about eight months. Know my way around fairly well. My name is Bill. What's yours?"

"Steve."

"Well, Steve, there's a youth hostel a few blocks from here. I'll walk you part of the way. I'm sort of heading in that direction myself."

"Thanks, brother. I appreciate it."

"Don't mention it. Always happy to help out a fellow Yank."

"You know," I said looking up at the overcast sky, "when I left California yesterday, summer was on its way in. Over here it feels like early spring."

"Oh, this is nice weather. At least it's not raining for a change. They tell me summer is just around the corner."

The light changed, and I stepped off the curb. Bill caught my arm and jerked me back, just as a taxi lurched around the corner and past the spot I had just missed stepping into.

"Whoa, boy!" he said. "You almost got creamed. You've got to look to the right, not the left, before stepping out. Those Limeys drive on the wrong side of the road. And cabbies are bonkers."

"Thanks, I'll make a note of that."

"Well, let's push on," he said.

We walked on a few blocks, then my guide said, "Here's where I turn off." He pointed out the way to the hostel, and waved as he walked on. "So long, California. Watch those cabbies."

The hostel was nearby, and I found it easily enough. It was in an anonymous brick building in the middle of a block. Inside, it reminded me of the YMCA, with its rows of dormitory beds, and shared bathrooms and showers. I checked in and paid for one night, found an empty bed, set my watch to local time, and fell fast asleep, awakening in the evening, refreshed enough to want to go out exploring.

A pub seemed a likely spot to visit first, so I tagged along with a guy who was also staying at the hostel. He knew of one in the neighborhood, and when we entered it, it struck me as being quite different from an American bar. Oh, it was noisy and smoke filled all right, but that was the only similarity. The place had the ambience of someone's living room. There were carpets on the floor, sofas and tables and easy chairs scattered about, lace curtains in the windows, and paintings hung on the mahogany walls. People sat around at tables and in chairs socializing. We stepped up to the bar, where there were no stools, and everyone stood to drink, some resting a foot on the rail. On the wall behind the bartender were shelves containing bottles of liquor and bottles of beer.

"What'll it be, guv?" asked the bartender. I ordered a Watney's, and watched him take a bottle from the shelf, pop off the cap, and pour it into a glass for me. I took a sip. It was room temperature warm, and sweet.

"That'll be 'alf a quid, guv'ner," he said.

I stared blankly for a moment, then pulled out a fistful of bills and coins from my pocket, and placed it on the bar. The barkeep picked out one of the large, colorful bills, took it, rang up the sale, and handed me back a coin—my change.

I took another sip of beer, and said to my companion, who had ordered a Double Diamond, "I think warm beer is going to take some getting used to."

"Well," he said, "have another and start getting used to it now."

"No, I don't think so," I said, sliding the half empty glass away. "I think I'll go out and do some sightseeing."

"Okay, then. See you back at the ranch."

Outside in the cool evening I wandered, taking in the sights and watching strangers as they went about their business. Then I spied a familiar face and form, that of a slender young lady of medium height, as she stood on a curb waiting for the light to change. She had shoulder length brown hair and was dressed in tight fitting jeans and a long sleeved off-white blouse. I strolled on up and said hello. She stared at me dumbly for a few moments, then recognition came to her eyes, and her smile followed behind.

"Hey, don't I know you from somewhere?" she said, searching my face for a place to file it.

"Yeah," I answered, "Santa Rosa J.C."

"You're kidding!" she said with a look of surprise. Then the synapses that had been spinning in her head, scanning bits of stored memory information, suddenly found the match for my face. Her whole face lit up in recognition. "Yes, you're right! We had a class together. I'm sorry, but I've forgotten your name."

"Steve Dupree—and yours?"

"Rhonda. Rhonda Sykes. When did you get here, and how long are you here for?"

"Just got in this morning, leaving tomorrow. I'm on my way to Germany. What about you?"

"I just arrived yesterday. I'm on a thirty-day sightseeing tour of England. What a small world! We almost came over on the same flight. Where are you staying?"

"At a youth hostel near here."

"I've got a cheap hotel room. So what are you doing right now?"

"Nothing, just wandering around."

"Have you eaten yet?"

"No, I haven't."

"Well, if you don't mind keeping me company, let's go get some dinner and maybe hear some music somewhere."

"That sounds great to me," I said. "You're a day ahead of me here, so why don't you lead on."

We walked along together in the London evening, talking about ourselves and Santa Rosa, and of our summer plans, while she led me down busy streets to an English hamburger franchise called Wimpy's, named after a character in Popeye cartoons. It was the English version of McDonald's. She ordered a cheeseburger, and I the fish and chips. After the meal, she said, "Let's find some music." We came upon a nightclub called The Great American Disaster, paid a cover charge, and went inside. It turned out to be the British version of an American club, on two levels. The lower level had a brightly lit stage and an area in front of it for dancing.

Tonight there were no dancers, or maybe it was just that it was too early in the evening yet. The group onstage was a pair of American folk singer types with acoustic guitars, singing versions of popular American songs. Rhonda seemed to really dig the scene, but I thought for a woman who was on a month long tour of England, she wasn't straying far from American culture. She wanted to hang out here for the night and do some dancing later on, but I wasn't interested, so I said goodnight and wished her a nice summer, and wandered the streets again, trying out another warm beer at another pub. Then with jet lag again sneaking up on me, I decided to head back to the hostel and catch some shut-eye.

In the morning I showered, changed clothes, and checked out of the hostel. Before leaving, I asked the girl on the desk if she knew the cheapest way to Germany. She said I should check Victoria Station for a rail and ferry package. I thanked her and headed off in the direction of the station. At the information kiosk I was told there would be a train leaving in the afternoon that would connect with a ferry at Dover and with another train in Oostend, Belgium. I bought a ticket at the counter, stored my luggage in a coin-operated locker, and went off in search of breakfast. I found a brightly lit cafeteria and had a cheap if unspectacular meal. Then I set off to see some sights.

I climbed aboard a double-decker bus, and took it as far as Buckingham Palace, where I was in time to watch the changing of the guard. Then I hoofed it on over to Piccadilly Circus, and to Trafalgar Square, with its pigeon-covered statue of Lord Nelson. I would have liked to have seen and done much more, but my forty-eight hours grace period was rapidly ticking away, and I had to catch a train soon. I made the long trek down to Buckingham Palace Road and a few more blocks to Victoria Station, where I boarded the train just as it was about to leave.

We pulled out of the station, passed through London, and headed into the countryside to the southeast. I watched out the coach window as we rolled through field and forest and little villages, and I thought about Robin Hood and Sherwood Forest. Then as we passed through Canterbury, I remembered Chaucer and the *Canterbury Tales* from my English Lit class. The afternoon was about spent when we reached the famous white cliffs of Dover. There was just enough time to catch the ferry, whose diesel engines were humming impatiently, decks vibrating, and straining at the ropes on the bow that kept her fastened to the dock. I was barely aboard and seated when lines were cast off, the vessel backed away from the dock, blew exhaust smoke from her stack, and we lumbered out into the English Channel on a cold, blustery grey evening. I stayed atop the main deck, biting wind blowing through my hair and against my face, for as long as I could stand it, watching Dover's white cliffs recede over the horizon. Then I ducked inside the passenger cabin to warm up with a cup of coffee at the bar.

The channel crossing was a choppy one, taking up the evening hours, and I stayed inside, out of the cold and wind, drinking coffee, writing postcards, and eating some fish and chips that were neither warm nor tasty, but they filled the gap. As we approached the low-lying coast of Belgium in the fading light, I went back out on deck to watch our approach. We pulled into the harbor and the ferry shuddered as the engines reversed and we sidled into the dock with a bump and a grind, and tied up and made fast. There was only time for those passengers who were continuing on to make a mad dash for the nearby railroad station. People piled into various trains and railcars, but I didn't know where to go, and so I rushed around, asking if anyone spoke English. I noticed the cars had different names on them such as Koln and Essen, and I assumed those were destinations, but not a one of them was marked "Munich." Then I spotted a British gentleman boarding the train, showed him my ticket, and asked if he knew which car was mine. He smiled patiently and pointed one out.

"Over there, lad. You want the one that says *Munchen*. That's the German word for Munich."

I thanked him and hustled on over to the coach, just as the train began moving. I hopped aboard, made my way down the aisle, and found a compartment with a vacant seat. I tossed my guitar and pack in the overhead, and settled in as we rolled out of the station. I looked around at the others in the compartment and asked if anyone spoke English, but they just shook their heads no. The night had descended now, and my world became an endless succession of station stops, unfamiliar landscapes rushing by in darkness, and names of cities we passed through: Bruxelles, Bonn, Mainz,

Mannheim, Stuttgart, Ulm, Augsburg. I dozed fitfully, but could not sleep for just as I was about to go down for the count, the train would come to a stop, lights would flick on, and passengers would come and go. A conductor came around frequently, waking anyone who might be sleeping, to check and punch tickets. Finally, I gave up trying to sleep, and just sat upright in my seat in a kind of daze, watching with disinterest each new stop and each new interruption.

After a while, the night took on a dream-like state, and I quit checking my watch, for it seemed pointless. But then the dawn of a new day filtered through the glass window, the world outside became brighter, I could make out bits of landscapes, and finally the station sign that read *Munchen.* We were in Munich station. The car was uncoupled, and we were left behind as the train continued onward.

Sore and stiff, deprived of sleep, and with an aching head, I collected my gear, stumbled out of the coach, and stood on the concrete platform of the station, a stranger in a strange land. First I changed a traveler's check into deutschmarks, and then I shuffled over to an information kiosk, pulled the letter from Vic from my shirt pocket, and handed it to the woman seated there. I pointed to the return address, and pantomimed, "Where do I go?" She directed me to a ticket window, where I played the same game of charades. The man nodded, "*Ja, ja.*" He said something else I didn't understand, but then he said the ticket price, and I handed him a bill, which he took, and handed me back change along with the ticket. I looked closely at it. The destination said Murnau. Then the man at the ticket booth held up one finger and said, "*Ein stunde.* One hour." I nodded, looked for the platform that had a sign saying Murnau, and waited on a bench for an hour, too exhausted to even read. Just sat there until the train pulled in and I got on board. I hadn't a clue where Murnau was, but supposed I'd have to change trains again once I got there.

The train with its coaches painted a dull olive drab chugged out of Munich Station, and through the city, and then began its slow ascent into the mountains. We were hardly outside the city when I began seeing pine forests rolling by us, and later a lake. We continued to climb, higher and higher into the mountains, and the forests became thicker and the passes narrower, and in the bright crisp Alpine sunshine, I felt my spirits begin to revive and my heart beat faster in anticipation of what lay at the end of the line. I shared the compartment with just one other person, an older gentleman wearing an English style business suit, and reading an English language newspaper. I decided to strike up a conversation.

"Excuse me, sir, but do you speak English?"

He put down the paper, folded it in his lap and turned to me.

"Well, I should hope so," he said pleasantly, "After all, I am British you know. I'm over here on business. Are you on holiday?"

"Well, I suppose I am." Then I gave him a sketchy version of my plans to meet up with Vic and Star in Bad Kohlgrub. It was good to have someone to talk with after the long night. Then I mentioned I hadn't eaten anything since the evening before, and asked him if he thought I could get some food on the train.

"They'll probably be around soon, taking breakfast orders," he said with the certainty of someone who had traveled this way before.

"I hope so," I complained. "I'm starved."

"It'll only be a Continental breakfast, no doubt."

"What's that?" I asked.

"Coffee and rolls."

"Oh," I said, disappointed. But I imagined nice big, warm, sweet Danish pastries. Instead, we were served a couple of white dinner rolls with butter and jam, which I wolfed down. The coffee came in a small cup, but it was strong, and the cream was thick and sweet, and I savored every drop. I put down the cup, relaxed in the seat, and watched contentedly as pine trees and tiny villages and farms passed by. We reached Murnau mid-morning, I said goodbye to my traveling companion, he wished me a safe journey, and I stepped off onto the platform and watched as the train pulled away, I noticed I was the only passenger who had gotten off, and I stood there a few moments on the platform alone, looking all around. The station was a small one, and I could see some of the woods beyond, could feel the crispness of the morning, and smell the forest smells and the freshness of the thin Alpine air.

I walked off the platform and into the station itself, and I bought a chocolate bar at a snack stand, for I was still hungry. The chocolate was smooth and rich, and I devoured it. I walked over to the ticket window, showed the return address on Vic's letter to the plump woman behind the counter, and indicated I wanted to go there. She smiled broadly and nodded.

"*Ja ja*," she said good-naturedly. "*Bad Kohlgrub. Fumph mark*." She held up five fingers for emphasis. I handed her five deutschmarks, and she gave me a ticket.

"When does the train come?" I asked.

"*Nichts train*." She shook her head and pointed to the street outside. "*Autobus. Swanzeig minuten*." She opened and closed her hands twice, showing twenty fingers.

"A bus in twenty minutes?" I asked.

"*Ja,*" she said again with a friendly smile. "*Autobus.*"

I said thank you, she smiled and said, "*Bitte*."

I waited outside in the sunlight, enjoying the mountain greenery and checking my watch. Right on schedule, a short but wide Mercedes Benz diesel bus with room for about twenty passengers pulled up and stopped, its engine idling. I climbed aboard with backpack strapped on, and guitar in hand, and handed the driver my ticket. Then I found a seat and put the guitar on the floor, and the pack on the seat next to me. The other passengers seemed to be mostly happy vacationers, all German, Their eyes were all upon me as they talked and joked among themselves, pointing at me, obviously commenting on my appearance: cowboy hat, fringed leather jacket, long hair tied in a ponytail. But it all seemed good-natured and not at all antagonistic. "American?" asked the man across the aisle, smiling.

"Yes," I smiled back, "American."

"Oh, *ja, ja.*" They all understood.

We drove through the village of Murnau and along forested mountain roads, passing little villages in the process. Then the driver pulled off the road and into another little village and sang out, "Bad Kohlgrub!" He pulled over in front of a post office, and stopped there with the engine idling until I had managed to grab all my gear and squeeze out the door. The bus drove off and I looked around.

The post office stood at the end of the village, which was rolled out before me heading uphill, with green hills at the other end, beyond which were mountains. I began walking up the main street. Although the village looked old, still the street was of asphalt, not cobblestone, and the little gingerbread houses and shops seemed to be replicas of much older times. The village seemed a little touristy, but in an understated way. I observed a bakery and a camera shop, and a little shop with a rack of postcards outside. A quaint hotel sat on the corner of a side street, and I noticed the townsfolk were dressed in clothing that either seemed to be geared toward tourism, or else this place was just so isolated and steeped in tradition, fashion hadn't yet caught up with the twentieth century. The women wore dirndl-type dresses and the men lederhosen and peaked Alpine hats. The Volkswagens and Mercedes-Benzes parked along the street contrasted with the impression that I had stepped into another century.

I stopped a man on the street, once again pulled out Vic's letter, showed it to him, and asked if he could direct me. He nodded in understanding, and pointed up the street in the direction of the church with the onion-dome spire, which stood on a hillside at the other end of town. I thanked him and continued on my way, past some more shops and into the town square, where a fountain stood in the center. Then, from the far end of the village, I saw two figures, a man and a woman, racing downhill toward me, taking long strides. The woman was of medium height and slender, with long brown hair held in place with a colorful scarf. The man had a beard and long hair, and was clothed in jeans, a Navy blue military coat with brass buttons, and sporting a grey top hat, like one wouldsee at weddings or other formal social occasions. He was above average in height, thin and angular, and his gait was quick and rolling, taking long strides, his legs almost kicking out to the sides as he hurried. As he got closer, he smiled, waved, and shouted out.

"Hey, Steve!"

The woman waved too, smiling brightly. I quickened my pace toward them, my backpack bouncing and nearly throwing me off balance. And then, in the middle of the town square, we came face to face.

"Good old dependable Steve Dupree," said the woman, as I set down my guitar case.

"Hi, Star," I said. "Hi Vic."

"Hey, Dupree!" Said Vic gripping my hand firmly and giving it a shake. "Welcome to Bavaria. Let's go get us a beer."

CHAPTER ELEVEN

Alpine Idyll

I awoke to a sound both strange and yet familiar, a sound that cut through the fog of sleep, and just before I opened my eyes, in that state between sleeping and waking, I heard it again, wondering if it was a part of the dream I'd been having. The dream involved Marty Power. He was playing the banjo and singing a song he'd worked out shortly before leaving for L.A. How did the song go?

> *Oh the cuckoo, she's a pretty bird, and she wobbles as she flies.*
> *But she never hollers cuckoo till the fourth day of July.*

Then I heard it again. *Cuckoo! Cuckoo!* I opened my eyes. It was truly a cuckoo bird I was hearing. It sounded just like a cuckoo clock. But of course! I was in Germany, in the Alps, no less. *Cuckoo*! *Cuckoo*!

I was fully awake now, and I began to take notice of my surroundings. The sun glistened on the silvery rain I could see through the slats of the barn as I peeked outside. The rain pattered softly on the barn roof, and on the fresh green grass, in the rustic morning of cuckoo birds. I smelled the fragrance of fresh cut green hay, which was piled up high beneath the sleeping bag where I lay snug and rested after two days of jet lag. I gathered up my thoughts and tried to recall the events of the previous day.

I recalled the scene in the village square, the late morning reunion with Vic and Star. After hugs and handshakes, Vic had said, "Let's go get a beer!" So I had followed him down the street and into the frescoed *gasthaus,* where villagers were sitting around wooden tables having breakfast, or sipping coffee, and enjoying lively conversation, which suddenly quieted as we entered the room, and all eyes fell on me. I set down my backpack and guitar by the table Vic had picked out for us, while he greeted everyone with a hearty "*Gruss Gott*!" He hailed the waitress in the blue dress and apron and ordered for us.

"*Drei pils, drei scheinken mit eiren, und ein tomatensap, bitte.*"

"What did you say?" I asked in amazement of his linguistic powers.

"Oh, I ordered us some ham and eggs and beers, and a tomato juice for myself."

"I thought you were a vegetarian," I said.

"I was," he said unapologetically. "But if I stuck to it over here, I'd probably starve. This country is strictly meat and potatoes and cabbage. As a matter of fact, most of the meat is pork, but it's good quality, especially the hot dogs."

"Well," I said philosophically, "when in Rome—."

"That's the spirit, Steve," said a smiling Star. "Except this is Bavaria, not Rome."

"That's right," concurred Vic. "Only here they pronounce it *Bayern.* They don't even consider themselves German. They say, '*Ich bin Bayrish,*' which means, 'I'm a Bavarian.' They're proud of their heritage. Of course the northern Germans just laugh at them. They're considered the hillbillies of Germany."

The beers arrived, and they were in half-liter glasses. "Jesus," I said, "check out the size of those beers!"

"Those are the small ones," said Vic. "You should see the liter mugs, which I'm sure you will if you stick around for a while."

Vic uncapped the bottle of tomato juice and said, "Watch this." He took a sip of beer, poured the tomato juice into the glass, and held it proudly aloft. "*Prosit,*" he said, clinking his glass against mine, then downed nearly half of it in one long gulp. Then he slyly glanced around the room to see who had noticed him.

"It blows their minds when they see me drink a tomato beer. They call me the 'Crazy American.'"

"You just like to get a rise out of people, Vic," said Star, embarrassed by the scene.

Now our food arrived, Star said, "*Danke schon*," and opened her purse to pay.

"Star's the one with all the bread," explained Vic, as he reached over and pinched her leg. "I get my room and board in exchange for doing odd jobs, but as a *zimmermachin*, Star makes the money. We'll go over to the hotel later, and see about putting you up. We told them you were coming, and Hans—he's the son—said you could probably stay in the barn for a while. We can drop in on Albert and Fred before we head up the hill. They only live a few blocks from here."

We dug into our food, and I discovered how hungry I was, as Vic filled me in on events of the past year, and all about their adventures abroad. They had flown from Montreal to London, and then caught a ferry to Ireland to look up Paddy O'Brien, and they had reunited in Dublin. Paddy was now playing the five-string banjo, and so there had been much partying in the pubs, and much jamming, with Paddy teaching Vic traditional Irish songs, mostly about drinking and rebellion. Then Vic and Star had gone to Holland, and rented an attic room in the village of Edam, near Amsterdam. They would hitch or take a bus to Amsterdam several times a week to busk in bars and restaurants, returning each night to their *kamer*. However, largely because he couldn't keep a low profile, Vic was to discover the villagers of Edam weren't as tolerant as the citizens of Amsterdam, and soon tired of the longhaired, unkempt, dope smoking American hippie. There was a plan being hatched to have the foreigners run out of town and deported. Having gotten wind of the plot, Vic and Star split in the middle of the night, and headed for the border. The Dutch couple they rented from gave them a Citroen to help speed their departure. Steve had heard of a possible gig in Barcelona, so they headed for Spain.

The Citroen somehow made it across Belgium and France with no brakes and a bad engine, but was confiscated at the Spanish border owing to its condition, and the fact that Vic had no documents of ownership or auto insurance. So he and Star continued on by train. But when they arrived in Barcelona, the promised gig failed to materialize, so it was touch and go for a while, with Vic busking in the streets, and Star teaching English.

At one point, they were reduced to sleeping in a friend's VW bus at night. But Vic was undeterred, and aggressively sought out a real gig, finally landing a residency in a club named The Red Lion, on the Ramblas. He was able to save a little money singing there until the *Guardia Civil* came looking for him, and again he and Star lit out in the middle of the night, this time for Germany. They had successfully weathered the spring in Bad Kohlgrub, summer had arrived, and now Vic was making plans to go on the road again—with me, no less.

By the time he had finished his story, I had finished my breakfast and beer.

"Ready for another beer, Steve?" said Vic.

"No thanks. That one made me sleepy. Another would put me right out."

"Okay, then, let's head up the hill and get you settled in. But first, let's go see the Fischers."

"Who are they?" I asked.

"Albert and Fred. They're living with their parents."

"I thought they were Americans," I said.

"They are. Their father is a German Jew. He escaped from Germany after the Nazis came to power and started rounding up Jews and intellectuals. He slipped across the border into Switzerland and made his way to the States, where he had relatives. Well you know the saying, like father like son? Now his sons have fled the States to escape the fascist Nixon regime. Kind of ironic, huh?"

I collected my things, and we walked out of the *gasthaus* and up the main street of Bad Kohlgrub, while Vic explained to me how the village derived its name from the mud baths that tourists came here to indulge themselves in. The village relied on tourism—skiing in the winter, and the mud baths in the summer, as well as hikers and sightseers. Unlike much of Germany, most of the Bavarian villages had escaped destruction during World War II, so many of Bad Kohlgrub's shops and chalets predated the war, and some of the buildings were centuries old. We crossed the village square, with its ornate fountain, and took a side street to the Fischers', which turned out to be a simple but fairly modern tract house. Albert and Fred were home, along with their parents.

Their father, Otto, had retired from his job in the States and had returned to the village of his youth, bringing his wife along. The sons had only been hiding out in Bad Kohlgrub for a few months. They were both in their early twenties, and had long hair. Albert had dark curly hair and a matching beard, and Fred sported a mustache and goatee. I thought they looked a little like Lenin and Marx, or maybe the Smith Brothers, whose bearded faces graced the cough drop packages of the same name. There were introductions all around, and we were subjected to some political rhetoric about Nixon and the Vietnam War from Albert, and then Vic asked them if I could take a shower. Yes, of course, they said, and afterwards we headed up the steep hill to Vic and Star's hotel, where there were more introductions with the hotel owners. After some visiting with Vic and Star, with guitar playing and singing, I was shown to my new quarters—a haystack in a barn. These were the surroundings I awoke to in the morning.

The rain stopped falling, and the sky cleared, and I hiked up the hill on soft wet earth carrying my guitar, and knocked at Vic and Star's door. They were awake and dressed, and as eager as I was for the day to unfold. We had coffee in the room, strong and rich with cream, and black bread with jam, as Vic outlined his plans for us.

"A little string band could really clean up over here," he enthused. "After Annie and my cousin show up we'll need to get a traveling van and get a circuit happening. Star and I have a little bread saved up for a vehicle. How about you, Steve—got any dough?"

"I've got a hundred bucks or so left," I said. "And I should be getting my last G.I. Bill check in the mail soon."

"Great! Meanwhile, let's work up some songs together."

I unpacked my guitar and we kicked around some songs we already knew, and I showed him some of the songs Uncle Zeke's Band had been doing, which we agreed on. Then I showed him a couple of my original songs, but I sensed he wasn't thrilled about them.

"They don't really fit the style I'm shooting for," he said, trying to let me down easy. "You need to write for the band. Let me show you what I mean. Here's a new one I wrote specifically for the band to do."

On his 12-string guitar he played for me a bluesy up-tempo piece that had a backwoods lyric quality. I got the message, and I understood his vision right away.

"I like it," I agreed. "Let's work it out."

After awhile, Vic put down his guitar, filled up his pipe and lit it, and said, "I think we're about ready to get in the wind. Let's go up to the Linderhof and busk."

"What's the Linderhof?"

"It's a neat little castle near Oberammergau. Mad King Ludwig built it and another one with the Bavarians' taxes for his amusement, and sort of broke the Bavarian bank in the process. I hear they ran him out of town or killed him or something, but the castles are still around, and they're good tourist attractions. So in the long run, I guess it was a sound investment. We ought to do well there, what with all the summer tourists."

Vic put his guitar in its case and closed it up. The handle had long ago broken off, and in its place, he'd fashioned a long belt for carrying the guitar over his shoulder. He slung it onto his shoulder now, glanced at Star, who was sitting in the chair mending a pair of jeans, and announced, "Me and Steve are goin' busking. We'll be in late."

"Okay," she said smiling as she stood up to kiss him. "Have a good time."

We headed down the hill and through the village to the *banhoff*, or train station, where after a short wait, we caught a train headed for the Austrian border. Fresh cool mountain air blew in through the open coach window, and the clack-clack along the iron tracks provided an auditory background to Vic's guided tour.

"Check out the view, Steve. Looks like we're in the land of Heidi, eh?"

From the moving carriage I looked out onto a day of sunshine, blue sky, and fleecy white clouds. Below us was a narrow green valley framed by jagged snow capped peaks and carpeted with a little village of white and brown chalets and cottages, and an onion domed church with a small cross atop it. Outside the village were small farms with large barns, with sheep and cattle grazing, and stacks of new-cut hay ready to be bundled up and stored away. As we came into another village, Vic announced, "This is our stop," and when the train slowed to a halt, we hopped off and onto the station platform, guitars in hand, Vic leading the way and shouting, "*Gruss Gott!*" to everyone we encountered. We then caught a bus filled with happy vacationing Germans from the north who, like us, were heading for Linderhof.

Linderhof was not so much a castle, as a palace, and an impressive one at that, sitting royally in an Alpine valley, looking stately with large fountains in front. It was ornately finished on the outside, and I could only wonder at how it looked inside. We set up in front of the wide steps leading into the palace, took out our guitars, and as soon as a group exited from a tour, we began singing songs. After three songs, Vic passed the hat, which today was his beret. Then as another tour group formed to go inside, we went about our routine again. We managed to get four sets in before Vic spotted security guards coming our way, and gave me the signal to pack up. Vic pocketed the money and we headed for the tour bus area and anonymity, and when he spotted one leaving for Oberammergau, he said, "Let's catch this one. Maybe we can busk at Jimmy's Bar."

"Where?" I asked.

"Jimmy's Bar. It's just outside of Oberammergau. Jimmy's an American—an old retired army sergeant. He's kind of a redneck, but he likes it when I sing country songs. He makes a living off the GIs who are stationed at the local army base. It's as close to a down-home bar as you can find around these parts. And he's got the only place around where you can get a real American hamburger. Makes them himself."

So we caught the bus into Oberammergau, seven kilometers away, while Vic explained that the world-famous Passion Play is held there every ten years, and all the villagers take part in it. And that Oberammergau is also famous for it's woodcarvings. Then he added, "There's still some old Nazis living there, too, and they don't like to see us hippies hanging around. But I say, fuck 'em."

We were soon in Oberammergau, walking through the narrow old streets, admiring the hand painted murals, and the woodcarvings on the sides of buildings and for sale inside the tourist shops. We walked to the outskirts of town and over a footbridge that spanned the narrow Ammer River as it wound its way down out of the Alps.

Then we arrived at Jimmy's Bar, a wooden building set off by itself, an American Schlitz beer sign in the window. We strode on through the doorway and met Jimmy, a middle aged man who even in civilian clothes looked like a soldier, especially with his leathery face and white sidewall haircut graying around the temples.

"Hi Vic!" said Jimmy with a toothy grin. "Who's your long-haired friend?"

"Name's Zeke," I said.

Vic shot me an angry glance. "That's a joke," he said, turning back to Jimmy. "This is Steve Dupree, an old partner of mine from California. We're putting a band together to go on the road with."

"Sounds good," said Jimmy. "What'll you fellas have—burger and a beer?"

"You guessed it," said Vic. "I was just telling Steve about your burgers."

"Best around. Everything on 'em?"

"Yeah," said Vic.

"Hold the onion on mine."

"Say, Jimmy, you think we could come back later and do some playing?" asked Vic.

"Sure, why not. Just make sure you play "Detroit City" for me".

When our orders came up, I pulled out my German change, trying to sort it out, but Jimmy waved me off. "Forget it," he said. "It's on me. Just come back later and sing us some country songs."

Vic suggested we wander around town some more while we killed time, waiting for the bar crowd to show up. As soon as we stepped outside, though, he suddenly turned on me.

"What's this bullshit about you calling yourself Zeke? If you think you're going to be the front man of Uncle Zeke's Band, you can forget about us working together, period. I ain't a sideman for you or anybody else."

"Hey, relax, man. I hadn't planned on being the leader of anything. I just like the name, that's all."

"Yeah? Well, you aren't using it. If anybody's going to be Uncle Zeke, it's me."

"Okay, okay. I won't use the name. We can all be Uncle Zeke, okay? I just want to play music."

"Well—alright. As long as we understand each other," he said. Then in a conciliatory gesture, he pulled out a little chunk of hash he had in his pocket that he said he'd been saving for a special occasion, and suggested we smoke it, to which I agreed, since I'd never smoked hash before.

"It's hard to get pot over here," he said, crumbling the hash into his pipe. "so everyone smokes hash. I scored this off one of the GIs at the Army base." He lit the pipe, took a hit, and passed it to me. I hit on it, coughed at its harshness, and passed it back. A couple more rounds and we were stoned sufficiently to wander around the village for a while and enjoy the warmth of the day.

Back at Jimmy's Bar later, we sat around playing and singing and drinking beer with the soldiers. After doing "Detroit City" for him (*"I wanna go home, I wanna go home, oh how I wanna go home")*, Jimmy put out a tip jar for us, and the money started trickling in.

"Hey Vic," shouted a GI, "how 'bout playin' that song you wrote about L.A.?"

"Oh, you must mean 'My Smoggy Mountain Home'," Vic chuckled, and launched into the song, while I tried to follow his chord changes.

"How I miss my home way up on Smoggy Mountain,
How I miss the lovely streets of old L.A.
And I miss my job back at the old defense plant
But most of all I miss the weekly pay
I miss the movie stars in all the topless bars
Waiting patiently to be discovered
And I miss the stops by all the nice policemen
And the ones that in the helicopters hovered."

"Haw haw! That's pretty good you guys. What're ya drinkin'?"

And so it went for a while. Then the girls wandered in. They were American, and sat at a table over in the corner of the room and watched us watching them until Vic announced that it was time for a break, and we sauntered on over to meet them.

"Have a seat guys," said the buxom one, whom I soon found out was named Sheryl, aged twenty-two, from San Francisco.

I sat next to her, while Vic sat next to Barbara, aged sixteen, from—Oberammergau? Yes, exactly. She was the Colonel's daughter, offspring of the commanding officer of the army base. And Sheryl was the Colonel's maid. They were both attractive brunettes, and almost seemed like sisters. Vic had told me that in Germany kids start drinking early, and it wasn't uncommon to see a sixteen-year old in a bar. So Jimmy didn't bother with checking the girls' IDs. After some small talk, we excused ourselves to play another set, and made it a short one so we could chat up the girls before they got away. After some more small talk, we packed up the guitars and all went for a walk. I took Sheryl's hand, as we walked ahead of the other two, over the little footbridge, and out into a meadow beyond the village lights, where we held each other and shared a little about ourselves and how we'd ended up here in Bavaria.

Sheryl had taken a trip to Europe as a college graduation gift, and had decided to prolong her stay. Running low on funds, she'd taken the job as the Colonel's maid. It wasn't just the chance to see more of Europe that had caused her to stay on, but this was the first time she'd been away from home and now she wanted to "find herself." That is, to do some soul searching about herself, her values, what she wanted from life. And in the process, she'd found a friend and confidant in Barbara. But there was also another reason for being here. She'd broken up with her fiancé, and needed to sort her head out about that. I told her about my failed relationship with Vicki, and then we understood each other without having to talk anymore. So we kissed instead. All too soon, it was time for her to go, before the Colonel discovered they'd overstayed Barbara's curfew. But we promised to meet again the next day in front of Linderhof around noon. Then we walked the girls to as close to the Colonel's house as we dared before saying goodnight.

"Don't let Star know about Barbara," said Vic. "We'll keep this to ourselves."

We walked on to the *bahnhoff,* but we'd stayed out too long, and had missed the last train, so we were stuck, and my heart sank.

"We blew it!" I said. "What'll we do now?"

"Don't sweat it," said Vic. "We'll just ask around town to see if somebody can put us up. There are still some bars open. If that doesn't work out, we'll just find an empty field to crash in. I've done it before."

I wanted to believe in Vic, but the prospect of spending the night in a field on the hard ground made me shiver, and I buttoned my fringed jacket and turned its collar up, and stuck my hands in my pockets. But at the first bar we came to, Vic cornered a German hippie outside the door, joked around a little, and then asked if he knew where we might spend the night out of the cold. The tall, thin, bearded guy's face lit up in the glow of a street light and my heart lit up as well when he exclaimed, "But of course! You must come with me and spend the night. I live not far from here." And he said all this in very good English with a slight British accent. We walked through the village again and up a mountain trail into a thick forest, where we came to his little cabin in a clearing. He lit an oil lamp and showed us a little room where we could bed down on the hardwood floor. The little room, not much bigger than a closet, was of unfinished rough-hewn wood, and in a way it reminded me of Ed and Sue's place in the Mendocino woods.

Vic said, "Goodnight, man, and thanks again," to our benefactor, who then blew out the oil lamp and said, "*Guten abend.*" I tried to gather my jacket around me like a blanket and fall asleep on the hard floor, but the night was cold, colder than it had ever been at Ed and Sue's. We were, after all, in the Alps, and summer or not, I felt too frozen to sleep. But I made an effort to do so, dozing off from time to time, and awoke in the dawn, stiff and sore, but thankful to at least have a roof over my head. Vic and I took the first train back to Bad Kohlgrub, and I grabbed a nap on the haystack before we set off for Linderhof again.

The girls were waiting for us by the great pool in front of the palace, and we managed to get three sets in before the security guards caught up with us and chased us off. Vic and I both knew this would be our final appearance at King Ludwig's palace.

"We hadn't even get to play the main room," Vic joked.

We all went off for a walk in the nearby woods, and Sheryl and I spent the time getting to know each other better. I really liked her. She had a wonderful smile, was attractive inwardly as well as outwardly, having a great enthusiasm for life, an open honesty, and a nice sense of humor. We found a fallen log to sit on, and I took out my guitar and sang songs to her in the quiet glade. From the moment we met, there had been an unspoken agreement between us that if we were to have a romance, we would have to skip the formalities and cut right to the chase, because we didn't have a lot of time to waste. We only had now, maybe tomorrow, maybe another day. We really could only live in the moment, so we filled those moments as fully as we could. This was the first relationship either one of us had had since our former lovers, but we plunged on in, becoming as intimate as time and opportunity would allow.

The day suddenly darkened, as if a curtain had been drawn across the sky, and menacing clouds gathered overhead. Then a bolt of lightning flashed, followed by a loud thunderclap. I quickly packed up my guitar.

"Let's find some shelter," I said, helping her to her feet. We ran from the clearing toward the forest, which seemed to offer the only protection from the storm, and hid beneath some sheltering trees. The sky opened up above us, pelting the trees with raindrops, but missing us. We huddled close together, protected by a large pine, and I kissed her hard, feeling both peace and desire wash over me. My hand reached under her blouse and held one of her breasts, caressing it, and I felt her warm breath close to my ear. The storm blew out as suddenly as it had blown in, as storms will do in the mountains in the summer. I asked Sheryl to come back to Bad Kohlgrub with me, and she said yes.

"I'll have to go by the house, change, and leave a note," she said, running her hand across my cheek.

We caught the bus to Oberammergau, walked up to the Colonel's estate, and since he was out, she invited me in. It was a cavernous house, filled with many rooms.

"You'll have to see the trophy room," she said with a look of distaste. "It's really weird." We walked inside and I was taken aback as she announced, "Welcome to the Death Room." It could have been a comfortable den or study, filled with books, but instead was filled with stuffed heads and carcasses and skins of all manner of wild animals, mounted on the walls and mantelpiece, as well as photographs of the Colonel posed with his kills—everything from lions to tigers to deer. You name it, he'd killed it. I could see why he'd made the army his occupation.

"Maybe he wants to be Hemingway," she allowed.

"I remember now why I decided to become a vegetarian," I added. "Let's hurry up and get out of this place. It's too creepy."

We caught the afternoon train from nearby Oberammergau. Sheryl had packed us a lunch, and we ate it on the train, looking out the window to postcard scenery flashing by. We climbed the hill to my barn and then sat outside on the grass, talking and gazing down onto the village of Bad Kohlgrub, and far off into the distance toward Munich. On the horizon dark clouds appeared, and began marching our way, rain misting down to the ground, like an invading army. We watched for a long time until the storm reached the outskirts of Bad Kohlgrub itself, so we retreated into the barn and made love on my sleeping bag atop the haystack, while rain beat against the roof, and little puffs of wind snuck through the slats on the side of the barn. During the night, Sheryl lost a little wire hoop earring in the haystack, and lamented that she'd never find it again. But in the morning's light, I stuck my hand down in the hay, and pulled it out. "Simple," I said nonchalantly. "Just like finding a needle in a haystack.

Vic had discovered a discotheque outside neighboring Murnau on the *Staffelsee*, a mountain lake, of average size, that in the daytime was host to boaters, swimmers, and picnickers. On Friday, he decided we'd try busking there. So we took the bus down there, guitars in hand, and walked on into the disco near nightfall. Vic made the pitch to the bartender, something to the effect that we were a couple of folksingers from the States over on a tour, and could we try doing a few songs here, out on the dance floor? The bartender conferred with the DJ who spun the records, and then returned to Vic.

"Come back in an hour or so," he said, "when it's busier. You can play a few songs in between the dancing, for fifteen minutes every hour."

We went down by the lake, buying a couple of beers from a local brewery on the way, and drank them while we practiced songs. Then we returned to the disco, and after the DJ had spun some records, he introduced us to the crowd in German, and we walked to the middle of the dance floor and put on our show. Then Vic passed the hat. We did two sets that night, then divided our money, had a beer on the house, and left. As we were leaving, though, we heard a commotion coming from the pier nearby, of singing and laughing and talking in loud German voices, so we went to investigate. We stumbled upon a group of teenage boys, and when they spied us carrying guitars, they pointed at us, laughing, and made air guitar motions. Vic spoke a few words of German to them, and told me that they were a soccer team that had just won a game and were celebrating. The kids, discovering we were Americans, decided to try out their high school English on us. They offered us beers from the case that was set upon the ground, and one of them said, "Come, you must sing for us now. *Musik machen, ja!"*

We happily obliged them, and soon we were all singing and drinking and laughing and yodeling, until the police showed up and began having words with the kids, who just laughed at them, and it sounded like they told the cops to go bugger off. But Vic and I decided not to stick around for the outcome. Vic said, "Let's catch a taxi back home, they don't cost much." And so we did. We'd done so well at the disco, Vic said we should try it again the next night.

I knew Saturday was Sheryl's day off, so I got word to her to meet me in Bad Kohlgrub, and accompany us to our disco gig in Murnau. The three of us took the bus to Murnau and Sheryl passed the hat for us when we sang. Back in Bad Kohlgrub, while on the way to the hotel and barn, Sheryl and I made a detour by the little church that sat near the foot of our hill on the edge of town, and we made love on the churchyard lawn, underneath the stars.

Life went on in this way for a while, me stealing moments with Sheryl when Vic and I were in Oberammergau, and her making secret trips to see me, while Vic and Barbara also had a thing going on. But eventually Barbara found out about Star, Star found out about Barbara, and the Colonel found out about all of us and forbade his daughter and his maid to see either of us again. "They only play music to support their habits," he declared.

"What habits?" I asked.

"Hmmm—maybe eating," commented Vic. "I know I'm hooked on at least two meals a day, and sometimes I get cravings for a third."

So it was over for Vic and his not-so-secret girlfriend. But Sheryl and I continued to see each other on the sly. And when we'd meet, she would always have a sack lunch prepared, or a little gift for me, like a novel by Hermann Hesse or Richard Brautigan. Once we took the train up to Garmish so I could buy some new guitar strings from a music store, and we sat at the outside table of a *gasthaus* sipping coffee, and she pointed out the *Zugspitze* to me, the highest mountain around, just across the Austrian border.

Days became weeks as Vic and I continued our leisurely routine of busking, and hanging out in the *gasthaus* and the beer garden in the woods with Albert and Fred, and Fred's girlfriend from South Africa, and Hubcap and Star, and sometimes Sheryl. Vic and I would occasionally spend time of mornings hanging out in the little church in the village, whose door was always left unlocked, reading books, until the rector spotted us one day and from then on the door stayed barred to us. And meanwhile we waited for news of Annie and Marty, but no word came and neither of them showed up. It was as if they'd dropped off the face of the earth. That is, until the day that Annie suddenly appeared, unannounced.

We found her at a table in the village *gasthaus,* alone with her meager belongings—a travel bag, a sleeping bag, a mandolin, and her cherished violin. She looked like a little lost waif from a Dickens novel. Her long hair fell down over her back, tied up with a bright red scarf, she wore a hand knit poncho over her peasant blouse; while blue jeans and hiking boots, as well as her ever present granny glasses, completed the picture. Her blue grey eyes lit up in recognition and her small mouth widened in a smile when she saw us.

"Star! Vic! Zeke!" she exclaimed as we entered through the doorway in that order of appearance. "You're here!"

"Annie!" cried Star, rushing over to hug her. "How long have you been here?"

"I don't know," she said. "It seems like hours. I met a blond-haired woman from South Africa named Alice who said you guys hang out here. So I just planted myself here, passing the time with a book and a cup of coffee."

Vic and I both gave Annie hugs, and we all sat down to join her. Vic ordered half liters of beer all around, and then popped the question that was on all our minds.

"Where's Marty?"

"I don't know," she said. "I stayed with Steve's folks in La Mirada while I waited for my flight, and I tried to find him, but couldn't. No one would tell me where he was. I checked out an address that was supposedly where he was staying, but he wasn't there either. I'm surprised you haven't heard from him."

"Not a word," said Vic.

"And what about you?" I added. "What took you so long to get over here?"

"That was the weirdest thing," she said. "The flight was postponed, and the airline was very secretive about the whole thing. So I called your parents, and they picked me up at the airport in L.A., and let me stay with them. We thought it would only be for a day, maybe two at the most. The airline was supposed to call me at your parents' house when the flight was rescheduled, but they never called. Every day I would call the number they had given me and ask, and each time they were evasive. Finally, I got a call telling me to report to LAX at a certain terminal at a certain time, and to keep the information to myself. It was all very mysterious. Then two uniformed people escorted me to the plane. All I can think is that the airline was going out of business, and maybe I had caught the last flight out." Then she smiled. ""But I made it, I'm finally here, thank God."

"Maybe that's what happened to Marty," said Star. "Maybe he couldn't catch the flight."

"Yeah", said Vic. "But that doesn't explain why we haven't heard from him. He has my address."

"I guess what really matters now," said Star, "is that Annie's here, and now there's four of us."

"I'll *prosit* to that," said Vic, clinking his glass to ours in turn.

The other patrons of the *gasthaus* noticed that there were now four of us, and grumbled amongst themselves. They had watched for months as one after another longhaired hippie moved into Bad Kohlgrub, and now with Annie's appearance, it seemed to tip the scale of tolerance. We were multiplying too rapidly for the staid citizens of this little burg. It was another invasion of foreign occupiers. We had overstayed our welcome. Of course, we didn't know that yet. We carried blithely on with our business of music making and hash smoking, and the hotel owners were not put out at first with Annie. They liked her, and the mother doted over her, and they agreed to put her up in a little shed out back for the time being. But it wasn't long before the townspeople began griping to the owners about our presence being bad for the tourist business.

That afternoon, after Annie had settled in, and we'd all had a meal together, I took off and met Sheryl in Oberammergau, where we spent the evening like a twenty-dollar gold piece—walking, talking, enjoying a quiet beer at a sidewalk café, and making love in a moonlit secluded field of tall grass and wildflowers. We were summer lovers in the fullness of its season, all too well aware that the season was slipping away, and so we grabbed every moment we could, and lived it to the fullest measure.

A couple of days later, after breakfast together in his room, Vic called a meeting to discuss our future together.

"We need to be getting in the wind soon," he announced. "We're starting to become unwelcome around these parts. These Bavarians treat you real nice up front, smiling in your face, but behind your back they're just Nazis and capitalist pigs."

"Well, which are they," I said, "Nazis or capitalists? They can't be both."

"Shut up, Dupree, and let me finish. The hotel owners are starting to ask how much longer we plan on being here, and we've told them we're leaving soon. Now we haven't heard anything from Marty, and although I'd love to see my cousin again, we just can't wait around any longer. We need to start getting ready to pull up stakes. First we need to work out some more songs, so that we can be a working band, and then we need to get a Volkswagen bus so we can travel. We can all pool our money. Star and I have a little bread saved up. How much bread have you got left, Steve?"

"Well, counting the GI Bill check I got in the mail, about a hundred and seventy-five dollars."

"Good. How much bread have you got, Annie?"

"I've got about a hundred and fifty, but I'm saving it for an emergency."

"If we stick around here much longer," said Vic, "it will be an emergency. Come on now, don't hold out on us."

"Well, I guess if you really need it . . ."

"We do. And we're all in this together, whatever happens. Okay, we'll start looking around for a VW. Since Star doesn't play any instruments, except tambourine, she's volunteered to be our cook and bottler."

"You mean bottle washer, don't you, Vic?"

"No, Dupree. A bottler is someone who passes the hat for you when you busk."

"I've done it for Vic," Star said proudly. "He usually does better tips when I do."

"That's cause you're so goddamned pretty", Vic said as she blushed.

So we pooled our money, and shopped around, but the closest thing we could find to a used VW microbus was a VW Variant, a small hatchback station wagon. It was just big enough to fit the four of us with our instruments, and our baggage. We picked it up from a used car dealer in Murnau, who provided us with the necessary papers, tourist plates, and insurance. We also bought a used four-man tent with the plan of camping out all summer. But as it turned out, there were no instructions on how to put it up, and not enough tent poles, so it mostly just took up space in the back of the car. We rehearsed frantically, adding Irish songs, folk songs and country songs, as well as Vic's originals. He and I even wrote a song together one day, cobbled together from a partial song I'd been working on, and another Vic hadn't finished. Since we were about to get in the wind, that's what we wrote about, and called it "Traveling Song." When we showed the song to Annie, she added some instrumental flourishes, so now we had a genuine Uncle Zeke collaboration. We were ready to get in the wind, as Vic put it, and now the villagers gave us a push in that direction. We were evicted.

The hotel owners called us into the kitchen and tried to tell us in a diplomatic way that we had to move out, whereupon Vic rubbed his fingers together in the time honored tradition of expressing money changing hands, and called them money-grubbing capitalists. That put the cap on it. We were told to leave immediately, in no uncertain terms. So we packed up all our belongings, including pots and pans, a Coleman stove, and eating utensils, loaded them into the VW, and pulled out of town and into the countryside, intending to camp somewhere. For a while we busked around Murnau, Oberammergau, and Garmish, and bummed showers off Albert and Fred and Hubcap, and anyone else we could think of, including people we would meet along the way. We slept under the stars in the forest, and ate simple meals prepared by Star and Annie. It was an easy life, all things considered. Near the end of July we found a cave to stay in overnight, but it was wet and slippery inside, and I dropped my guitar, sustaining a large crack in the body. We took it to a violinmaker in Oberammergau, and he fixed it up like new for just a few deutschmarks.

Sheryl's life was also going through rapid changes during this time. The Colonel was being transferred back to the States, had sent his wife and daughter ahead, and was taking up residence in the Bachelor Officers Quarters on the base. Sheryl moved in there too, to a private room, while she contemplated her next move. She no longer had a job, and after pondering whether to stay in Europe a little longer, she decided to return to San Francisco. We were pulling out too, leaving soon for Munich, so she and I had only time for one more date. I snuck onto the military base, and to the Bachelor Officers Quarters. After bumming a shower from her in her room, we made love on an army bunk. Suddenly, there was a loud rapping at the door. It was the colonel.

"Sheryl!"

RAP! RAP!

"Sheryl, are you in here?"

RAP! RAP!

"SHERYL!"

We held our breaths and moved not a muscle. After what seemed like a long time, we heard footsteps marching away and down the hall. We exhaled, and then decided to sneak off-base and into town. We spent precious hours together down by the Ammer River, and then I had to get the VW back to Bad Kohlgrub to pick up everyone at the Fischers'. We had a final long kiss, a desperate goodbye with promises to write. But just as I was starting up the car, Sheryl said we could rendezvous in Munich in a few days, when she was due to catch a train north to Frankfurt.

I picked up the band at the Fischers', and Vic said to everyone gathered there—Albert, Fred, Alice, and Hubcap—"We'll probably see you in the spring. We're going to set up a traveling circuit between here and Amsterdam."

But we never saw them again.

We pulled out of town in the late afternoon, the good citizens of Bad Kohlgrub no doubt marking this day on their calendars as one to be celebrated henceforth as a holiday, and headed down out of the Alps. We came down the mountain road into the foothills, passing forests and fields and farms to the valley floor and onto the Autobahn that pointed straight toward Munich and our future.

CHAPTER TWELVE

Down From The Mountain

The swift midsummer Isar River, born out of the melting snows of the jagged Austrian Alps, ran freely across the German border with no guards to challenge or detain it, for its business was to wander and flow. It went quietly about its business, becoming wider as it flowed past Mittenwald, to the east of Garmish, resting for a moment in a lake, then continued its journey down through Alpine valleys and past the towns of Bad Tolz and Geretsried, and into the foothills where forests are patched with green and golden farmland. While hurried motorists rushed by at dangerous speeds on the Autobahn, the Isar gave no notice, sparkling silvery in the sunlight as it made its way into and through Munich, and leisurely onward to join with the Danube, which flowed to the sea.

Along the portion of the river which flows through Munich was the Englischer Garten, a three mile stretch of lush park packed with picnickers, dog walkers, sun bathers, tourists, students from the local university, and, oh yes, four American hippies who were playing songs and drawing a small crowd. They called themselves Uncle Zeke's Band. Vic stood in the center, playing guitar, looking scruffy in wrinkled shirt and vest, too-short baggy pants, army boots, and a grey top hat. To his right stood Annie, playing the violin with deep concentration and looking colorful in a red scarf, Gipsy blouse and patchwork skirt. To Vic's left, playing the other guitar, I stood, also looking thin and scruffy with wispy beard, wrinkled denim shirt, blue jeans, fringed leather jacket, and black cowboy hat and cowboy boots. Off to the side, smiling at everyone, was Star, quietly unassuming in long hair and understated beauty, clothed in earth-tone colors of brown and green. Occasionally, she would take a dark blue beret in hand and pass it around through the crowd, collecting tips.

The Englischer Garten (or English Garden), was where we spent a good deal of our time of sunny August afternoons. Other times, we might have been busking in nearby Schwabing, an area near the university, filled with students, which reminded me of Telegraph Avenue in Berkeley next to the U.C. campus. At night we could be found gigging at the Song Parnaus, or one of the other folk clubs, bars, and eateries in the heart of Munich. Sometimes we would also busk in the public rooms of the Lowenbrau, Paulaner, and Augustiner breweries, where we would be treated to more rounds of liter mugs of beer than we could drink.

A few days after we had arrived in Munich, I rendezvoused with Sheryl once more. We met up at Munich Station, where a train would be taking her to Frankfurt later. She'd packed a picnic lunch for us, so we drove around looking for a place to eat it, passing ruins and rubble left from the bombings of World War Two. We wound up at the Montopteros, where we had our final visit, and kissed for the last time. She gave me a going away present, a copy of Hermann Hesse's *Narcissus and Goldmund*, a novel set in medieval Germany. Then it was time to take her back to Munich Station.

"Well, goodbye," she said. "It's been a really nice experience."

"For me too," I replied.

"I wish you success and all the happiness in the world."

I didn't know what else to say to her, other than that I'd enjoyed every moment spent together, and that I'd miss her. Then she boarded her train, and as it pulled out of the station she lowered the coach window and waved goodbye to me. I watched the train until it rolled out of sight, before driving back to the beer garden, where Vic and the others were waiting.

For the first week that we were in Munich, we camped out every night. We'd get on the Autobahn and drive back up into the foothills, and find a secluded part of the forest to bed down in. We'd decided at the outset that the station wagon with its seats folded down could accommodate two of us, while the other two could sleep on the ground. We'd take turns, so that each couple would spend every other night in the car. Annie and I tried setting up the massive tent one night when it was raining lightly, but to no avail. We ended up just laying it out on the ground and crawling inside it as if it were a huge sleeping bag. It kept the rain off us, at least. After a week of this, we began looking for better lodgings.

One night, while we were playing at the Song Parnaus, Vic met a university student who had taken a liking to us. Always the opportunist, Vic hit him up for a place to crash, and he said we could sleep at his apartment in Schwabing, on the couch and the floor in our bags. It was a step up for us, because now we also had a place to shower and clean up. On our first morning there, I awoke and gazed out a sliding glass door to the small back yard of overgrown grass and plants and flowers, saw that the sun was shining, and felt very cheerful about my situation in life. I was a free man in a traveling band, unencumbered by the trappings of a materialistic life. I got dressed and had a cup of the coffee that Werner had made for us, and then began browsing through his record collection. I was surprised to come across an album by Norman Greenbaum, who had hosted the open mikes at the old Rosewood Forest in Santa Rosa. There was a photo of Norman and his wife on the cover, standing in front of their farm in Petaluma. It seemed to be a small world after all.

Our gig at the Song Parnaus was unique, in that we were only one of several bands and performers on the bill each night. With so many acts, we were paid only ten deutschmarks, not a great sum, but I rationalized it was better than busking. Besides, the audiences were very generous with their attention and their applause. But Vic bristled at the idea after mulling it over in his mind for too many nights. He decided we were being cheated.

"These cheap bastards are ripping off all the musicians," he complained. "We need to organize a strike."

He tried to whip up support among the musicians to organize, but didn't get any takers. As one of the folksingers pointed out, "A strike would do no good. There are plenty people would play for nothing, *und* anyway, ten marks *ist* ten marks."

So Vic went to the manager, the guy who hired the acts, and said that if we didn't get a hefty raise, we would refuse to play. That of course turned out to be our last night at the Song Parnaus, but we still had another folk club where we hadn't been fired, and there was always the busking.

Busking in the streets, however, was not an option. We had tried it early on, but had hardly set up when a friendly German approached us and said, "*Das ist verboten.*" Of course we knew what v*erboten* meant, as we'd seen plenty of signs telling us the things that were *verboten*, like No Parking signs. Vic's reply to that was, *"Ja, ja. In Deutschland alles ist verboten."* Nevertheless, one day we spotted some Americans playing on a sidewalk, so we went to investigate. They were singing religious songs, and it didn't take long to find out that they belonged to a cult called the Children of God. They were also busy handing out literature prophesizing the end of the world. We noticed that their guitar cases were closed, so they weren't really busking. This gave Vic an idea though.

"Let's take some of those pamphlets and pick out a corner somewhere and sing some Jesus songs. Star can pass the hat for us."

"We'd never get away with it," I replied. Annie and Star backed me up, so Vic dropped the idea.

We hadn't been in Munich long before we realized our time there was running out. We noticed the police had stepped up their patrols around town, and were checking the passports of hippies and young foreigners. We discovered that it had to do with the 1972 Olympics that were being held in Munich soon.

"They're cleaning up the town," said Vic. "They don't want any lowlifes or hippies giving the place a bad rep, so it's only a matter of time before they start hassling us. Star and I have working papers, so we're sort of legal. But they could really fuck with you and Annie. Maybe we should get out of town for a while. I've heard of a club up in Dusseldorf, Danny's Pan, where we could probably gig. We could do some barnstorming along the way, set up gigs for the return trip, and get a regular circuit going. In the spring we could head on back to Bad Kohlgrub for some R and R."

"Sounds good to me," I said.

"Me too," Annie chimed in.

We played our last gigs at the folk club and a bar, thanked Werner for his hospitality, packed the car good and tight, and hit the road. Star had made us some salami sandwiches on black bread, and cheese sandwiches on rye. Vic bought a gallon of Chianti with money from the kitty (we were pooling all our money together now, which went into a bag that Star carried). Being the designated driver (the only one with a license), I gassed up the car, ("*Voll mit normal, bitte")* and we got in the wind. I kept to the slow lane of the Autobahn as BMWs and Mercedes Benzes blew by at suicidal speeds in the fast lane, while we watched the glass and steel, concrete and rubble of Munich fade in the distance.

Vic wanted to hit some university towns along the way, where there were sure to be folk clubs, so we looked at a map and marked off Heidelberg, Tubingen and Reutlingen. With Star navigating, we set a course for northwest, passing Augsburg and Ulm and turning south at Stuttgart. Vic and Star were snuggled up together in the backseat, reading and looking out the windows, Vic occasionally nipping off the wine and sometimes passing it around. Annie sat beside me, wound up at first talking, singing and pointing out sights. Then she settled into the rhythm of the road, quietly watching the world pass by outside her passenger window. I sat behind the wheel, watching the traffic and caught up in thoughts of Bavaria and of Sheryl, trying to recall the warmth of her lips and the light in her brown eyes.

We hit Tubingen first, and I wheeled tentatively through its medieval gate to behold a scene out of the Hesse novel I'd been reading, of old narrow cobblestone streets and tall narrow brick buildings in the Alt Stadt. Tubingen had been spared the carnage of World War II, and stood much as it had for centuries. Over on a hilltop on the edge of town was a great crumbling stone castle that we took the time to explore, snapping photos. Over a wooden bridge across a moat-like waterway we found a place to park the VW where there were no *Parken Verboten* signs to be seen, then we set out to explore the town. In the village square with its community fountain, Annie and I browsed quaint little shops, spying an old bookstore with a brass plate on the hard oak door that announced *Hermann Hesse Arbeit Hier 1902*. Hermann Hesse, whose novel Sheryl had given me, had worked at this very shop in 1902, a fact I shared with Annie. We wanted to go inside, but as it was already evening, the shop was closed for the day. We met up with Vic and Star, who had been doing their own exploring, and Vic said, "I found out where the university is. Let's go over there and see if there's a coffeehouse or a cafeteria we can busk. We'll get something to eat, and then ask about some gigs."

We found the cafeteria and played for a meal, then went to the student center, where a dance was taking place. Vic spoke to someone in charge, so we managed to get up on the stage and do a quick audition set, after which Vic booked us a gig for some time in the fall. Later we busked at a pub, drank beers and made new friends. One of them invited us to stay at his flat. There we kept the party going a while longer, playing and singing before crashing on the floor in our sleeping bags. Earlier we had met a guy named Wolf who worked at a jazz club, Die Jazz Keller, and he said he'd get us a booking there also in the fall. For our first day on the road it seemed we'd done well for ourselves.

We blew through neighboring Reutlingen early the next day and spoke with a club owner, auditioned for him, and set up yet another gig for the same time frame that we'd be in Tubingen again.

I picked up the Autobahn again at Stuttgart and took it northwest to Karlsruhe, where we turned north. We were in the Rhine Valley, and our road now followed the course of the Rhine River. We watched farmlands out the windows and then pulled off at a rest stop to drink strong coffee and use the restrooms. I wheeled the car into a space in the parking lot that was surrounded by a caravan of travel trailers pulled by Mercedes-Benzes.

"Looks like the Gypsies are here," said Vic, pointing with his pipe. "They get a pension from the government because they were persecuted during the war, put in concentration camps and gassed. So now they travel in style. No more horse-drawn wagons for them. This should be very interesting."

We piled out of the car and into the cafeteria line inside the building to pick up our coffees. The Germans behind the counter were suspicious, watchful, eyeing us with undue interest. And they didn't take their eyes off the Gypsies for an instant.

"You can bet they'll walk out of here with at least some silverware", Vic chuckled slyly.

We had to take a turnoff near Mannheim to get to Heidelberg, our next destination, leaving the Rhine for the smaller Neckar River.

"Alright!" said Vic. "I've always wanted to see Heidelberg. This is where the play *The Student Prince* takes place. We ought to do well here."

Across the river from the medieval city of Heidelberg, an imposing castle stood atop a high hill, which dropped down steeply to the water below. We passed under it and over a narrow bridge that spanned the river, and drove through the old city gate and into a scene of cobblestone streets, ornate fountains, and weathered stone and wood buildings that hosted pubs, beer *kelders*, a folk club, a jazz club, cafes, *rathskellers*, and of course souvenir shops. Crowding the narrow streets were students, tourists, and GIs from the neighboring army bases. And if that weren't enough to pique our interest, Heidelberg also boasted the oldest university in Germany. We looked around us, and didn't really know where to start, there were so many choices. The first thing to do, we decided, was to ditch the car and set out on foot.

"Let's go busking," said Vic.

We got out our instruments and walked along the cobblestones of Hauptstrasse to the Marktplatz, a wide square enclosed by close-quartered old buildings, and set up in front of a fountain. Soon we drew a crowd of shoppers with children in tow, as well as students and tourists. They were like bees to honey, attracted to our appearance as much as by the music we made. Star dutifully passed the hat among the crowd, while Vic left his guitar case open to catch tossed coins. When we finished, we put all the money in the kitty, and hung around to talk with the people who had stayed, making new friends, and getting tips on where to busk, what sights to see, and how to find the local folk club. We were also informed that we didn't have to worry about the police rousting us, for we were breaking no laws here. Heidelberg had long been a haven for buskers, wanderers, and eccentrics. The troubadour tradition was alive and well here in this little oasis where time had stood still, and the fifteenth century rubbed shoulders with the twentieth.

Vic's main objective was not to busk, but to find real gigs, and the folk club seemed to fit that bill, as did the university. The folk club was nearby, and soon we were climbing up a flight of stairs leading to the second floor of an old building, where the club was located in a dark room smelling of stale cigarette smoke. The room was crowded with chairs and tiny round tables, a small stage, a bar, and grimy walls covered with posters, handbills, and photos of folk singers. Behind the bar stood the owner, stout, mustached, and wearing wrinkled clothing. It looked as if he hadn't yet shaved today, and he eyed us coldly. He spoke to us curtly in German, and when there was no response, repeated himself in English.

"What is it you want? We are not yet open for business."

Whereupon Vic launched into his smooth fast-paced monologue about us being a band from the States out on tour, and we were considering playing his club as it looked like such a fine establishment. At this, the proprietor's attitude changed, and he became almost friendly, showing some tentative interest. Vic asked if we could audition, and we pulled out our instruments and played one of our up-tempo songs. That capped the deal, as the barman now pulled out his calendar and wrote our name in it, on a date some weeks hence. Then Vic negotiated the payment, and part of the deal was that we'd be lodged in the adjoining hotel that he also owned. The two shook hands on it, and we hit the street again, where we found a pizzeria to sing in for food, and a pub to busk for tips and drinks. It was an English pub, with all the British trappings, including Watney's and Double Diamond beer on tap. The bartender there liked us so much, he told us to come back again the following night. I was beginning to fall in love with Heidelberg.

That night we camped outside of town, along the Neckar River, in a rest area, with Alice and I in sleeping bags on the ground, and awoke in the dawn to a light rain beginning to fall. So we quickly got dressed, rolled up our bags, and crowded into the front seat of the VW until the rain quit and the sun broke through the clouds. Then Star fired up the Coleman stove and made breakfast. Before heading back to town to do some more busking, we drove up to the Schloss, the castle on the hill that had once served as a lookout tower and fortress, but was now a tourist landmark. We explored around the ramparts, and Annie and I met an old artist who had staked out a corner of the ramparts as his workplace to sell his paintings to tourists. After talking with him, we found out that he was related to Hermann Hesse in some way. In the meantime Vic had spotted a young American wandering around.

"Hey, man, where're you from?" he said.

In the course of conversation he found out the guy's name was Billy, he was twenty-two, and he lived here in Heidelberg close to the Schloss. Vic immediately hit him up for a place to crash, and Billy graciously led us over to his apartment, where he made coffee for us and let us use his shower. Billy had long hair and a beard, but it was trimmed and he was well groomed, and dressed in clean comfortable college student attire, denim and corduroy and desert boots. His flat was a simply furnished but comfortable place, and he told us about his European wanderings, which seemed to be coming to an end.

"My mother wrote and said I should come back home in time for the fall semester and finish college. She doesn't understand what I'm doing over here, that I'm learning about myself and finding some direction to my life. All she can talk about is graduating from the right university and getting a secure high paying job. But there's more to life than that."

When Billy left the room for a moment, Vic turned to me, and rubbing his thumb and forefinger together, said slyly, "I smell money."

Back in town that evening, we repeated our routine of the night before, busking in a café, the pizzeria, and the London Inn Pub. We also located the university, found someone to audition for, and added another booking to our calendar. At the end of the night, we returned to Billy's place to crash on the floor.

In late morning, we said goodbye to Billy and set out on the road again, hooking west at Mannheim to the Autobahn, which again followed the course of the Rhine northward. Near Koln we pulled off for gas, and Vic and I wandered into a pub to take a leak. As we entered the room, all heads turned toward us and before we could take two steps toward the *Herren* sign a voice boomed out, stopping us dead in our tracks.

"*Ein moment, bitte! Wo gehen sie?*"

We turned sheepishly toward the sound of the voice to behold a burly red-faced bartender who was advancing toward us menacingly. I pointed toward the men's room and said, "*Toilette?*"

"Yeah, we're just going to take a leak, man," added Vic.

The beer-bellied ogre took another step toward us, shaking his fist.

"Nein! Das ist verboten!"

"I think we're supposed to buy something first," I said.

"I think he just doesn't like the looks of us," Vic replied.

Now the bartender was shouting *"Raus!"* while the old men planted on bar stools either laughed or glared at us. We'd had enough of this welcoming committee and turned to face the blustering bar man, clicked our heels in unison and gave the Nazi salute. *"Sieg heil!"* we shouted, just before we split. It felt very satisfying.

"Crazy krauts," said Vic. "They're either so nice to you it's embarrassing, or else they're trying to run you out of town."

We found a restroom elsewhere, in a nice little *gasthaus* where we also bought some lunch before hitting the highway again.

We pulled into Dusseldorf in the evening. It was a modern industrial city, completely rebuilt after being bombed into rubble during the war. However, the allied bombers purposely missed some old churches, and much of the Altstadt, the old section that the Rhine flowed through. And here it was that we found ourselves, driving around looking for busking spots. Vic pointed out a pizzeria and said, "Pull over here, Steve. This looks like a good spot."

We parked half a block from the restaurant and walked on over, and when we opened the door were surprised to find a Dixieland band set up on a stage in the back of the room. They sounded so authentic it was hard to believe they weren't from New Orleans, rather than Dusseldorf. We located a table and ordered beers and found them to be dark and bitter, unlike the light beers of Bavaria. When the band took a break Vic chatted up the musicians and their manager, and talked them into letting us do a guest set of three or four songs. We knew there would be no busking or gig for us here, but we wanted to play anyway just for the hell of it. Vic asked the band's manager about Danny's Pan, and yes, he knew of it and gave us directions. It was located on Graf-Adolf Strasse, on the edge of the Altstadt, not far from where we were.

From the exterior, Danny's Pan was just another doorway on a crowded modern street filled with shops, department stores, pubs, cafes, and the German version of a lunch counter. We might have missed it, save for the sign above the door that showed a rendering of Pan with his pipes, and read "Danny's Pan, *Kleinkunst-theatre*". The sound of music and loud conversation spilled out onto the street as a young couple exited, and before the door could close, we stepped inside to a dimly lit smoke filled room. A spotlight from a booth on the near side of the room arced across the tables and chairs inside and lit up a good sized stage which was back dropped by a red curtain, and which had an apron around the front. In one corner sat an upright piano, turned diagonally toward the audience. On the piano stool sat a young German, wearing a black bowler hat, and a white shirt with red garters on his sleeves. He was playing some spirited versions of Scott Joplin rags, and we found out later that his name was Ragtime Charlie. I took a good look around the room and noted papered walls of a dirty faded red, and couples sitting around little candlelit tables. A bar ran along the left side of the room. Just inside the doorway in the foyer that led into the room a dark haired young lady sat in a chair and collected admissions. Across from her on the wall was a schedule of performances, and glossy photos of the acts that were appearing this week.

"*Guten tag,"* Vic said to the woman, whose name we later learned was Christine.

"Guten abend", she replied. "*Wie geht es?"*

"*Gut, danke. Sprechen sie English?"*

"Oh," she said with a little laugh, "you are English?"

"No, sister, we're Americans, and musicians. We have a little folk group called Uncle Zeke's Band, and we'd like to see the owner about playing here."

"The owner? Danny? He is not here now. Perhaps you would like to speak with the manager."

She called over to one of the men behind the bar, a slight and pale man in his thirties, with short thinning black hair. He wore pegged black slacks, a stylish black leather jacket over a white shirt, and high-heeled black Italian boots. He strolled toward us effeminately.

"Ja? Was ist los?" he said suspiciously in a soft voice, and his words had a French accent behind them.

Christine spoke to him in German, whereupon his demeanor noticeably changed. He smiled at us, bowed ever so slightly, and offered his hand first to Vic and then to me. It felt cold and limp, but there was warmth in his voice.

"Ich bin Maurice," he said.

He spoke some words to Christine, who then translated them to us.

"Danny is at his restaurant, some blocks from here. Maurice says he will send you there by taxi, and there you may speak with Danny."

Maurice nodded and smiled and excused himself while he went to phone for the taxi, a black Mercedes Benz that arrived shortly. We were then whisked away by a madman driver who raced through busy traffic, weaving in and out of lanes, blowing his horn, running red lights, and cornering nearly on two wheels. Our wild ride ended as quickly as it had begun, with brakes squealing as we came to a sudden stop in front of a modern upscale eatery. We paid the fare and were deposited, instruments in hand, onto the sidewalk. We went inside and Vic introduced himself to the hostess, who led us to a dim lit booth in the back where we came face to face with the mysterious Danny. He rose, smiling, to greet us.

"Please, sit." He gestured graciously with an open palm. We set our instruments down and crowded in around him.

"I am Danny," he offered, shaking our hands in turn. "You are the American folk group?" He studied us skeptically, owing perhaps to our scruffy appearances. Like Maurice, he had dark hair and eyes, and wore a tight fitting black leather jacket over a white shirt, black pants, and Italian boots. Unlike Maurice, he carried himself with an air of confidence and authority

"That's right," said Vic, "We're Uncle Zeke's Band."

"And which one of you is Zeke?"

"I am, I mean we all are, sort of," said Vic, turning his gaze to me and then back to Danny.

"Then who is the leader?"

"I am," said Vic.

"Ah zo! Then I will conduct my business with you," he said, pulling a cigarette from a slim case and holding it effeminately between his fingers. "What can I do for you?"

"We'd like to play in your club, Danny's Pan."

"Oh?" He paused, studying Vic intensely. "And how long are you going to be around here?"

"We're living over here. We plan on staying a long time. Star and I have working papers. We're on our way to Amsterdam for a few days, then we'll be back, and we plan on getting some work here."

"*Ah, zo.*" Danny now lit his cigarette with a flourish. "Well, I see that you brought your instruments with you. Perhaps you would like to play a few songs for us, so we can see how talented you are."

"You mean right here?"

"Why not?" said Danny, sweeping his arm grandly toward an open space in the front of the room, where diners could easily view us. We obliged him, and after a few songs he applauded and waved his hand, as if to cut us off.

"That will do. You are very good, especially the girl with the violin. Annie is your name? Yes, I think we can use you. Stop by here tomorrow night, at say twenty hours, and let us hear some more. I'll pay you fifty marks and give you a meal for your trouble."

Vic told him we had a deal.

"Fine. I'll have a photographer on hand to take some publicity photos of you, and by then I'll have had a chance to look at my calendar to see when we can book you."

We thanked Danny as we left the place and I said to Vic, "That was easy."

"Yeah," he agreed, "You just got to know how to deal with these people. Most club owners are thieves. I think these guys are a couple of fags, especially Maurice. Anyway, just let me do the talking and I'll negotiate a good deal."

"Being in that restaurant made me hungry," said Annie.

"Let's get something to eat, Vic," said Star, hooking her arm in his.

"Well, the night is still young," said Vic, slinging his guitar strap over his shoulder. "What say we look around for a place to busk where they'll feed us?"

"I'm all for that," said Annie.

"You're always the trooper, Annie," said Star as we headed on down the sidewalk and into a nearby pizzeria where we sang for tips, a meal, and glasses of wine. Later, in a pub, we met a university student who let us crash on the floor of his cramped high rise flat.

We spent the next day killing time, exploring the Altstadt, practicing in a park, and just hanging out until it was time for our gig at Danny's restaurant, which paid off with a ten-night booking at Danny's Pan. Vic asked if Danny could provide lodging as well, and Danny said of course we could stay in a couple of rooms at the club. We had a full week before we were scheduled to play at the club, so Vic suggested we get in the wind and head up to Holland. We started out in the morning, and as we drove, Vic puffed on his pipe as he educated me about the Netherlands.

"Holland isn't the name of the country, it's just the province that Amsterdam is located in. The country is the Netherlands, which means lowlands. A lot of the country is below sea level, which is why they built dikes. The Dutch are related to the Germans, only they were the less warlike tribes, so they got pushed out to the marshes at the edge of the sea centuries ago. We'll see dikes where we're going, built to hold back the sea, and the windmills that drained the water off. Most of Amsterdam has been reclaimed from the sea, which is the reason there are so many canals."

We followed the course of the Rhine north, as we skirted the industrial centers of Duisburg and Essen. Rolling hills gave way to stretches of flat land as we neared the border with Holland. In our travels so far, we had been from one end of Germany to another, and had even crossed the border into Austria at Garmisch, just to say we had been there. Now we were about to cross into another country, and as we did, Vic became anxious, digging around for passports and working papers to show at the border. We eased into line at the inspection station at Nimegen.

"Let me do the talking," said Vic cautiously. "This is a smaller border crossing, so it might be okay. But sometimes they question you about how much money you have and whether or not you have a return ticket to the States. Since Star and I have working papers for Germany, the worst they could do is send us back there. You and Annie might get hassled, though."

But we weren't hassled. Everything went smoothly, the guard lazily flipping through our passports, handing them back without comment and waving us on. I could feel an almost audible sigh of relief from inside the car as we drove carefully away and into the Netherlands. Although I'd never been here before, it seemed oddly familiar to me, as if from a half remembered dream, and as we drove into a small Dutch village, Star said, "Oh look—a windmill!" It stood next to a small café, so I parked the car and we took some photos, and then Star said, "Let's go inside."

Inside, the café was quite homey. There were lace curtains on the windows, carpets on the floor, tablecloths on the tables, and comfortable armchairs by the fireplace, giving the impression we were in someone's home, which was probably the case. Our hostess, an older woman wearing a lace cap and an apron, was all smiles and amiability, welcoming us with words of English. To show off, Vic hurled some badly-pronounced Dutch her way, which she politely pretended to understand, while showing us to a table and handing us menus. The choices were limited, as this was a café and not a restaurant, so we settled on *broojies* (rolls filled with meat or cheese), *frites* (french fries), and cups of coffee, rich and dark, served with little pitchers of thick cream. Vic brought out his pipe, made a show of filling it, and then lit it with a match.

"Let's get up to Amsterdam before nightfall, and find a place to stay. There's no place to camp around Amsterdam, and the hotels are always filled in the summer, and we couldn't afford them anyway. There are some hostels, but they're crowded and you're likely to get your stuff ripped off. I don't like sleeping dormitory-style anyway. A friend of ours has a sleeping boat just across the harbor. It's like a hostel, only a little looser. What do you say we get in the wind?"

We rolled into Amsterdam with daylight to spare.

Across the IJ harbor, accessible by ferry, was a small suburb of Amsterdam, an area of docks and houses and canals. We parked alongside a canal that dead-ended where a large rusting barge was moored. It had once been a vessel of trade, plying the harbor and canals and the Amstel River, but was now converted into a sleeping boat, permanently docked, weather beaten with flaking paint, some flower boxes scattered around the deck, and a clothesline strung between the two cabins on which laundry flapped quietly in the gentle breeze. Pipe in hand, Vic jumped aboard with us following behind, knocked at a cabin door, and called out. "Hey Jan! Is anyone home?"

From inside a voice answered. "*Ja!* Who is dere?"

"Hey, man, it's me, Vic Power!"

There was a pause, and then the cabin door opened and a man in his early thirties appeared with a look of surprise on his face.

"*Ja*, Vic! It is you! Where hef you bin, man?"

Jan was about Vic's size, only stocky and muscular. His dark hair was shoulder length and his mutton chop sideburns grew all the way to his jaw line. He was dressed in a sheepskin vest over a turtleneck shirt, jeans, and work boots. The Cossack hat that Vic was wearing would have nicely complimented Jan's appearance. Only his accent betrayed the fact that he was not an American. Stepping out on deck, he turned and called down through the cabin door.

"Katje! Kom hier! Look who is wid us."

Katje's head appeared in the doorway, and her body followed, a wide smile playing across her attractive face, apprising us with big bright eyes. She was dressed much like Star, in hippie fashion, and also looked like an American. She was of medium height and build, and looked a little younger than Jan. Her brunette hair flowed thickly over her shoulders, and a little beyond.

"Vic en Star," she said cheerfully, "how nice to zee you again. Where hef you bin, en what are you doing now?"

"We've been down in Germany. We just got into town, and we have to be back in Dusseldorf next week for some gigs. We thought we'd line up a few things in Amsterdam as well."

"Who are your friends?" asked Jan.

"Oh, these are some partners of mine from California, Steve and Annie. We have a band together."

After some more small talk to break the ice, Vic cut to the chase.

"We need a place to crash for a few days. We were hoping you might be able to put us up."

Jan gave a quick glance to Katje, and then addressed Vic.

"You hef come at a bad time my friend," he said apologetically. "It is summer, en you know how dat is. We are very busy. I wish we could help you out. Maybe if you come back in de fall . . ."

"Oh, that's okay brother," said Vic, trying to hide his disappointment. "Just thought we'd ask. We'll find something."

"Well, den," said Jan, smiling, "let's go down below and smoke some hash, *ja*? One of de Americans has some Lebanese shit."

Down below, the hold was dark and dank, musty, and stunk of dirty clothes, stale cigarettes, hash, spilled beer, and body odor. A few American and European hippies lounged around lazily on battered chairs and bunks, residue of smoking paraphernalia scattered about along with paperbacks, newspapers, rucksacks and sleeping bags, and bits of half-eaten food. Jan bought a chunk of blond hash from an emaciated bearded hippie, and we smoked part of it, mixed with tobacco in a chillum. With much coughing and hacking, we passed it around and were soon stoned. Vic regaled Jan with stories of the road and his adventures since leaving Holland the previous year. Later we climbed back up topside and breathed fresh air under a darkening grey cloud sky, saying our goodnights, which I somehow knew were really goodbyes.

We raced the sun across the harbor and lost, watching the lights of Amsterdam winking on, white and yellow and neon, and as we drove around the Centrum, Vic pointed out sights with a running narrative. Meanwhile, I had my hands full with trying to maneuver the narrow one-way canal streets that wove through the heart of the city.

"Amsterdam has a major housing shortage," said Vic. "They've also got major traffic problems. During the day, delivery trucks sometimes block these narrow streets for hours. Gas is expensive, too. That's why so many people get around on bikes and motor scooters."

There were no delivery trucks blocking the way tonight, but nevertheless it was slow going until I finally found a space to park, where we left the car and set out on foot. Instruments in hand, we followed Vic as he searched for some of the places he'd played at the previous year, but came up empty on the first two because they'd gone out of business. On the third try we found the Folk Fairport on Prinsengracht, facing the tree-lined canal of the same name. The folk club was filled with young people from all over Europe and the States, as well as the locals. It was a real melting pot of nationalities, as all of central Amsterdam turned out to be. Vic tried to get us an audition, but they had scheduled performers for the night. We were told to come back the following afternoon to audition.

So we moseyed on back to the car, taking in the sights and sounds of Amsterdam after dark, in the cool night of the waning summer, with the green-leafed trees just beginning to fade into yellow.

The cosmopolitan city of three quarters of a million people was vibrantly awake and alive as we passed brown cafes with lace curtains drawn open, and caught snatches of laughter and music spilling out of clubs and pubs. Amsterdam was a city of color and contrast with the old mixing in with the new: Dutch couples strolling along beside tourists, and young travelers and hippies from all over with rucksacks on backs, crowding down tree-lined canals and busy boulevards. The sounds of trams clacking along tracks in the middle of streets mixed with the warning bells of bicycles, and the vroom sound of motor bikes and scooters, along with the carnival-like music pouring forth from the barrel organs and calliopes along the streets, with the old Dutch men winding the cranks that produced the sounds while shaking little tin cups, hustling for tips. The smells wafting along the breeze off the North Sea were of raw fish from herring carts, and fresh hot *frites*, with mayonnaise for dipping sauce and served in little conical paper cups from corner stands, and also the freshly cooked *broojies* from stands, mixing with the spicy smells of Indonesian restaurants. A couple of Dutch Policemen, (or *Polite*) strolled casually past us, hands clasped behind their backs, their hair long, nodding and smiling at people. The Polite, like the spelling of their name, were mostly polite and respectful, and inclined to look the other way when they saw someone smoking hash. They were a nice change from the uptight cops we had had dealings with in the States. We continued walking, past tall narrow brick and mortar buildings standing close together, row upon row, some of which dated back to the 16th Century. Finally we came to a fast food stand near the

Central Station, where we ordered burgers and *frites* and a six-pack of Heineken beer, while Vic planned our next move.

"I guess we'd better plan on camping out tonight. We could camp in the Vondel Park, but people rip you off when you're sleeping. I think we ought to drive out of town toward Edam and see if we can find a spot."

As we drove, I discovered just how small and cramped Holland is, for the villages outside the city were small and close together, with no open land for gypsies like us to hide out for the night, so we settled on parking atop a dike, and layed our bags out under the dark starless sky, with the sea on one side of us, and the land further down the hill on the other. Occasionally, the moon would peek out through the clouds as they moved along on the North Sea breeze. In the gray damp foggy morning while we still lay cocoon-like in our bags, we stirred to the sound of an approaching Volkswagen, which was painted white and blue and had a revolving red light on top. We scrambled out of our bags and into our clothes, and a panicked Vic reached inside a pocket of his blue nautical coat with the rows of brass buttons, dug out the leftover chunk of hash from the sleeping boat, popped it in his mouth and swallowed it. But these were Dutch cops, not American ones, and they weren't about to search us for drugs, or rough us up before handcuffing and arresting us. They merely wanted to politely but firmly suggest we find another place to camp, preferably the Vondelpark in Amsterdam. Then they wished us a good day and drove off.

"That was a close one," said Vic, and I noticed his eyes were turning red and glassy, and a crooked grin showed above his beard. Then he added, "I think I'm coming on to this dope."

"Oh, Vic," said Star disapprovingly, and then she laughed, and Annie and I joined in.

"Let's go back to Amsterdam and find some public showers," said Vic with slurred speech and a stoned grin. "This afternoon we can drive out to Edam and look up some friends who we stayed with last year. Maybe they can put us up for the night."

But that was wishful thinking on Vic's part, for clearly he had worn out his welcome there. We sat around the Dutch couple's modest home with the open curtained windows, drinking tea and making small talk, but the conversation was strained. Eventually

Vic realized they weren't going to roll out the red carpet for us, so we took our leave and drove back to Amsterdam through the touristy fishing port of Volendam. We ended up staying at the Student Hotel at Kromme Wall 20, a canal street near the Central Station. It was a good location for us, as we could walk from there all around the Centrum, digging up busking spots. The hotel had the usual hostel dormitory setup, but Vic negotiated with the owner for semi-private rooms in an adjoining building. Each room had two sets of bunk beds and a sink. The toilet was in the café of the main building, where we would breakfast on coffee and rolls each morning.

Our week in Amsterdam flew by in a flurry of activity that included sightseeing, busking, and hustling up future gigs in clubs like the Folk Fairport, De Melkweg, and the Great American Disaster. We also managed to squeeze in an impromptu gig at the Lowlands Weed Company, a houseboat converted to a marijuana teahouse, where we were not only paid with guilders, but with some pot as well. Our audience was made up of laid-back hippies lounging around on chairs and cushions. Then our time in Holland came to an end and we beat it back to Germany, where we had gigs waiting for us in Dusseldorf. As the summer of 1972 faded away, Vic's plans for a traveling circuit from Munich to Amsterdam were becoming a reality.

CHAPTER THIRTEEN

In the Rhineland

We began our ten night's run at Danny's Pan in Dusseldorf on Friday, September 1, 1972. The little Frenchman Maurice had given us a key to the place, since we were to be lodged there as well. Danny had offered us two rooms to use, one upstairs above the stage, and the other downstairs on the opposite side of the room, beneath the lighting booth. The upstairs room was relatively clean, and furnished with a bed, a chair, and a nightstand. There were no windows, but an overhead light kept the room well lit. By contrast, the downstairs room, a cellar, was dark and dank and moldy smelling, with a dirty mattress, overflowing ashtrays, empty and broken beer bottles, and cockroaches that scuttled away when the bare bulb hanging from a ceiling cord was switched on. Vic compared the rooms and said that as bandleader, he would choose the upstairs one for himself and Star. Annie and I stored our gear in the dungeon.

In the foyer of the club our photos, which had been taken in Danny's restaurant the last time we were in town, now graced the wall, and our name, "Uncle Zeke's Band: *die Amerikanicshe trio*," appeared on the schedule, and also on little hand bills at the door. We felt like we'd arrived, or at least were climbing up from the streets.

That first night set the tone for the rest of our stay. A young German folksinger named Buddhix opened for us. Buddhix was his stage name, a contraction of the words Buddah and Asterix, a German comic strip character. Buddhix was tall and slim, with dark shoulder-length hair and wore black-rimmed glasses, like

Buddy Holly. He looked a little like Peter Fonda and dressed in a peasant shirt, brown corduroy pants, and calf-length lace-up boots. He wrote and sang songs in English, most of which were political in nature (he was a pacifist and opposed to Richard Nixon and the war in Vietnam). He had also written a moving song about his father, who had been a Luftwaffe fighter pilot in World War II, and had survived to become a pacifist himself. Buddhix opened several shows for us, and we became good friends, and Vic especially took a liking to him. Later on, we would get together for jam sessions before or after the show. During our performance, with the spotlight shining down on us, and the audience clapping and cheering and whooping it up, and giving us an encore ovation, we were pretty full of ourselves. After the place had closed, and everyone had gone home, we moseyed on over to the bar and poured ourselves glasses of Altbier, the strong bitter brew they served on tap. Then Vic hit the hard stuff, pouring himself a couple of shots of Johnny Walker Red to chase the beer with.

"Aha!" he said. "They left us the good stuff. Mighty neighborly of them. I tell you, Dupree, stick with me and I'll take you places. Yessiree, we'll be living the good life. This here is hillbilly heaven."

In the morning we breakfasted on muesli and fruit that Star fixed for us, and Vic had some of the Altbier for desert. Then we decided to go out for coffee, and found a diner down the street. While we sipped the strong brew in small cups, we watched events unfolding on a television screen that were taking place in Munich. The broadcast was, of course, in German, but as they say, a picture tells a thousand words, and from what we could figure out, an Israeli sports team had been kidnapped at the Olympic village by terrorists. Apparently there was some sort of standoff taking place.

"Looks like we got out of Munich just in time," said Vic. "I sure wouldn't want to be there now, with cops swarming all over the place."

I was thinking that maybe the Israeli team could've used even more cops swarming all over the place.

After our third night at Danny's Pan, it became apparent to Maurice that Vic had nearly drained the bottle of Johnny Walker, and from then on kept the liquor locked up. We were still allowed the tap beer, but Vic was indignant.

"Tight ass son of a bitch," he groused. "Old Maurice is locking up the good stuff for himself so he can have his own private stash."

"That's okay," said Star. "You know how you get when you drink whiskey. You're just like an Indian on the stuff, you go wild."

"Yeah," he allowed, "maybe I should stick to beer." Then he pulled her close to him, kissed her, and slapped her on the ass, good naturedly.

During our stay at Danny's Pan, we played four sets a night, six nights a week, with Monday off. In the beginning we had only enough material for three sets, and had to repeat songs at the end of the night. But during the day we would rehearse and add new material. Vic was also inspired to write a couple of new songs, which he'd play for us, and Annie would work out violin solos for them. Soon we had four sets together.

On our night off, we took a taxi to the Altstadt and walked down the narrow streets and alleys looking for *rathskellers* and pubs to busk. We discovered there were plenty of the latter. We played for a meal and drinks at a cavernous old restaurant that must have been built in an earlier century, and at the end of a night of busking, we split the money four ways. In the beginning, everything had gone into a kitty from which we'd take out expenses. But during our stay in Dusseldorf we realized that Vic was constantly dipping into the fund for pipe tobacco, beers and other luxuries, to the detriment of gas and food money. So our experiment in socialism ended, and we had consensus on the new arrangement. By the time the ten days were up, we had money in our pockets, gas in the tank and a fund set aside for traveling expenses. It was time to get in the wind again, and so we headed south down the Rhine valley toward Heidelberg.

Our first gig was at the university, in the student center. Vic hustled us a place to crash that night with one of the students, sleeping on the floor in our bags. On the first of the two nights we were scheduled at the folk club off the Markplatz, all seemed to be copacetic. We played to a small but appreciative crowd, the stout, mustachioed owner—this time in clean unwrinkled clothes and freshly shaved—smiled cheerfully at us and offered us drinks on our breaks. After we'd finished, and the club was darkened and emptied, we were to be lodged in the hotel next door. As we started down the stairway however, the owner told us "*Nichts, nichts.* Leave the instruments here please. You don't need to take them to the hotel."

"Yes, we do," argued Vic. "We're not leaving our axes here. Where we go, they go."

"*Ja, ja*. But they will be safe here," countered the barman, in an agitated voice.

"Maybe so, but we're taking them with us anyway," said Vic as he headed down the stairwell.

The man followed us down, swearing in German and shouting at us that he didn't want his hotel guests to see us carrying our instruments inside, and besides, he was worried about our keeping them awake with our loud music. But Vic could not be budged from his position, and we all backed him up. In the end, though, the owner won the argument, because he told us we were finished, *kaput.* We wouldn't work in his club tomorrow night or ever again. And furthermore, when we checked out of the hotel in the morning, we shouldn't bother to ever come back.

So our next night in Heidelberg, we were reduced to busking again, and at the London Inn we met a couple of GIs from the nearby Army base who had an apartment in town. They agreed to put us up for the night. But before crashing on the floor and the couch, we stayed up late, singing songs and smoking hash with them. The two GIs, Dean and Michael, were off duty for the weekend, so we stayed there another night, getting in some busking around town. When they left for the base on Monday, they left the place to us, and so we had one more day there before heading south again.

In Reutlingen, we played a sort of disco-type club before moving on the next night to the university at Tubingen, where we performed on a big stage and were again put up by a university student. Then came our two nights engagement at Die Jazz Kelder, a dimly-lit cellar that usually hosted jazz bands. I can't say the jazz fans and students were wildly enthused about our performance, but as we were at least different, therefore unique, they treated us warmly, for the most part. Vic managed to get into an argument with one of the patrons, but it was a small tiff. After the gig we crashed on the floor of Wolfgang's tiny basement flat. Wolf was a bartender at Die Jazz Kelder, a university student, and it was he who'd gotten us the gig there the last time we'd been in town. On our second night at his place, as we sat around talking and stoking the coal burning heater late at night, the door suddenly flew open and in burst an angry old grey-bearded man, red of face, swearing loudly at all of us, and especially Wolfgang, bombarding him in a language we didn't understand. Wolf yelled back at him in equally loud and incomprehensible words, and then the man was gone as suddenly as he'd appeared, slamming the door on his way out.

"What was that all about?" said Vic, knocking the ashes out of his pipe and into the stove.

"That was my landlord," answered Wolfgang, clearly upset. "The *swinehund* just evicted me for having visitors in here."

"Oh, I'm really sorry," said Annie with sincere concern.

"Fuck him!" said Vic. "The fucking Nazi. He can't get away with that."

"Yes he can," replied Wolfgang with resignation in his voice. "He just did. He said I have to be out today."

"What will you do now?" asked Star.

"Oh, I'll be okay. I'll go stay with friends for a while, until I can find a new place. I didn't like it here anyway. You see what a bastard he is, *ja*? Well, it is okay. We smoke some more hash, *ja?"*

"Good idea," said Vic, refilling his pipe, mixing the tobacco with the strong hashish he'd scored from the GIs in Heidelberg.

We headed back to Dusseldorf by way of Heidelberg again. Vic bought a gallon jug of Chianti from our funds for the drive, I slid behind the wheel, and off we went. We stayed again with Dean and Michael, both of them great guys, perused their collection of records, and found one by Ramblin' Jack Elliot, that we played over and over, learning a couple of more songs for our repertoire. Then Vic added yet another new one that he wrote one afternoon while we hung out there. We busked again while we were in Heidelberg, and we could feel the changing of the seasons, as we now buttoned up our coats when we went out at night.

Then it was back to Dusseldorf, for another ten-day engagement at Danny's Pan, with Buddhix opening for us on some nights, Ragtime Charlie on other nights, and a German folksinger named Hans Keller one night. Again the audiences loved us, and especially loved Annie, whom I felt was now the star of the show. They loved the way she looked and sang, and the way she played violin so gracefully and so unaffectedly. Vic of course believed he was the star, based on all the encores we got nightly. What he didn't understand was that our audiences were just very demonstrative, and they gave ovations to most of the headliners that played there. As before, on our night off we took a taxi to the Altstadt to do some busking.

After we had passed the hat and sat down to eat in a pizzeria on the Berliner Allee, Vic noticed an 8"x10" flyer tacked to the wall by the doorway.

"Hey, look!" he said. "Check this out. Bill Haley and His Comets are over here in Germany! I didn't know he was still around."

I hadn't known that Bill Haley was still around, either. In fact, I hadn't known whether he was even still alive. But I remembered who he was—the father of Rock and Roll. It was Bill Haley who'd had the first rock record to reach number one on the Billboard charts in 1955 with "Rock Around The Clock", after it had appeared during the opening credits of the movie, *Blackboard Jungle*. And in doing so, he had become the first rock idol, at the unlikely age of thirty. Bill and his band had created quite a sensation, and other records quickly followed, like "Crazy Man Crazy" and "See You Later Alligator." Columbia Pictures had rushed out two movies in 1956 to cash in on the rock phenomenon, both featuring Bill Haley, and rock's first concert promoter, Alan Freed, who had coined the phrase "rock and roll" to describe the new music.

When Bill and the Comets toured England and Europe the following year, they brought the house down everywhere. In London, teenagers rioted and tore up seats, sang along, and danced in the aisles. But Bill's reign as the King of Rock ended abruptly when Elvis Presley, ten years his junior, came out singing, swinging, and swiveling his hips to "Hound Dog" and "All Shook Up." Bill couldn't match this young upstart in terms of raw energy and sex appeal, and suddenly his ride was over. His star hadn't faded so much as had burned out, ironically, like a comet. But now, apparently, he was back. I studied the flyer in disbelief, but yes, there he was in glorious black and white, his ample body taking up most of the flyer's space—Bill Haley. Bill with his moon face and lazy glass eye, Bill with his trademark spit curl to one side of his forehead, Bill holding a large hollow body Gibson electric guitar, his body stuffed into a tuxedo jacket, white shirt and tuxedo bow tie—Bill Haley the founding father of rock and roll was alive and well and playing in, of all places, Essen, Germany, just north of Dusseldorf.

"It says here that the show's being promoted by Rock Concerts. I wonder if they're Americans," said Vic.

"Man, I always dug Bill Haley. Maybe we could go see him," I suggested.

"Nah," said Vic. "It's up in Essen, and we got no business there. It's just a big ugly industrial city."

A little later, as we were walking along a narrow street, we watched a Mercedes Benz van pull over to the curb across from us. Two men quickly exited it, carrying bundles of what looked like flyers in their arms.

"Man, you won't believe this!" said Vic. "Look what it says on the side of that van."

I took a good look at the two words stenciled prominently on the side. ROCK CONCERTS, in big bold letters, next to which was a large poster of Bill Haley and his Gibson guitar.

"I smell the Big Time," said Vic, slinging his guitar case by its strap onto his shoulder. "Let's catch up with them."

We rushed across the street, and Vic shouted, "*Chuss! Sprechen sie Enlische, bitte?*"

The two men who were dressed in business suits turned and eyed us curiously. The taller one, who was middle-aged and a little overweight, answered Vic directly.

"Yes, we speak English. What can I do for you?"

"Well, I noticed the sign on your van. Are you with Rock Concerts?"

"Yes, we are Rock Concerts. I am Manfred, and this is my partner Karl."

Karl, the smaller and younger of the two, nodded his head politely. "*Guten abend,*" he said. "Did you wish tickets for the Bill Haley show?"

"No, not exactly," said Vic. "We'd like to be in the concert. Do you promote any other bands? We're an American group called Uncle Zeke's Band, and we're in the market for a manager."

Manfred eyed us skeptically, for we were a scruffy looking lot, evidently in need of a tailor, a barber, and a bath.

"So you are American musicians," he said, sounding unimpressed. "And what brings you to Dusseldorf?"

"We've got a ten night engagement at Danny's Pan. We're the headliners. Why don't you come hear us tomorrow night? Tonight's our night off, so we're just out seeing the sights."

"I see. With your instruments, of course," he said dubiously.

"Well," said Vic sheepishly, "we were just doing a bit of busking, to keep our chops up."

"And what kind of music do you play?" asked Karl.

"Oh, folk and bluegrass, mostly," I said.

Vic shot me an angry look as he interjected, "We do a lot of stuff."

"Well, the show we're doing with Bill Haley is a Rock and Roll Revival show, and we already have two bands opening for him. So I don't think we'll be able to use you. But good luck with your group." Then Manfred turned as if to walk away.

"Wait!" said Vic. "You haven't heard us yet. We're really good. The audience loves us at Danny's Pan. Stop by tomorrow and find out for yourselves. Do you know where the club is?"

"Yes," said Manfred without interest, "we are familiar with it. What time do you perform?"

"Around ten. Right after Buddhix."

"Ten," Manfred repeated. "That's twenty-two hours. Perhaps we can come. We'll see."

"Okay. Thank you," said Vic. "Don't forget."

"Chus," said Karl, waving as they moved along the sidewalk.

"*Guten abend,"* I added.

"Well," said Vic smugly, "I think we're headed for the Big Time."

We were naturally nervous the next night at Danny's Pan, knowing that the guys from Rock Concerts might be in the audience. But I couldn't see them, because when I looked out into the smoke-filled room, the harsh light from the spotlight made me squint, and I could only make out the faces at the tables nearest the stage. Nevertheless, we were keyed up, and put on the best performance we could muster. The audience shouted *"Mach schau!"* And we put all our energy into fast songs like "Cotton Fields", dancing around and swinging our guitars.

> "*When I was a little bitty baby my mama would rock me*
> *in the cradle*
> *In them old cotton fields back home . . .*"

Finally, after several encores and standing ovations, we went offstage for the night, and retired to Vic and Star's room, where we sat drinking glasses of Altbier. There came a knocking at the door, and when Vic opened it, Manfred and Karl stood before us, all smiles and still dressed in smart business suits.

"We are impressed," said Manfred as we invited him in. "Maybe we can do something for you. We are thinking of managing you, but there are details to be sorted out first. Who is the leader of the band?"

"I am," said Vic without hesitation.

"Good. We will deal with you. It is late tonight, and Karl and I will need some time to make plans. We will return tomorrow and then we will talk some more. But for now, just let us say that we plan to use you in the Bill Haley show."

We all agreed that was good news.

The following night, just before the show, a reporter and photographer from a local entertainment magazine stopped by to interview us for a feature story and to shoot some photos. Vic did most of the talking, embellishing the facts, and making up stuff to make us sound more important, and also to expand more on his own role in the group. I didn't care, just so long as they spelled my name right. The pair thanked us and said that the article would appear in a fortnight, about the time we'd back at Danny's Pan again. Of course we were excited about the publicity, but more importantly the interview was taking place around the time that Manfred and Karl showed up. This might have sealed the deal for us, because now the two were more lavish with their promises.

"We have exciting plans for you," said Manfred, and then he outlined what those plans were to be. For starters, we would be the first opening act in the rock revival show in Essen October 1st, followed by another show with Bill Haley in Stuckenbrock the following weekend. In between, they would book us into a disco, put us up in a cottage in the country, and in the future—well, who could tell? Big things were hinted at—clubs, shows, maybe a recording contract. They had connections, he said. But first we would do the show in Essen.

Being on the road as we were, we had two mail drops where we could pick up our mail. One was the American Express office in Amsterdam, and the other was Danny's Pan. The next morning we received a letter addressed to Vic.

"Hey, look at this," Vic exclaimed, "a letter from Marty."

We all turned toward him, waiting for him to share the news. But when his face took on a serious look, I knew something was wrong. Vic raised his eyes slowly.

"He's in the Army," he said. "He got drafted in July. That's why he never showed up. The good news is he won't be going to Vietnam. They put him in Special Services and are sending him to New Mexico, probably because he's a married man. But there goes our banjo player. Guess we'll have to carry on as a trio. Banjo players are pretty rare over here."

"What about Paddy O'Brien?" I suggested.

"Forget it," said Vic. "When Star and I were over in Ireland last summer we asked him to go on the road with us and he turned us down flat. He's got it made over there in Dublin. He lives rent-free with his mother and hangs out in pubs playing his banjo and drinking Guinness. And he's on the dole, so he doesn't have to work. It's hillbilly heaven to him. I know you're disappointed about my cousin, Dupree, and you've got your mind set on a banjo player, but we've got to be realistic. Paddy's a lost cause."

"Well, do you mind if I write to him and invite him to join us?"

"Not at all, man. It's your nickel. Just don't get your hopes up."

But I did have my hopes up, and I wrote Paddy a long letter, waxing eloquently on our status as future stars. I told him about our gigs at Danny's Pan, and about our new managers and the Bill Haley concerts, and in general painted him a very grand picture indeed. Then I walked down to the post office and sent it off, giving Danny's Pan as our return address.

We finished another successful run in Dusseldorf, and headed north to Amsterdam once again, this time to prearranged gigs and a good idea about where we'd be staying, and this time it wouldn't be on top of a dike.

We rolled across the border checkpoint at Nijmegen with no trouble, the guard merely glancing at our passports before handing them back and waving us across.

Once in Amsterdam, we checked into the Student Hotel on Kromme Wall, and Vic wrangled a deal from Jaap to let us stay in two rooms again in the adjoining building. Vic and Star would have bunk beds in one of the rooms, and Annie and I would stay in the other. As before, we would make use of the restroom in the restaurant, and clean up at the public showers across the IJ harbor.

Our days in Amsterdam were filled with sightseeing and walking along tree-lined canals, whose leaves were now turning colors and beginning to wither and fall. Houseboats of all sizes were moored along the canals, some of them very colorful looking. The Student Hotel was in the Centrum, near the Central Station, so most everything we wanted to see was within walking distance. If we needed to venture further out, we had only to hop aboard one of the many trams that ran down the center of streets and fanned out in all directions. Sometimes we'd find places to busk during the day. We didn't have to venture far, as there were so many restaurants, pubs, coffeehouses, and youth centers that had live music, or potentially could. Our nights were taken up playing our existing gigs at the Folk Fairport, the Melkweg, and De Kosmos, and adding new places like the pub De Moor, and a youth center near the Vondelpark, which was furnished with Persian rugs and tapestries, and couches and cushions on the floor, and had a smell in the air of incense, hashish, and tobacco. Amsterdam was like a hippie Grand Central Station, crammed with travelers from all over the world, many of them Americans. We'd see them walking along with rucksacks and sleeping bags, or hanging out at the Dam (the monument across from the Queen's palace), and in all the clubs and bars. The hostels and the sleeping boats and the cheap hotels were filled to capacity. We were in our element. At night, Amsterdam took on the look of a carnival, the footbridges and drawbridges over canals lit up, and all the city sparkling in neon finery. Shallow bottomed tour boats cruised the larger canals, and all colors of twinkling, sparkling lights shone and shimmered in the reflection of the canals. It seemed the city never slept, for even after the bars had closed down for the night, the private clubs remained open, with parties continuing sometimes until daybreak.

Of mornings, we would have a Continental breakfast at the hotel, and for the most part our other meals consisted of fast foods—*broodjes*, *frites*, and the like, although sometimes we'd busk for a meal in a cafeteria or a nice restaurant. We were living each day to the fullest, and hardly noticed that our time there was almost up.

Autumn had arrived, and the change wasn't only felt in the cooler, crisper nights and the recurrent rain sneaking up on the sunny days. We could feel the change in our fortunes as well, and the shows in Germany were like a marquee in the distance with our names emblazoned in neon glory. Vic smelled the Big Time. He could almost taste it. It was what he'd been chasing since I'd first met him more than ten years before. Summer had left the building, and September was about to shut its door as well. It was time to get on the road again and hook up with Rock Concerts and the legendary Bill Haley.

CHAPTER FOURTEEN

Night Of The Comets

The offices of Rock Concerts were located in Dortmund, in the industrialized north of Germany, near Essen and to the northeast of Dusseldorf. After leaving Holland, we drove through a landscape of smokestacks, factories, and smog filled skies, arriving in Dortmund after nightfall, lost, unable to find the address we'd been given, or to get an answer from the phone number we had for them. Finally, hungry and tired, we stopped at a *gasthaus* and ordered food, and while we ate, asked the few customers there for directions, and received only blank stares or shaking of heads coupled with the word *nein.* But then a short, middle-aged man in a business suit who was nursing a drink at the bar replied, *"Ja,* I speak little English."

He studied carefully the little piece of paper Vic handed him with the address of Rock Concerts' offices, and also shook his head.

"Nein, is not in Dortmund. Too far. Too late at night. You go tomorrow."

But Vic, never one to take no for an answer, pressed him further. When he mentioned we were musicians and that we were going to be in a concert with Bill Haley, the man suddenly became interested in our plight, treating us like old friends and buying us beers. Then Vic mentioned that we had no place to stay for the night, and he became the very model of generosity.

"*Nein, nein. Kommen mit mich. Alles welkom. Mein haus ist mein schloss, und ich bin die Konig. Ja, kommen."*

"What did he say?" I asked.

"I think he said his home is his castle, and he's the king."

Everyone laughed at that, including our new friend, whom we followed in our VW down winding streets into the suburbs to a modest tract home, and parked at the curb in front. We followed him to the door, instruments and sleeping bags in hand, and then stood inside the doorway while his embarrassed wife argued with him, and he gestured toward us pleadingly.

"King of the castle, eh?" Vic whispered to me.

The king put up a losing fight before surrendering. He turned to us sheepishly.

"Sorry. No *schlafen* here tonight."

Then with gestures and broken English, we understood that he was offering to put us up in a hotel for the night, and wouldn't take no for an answer. Of course, the thought of saying no never entered our minds. So once again we followed him in our car, as he led us down winding streets and back into town to a modest hotel, where he arranged two rooms for us and picked up the tab. The woman at the desk viewed us with distrust and disapproval, but money was money, and the man had paid in cash. We said goodbye to our friend with many thanks and handshakes, and with his dignity intact, he left us. We were grateful for clean sheets and hot showers, and in the morning set out again to find Rock Concerts.

I telephoned from a corner box, and Manfred answered at the other end, and with his directions, we soon found his office. A secretary ushered us in and told us to sit. Manfred and Karl were both in the room, along with a younger man, in his twenties, who was dressed casually in slacks, white sport shirt, and a tight fitting waist length black leather jacket. He had longish black hair, shining blue eyes, and a disarming smile on his handsome face.

"Pleased to meet you," he said as he stood and nodded to each of us. "My name is Rolf."

We soon figured out that Rolf was a financial partner in the organization.

"Well, let's get down to business, shall we?" said Manfred. "Tomorrow night you will play at the Gruggahalle in Essen, which seats ten thousand people. You will go on first, and just do three of your fastest and loudest songs. *Mach shau,* right? Then you will come offstage before anyone has a chance to think, 'man, this does not sound like rock and roll'. If you do well, we'll put you on the next Bill Haley show that we're doing in Stuckenbrock next Saturday. You will be at the Gruggahalle at sixteen-thirty hours for the sound check, and then go onstage at twenty hours. We have booked you at a nightclub, a disco really, on Monday night. Beyond that we have many plans for you. We have many connections. We will take twenty-five percent as commission and management fees, and we will guide your career. First, we need to get you working papers."

It all sounded great to us, like we were part of a rags-to-riches story in the making.

The Gruggahalle was a massive sports arena. We drove into the vast empty parking lot, and pulled up close to the door, where we noticed two men talking, sports bags on the ground beside them. Both were big men with pale faces puffy and bandaged. One man sported a black eye.

"Hey, check out those pugs," said Vic. "They must have just had a boxing match. Man, what a way to make a living, beating each other up. Me, I'll stick with music. It's easier."

During the sound check, we stared out from the biggest stage we'd been on, into the cavernous stadium of empty seats, visualizing them as filled with boisterous fans. And we felt intimidated, for our voices and our instruments blared out of huge speakers, echoing off the walls and throughout the building.

"I hope they get those monitors adjusted better," complained Vic, "so we can hear each other."

We had a few hours to kill before show time, so we availed ourselves of the cold showers in the sports arena, and then drove around looking for a restaurant, but as this was a Sunday, and most businesses were closed, we settled for fast food.

Back at the Gruggahalle, we lounged in our dressing room, all keyed up and anxious, tuning and re-tuning our instruments, and rehearsing. Then Vic said, "Let's go meet Bill Haley." We found his dressing room just down the hallway, and as the door was ajar, we let ourselves in. He sat in the room alone in a big overstuffed chair, a Styrofoam cup of coffee in hand, looking tired and slightly bemused, a giant of a man in rumpled stage clothes that somewhat resembled a tuxedo, but at any rate were hopelessly out of fashion. He smiled cordially.

"Come on in. Make yourselves at home."

"Hi, Bill, it's great to meet you," I gushed. "I've always been a fan of yours."

"We're your opening act," added Vic proudly.

"Where are you boys from?"

"California," we replied in unison.

"What are you doing in Germany, Bill?" I asked.

"Same as you, playing music. We just did a tour of England, now we're touring Germany. They still appreciate us over here in Europe. We've got a record on the charts over in England that's doing well."

"Got any of the original Comets with you?" I asked.

"Oh, yeah, a couple. Rudy, he's the sax player. He's been with me from the beginning. And Ray on bass. He's been with me a long time now."

We soon ran out of small talk and began fumbling for words, so we excused ourselves and wished him a good gig. Then Vic said he wanted to meet King Size Russell, another of the acts on the bill.

"He's famous, you know," Vic confided to me. "He used to play with the Rolling Stones.

"No, man, I never played with them cats," said King Size, setting the record straight. "I never even met them."

It was easy to see how King Size Russell got his name, for he was so tall and wide of girth, he made even Bill Haley seem small. He was an affable, likeable black man from England who played piano New Orleans style and covered many of Fats Domino's songs. You might say that he did a Fats Domino tribute act. I thanked him for his time and Vic and I wandered back to our own dressing room

We had heard rumors that the promoters were worried about the turnout. It seems the entertainment writer for the local paper had slammed Bill Haley for being over-the-hill and out-of-date. In fact, the writer had derisively labeled him the "Grandfather of Rock and Roll." Presently Manfred knocked on our dressing room door, and thrust his flushed face inside.

"It's show time," he announced "Go out there and do your best. Remember, now, just three songs. Get on and get off."

He led us out onto the stage, and we took our places at the microphones, which by bad planning were spaced out across the stage, one in the middle, and one at each end, instead of all together in the center. The result was that we couldn't see each other without turning our heads at all angles, and so I felt conspicuously alone on my end of the stage. We also couldn't hear each other over the din of the crowd. The only sound we could hear was our music spilling out of the monitors, which bled into the sound from the main speakers, and then echoed back from the far walls of the hall. We launched into "Cotton Fields" and it sounded all jumbled up. I couldn't hear what Vic and Annie were doing. All I could hear was my own voice and a jumble of noise. It sounded like this:

> "*When I was a little bitty—when I was—when I—baby—little bitty—when—*"

So we hunkered down and played by instinct, and all the rehearsals we'd had and all the performances we'd done helped us stay in synch. I tuned out all the noise as I concentrated on my own part. We got through the song and two more, and then beat a retreat off stage, to a thundering of applause. Manfred was right. We hadn't been on stage long enough to bore the crowd or have them wonder why we weren't doing rock and roll. We also weren't onstage long enough to realize that the seats were only half filled. All we could see was the glare of spotlights and some sort of sea of faces that had no connection to us or what we were doing up on the stage. It was nothing like the intimacy of a coffeehouse or a folk club. Nevertheless, it had been a rush, a high, not unlike the effect of a drug.

After stashing our instruments in the dressing room, we watched the show from back stage as first Fumble, and then King Size Russell performed to an increasingly impatient crowd. "Bill Haley! Bill Haley!" they chanted. Finally the headliners, Bill Haley and His Comets, walked onstage to a thundering roar of approval, most of the band looking very over-the-hill, and outfitted in 1950s stage attire. But they still knew how to "rock the joint."

One o'clock, two o'clock, three o'clock rock.
Five, six seven o'clock eight o'clock, rock.
Nine, ten, eleven o'clock twelve o'clock rock.
We're gonna rock around the clock, tonight!

And they were off and running. I decided to watch the show from out front, especially since there were so many empty seats, so I brushed by the security guard at the edge of the stage, and found a seat in the front row. As I watched the band, I realized what an anachronism they were, as if they had just stepped out of a time warp. But they knew how to *mach shau* as they belted out all their hits. Ray climbed up on his big double bass, plunking it, then playing it upside down, then laying it down on it's side and riding it like a horse, while still plunking away. Rudy Pompilli honked his tenor sax while swinging it up in the air, then while down on his knees, then while stepping over Ray, who was still riding his bass. Bill Haley swayed back and forth and pointed his guitar at the audience like a machine gun. I sat spellbound, but at some point decided I'd better return backstage. However, the security guard didn't recognize me, and blocked my way with his body.

"*Nein! Nein! Ist verboten!*" he said firmly.

"But I'm on the bill," I protested. "I'm with Uncle Zeke's Band. We were just onstage, the opening act."

But apparently the muscular guard with the buzz cut hair didn't understand English, for he kept shouting "*Nein!*"

Just then, though, the young German promoter Rolf looked over my way from behind the stage curtain and came to my rescue. He said a few German words to the guard, who let me pass.

"Man, what were you doing out there?" said Rolf.

"Just trying to see the show."

"Well, just stay right here and watch it. Don't get lost again. Bill is almost finished anyway."

But he wasn't quite finished, for there were the encores to do yet. The band filed off stage, while the crowd rose in their seats, clapping hands, stamping feet, whistling, and chanting "Bill! Bill!" And "*Noch ein mal!*" ("Once more!) The promoters frantically rounded up the band members, pleading with them for an encore before a riot ensued. Someone grabbed Bill and led him back onstage, minus his guitar, which he had left in the dressing room. Bill appeared disoriented, lost, in his own world. Grasping the situation, I raced to his room, extracted the big Gibson guitar from its case and hurried back, walked onstage, and placed it in Bill's hands. I plugged the cord from the amp into the guitar, as Bill stared blankly ahead into the bright lights. Then as if a switch had been thrown somewhere, he wound himself up and started the show all over again.

"One o'clock, two'clock, three o'clock, rock . . ."

And they were off to the races again with repeats of "Rock Around The Clock," "See You Later, Alligator" and "Rock The Joint". The crowd, such as it was, went wild. Meanwhile, we hung around in the wings, awaiting further instructions from the promoters. I ducked out long enough to say goodbye to some of the Comets.

"See you later, alligator," I said shamelessly.

"After a while, crocodile," said Rudy, his sax tucked in the crook of his arm.

The Rock Concerts promoters were disappointed by the turnout of only five thousand people, since they'd expected a sellout. We were looking forward to the thousand deutschmarks they'd promised to pay us, since our VW needed some major repairs, but now they told us they could only afford to pay three hundred. This did not sit well with Vic, who began arguing with Manfred, complaining we were being ripped off.

"Promoters always stiff the opening acts," he groused to me later. "I know they made a fortune off us."

However, it was not all bad news, as Manfred outlined his latest plans for us.

"We're putting you up in the master suite of a very expensive hotel, just outside of Essen. We had the room reserved for Bill, but he's decided not to take it, preferring to stay at the other hotel with the rest of the band. So, since it's already paid for, we're giving it to you." Then he added magnanimously, "You see how we take good care of you. Stick with us and you won't regret it."

The hotel turned out to be a remodeled old castle, complete with moat and drawbridge, and extensive grounds. I was stunned by all the opulence, but Vic was un-phased. He said it was the kind of lodgings we deserved. He also said that as leader of the band he and Star deserved the master bedroom. Annie was relegated to the couch in the adjoining room, while I slept on the floor. But I didn't much care, for we had a bathroom and shower at our disposal. In the morning, after a breakfast of ham and eggs and coffee, bread and jam, I strolled through the large garden on the castle grounds, enjoying the quiet of a grey morning, listening to the chirping of birds, and feeling thankful for my lot in life.

The following night we played at the disco, which was housed in yet another converted castle, for which we were paid one hundred fifty marks. We played short sets in-between dance records spun by a deejay, much as we had done in Murnau a few months back, and received about the same level of response—polite indifference. This was not our kind of venue. We knew it, the audience knew it, and now our managers knew it, as they mentally crossed the place off for future gigs. But still, there was another rock revival concert coming up in a few days in Stuckenbrock, and for the rest of the week we hung out at the cottage in the country, drove into town at night to busk, and killed time while awaiting our big break.

Saturday night found us sitting around in another dressing room, marking time, waiting to go onstage again, this time on a much smaller stage. A makeshift stage, in fact, set up in front of the restaurant at Safaripark, a wild animal park outside of Stuckenbrock. The audience was much smaller than the one we'd had the previous week, and the promoters ran around nervously, worried about their investment, while we merely waited to go on, sipping beers, snacking on the junk food that had been provided for us. Our dressing room wasn't very glamorous either, merely a break room for the park's employees. Vic insisted that we were now in the Big Time, but as far as I was concerned, we were still the scruffy-looking lot who had been busking for a meal the night before. Vic's rumpled pants were still too short, my jeans were getting threadbare, and I needed a shave and a haircut in order to appear respectable in polite society.

"Let's go over 'Cotton Fields' again," I said.

"I've had my belly full of that song," said Vic. "This better be the last time we ever do it."

"Why don't you sing your new song," Star suggested. "You know, the one about Nixon."

"Oh, you mean the 'Goosestep Rag'? Nah, it's not upbeat enough. You know what Manfred says, '*mach shau'*." Then he said to me, "And that's why we're not doing any of your songs either, Steve. We're going to hit 'em with three fast ones again, and then get offstage. And this time they'd better not stiff us on the bread."

Tired of waiting around in our room, Vic decided we'd pay a visit on the Comets, and maybe smoke some hash with them. But only the guitarist, a guy in his twenties, took us up on our offer, and then with the stipulation that we only smoke it in the bathroom with the door locked.

"Bill won't let us touch that stuff," he said as Vic lit the joint. "He'd fire me if he caught me smoking. But hey, you guys are cool, and I haven't smoked any shit since the tour started." Then after taking a hit he remarked, "I think it's a real honor for a young guy like me to get to play with these cats. They're legends, and this is a good opportunity for me."

We followed the guitarist back to the band's dressing room, and then sipped some of their whiskey. On our way back to our own room, Manfred collared us and said excitedly, "Where have you been? You're on in a few minutes. Just stay put until I return."

He quickly returned, as promised, and we strode onto a stage that faced a crowd of only two thousand people. But this time, we were close together and could hear each other, and so our three songs went off without a hitch. Then we all watched the rest of the show from backstage, and the audience clearly loved Bill Haley and His Comets. However, on this night Bill was less animated, and seemed almost bored, giving the guitarist and the sax player solos, and then giving the drummer such a long solo that Bill walked off stage for the whole thing. Vic was impressed, though.

"Bill's a good band leader," he said. "He lets each of his guys have the spotlight for one song."

I began to wonder if that was the way he saw Annie and I in Uncle Zeke's Band, deserving of only one song apiece.

After all the encores had been played, and the crowd dispersed, we joined the Comets in their dressing room to sign autographs for the fans, eat their food, and help drink their whiskey and beer. I'm sorry to say they drank us under the table, though we tried valiantly to keep up. Afterward, Star and Annie managed to find our car without any trouble, but Vic and I weaved and stumbled the whole way there and I still don't know how I managed to find the hotel, but I did and stumbled to my bed where I quickly passed out.

In the morning, severely hung over, we stumbled downstairs to the restaurant and breakfast, downing large quantities of coffee, while listening to stories of the road from some of the members of Fumble. Then we met with the promoters to collect our pay.

"I'm afraid we had a poor turnout," said Manfred. "We can only pay you five hundred marks this time."

"But you promised us twice as much," said Vic angrily.

"Sorry, boys, that's the best I can do. Before I can pay you though, I'll need to have Vic sign this receipt."

The paper he handed to Vic was written in German, but the amount filled in at the bottom was easy to read—one thousand deutschmarks.

"I'm not signin' nothin'," said Vic. "You promised us a thousand marks, that's what it says right here, and that's what we want."

"Then you won't get paid at all," said Manfred.

"Just sign it, Vic," I said, "and take the money. Then let's get out of here."

After some more arguing, Vic took the money and quit our association with Rock Concerts. But then Rolf, the young promoter, took us aside and said, "Here's another hundred marks. I know you need it."

"Thanks, Rolf," I said. "We appreciate it."

"Yeah," said Vic, "but it won't buy us a van. We need one, and we were counting on this money to buy one in Amsterdam. Our station wagon is about shot."

"How much do you need?" Asked Rolf.

"I figure about a thousand marks."

"Well, maybe I could lend you another hundred. I'll give you my address, and you can return the money later. I know how it is in this business, I used to be a musician myself."

"That's really nice of you, Rolf," said Annie.

"We'll pay you back as soon as we can," I promised. But we never contacted him again.

Our next move was back to Amsterdam. In front of the American Express office was where all the hippies and travelers conducted business, buying and selling, offering rides and seeking rides, things of that nature. We parked our VW Variant nearby and took turns holding up a sign advertising the car for sale. We got rid of it in a few hours, and a couple of days later bought a used VW microbus, complete with a mattress inside for sleeping on. After several days of gigging and busking, and setting up future gigs, we headed back to Dusseldorf and Danny's Pan.

CHAPTER FIFTEEN

Stormy Weather

I lay in bed in the room above the stage at Danny's Pan, sweating, burning up with fever, and sometimes hallucinating. My head throbbed, my throat was swollen, and I coughed violently. Somewhere in the recesses of my feverish brain, I could hear the sound of music. It seemed to be coming up through the floorboards. It sounded like a guitar and a violin, and someone singing about goose-stepping in a Nixon parade. I slipped back into unconsciousness, and when I awoke the room was dark, the sleeping bag was wet with cold perspiration, but the fever was gone. I felt weak, drained, my head still hurt. I fell asleep again for an interminable amount of time When I next opened my eyes, the headache was gone, and though I still felt weak, I could sit up and look around, and then I understood where I was and how I'd gotten there.

What had begun as a cold a few days back had turned into a hacking cough and a throbbing headache, and I became concerned enough that with Annie and Star's help I persuaded Vic that I needed to see a doctor. We found ourselves at a clinic where I was examined, and the doctor, showing great concern, said I had pneumonia, with a temperature of 103 degrees, and should be hospitalized immediately. Vic began protesting that we couldn't afford the bill and wasn't there some other way to get me well? Yes, the doctor replied, I could be put to bed immediately in a warm, dry room, and attended to until the fever broke and the coughing and sore throat cleared up. I needed at least a week of bed rest. Vic agreed that we had just such a place, and that they would take good care of me, and somehow I was able to drive back to the club and crash down in the dungeon for a while. But the dungeon was dank and cold, and this being November, I couldn't keep warm. So after threatening to put myself in the hospital, Vic relented and let me stay upstairs where it was warmer. I soon fell into a long period of waking and sleeping and delirium. But on the third day, I felt well enough to get out of bed. That's when Vic informed me that I would be docked two days pay for not performing onstage.

"Are you fucking kidding?" I said.

"Hey, Dupree, no play no pay. I'm not running a charity here."

"What about Star?" I said. "She doesn't play, but she gets an equal share."

"Leave Star out of it."

"No, I won't. What does she ever do, besides be your girlfriend?"

"She's our cook."

"Yeah? When's the last time she did any cooking around here? She either makes us sandwiches, or else we eat out."

While Vic was shooting me daggers, Annie was trying to smooth things over.

"Come on, you guys, don't fight about this. We're all in this together. I don't see why Steve can't get paid. He couldn't help it if he was sick."

Vic gave me a long, hard look, and then relented. "Okay," he said, "but just this one time. Next time you'd better show up on stage, no matter how sick you are, or you don't get paid."

The crisis blew over, but after that I began to see Vic in a different light. His halo looked a little tarnished.

Feeling mostly recovered now, I wrote another letter to Paddy in Ireland, exaggerating and painting a beautiful picture about our gigs with Bill Haley and our residency at Danny's Pan. I asked him again to join the band, and I gave him our mail drop address in Amsterdam to reply to. Then I posted it.

During our run at Danny's Pan we met an older man and his wife who were in the audience, and who asked us to play for a private party at their estate outside of town. They would pay us well, and put us up in a nearby hotel. Vic said yes, of course we'd do it. After that gig, we headed south again. It was well into autumn now, the days were grey and cold and sometimes rainy, the leaves, now brown, shook loose and fell to the ground, and Vic began to talk about how we should start looking around for a place to winter in. But first there were gigs to play in Heidelberg again, and then in Tubingen.

After wrapping up our gig in Tubingen our next stop was to be Amsterdam, but suddenly on the Autobahn the van started acting up, running rough, and so we pulled into Frankfurt and found a garage to have it checked out. Bad news. The VW needed two hundred marks worth of work done.

"Will it make it to Dusseldorf?" I asked.

"I don't think you'll make it out of Frankfurt," was the reply. "Why don't you leave it with us overnight, and we'll work on it first thing in the morning."

Vic and I conferred and checked our funds. We had less than fifty marks between us.

"What are we going to do?" I said anxiously. "We need the van to get to Amsterdam, where we have gigs, but we don't have any bread to get it fixed."

"Looks like we stay here tonight, and go busking tomorrow. We can try the subway first."

"Where will we sleep? We don't have money for a hotel."

"Star and I can sleep in the van. We'll just have to find some place for you and Annie. We'll ask around."

We told the mechanic that we'd leave the van for the night, and to go ahead and fix it. And would it be all right if two of us stayed with it tonight? Of course, that would be fine was the reply.

"Know of any place where someone can spend the night cheap?" Vic asked

Yes, said the mechanic, there was a youth hostel nearby. He gave us directions. We left the van and walked to the address, found the hostel, and realized we had just enough money to put Annie and me up for one night. We were told to come back after eight, when we could check in. The four of us then found a cheap place to eat with the last of our funds, and I worried aloud about being down and out in Frankfurt. Vic didn't seem bothered though and said, "Well, Steve, you can always split to California and go back to work at the record shop."

"What?" I said. "And give up show business?" And then I felt better.

Annie and I slept the night at the hostel in segregated dormitory rooms, and in the morning met up with Vic and Star. We didn't have enough money between us for a cup of coffee, but we grabbed our instruments and walked down to the Metro and into the bowels of the subway, and played and sang our hearts out for a couple of hours. Finally we decided we had made enough money to take a break and go have some lunch. But we were still a long way from our goal of two hundred marks. As we climbed back outside and into fresh air and began walking down the sidewalk, a voice called out to us. We turned to see a tall black woman hurrying our way.

"Excuse me," she said in perfect American with no trace of accent, "Are you musicians? I mean are you a band?"

"Yeah, sister," said Vic. "How did you guess?"

"Well, I saw your instruments, and I wondered if you're playing anywhere tonight."

"Why," said Vic, "know of any place where we could play?"

"Yes," she said with a wide smile. "I own a club, an American bar, and I need a band for tonight. The group I had lined up cancelled on me at the last minute."

We all looked at each other in disbelief. The woman continued.

"I'll pay you two hundred marks, feed you, and put you up for the night."

We were so stunned that even Vic had to pause before answering.

"Sure. What time do you want us?"

"I'd like you to play from nine to midnight. Come a little early, and I'll fix you up with dinner. There's a room above the club where you can sleep afterward."

I thought to myself, what are the odds of something like this happening? Maybe this is how it works, how the universe takes care of you when you're trying to do noble work, like making music. All my doubts of the previous night, when I had been at my lowest, now vanished. We counted the money we'd made in the subway and found it was enough for the food and gas to get us to Amsterdam. And the two hundred marks we were being paid would get the van fixed. We did the gig that night, and while talking with the woman, found out she was an expatriate from the States, and had been running her club for several years. She'd been married to a German, but was now divorced. The next morning, our van repaired and paid for, we got in the wind again.

It was now late November, and although by the calendar it was still officially autumn, it felt like winter to me. I sat behind the wheel of our VW microbus, dressed as warmly as I could manage with a sweater and my fringed jacket, and gloves on my hands that gripped the steering wheel, yet I still felt uncomfortably cold. I could feel the chill coming through the metal floor of our unheated vehicle, freezing my feet, even with two pairs of socks on.Vic had said that we needed to hole up somewhere for the winter, so we wouldn't have to be on the road all the time. Snow would be coming soon, and we didn't want to be driving in it, let alone camping out. But first we had these gigs to do in Amsterdam, our only source of income at the moment.

We approached the same border crossing where we'd been waved across before, so I didn't foresee any problem. But Vic was visibly nervous.

"Tourist season is over now," he reasoned, "so they might not let us in. They like tourists in the summer, spending their money freely, but if they think you're just here hanging out with no money, and no return ticket home, well that's another story. The Dutch pride themselves on being tolerant, but the bottom line is that they're just greedy capitalists like everyone else."

We took our place in line at the border check, and then it was our turn to be inspected.

The guard eyed us carefully. "Passports," he said, and I handed them to him, along with Vic and Star's working papers.

"What is the purpose for your visit?"

"We're tourists," I replied, forcing a nervous smile. He studied me, and then my passport. He did not hand the passports back. He told us to pull our van over to the building on the side, and to go inside.

"Tell them you've got five hundred bucks," said Vic, handing me the bag that contained all our money, about fifty marks. Then we all went inside and were grilled by a no-nonsense official who looked at all our papers, counted our money, and asked if we had return tickets to the States. We did not.

"Den you cannot enter De Nederlands," he said with finality. "You must return to Germany." With a quick forceful motion, he brought the stamp in his hand down on all our passports, one after the other. I looked at mine. *Niet Toegang.* No entry. Then he told us to turn our van around and head back the way we came, which we did. I drove the VW back down the road until we were out of sight of the border crossing, and then pulled over.

"Shit," I said. "What are we going to do now? We have to get to Amsterdam. We can't just go back to Germany."

"We'll try again," said Vic, a worried but determined look on his face. "Get out the map. Let's find a smaller border crossing where they might not be so strict. We should have thought of that in the first place anyway. This is the main road, and of course they're going to hassle hippies this time of year."

"Okay," I agreed. "Looks like we haven't got a choice."

We drove off the main road to a secondary one and found the next border crossing a few kilometers away. As it was a smaller road, and didn't get as much traffic, we didn't wait in line, but just drove up to the guard post, slowed and stopped. We handed over our passports, and held our breaths, hoping he wouldn't look inside the passports, but only at our photos. But he did look carefully at every page, and stopped when he saw the *Niet Toegang* stamp, He closed each passport in turn, holding them in his fist for what seemed to be a long time before handing them back to us. Then he brusquely stated that we could not enter the country, and to turn around and go back. I was about ready to give up and to head back to Dusseldorf where we could at least busk. But Vic said no, we had to try again. So out of sight of the guard post we got out the map again and followed it to yet another border crossing, this one even further out of our way, in the quiet countryside.

The third crossing was even smaller, and the guard more laid back. He took our passports, lazily opened them to the first page, which held our photos, and closed them again, handing them back. But he wasn't through with us quite yet. He wanted to inspect the vehicle. I smiled and said, "Go right ahead."

Vic, who was in the back with Star, lounging on the mattress, opened the side doors for him, and welcomed him to look around, then started joking with him, saying things like "If you're looking for hashish or marijuana, we don't have any. That's why we're going to Amsterdam, to get some."

The guard actually smiled, and Vic, encouraged by this, gave him a tour of the inside of the van, showing him our instruments and building us up as a somewhat famous band from the States that had some important gigs in Amsterdam. He showed him a poster of the Bill Haley concert with our name on the bill, and then dug out a photo of Vic and me with Bill, arms around each other. That capped it. The guard was satisfied with his search, and wishing us a pleasant day and success with our music, waved us on our way. Once out of sight, we all began to breathe easier, and even had a good laugh about our experience, and how we'd pulled the deception off. Then Vic expressed what was on all our minds.

"You know what this means now, of course. We can't go back to Germany. We'd never get across the border to Holland again. We're stuck here for a while. But Amsterdam is a good place to winter in. It won't get as cold as Germany, and there's plenty of gigs. But we'll need to find a place to stay at for the long term. We may have to stay in Amsterdam till summer."

And so we settled in at the Student Hotel at Kromme Wall 20, on the tree-lined canal, but now the trees were bare and the sky was grey and overcast with dark clouds that blustered by on currents of North Sea wind. Since the tourist season was long over, Vic was able to make a better deal with Jaap on our rooms, which were adjacent to the hotel, and for which we paid on a weekly basis. We'd had to rent the first week partly on credit until we'd played a gig or two and done some busking. During the day we parked our VW on the little cobblestone street that bordered the canal, the front wheels resting against a small railing that kept it from rolling into the water. On some canals where there wasn't such a barrier, little Citroens and Volkswagens had sometimes been driven or pushed into the dark and dirty water, and then had to be dredged up by one of the cranes attached to a barge whose job it was to periodically clear the canals of trash and errant bicycles and such. When we'd go out into the streets of Amsterdam in the daytime to wander and explore or to have a beer or eat a meal, the VW would stay parked in its spot. And at night when we'd take our instruments to go out busking, we would go on foot and leave the van in its spot, for it was easier than looking for another parking spot, and besides, gas was expensive. But on nights when we had a gig farther than walking distance, we would usually take the VW and hope to find the same spot vacant when we returned much later on.

One night when we returned around three in the morning, I spaced out and left my Martin guitar on the ground, next to the van. When I woke up at noon, and missed seeing it, I was certain that it would be long gone, stolen. But to my surprise and relief, it still sat in plain sight, right where I'd left it. I felt like I had a guardian angel watching out for me.

During our first week back in Amsterdam, I found a letter from Paddy O'Brien waiting for me at the American Express office on the Damrak, near the Central Station. It was short and to the point. Paddy said he'd join us in Amsterdam and play banjo in our band if we would send him the money for the airfare. This was great news, and it was at first hard for Vic to absorb it, he'd had it so set in his mind that Paddy was a lost cause, but when it did register with him, he lit up in a smile.

"How much money does he need?" When I told him the amount, he said, "Let's take up a collection and get a money order off to him right away. He can sleep in the van for a while, until we figure out better accommodations."

It took another week for Paddy to show up, and in the meantime we played gigs at De Moor (a little neighborhood pub nearby), and Om Shanti, a little hippie teahouse, and another bar named the Famos. And we busked at the Mensa (the university's student cafeteria), as well as some bistros and bars. The weather turned colder, rainier and windier; the gusts of a near gale force wind pushing against us as we walked along the streets one bitter night. Our hotel was near both Chinatown and the Red Light District, and sometimes we walked through there on our way to the Damrak, and I'd notice the painted whores sitting bored in red-lit windows, or the older sad-looking ones shuffling along in the daytime, their faces pale and haggard, looking beaten down. But beyond the Red

Light District were friendly pubs and cafes for us to busk at, or just sit quietly and enjoy a beer or a meal.

Vic struck up a friendship with Jeff, a bearded American who worked at De Moor as the house dealer. Many of the youth clubs and pubs in Amsterdam had an official dealer to sell hash to the customers, someone who was trusted and wouldn't cheat, or charge more than the going rate. This kept potential problems and bad vibes from breaking out over questionable drug deals. Jeff lived in the neighborhood in a *krak haus*, or "cracked house," as he called it. It was a squatters' building, and it was going to be torn down in a few months, due to urban renewal. But for now, American and European hippies squatted there, with the unofficial blessing of the local authorities. Vic put out the word to Jeff that we had a friend coming over from Ireland to join us any day now, and we'd be looking for a better place to stay than the Student Hotel. Jeff said he'd keep his eyes open, and in the meantime, why not have a few tokes off the hash pipe, courtesy of him? After all, we were fellow Americans, just hustling from day to day, and besides, he liked our music.

Thanksgiving showed up, and we celebrated it together over a meal at a Chinese restaurant. The day had started out blustery and drizzly, but with the afternoon came the sun, peeking out through puffy grey clouds. I took this as a good sign, and felt very thankful indeed. Thankful that we were in Amsterdam, and that we had a comfortable place to stay with beds to sleep in, thankful that we were off the road for a while, but mostly thankful that I was making music for a living, and in a band with kindred spirits. It seemed to me I had everything, needing nothing. I looked forward to seeing Paddy again, and to playing music with him, and to hearing the sound of a banjo in the mix with our guitars and violin.

And then the day came that Paddy arrived. We found him waiting for us in the cafe of the Student Hotel, his banjo and a suitcase on the floor next to his table. His blond hair was darker than when I'd last seen him, and unkempt looking as it hung down on his shoulders. His face was framed by a light beard, and when he smiled that wide smile of crooked teeth, his hang dog face lit up and his nose crinkled.

"Vic! Star! Dupree!" he said. "It's about time yez showed. I'm after havin' a dry t'roat an' cud use a pint o' the barley. And who's the pretty colleen with the fiddle case?"

There were hugs and handshakes all around, and then we all went down to De Moor for a drink.

CHAPTER SIXTEEN

Land Of The Wooden Shoes

There was one thing about Jeff that I found strange, yet intriguing—he wore wooden shoes, Dutch wooden clogs painted black. I knew that the wooden shoes were traditional in Holland, and some of the old farmers in the countryside still wore them, for they were good for walking in the soft wet fields. But they were obviously not made for the city cobblestones. Yet now that I noticed them on Jeff, I began to notice them on the feet of other hippies, Dutch or otherwise, who had been living in Amsterdam for some time. Jeff had been living here too long, he said. He wasn't ready to spend another long cold wet winter in Amsterdam in the "cracked house," coming down again with the croup, an affliction that seeps into the lungs from all the fog and moisture and chill of the winter. This year, he said, he was getting out of town. He was going to New Zealand, on the bottom side of the world, where summer was just now coming on. He had just about enough money saved up to go. He wanted to leave Holland by Christmas.

"What are you going to do about your room in the cracked house?" Vic asked.

"A friend of one of the other guys that lives there is planning to move in."

"What if we get there first?" said Vic.

"I see what you're getting at," said Jeff. "If you got there first, and I were to give you my key, that would be that. First come, first squat. Sounds okay to me."

They shook hands on it. We went over to see the place next day before Jeff went off to his job of selling hashish. The building was only a few blocks from us, located at 44 Konigstraat, in a quiet old neighborhood where a little canal dead-ended. It had once been a four-story pickle factory, but had been abandoned in preparation for the wrecking ball. That was before the squatters moved in. Jeff lived in the basement. We knocked on his door, and when it opened, we had to drop down a few steps into the dim room. There was a single small curtained window that faced the street, and a lamp in a corner that partially lit the room. A large oil-burning heater in another corner provided warmth.

A large mattress sat upon a platform beneath the window, and another mattress lay on the floor in the back room, which was accessed through an opening in the wall where a door might once have been. The place was dark, dank, and squalid. But the price was right—zero rent. All the tenants of the building kicked in a little money each month to keep the electricity and water going. Down in the basement, where we were, there was no running water.

"It may not be pretty, but it's home," said Jeff. "It won't be home much longer, though. I got my plane ticket and I'm leaving next week." That meant he would be gone just before Christmas, which would make for a nice Christmas present for us.

After our little open-house tour by Jeff, we walked back to the Student Hotel. Paddy had been around a couple of weeks now, sleeping in the VW at night where it was parked out front of the hotel, facing the canal. After waking late in the morning, we would all have rolls and coffee at the hotel cafe, then retire to Vic and Star's room to work on songs with Paddy. Now that he was in the band, we had more Irish folk songs, and instrumentals for Paddy and Annie to do solos. We were developing a better sound, a fuller one, and so we were getting more gigs, and better ones. But we needed to, because now there were five of us, which meant another mouth to feed.

Our first gig with Paddy was at The Great American Disaster on the Singel canal, within walking distance. I closed my eyes while we were playing the instrumental "Grandfather's Clock," listening intently to the banjo and the fiddle, Vic's 12-string and my 6-string guitar, how it all blended together, and it felt and sounded like a well-oiled machine, with everything working in sync, and I was happy just to be a part of the machinery.

We moved over to the *krak haus* on Koningsstraat two days before Christmas, beating out the other potential squatter by hours. When he arrived, we had already unpacked the bus, and moved our stuff in. He was bummed out, but what could he do? He would just have to find another squat. Vic looked the place over, decided the back room was a better one, because of the privacy, and said that as leader of the band he would take it for himself and Star. Paddy and Annie got the big bed in the front room. I slept on the floor until I was able to cop a mattress from somewhere a few days later. I laid it on the floor, up against the wall, underneath a mural that someone had painted, and rolled out my sleeping bag. My leather jacket would double as a pillow. There were some worn Persian carpets on the floor, and a tapestry hung from another wall. The big oil-burning heater in the far corner provided heat, but we couldn't turn it up past the number three on the dial, or it would start belching smoke into the room, so we could never really get the place comfortably warm. The heater came with a five-liter can of heating oil, which we could refill at a petrol station. This was to be our new home, and it suited us. Now we had a place to practice, to cook meals with the Coleman stove, and to sleep at night protected from the elements.

A few doors down, on the corner, there was a bar named the Branderij. It was a smoke-filled, dingy, rough place, with a pool table in the center, a bar along the side, and a small stage in the back. We heard rumors and true stories of fights and knifings and shootings there. It was the kind of joint where one walked softly, and didn't make a lot of eye contact. It was a place where Interpol would come sniffing around every once in a while looking for international fugitives. The owners were Americans of dubious character, rumored to be serious drug dealers. The owner we dealt with was thin and wiry and bearded, and had dark eyes and a dark and mysterious air about him. He reminded me of a biker, with hard, dangerous vibes. But he liked us, and let us play there sometimes on the little stage, and we had use of the bathroom whenever we needed it. We still used the public showers across the IJ, though. Sometimes Vic and Paddy, who were drinking buddies from back in Morning Glory days, would hang out there and have a beer or two. We spent Christmas Eve at the Branderij, playing songs, and drinking and smoking hash, and I spent Christmas day down at Die Kosmos, a New Age hippie teahouse and vegetarian restaurant that included a sauna room for really mellowing out.

I had sent a Christmas card to Sheryl at her parents' address in San Francisco. Two days after Christmas, on a Wednesday, I found a letter waiting for me at the American Express office. It was from Sheryl. I walked down to the war monument at the Dam across the boulevard from the Royal Palace, sat down, carefully opened the envelope, and read its contents slowly, drinking in the words, her essence of thought and feelings set down through her own hand onto paper. And a warm feeling washed over me that dispelled the cold of the winter day. She wrote of her trip home, how she'd landed in New York, and taken a Greyhound to The City. She spoke of us, and how much that time together in Bavaria had meant to her. And she wrote of an uncertain future, how she hadn't settled yet on what she wanted to do with her life. For now she was working in a health food store, and considering whether to go to graduate school. She sent me her love. I folded the letter back into the envelope, stuck it in my shirt pocket under my sweater, and walked back to the cracked house, stopping on a bridge over a canal to gaze for a long time at the murky water, and remember Alpine summer days. Then I walked on.

New Years Eve found us busking in pubs for celebratory drunks, and taking the following day off to recuperate. It was the year of 1973 now, and it presaged new beginnings. Vic was indefatigable in hustling up gigs and places for us to busk, and as the year began we were constantly adding to our circuit, expanding now to places outside of Amsterdam: Haarlem, Utrecht, Purmerend, Zaandam. And more clubs in Amsterdam, with names like the Kater Keller, YMCA Clubhouse, O'Henry's, the Youth Center on Wyde Kapelsteeg, and the Continental Bodega. And there were the regular gigs at De Moor, the Folk Fairport, Melkweg, and others.

Our routine was to play our scheduled gigs, one or two a week, and go out busking the other nights, with Monday nights off. On the tenth of January, we played the Kosmos. Our next gig was for Friday night the twelfth. So Thursday night we went out busking.

On the way back to the cracked house, we stopped off at a little neighborhood brown cafe, and found a table. Vic and Star sat together, and Annie and Paddy, who were in a relationship now, also sat together. I was the odd man out, and sat between the two couples. Everyone ordered beers, but I excused myself, walked outside, and down to the little corner store, where I bought a bottle of Amstel. It was cheaper than paying for it at the cafe, and I was trying to save every guilder I could to buy a new pair of shoes. Mine were about to give out from too many nights of trudging cobblestone streets. I smuggled the beer back under my coat and discreetly opened it. Vic called me a cheapskate. That didn't bother me. What did bother me was the bartender coming over and chewing me out for having the bad form to bring my own drink into a pub. This was not allowed. I felt humiliated.

The lively group of young Dutch folks sitting at the next table had watched the scene unfold, and were now laughing good-naturedly about it. Vic struck up a conversation with them, and Star joined in. He bragged about us being a band and invited everyone to come down and see us at the Melkweg tomorrow night. The group resumed talking and drinking amongst themselves, but one woman turned in her chair to carry on conversation with Vic and Star. She spoke in perfect English, with just a trace of accent, and it was now that I really noticed her for the first time. She took my breath away.

She was a striking blond, with long fine hair that cascaded over her shoulders and down her back. Her lips were full and sensuous but wore no lipstick. The only makeup I could discern was the blue eyeliner that accentuated her ocean blue eyes. Her face had statuesque, well-sculptured features, and although she was seated, I could tell that her body was well proportioned—long and lithe and curvaceous and graceful. Everything about her manner was graceful femininity. She was sexy yet unpretentious, and her bright smile of perfect white teeth lit up her face in natural exuberance, and showed off her dimples. She looked to be in her early to mid-twenties, and I was as if struck dumb and mute. She was out of my league, I concluded, but I managed to screw up enough courage to open my mouth and watch, detached, as the words fell stiffly out into the space between us.

"What is your name?"

"Monika," she said. "And yours?"

"Steve," I croaked.

"Nice to meet you, Steve." She held out her hand to me and I took it. It was soft and warm, yet firm.

"Likewise." I let go of her hand, but could still feel her warmth in my palm.

"Don't forget," Vic was saying, using the pipe in his hand for emphasis, "tomorrow night at the Melkweg. Nine o'clock. You know where it is?"

"Yes," she said with a smile that could melt the heart of a pawnbroker, "I know the place. I'll try to be there, but I don't promise." Then she excused herself and went back to speaking Dutch with her friends, in a voice that sounded like music.

We finished our drinks and walked back to the cracked house. Annie and Paddy, who had a muslin tapestry around their bed for privacy, turned in. I crawled into my sleeping bag and lay on my back, staring into the darkness, and recalling Monika's face. I closed my eyes and still saw her face, especially her eyes and her mouth. I fantasized about her, and could almost feel her in my arms. But it was only imagination, for I knew she'd never go for a guy like me. Or so I thought.

The Leidseplein was a great square within the ring of canals of the Centrum, walled in by buildings old and new, many of which housed pubs and restaurants and outdoor cafes, theatres and cinemas. Tram tracks ran like a maze though it, and at night it was all lit up in festive colors like a carnival. We sometimes walked or took the tram out there to do a bit of busking. There was a gay bar there that especially loved us and our music, and the bartender would set us up with drinks while someone passed the hat around for us. There was always a party atmosphere in the gay bar, and it was nice to come inside to its warmth and friendliness from a freezing cold or stormy, rain filled night. When we were in the Leidseplein, we would make it our last stop before heading home. One night on the Leidseplein as we were walking along, instruments in hand, a woman stopped us and asked us what we were doing.

"Playing music," said Vic. "We're musicians."

"Yes, but what do you do for a living? Are you students?"

"No, we're musicians."

"But you can't make a living at music," she insisted. "You must do something else."

"Nevertheless, here we are, as you can see, with our instruments, and this is how we make our living."

Then, after she left, shaking her head in disbelief, Vic turned to me and said, "That's what Star's dad tried to tell me before we left the States. 'You can't make a living traveling around playing music in this day and age.' Guess he was wrong, eh Dupree?"

The Melkweg, or "Milky Way," as it translates to English, was situated off to one side of the Leidseplein, and one block over on Lijnbaansgracht, next to a canal. From the outside, it looked like an old warehouse, a small two-story red brick building with large windows and a peaked roof. Dozens of bicycles were usually chained up out in front. The letters spelling *"Melkweg"* were written in silver script above the windows under the roofline, and silver six-pointed stars were set around the letters. On the ground floor were steel double doors that opened to a ticket booth and waiting room, and beyond that were more double doors that led to a large listening room. A light booth was on one side of the room, and a stage took up most of the other side. In-between were a dance floor, tables and chairs, and a carpeted area with cushions and oversized pillows to sit on. On Friday night, we climbed up the side stairs onto the stage, stepped up to the microphones, and looked out into a crowd of friendly young faces. Following Vic's introduction, we launched into our set of acoustic, eclectic folk music.

I scanned the room looking for Monika, and found her standing on the dance floor in front of us. She was dressed in blue denim jeans and a brown leather jacket over a beige sweater. I smiled at her. She smiled back. My pulse raced. Toward the end of the set, Vic let me have my solo. I sang a love song I had written, and looked directly at her as I sang. She smiled, blushed, and looked away. Then she met my gaze again. I wanted the song to last forever, but forever turned out to be two and a half minutes, then it was Annie's turn to shine with a fiddle tune. I continued to let my eyes wander back to Monika until our one-hour performance was finished. A rock band was coming on next. We packed up our instruments and left the stage.

I sought out Monika in the audience, and found her still near the stage, talking with friends. I interrupted the conversation.

"Hi! I'm glad you could make it."

"Are you playing more later?" she said, turning toward me. I now noticed that she was about my height and nicely built.

"No, just the one set. Another band is coming on."

"You were very good. I enjoyed it. But I think that maybe Vic is an egotist. Is that the right word?"

"Yes, it is."

Then she introduced me to her friends, a couple she had come with. Noticing she didn't have a guy on her arm, I asked her if she'd like to have a drink, so we headed over to the bar and I ordered for us. There was nowhere to sit, so we drank our wine and chatted while we stood, and as the next band was taking the stage, I asked her if she'd like to go some place quieter and she said yes.

"Where should we go to?" I asked.

"You could walk me home, if you like. I live not far from here on the Nieuw Keizersgracht. Do you know it?"

"No, but you can show me the way."

We walked along together down the Kerkstraat, and near the Magere Brug, the narrow white wooden drawbridge across the Amstel River, that was always lit up cheerfully at night. She turned to me and said, "When you sang your song you were looking right at me. I felt as if you were singing just to me."

"I was."

She smiled, linked her arm in mine and we walked on. When we reached the bridge, I stopped and put down my guitar. We faced each other tentatively, and then I took her in my arms and kissed her. She pressed up close to me and said, "I wondered when you were going to do that." We kissed again, and we melted into each other's arms as if that was where we naturally belonged. She whispered in my ear, "Let's hurry to my flat. I'm getting wet."

As we crossed over onto Nieuw Keizersgracht, it began raining, so we hurried down to the corner her flat was on, in a five-story gabled brick building. It was student housing, she explained. She was a graduate student of psychology. We walked up the steps and into the building, and climbed a narrow, winding staircase to the second floor. I followed her down a hallway, and she unlocked her door, switched on the light, and led me inside. It was a single room with a twin bed and nightstand, and a loveseat under a window that looked out onto a courtyard. There was a sink in the corner, and a bookshelf took up a part of one wall, while shelves on another wall held a stereo and records, among other things. A table and two chairs took up the remaining space. She closed the door behind me and said, "Put your guitar down, and make yourself at home. I'll get us a drink. Do you like *jenever*?"

"Sure. Thank you." I sat on the edge of the bed, and the grey cat that had been lying there bolted away.

"That's Oedipus," she laughed, and then said something soothing in Dutch to the cat. She crossed the room and brought out a bottle of the Dutch gin and two small glasses, into which she poured the clear liquid. She handed one to me and set hers down on the nightstand, and lit the candle there. Then she lit another one that was on the table and turned off the light switch.

"There, that's better, don't you think?"

"Much better."

She sat on the loveseat, and I put down my glass and sat next to her, and began kissing and caressing her. She shuddered softly and whispered in my ear, "Would you like to stay here tonight?"

I said that I would, very much so, and she stood and undressed in the candlelight. I followed her lead, and could not take my eyes off her as more of her beautiful form was slowly revealed to me, until we both stood naked in the candle glow, and I thought how this moment was just too perfect, and maybe I was dreaming the whole thing. But I wasn't, because just then, we stepped into each other's arms, embracing and kissing, before snuggling into her small bed and making passionate love. Afterwards I slept peacefully, waking once in the pre-dawn to admire her face as she dreamt.

In the morning, she explained to me that there was a communal kitchen on her floor, as well as a communal bathroom and shower that I could use if I liked. After I showered, she fixed us a breakfast of rolls, meat and cheese, and coffee, and when I left, we promised to see each other again. She said she had classes during the day, and volunteered several nights a week at the Crisis Center near the Vondelpark. It was sort of an internship for her to practice her counseling skills on junkies and people having bad acid trips. You didn't have to look far to find them, she said, as the Vondelpark was a place where down-and-out hippies and street people could camp out at night, with the tacit approval of the authorities. I was entranced by the sound of Monika's voice as she spoke, for although she was fluent in English, she had just enough of an accent to sound exotic and sexy.

This was the beginning of my relationship with Monika, and I saw her every chance I got, Of course our schedules didn't match, but we worked it out anyway. Monika became my friend and companion and lover, and our relationship gave me a life outside of the band. Sometimes she would come to hear us play, and then after the gig I would walk her home. Other times after the band had finished a night of gigging or busking, I would walk over to her place and around back to the courtyard, where I could see the windows of her room, the light shining cheerfully inside, and I would stand there in the rain and the cold and throw pebbles against her window to get her attention. Then her face would appear between the curtains and she would smile and gesture that she was going downstairs to unlock the door. I would meet her at the front stairs, and we would go up to her room, where she would put away her studies, and we would spend a quiet time together, talking, listening to music, drinking wine or *jenever*, and then make love.

On Mondays, the band's night off, we would go out on dates together to restaurants and the cinema, or to pubs and cafes. Because she knew I was poor, she would always pay her own way. Even on our first date, she did so, saying, "This is what you call Dutch treat, isn't it?" Some nights, we would just walk around the city and she would point out places of interest and explain their history. "That is the Weeper's Tower," she said of the Schreierstoren, the old brick tower overlooking the harbor. "In the old times, when sailors would go off to sea, the wives and lovers would watch from the tower and wave goodbye and weep from sadness."

Of course there were nights when she'd be working at the Crisis Center, and I would just go back to the cracked house and sleep. And there were days when she didn't have classes when we would get together and sometimes ride around on her bicycle. And on the days when she was in class, I would walk around exploring the city by myself.

As winter settled in resolutely, days became much colder, with the canals freezing over. Occasionally snow would fall lightly, like the night we went busking along the big town square in Haarlem, outside of Amsterdam, walking along frozen cobblestones. When the flakes began falling, just before we reached the Ship Pub, the air actually warmed up a bit. Often on cold or wet days I would leave the cracked house and take shelter inside warm buildings, like the Tropical Museum, or the Anne Frank House on Prinsengracht. The first time I went there, on a February afternoon, I was alone in the building for a good fifteen minutes before a group of tourists showed up. I wandered through the small hiding place and thought about the two families who had taken refuge there from the Nazis before being discovered and shipped off to the death camps. It felt as if I were sharing the space with ghosts.

On days when I would stroll along the Nieuwezijds Voorburgwal, the pedestrian-only shopping street behind the Damrak, I would stop in front of a travel bureau and gaze longingly at posters of sun-drenched Greek islands and imagine being there. Next winter, I would tell myself. And when it wasn't raining or snowing, it was windy and overcast or foggy. Like Jeff, I came down with an upper respiratory infection for a few days, and wasn't able to go out busking one night, and so forfeited any pay. But no matter how poor I was in Amsterdam, I never missed a meal nor felt deprived. For the fact of the matter was that I was making a living at music, no matter how marginal, and that brought me a certain amount of satisfaction.

All through that long winter we continued to expand our circuit, adding places like the Paradiso, the big rock club on the Leidseplein, as well as clubs and youth centers outside of Amsterdam. Vic wanted bigger things for us, and was constantly hustling. He dropped in on a music publisher who showed some interest in publishing his songs, but wouldn't commit to doing so, although he did come to one of our gigs and listen. Undaunted, Vic borrowed a tape recorder from someone, and had us record a demo tape upstairs in the Melkweg one afternoon. Then he used the demo tape to get us an audition with a record label in Hilversum, southeast of Amsterdam. Vic was certain that our fortunes were about to change, but after the audition, that idea was quickly laid to rest, when a staff producer told us that he wasn't interested in signing us.

"What are you looking for?" I asked diplomatically.

"A hit record," said the company man. "They're few and far between. But don't give up," he added. "It's a long, hard row to hoe."

Vic didn't take the news in stride. He had a few sharp words to impart to the producer, and then sulked in the back of the VW all the way back to Amsterdam while Star tried unsuccessfully to cheer him up.

Often our good paying gigs were few and far between, and in those times Vic and Paddy would have a beer tab going at De Moor, which they would pay off when they were flush from a good paying gig. When things were really tight, we would play for a meal at the university's student cafeteria, and then play for drinks in their adjoining pub. And as each week passed, I watched the wrecking ball slowly getting closer to our neighborhood, as it tore down buildings along the path of where the new subway was to be dug. We knew we would eventually have to find another place to live, and so we began asking around, but came up with nothing. There was additional pressure on me to find my own place, as the pickle factory basement was okay for two couples, but I was one person too many. And so I put the word out that I was looking for a new crash pad.

As soon as Paddy had joined the band, Vic had decided that I should play bass again, and I agreed. We really didn't need two guitars anymore, since we had the banjo. But it took us a couple of months to save up enough money to buy a cheap Hofner electric bass and a small amplifier. I still took my guitar along when we went busking, but when we had a regular paying gig, we brought the bass and amp. Eventually, we were playing all around Amsterdam and Holland, and were approached one day by a young bearded Dutchman who introduced himself as Pieter Groothuis, (which translated to "Peter Big House") and offered to manage us.

"My partner Simon and I have an agency called Holland Folk Promotions, on Herengracht, and we've been watching you for some time," he said to Vic. "I think you're ready to take the next big step, and so we'd like to manage you." Vic and Pieter (who we began calling "Big House Pete") hammered out the details, and signed an agreement. In no time, Holland Folk Promotions had lined us up with some bigger gigs, and some live radio performances, and began beating the bushes to get us a recording contract. Pete also heard of a new music venue named Boddy's Music Inn. It was owned by a couple who also owned the Hotel Weigman, an American named Ted and his Dutch wife Nicky. The Boddys also doubled as concert promoters, bringing over bands from the States to play at the Concertgebouw, the big concert hall in Amsterdam. Boddy's Music Inn would serve as a place for the bands to practice, and they would be required to do a free show there after their big concert. On nights when there wasn't a big-name band in town, they would book other groups to play there. So without an appointment, we just walked into the Hotel Weigman and gave an impromptu audition. Ted agreed to book us, and we began playing at their club from time to time.

Spring took its time in arriving, for although the temperature warmed up little by little, most days were still overcast, and a cold wind from the North Sea often blew thick white clouds across the sky, sometimes with a near-gale force. By this time, Vic and Paddy were drinking to excess, and it began to hurt our reputation. At one gig, the money we were paid didn't cover our bar tab. The bartender renamed us "Drunken Zeke's Band." Vic and I argued about the excessive drinking, but his solution was to bring our own stash of beer the next time. When Vic wasn't fighting with me, he was at it with bartenders, club owners, and whatever other hands fed us. When they'd have enough of it, we'd become *personas non gratis*, and I'd have to slink back to the offended party the next day to apologize, and hope we would get the gig back. Sometimes this tactic would work, but my pleadings fell on deaf ears after we got fired from our live radio gig. Vic bitched that we weren't getting paid enough, and unless we got a raise, we weren't returning. As with the Song Parnaus in Munich, we didn't return.

On the other hand, the longer we stayed in Amsterdam, the more people we met and befriended. Some of them were American expatriates, others from European countries and Canada, and of course the local "Dutchies," as Vic called them. We ran across another band from the States, a duo called "Home Cooking." They consisted of a guitarist and banjo player, and mainly did bluegrass music. Because they worked some of the same joints as us, we'd cross paths a lot. One weekend our friend Buddhix, the German folksinger from Dusseldorf, showed up at the cracked house. Vic had written to him, so he was able to find us easily. He was up our way looking for gigs, and we did some song swapping, learning one of his songs, "Streets of Amsterdam," and put it into our repertoire. He stayed with us a few days, sleeping in the VW, and we showed him around to places like the Folk Fairport and Boddy's Music Inn.

I continued putting out the word that I was looking for another place to stay, and finally, late in March, a flat came my way in the form of another cracked house, out past the Rijksmuseum and the Heineken brewery, in an old quarter known as De Pijp. The coldwater flat was at 161 Govert Flinck Straat, a long narrow street with tall brownstone buildings, cluttered and jutting up toward the sky. The next street over was the Albert Cuypstraat, an open-air market that ran for several blocks. There were public showers on Albert Cuypstraat as well, which was a great bonus, as my new place didn't have a shower. But it had a small kitchen with a stove and a sink, and there was a shared bathroom down the hall, which made it an improvement from the place on Koningsstraat. The flat was on the second floor, and besides the small kitchen, it had one large room with a window that overlooked the narrow cobblestone street below. It was furnished with a single mattress on the floor, a couple of cushions under the window, and a radio. The Dutch hippie who had been living there, a guy I knew from one of the clubs we played at regularly, was moving in with his girlfriend in Haarlem, and generously offered it to me. Vic asked me to give the place up to himself and Star, trading me for the cold dank back room of the pickle factory, but I told him no, which led to some discord between us for a while. I had my own place now, and felt very prosperous indeed. Adding to my sense of prosperity was the fact that I'd finally saved up enough money for new shoes, and had bought a pair of desert boots at the Waterlooplein flea market for a few guilders.

Spring had hung out on the porch long enough, and was now knocking at the door. I stuffed all my belongings into my backpack, and with the pack on my shoulders and my guitar in hand I headed across town to my new place, climbed the stairs to the second floor, unlocked the door, and got settled in. First thing I did was to light a burner on the stove, to heat the place up. Then I got out my guitar and started writing a song for Monika.

CHAPTER SEVENTEEN

The Cobblestone Circuit

The winds of March blew in the rains of April, which had now softened. The air became a little warmer, and the sun shone more brightly, interspersed with clouds, and the smells of the harbor and the North Sea mingled with the smells of the earth coming alive, trees and tulips blooming, and there was no mistaking the fact that spring had at last arrived in Holland.

We had been knocking about Amsterdam for five months, and we'd settled into a regular circuit that gradually expanded ever further, as we discovered each new place to busk or a new gig to play. We were venturing out of Amsterdam more often, playing gigs in towns and cities to the north and south and east. We even picked up some regular busking spots in Haarlem and Utrecht, usually around the town centers. We would find a convenient spot to park the van, then stroll along the cobblestones to the little pubs and bars, and restaurants and bistros, and after we'd done a round of songs, Star would pass the hat and we'd be on our way again, to the next joint. We had a regular circuit in Amsterdam as well, and I was content to be hoofing it down alleyways and along canal streets, for now I had a comfortable pair of shoes, and it made a difference. We were still living hand to mouth, but with the warmer weather and Pete's promises of lining us up with "something big," we soldiered on. For a while, Vic and I even got along together, and it felt like more than just a truce.

There were exceptions of course, like the night we were playing a gig in a small bar in Amsterdam. At the break I went out looking for a bite to eat, a *broodje* or some *frites*, and stayed gone too long.

By the time I returned, the band was on it's second set, Vic shot me a murderous glare, and rather than join them onstage, I just stood with the audience for a while and enjoyed the show. After a couple of songs, I returned to the fold, but by then Vic was so worked up about it that he threatened to withhold my pay again.

But as I said, during the spring we mostly got on together, and when I wasn't needed for rehearsals or gigs, I spent much of my free time with Monika, and my relationship with her nurtured and soothed me, taking my mind off frictions within the band. Often, after a night of busking, I would wander along canal streets, seeing green leaves budding out on trees, the moon shining brightly, and the brownstone buildings and the canal boats reflected in the lightly-rippled shimmering water. I'd walk over the little Magere Brug drawbridge across the Amstel carrying my guitar, and over cobblestones and sidewalks to Monika's student apartment building, climb the steps and ring the doorbell. A voice would come over the intercom and I'd say, "*Erste etage*", and when a voice would answer on the second floor, I'd ask for Monika, and the door would be buzzed open and I'd climb the narrow stairs and meet her smiling face at her door. Sometimes, if the band had had an early gig, or I had a night off, I'd pick up Monika and we'd go out for a drink or to a café or a movie. But mostly we stayed in, and made love by candlelight and I got lost in her limpid blue eyes.

The *Polite* came sniffing around the Branderij on a regular basis, looking for desperados and criminal drug activity, and eventually they caught glimpses of Vic and Star entering or exiting the cracked house on Koningsstraat. Vic always made himself conspicuous, so it was inevitable that the police would nab him. It came one night in May, as Vic was entering the building while the cops were exiting the Branderij. They checked the passports of Vic and Star, also of Paddy and Annie, and gave the lot their marching orders. They were to vacate the premises, and get out of town ASAP. But where could they relocate to? There weren't many options available. At first Vic suggested he and Star move into my place, with Paddy and Annie moving into the bus, and me moving in with Monika. But I nixed that idea right off the bat. So it became a game of cat and mouse between Vic and the police, while he hustled up another place to stay. Vic got a lead on a hippie cooperative in Delft, so we drove up there to check it out. We could see right away that it wouldn't work out for us, and besides it was too far from Amsterdam, where we needed to work.

Then Big House Pete came through for us. When he wasn't managing or promoting us, Pete worked at a music store on the Haarlemmerstraat, and lived in the room above the store. He made arrangements to move in with a friend and gave up his attic space to Annie and Paddy. Behind the store was a small room for Vic and Star. So one day, we packed up our gear from the pickle factory basement and piled everything into the VW bus, and like the Anne Frank family going into hiding from the Nazis, we moved across town to the new hideout. I continued to stay at my flat on Govert Flinckstraat, but decided to lay low and keep out of sight. I hadn't yet met any of the other tenants of the cracked house, but now I made an effort to avoid them, as if I were a wanted man. When I played the radio (tuned in to Radio Caroline or the BBC), I kept it down low, as I did my singing and guitar playing. Before using the bathroom down the hall, I would crack the door open an inch and peer out to make sure no one was around. Of course I was just being paranoid, the police never came around my little neighborhood, or seemed to care who was living there, but for a while I played the fugitive-in-hiding game, and seemed to enjoy it in a perverse sort of way.

After the rest of the band was settled into their new safe house, where they were about as legal as they were going to get, Pete gave us some good news. He had lined up a spot for us on the bill at the Enschede Folk Festival, for the first and second of June. He was also trying to get us into the prestigious Cambridge Folk Festival, held in the summer. And he had been scouting out record labels on our behalf, and had found a producer from BASF Records who had agreed to hear us at the festival in Enschede, and if he liked us, might be willing to sign us to a contract. Vic reveled in the news. "I told you to stick with me, Dupree," he gloated, "and I'd put you in the Big Time."

Once Vic was convinced he was about to assume his proper place as a star, he began to resent having to busk. However, it was still a necessity of getting by, so we continued to pound the cobblestones. When we'd had the place on Koningsstraat, we had left the VW parked out front on the street. But now, we kept it near my flat, for two reasons: there was a place nearby where I could safely park it, and I was the only one who could drive a stick shift, or even had a driver's license for that matter. So I would pick the band up and drive to gigs, and sometimes to go out busking. We spent the next few weeks leading up to the folk festival routinely doing the regular gigs at places like Boddy's Music Inn, the Folk Fairport, De Moor, and out of town clubs, while making the rounds of our busking circuit, being careful not to hit the same place more than twice in the same week.

On the first weekend in June, Pieter Groothuis and his partner Simon drove down to Enschede, with us following behind in the VW. We parked, and then checked into the folk festival, which was held inside a large auditorium with a sizable stage. Among the groups on the bill were: Sonny Terry and Brownie McGee, Mike and Alice Seeger, and Chuck Pyle from the United States; Michael Chapman, Sandy Denny, and the Albion Country Band from Great Britain; and The Country Ramblers from Holland, to name a few. We hung around backstage, mingling with the other musicians and feeling important, before taking the stage to do our set. Vic sang all the songs, and Annie played an instrumental, and then we exited. Everything had gone off without a hitch for a change, Vic was on his best behavior and refrained from pissing anyone off, and so we considered the gig a success, as did our managers. We met the producer from BASF, a young guy named Jan who shook our hands and told us he enjoyed our music. Then he turned to Pete and said, "Yes, I think we can make a deal with you. I'll draw up a contract and we'll make an appointment next week for signing."

A few days later I got the message from Monika, who had a phone on her floor, that we were having a band meeting the following afternoon at the office of Holland Folk Promotions. When I walked in, everyone was seated or standing—Vic, Star, Annie and Paddy, and Pieter and Simon. Jan, the producer, was conspicuous only in his absence.

"I thought we were here to sign some papers," I said to no one in particular, as I found a place in the corner to stand.

"They've already been signed," said Big House Pete, turning his gaze away from me to Vic.

I must have looked puzzled because Vic turned to me with that very serious look he'd get when he wanted me to know he was in charge.

"Yeah, you're a little late, Dupree, so I'll fill you in," he said, looking down and making a big production out of filling his pipe with tobacco. "The contract is in my name," he continued, fixing his gaze back on me, but shifting his eyes back and forth to Star, as if for encouragement. "Jan and Pete thought it would be easier that way, you know."

"No, actually I don't know," I said in measured tones. "Why don't you illuminate me?"

"Well, you see, the record label only wants to deal with one person, and since I'm the band leader, they dealt with me. So I signed for all of us. The contract is in my name for a one-off single, and if it does well, we'll renegotiate for an album. What this means for you, Dupree, is that you're a hired hand now. I know we haven't been getting along real well lately, and I've had to take a lot of your shit. But that's all changed now. We're supposed to go into the studio in a couple of weeks and cut two sides. They'll be my songs, of course. But I'll let you play bass and sing harmony on them as long as you promise to shape up and quit being such a pain in the ass."

"What the hell?" I said angrily. I gave a pleading look to Annie and Paddy, but they sheepishly spoke up in Vic's defense.

"Sorry, Steve," said Paddy, "but Vic and I go back a long ways. I gotta side with him."

"He's right," added Annie. "We like you, but Vic is the leader, and he has been representing us and getting us a lot of the gigs."

"Hey, everything's cool," said Pete. "We're the same band, the same organization. It's just a matter of formality."

"So what's it going to be, Steve? Stick with the band or quit?" Vic said as an ultimatum.

I felt trapped. There was a long pause while I tried to sort things out in my mind. If I quit, how would I get by? I wasn't competent or confident enough to go out on my own. Besides, I really loved the music we made, and the whole camaraderie of being in a group.

"I just want to make music," I said finally in resignation, trying not to betray my anger. "I'll stick it out."

"Okay," said Vic. "But from now on, consider yourself on probation."

"I'm glad you're staying," said Annie.

I looked around the room and the expressions I saw written on faces were mostly of relief that this tense scene was over. Now we could get on to more important matters. The rest of the meeting was the working out of details—the songs we would record, where and when we would record, and Holland Folk Promotions' plans for us. I just listened, feeling stunned and vulnerable. I remembered that I'd put the band together, and had included Vic after the fact. But that's not the way he saw it, and I was certain he felt justified in his position. We had no gig that night, so I walked over to Monika's place later on, told her the story, and how betrayed I felt about the whole thing. I'd hoped she would give me some understanding and consolation, but her advice was something I didn't want to hear.

"You know that Vic is an egotist," she said curtly. "I don't know why you put up with him. He always treats you so shitty. You're a good enough singer to just do it on your own. You don't need him."

"But I like playing in the band," I countered weakly.

"Then I can't help you. You'll just have to go on putting up with him."

And so I did, for a while anyway.

We rehearsed Vic's two songs diligently every day for over a week, and got so tight with them we could do them in our sleep, and I probably did. Once we got into the studio in Hilversum, we found it to be a large and professional setup, which pleased us all. Jan had explained to Pete and Vic that we'd be recording at the end of someone else's session, and were included in that artist's budget. Jan wanted to record us live, no over dubs, and he emphasized we only had an hour to do it in. While we waited around in another room, Jan put down the bass part on the song he was producing for the other artist. When he had finished, and told us it was time to start setting up our mikes, I complimented him on his bass, a Rickenbacker, and his playing technique.

"Thank you," he said with a smile. "I enjoy playing bass. I play it in my own band, you know."

"You have a band?" said Vic.

"Yes, a pop group."

"I think pop music is lame," said Vic with an air of disdain. "It all sounds the same."

"I like pop music," I countered. "I always have."

"Well, boys, it's all good now, isn't it?"

He called us boys, although he was about the same age as us, and I couldn't tell if he meant to use that word as American slang, or if he was being deferential. I decided to believe the first impression, because I liked Jan. He was open, friendly, charming, and sincere. He was slender, had long hair stylishly cut, and wore the latest in European fashion. In other words, he was hip but in a classy way. He also knew his business. He capably set up all the microphones in the center of the room, two mikes for each person—one for vocals, the other an instrument mike. My electric bass was plugged into a direct box that went into the mixing board. Then he went inside the control booth with the recording engineer, and had us test for recording levels, after which he came back out into the main room to give us a pep talk.

"Okay," he said, "let's make a few passes on the first song. What's the name of it again?"

"'My Cabin In The Pines,'" said Vic, his voice tense.

"Yeah, dat's it. So we will try it out, for levels. I'll be behind the glass and will be able to talk to you over your headphones. So here we go, *ja*? Let's relax and have some fun, shall we?"

With that advice, he ducked back into the control room and we donned our headphones. I looked at Vic and he had the same expression on his face that I'd remembered from the Reverbs days when we were in studios. He was tense, serious, and his eyes conveyed anxiety. I closed my own eyes and listened in my headphones.

"Okay, boys, here we go—we're rolling."

Vic counted off, "One-two-three-four", his foot stomping off the count as well, and we were off and running. By the fifth or sixth take, we were warmed up enough that the next take was a keeper. Then it was on to the second song, and soon we were finished with it as well. Jan came back into the room and congratulated us, told us he and the engineer would spend some time mixing the tapes, and we should take a little break. When they were done, they would have us listen to a finished mix, and then a staff photographer would shoot photos of us to put on the cover of the single. I breathed an inaudible sigh of relief. It was over, and Vic hadn't screwed it up.

Jan had explained to us that the record would be released in September, and we would be paid according to record sales. We all took this as good news, but more importantly for me it was a vindication of my decision to stay with the band, keep my mouth shut, and just go along with Vic, whatever he wanted to do. We gathered outside with our instruments in hand, and posed for group photos against the side of the building that housed the recording studio. Not very imaginative maybe, but no matter, according to Vic we were on our way to the Big Time

Finished with the recording and attendant business, we drove down the road to a restaurant for a meal, and after the food was delivered, Vic gave us a talk.

"I've been thinking things over," he began. "I took a look at the calendar, and we've got nothing lined up for July. Our first paid gig isn't until the first weekend in August. The record won't be out till September, so we really can't use it right now to promote ourselves. I don't know about the rest of you, but Star and I have had a belly full of busking around here."

"What's your point, Vic?" I asked cautiously.

"Well, here's what Star and I were thinking—why not go on the road? Do some barnstorming, get out of Holland for a while."

"How can we do that?" I said. "There's a big stamp in all our passports that says we're not allowed in Holland. Once we split, we can't get back in."

"I've thought about that. We can go through Belgium. There's no border check between Belgium and Holland. It's perfect. We'll go through Belgium and do some busking across France. Star speaks some French, don't you dear?"

"Oui, mon amour."

"We could even barnstorm down along the coast of Italy, and still be back in Amsterdam for our paid gigs. What do you think?"

"Sounds like fun," said Annie.

"I could use a change," said Paddy.

"Count me in," I said.

"Okay, it's settled then," said Vic. "Let's plan on heading out next week, right after the Melkweg gig."

Later in the week I went over to Monika's to share the news of the upcoming single, and to tell her I'd be gone on the road for about a month. She seemed very withdrawn and uncomfortable with me, and after I explained our July travel plans, she hesitated before replying, and then said, "Well, maybe that's for the best."

There was a pause before she answered the question in my eyes, and when she did so, she stepped over to the window and gazed out onto the courtyard below and said quietly, "I've been unhappy with our relationship for a while, and I think this is a good time to end it."

"Why?" I asked feeling my throat choke up and a knot form in my stomach.

"I can't say why," she continued. "I just feel like I need a change. I don't really see our relationship going anywhere. I mean, here you are, an American traveling around. You could never stay in one place too long. I just want something better, that's all. Besides, I met a new man I want to date."

"Oh," I said quietly. No other words would come.

She turned to me now. "But it's not about you—you've done nothing wrong. You've been very sweet and dear and kind to me, and I'll always remember you that way. And I don't want you to be angry, in fact I hope we can still be friends."

"Of course we can," I said, stung and stunned. "And I hope you'll be happy."

"Thank you," she said, seemingly relieved, and then kissed me on the cheek. I wanted to take her in my arms and hold her tight and kiss her hard, but instead with an air of defeat I picked up my guitar, told her I would send her postcards from the road, and walked out of her flat and back out onto the sidewalk below, where I spent the next hour wandering along canal streets and remembering all the good times we'd spent together, before heading back to my lonely little room on Govert Flinckstraat. Maybe getting in the wind would be therapeutic for the pain I felt in my heart, and help me forget that I had once been in love with a Dutch lady, here in Amsterdam.

CHAPTER EIGHTEEN

Jumping Borders

Summer had arrived, and I knew irrefutably that it had done so, for when I opened my eyes, the morning sun was shining brightly on my face, and the air was warm. The dew on the ground was beginning to evaporate, and I could smell the richness of the earth beneath my sleeping bag and the fullness of the countryside, and I could hear the cheerful singing of birds and the buzzing of insects. I looked about at the rich greenness of trees and fields and realized that I was lying supine in a farmer's field somewhere in the north of France, and when I rolled over on my side, I saw our white VW bus parked on the other side of a fence, just off a country road. I was uncomfortably warm, so I stretched, zipped the sleeping bag open, and pulled on clothing, recalling the events of the recent past which had brought me, and the rest of Uncle Zeke's Band, to this place and time.

We had been delayed almost a week in Amsterdam with a couple of last minute gigs—a "beach party" in Zandaam and a birthday party gig in Amersfoort that Big House Pete had sprung on us, and they had paid well enough for us to hang around. But finally, at the end of the first week in July, we got in the wind, heading first to Antwerp, where we drove around until we spotted a likely pub to busk in.

Antwerp was in the north of Belgium, near Holland, and the Belgians there spoke Flemish, a dialect of the Dutch language. The bartender of the pub we walked into spoke very good English, and so it was easy setting something up. As it turned out, we didn't have to busk after all, as the bartender was also the owner and so he hired us to play a couple of sets. We discovered right away that he served Belgian ale on tap, brewed by Trappist monks, and so we liberally availed ourselves of strong sweet brew, although I held back, as I was the designated and only driver. Later we drove on into the night, crossing the border to France without incident, and turned off the main road until we found a quiet and likely spot to bed down. Now we were all up and stirring about, and Star fixed us an improvised breakfast. I consulted our map, and then we headed back to the main road, looking for a café where we could get a decent cup of coffee.

The highway we were on could have taken us into Paris, but Vic decided against going there. "Dealing with the Frogs is bad enough," he pronounced, "but the ones in Paris are even worse. I don't think they'll be very glad to see a band of scruffy American hippies. Let's just skip it and head to the south of France where things are a little less uptight."

So I charted a course that would take us southeast, through Reims, and soon we were in wine country, the green vineyards stretching on for miles. Outside of Chalons-en-Champagne, where the champagne grapes grew, Vic spotted what looked like a truck stop café, with lorries cluttering up the parking lot, and since it was about lunch time he said, "Pull over, this looks like a good place to eat."

We parked and filed inside, and were seated at a long table with other diners, and were given menus. Star translated for us, and when the food arrived, it was spectacular—a multi-course meal that began with a large bowl of salad placed on the table, family style, followed by loaves of bread, a large bowl of mashed potatoes, and a couple of carafes of red wine. Then we were served delicious platters of chicken in wine sauce, and vegetables, and for dessert we were presented with trays of grapes and cheeses, and coffee. The best part of the meal for me was that it only cost us a few francs each, amounting to about three dollars American.

Completely sated and satisfied, we headed down the road again until we came into the city of Dijon, where we parked the VW downtown and set off on foot with our instruments, looking for a place to busk, which we soon found in the form of a saloon that combined old and modern French style.

A chic bar with stools and a mirror on the wall behind it was on one side of the spacious well-lit room, and a floor-to-ceiling mirror ran across the whole of the opposite side of the room, where red upholstered booths were set along the wall. Down the center of the room were arranged small round tables and chairs, occupied by young couples, smartly dressed, sipping wine and beers and aperitifs, and smoking strong *Gitanes* cigarettes, which laced the room with wispy clouds of blue smoke. I spotted a beautiful blond French girl with full red painted lips smiling at me in a flirtatious manner. But when I returned her smile, the boyfriend who sat next to her in tight-fitting slacks and a white shirt with big lapels, opened at the second button to reveal a gold chain, sneered at me with a cigarette hanging from his lower lip. So I turned from her gaze as Vic and Star negotiated a busking session for us with the bartender. After a quick set and a pass with the hat, we were out the door and Vic said, "Let's get in the wind."

We headed south again, now in the Rhone valley and following the course of the river until we came to the old Roman city of Lyon. After finding a likely district and a place to park, we came across an outdoor café, where we played and sang. Star passed the hat, and then we found a restaurant to spend some of that money on glasses of wine and a meal. After settling up the bill and leaving a tip, we began walking out of the place when we were accosted by the waiter, who began arguing loudly with Star, claiming we hadn't paid anything. The manager joined in, and we could tell we were being clipped because we were Americans, but it was turning into such a big scene, that we knew our only recourse before they called the cops was to pay them off a second time. This not only wiped out the funds we'd just made from busking, but dipped into our savings as well.

As we walked away grumbling, with Vic shooting the waiter the bird, I watched as a couple of guys parked their Renault across the street, and began walking away. That they had forgotten to set the parking brake became obvious immediately, as the car began coasting away downhill. I yelled out at them, and at the same time began chasing the car as it picked up speed. I was able to catch it, yank open the door, jump in, and jam on the brake. Vic had been chasing the car as well, and just as I brought it to a stop, he jumped in front, and placed his hands on the hood, his feet braced apart.

As I climbed out, he said to me, "Hey, we did a good job stopping that runaway." I just looked at him stunned that he was already taking credit for something in which he was a dubious participant.

The two young guys came running over, and the one I assumed to be the driver was smiling sheepishly and thanking us. We could have made some new friends right then and there, but Vic began taunting him and calling him an idiot in French, which was one of the very few French words he knew. The driver's smile vanished in an instant, and he and his friend became suddenly surly, shouting back at Vic and me in words I couldn't understand, but the gist of which was obvious.

"Let's go," I said to Vic. "Now!"

Vic continued to taunt the Frenchmen as we walked rapidly back to the VW, with them in angry pursuit.

"Let's get out of this place," I yelled across the street to Star, Annie, and Paddy. They needed no further prompting. As we pulled out of Lyon, I felt that if we'd been on foot any longer, we'd have been run down by an angry mob waving pitchforks and torches. Bad vibes. We continued on south, through more wine country, as Vic recounted again how he had stopped a runaway car and instead of appreciation, all he'd gotten was verbal abuse from some "idiot Frogs." The sun was beginning to set as we put Lyon behind us, and again we pulled off the main highway and found a field to camp in.

It was another bright and warm morning that we awoke to, and after cleaning up a little, we headed out on the road again, off the main highway but still following the Rhone River toward Orange. Now a sense of déjà vu hit me as we entered the region of Provence, and I felt a sense of familiarity about the countryside, and the cliffs to our east, and the smells of the rich earth, and even the strong morning light, as if I'd been here before. Maybe it was only that it reminded me of Southern California, but a nostalgic feeling of homecoming washed over me.

Still north of Orange, we had just passed through a small village when a sudden rainstorm erupted, bringing a heavy downpour. Water began rushing along the road, like the kind of flash flood that hits the deserts of the American Southwest in the summer, and I could tell that the water was rising exceptionally fast. Just as I began driving into a low water crossing, I froze up and hit the brake.

"We'd better turn around," I said, and as I began doing so, the water rose halfway up the tires. Frantically, I turned the VW around and started heading back uphill, the flood following close behind us. We topped a hill, and around a curve in the road I spotted a restaurant.

"Let's hole up here for a while," I said as we pulled into the parking lot and came to a stop by the side of the building. Once inside, we ordered coffee and croissants as we watched the rain lash down and the water begin to flood the parking lot. Then there was a burst of activity as the owners broke out towels and tablecloths and stuffed them around the bottom of the door to hold the floodwaters back. A short while later, the storm let up as suddenly as it had struck, the sun broke through the clouds, and the water receded. With the water gone, and our bus no longer in danger, we piled back into it, and I steered back to the main highway, skeptical now about scenic country roads. Vic looked at the map and decided to bypass Orange altogether, and to just head straight to Avignon instead.

"It's a famous old city," he explained. "The Popes lived there for a time during the Middle Ages. So it's a tourist town, and there's bound to be some good busking there. Maybe we can even scare up a gig."

Vic had the right idea. Avignon turned out to be even more picturesque than I'd imagined, sitting on the Rhone and closed in by ramparts. The Palace Of The Popes appeared like a fortified medieval castle, standing atop a bluff from which it commanded a view of the Rhone Valley, all the way to the mountains on the horizon. From another viewpoint, the famous medieval bridge, the Pont Saint-Benezet, could be seen, still spanning about a third of the river before it abruptly ended, having been washed away by flood waters centuries ago. Our timing was good, as a summer festival was underway in the city, and we soon found a place to set up on a sidewalk in front of a café. As we were packing up our instruments later, an older American stepped up and handed me a ten franc note.

"I was going to donate this to the church," he said with a smile, "but I think you're doing a better job."

I thanked him, and as he melted back into the crowd, I felt proud and noble about the way I made my living.

We moved along to the large cobbled square in front of the palace, where throngs of people milled about, and other buskers had set up shop already. But there was room for us as well, and after finishing up there, we ran into someone we had known in Amsterdam, when he had lived for a while in a room above us on Koningsstraat.

He was a Gypsy and one-man band who dressed colorfully and so conspicuously that he made Vic look ordinary. He was of slight build and wore his black hair long, sported a wispy beard, and wore a red scarf casually around his neck. He had a large gold earring dangling from one ear. He tuned his guitar in an open tuning and had rigged a device that strummed an open chord by means of a pick attached to a lever that was controlled by the tapping of his foot on a jerry-rigged drum and tambourine. At the same time, he played two flutes simultaneously, one in each corner of his mouth, fingered by both hands. A nice-sized crowd had gathered around him, and his beret, which lay at his feet, was filled with change and franc notes of all denominations.

When he took a break, we all had a reunion over wine in a café, and Moro, as he was called, invited us back to his flat, which was actually rented by a friend of his. But he said we could spend the night in the cramped room (although I elected to sleep in the VW bus), and clean up and shower. Moro told us he was vagabonding around the south of France and the Mediterranean during the summer months. He planned to go to South America in the fall or winter before returning to Holland or Germany in the spring.

We pulled up stakes the next afternoon, with a plan to reach Aix-en-Provence that evening. But along the way, driving through Van Gogh countryside, we spotted a theme park that turned out to be a cross between Disneyland and Knott's Berry Farm. It was the French version of the American Wild West. Vic said, "Stop the van! I smell a gig."

So we pulled into the place and looked it over. A big American flag flew from a pole in the center of a log frontier fort. Included in the theme park, besides the cowboys and Indians on horseback and the staged "shootouts," were a replica nineteenth-century train on tracks that ran through the park, a stagecoach, and a replica Western town, which included a saloon. Vic made straight for the saloon, and we followed, instruments in tow. It didn't take Vic long, with Star's help, to negotiate a deal with the boss. He would pay us one hundred francs to play bluegrass and country music in the saloon for a couple of hours. Later, we watched some of the shows, like the dancehall girls and the stagecoach holdup and shootout, and we dined on American hamburgers and fries and downed glasses of red French wine. That night, we encamped outside of Aix and I slept under inky skies filled with glittering stars that reminded me of Van Gogh's *Starry Night*, for this was the countryside in which he had spent so much of his time, and these were the same stars he had once painted.

Next morning, we drove into the heart of Aix-en-Provence. We picked up beer and cheese and cold cuts and a baguette of fresh French bread at a little market, and found a square to eat our picnic lunch, where we made a plan of action for this beautiful cloudless summer day. Vic, of course, was on the lookout for more busking opportunities and possible gigs, so he suggested we drive around some more, until we found a likely spot. Our search ended on the Cours Mirabeau, and so we stashed the bus around the block in a parking lot, and hoofed it on over to the wide boulevard, which ran for several blocks east and west.

The Cours was shaded by rows of towering plane trees, looking as if Cezanne had painted them, and they formed a cool green canopy where they met overhead in the middle of the boulevard. At one end of the Cours was a large ornate fountain. A smaller one resided at the other end, and two more were situated in between. On the south side of the boulevard were seventeenth—and eighteenth-century buildings, many of them hotels with wrought iron balconies. However, on the north side, our attention was drawn to the many shops, restaurants, and sidewalk cafes, and it wasn't long before we were performing up and down the Cours, with Star dutifully passing the hat.

As it turned out, Aix was a university town, and also boasted an American School and an art college, and so it wasn't long before we began meeting American students, and so we were able to bed down for the night in town like regular members of society, with bathrooms and showers at our disposal. Vic and Star and Paddy and Annie were ensconced in the large house of a young woman who was studying at the American School. We had met her at one of the outdoor cafes on the boulevard.

I ended up spending the night with a young art student named Chris. He was tall and slender, and wore his blond hair fairly short. You could tell he was an American by his casual dress and his directness of speech and his flat Midwestern accent. He rented a simple apartment near the corner of Rue Fontaine D'Argent and Rue de la Mule Noire. It was on the second floor of an old building that had windows with painted shutters and a red-tiled roof. Around the corner, two sculptured faces protruded from the side of a wall, and water spouted out of their mouths into the fountain below. The fountain gurgled softly day and night. Besides a bathroom, Chris' place consisted of three other rooms—a bedroom, a kitchen, and another room he used as a study and studio. He thoughtfully rearranged his paintings and books and art supplies to make a place for me to roll out my sleeping bag for the night.

Then we took a walk down some narrow cobbled streets to where his friend John, another American art student, had a flat. We were introduced, and the three of us passed the time chatting about art and music, and of course about ourselves. John suggested that Uncle Zeke's traveling band hang around at least through the weekend, as tomorrow would be Bastille Day, and the place would be crawling with free spending locals and tourists. He predicted that it should be a windfall for our little group, but I figured Vic had already come to that conclusion.

We spent the next afternoon along the Cours Mirabeau, among the throngs of Bastille Day celebrants, busking and filling our coffers. At the far end of the boulevard, in front of the great fountain, an impressive stage had been set up during the day, complete with a sound system and light towers. Then in the evening hours, classical musicians inhabited the stage, as well as ballet dancers and long-winded orators. And when it was dark enough, fireworks lit up the sky, just as they do in The States on our Independence Day. We met more Americans that night, Vic and Paddy got rip-roaring drunk, and I got a buzz on myself, since I didn't have to be driving anywhere. Later, the couples went back to their crash pad at the big house, and I spent the night sleeping on the floor of Chris' cramped flat.

We pulled out of town in the early afternoon, Vic and Paddy and I nursing hangovers. Vic decided to have a "hair of the dog," so we bought some wine before we hit the road, but I waved the bottle away when it came around, as I had my hands on the wheel and my eyes on the road. And that road led southeast, through the countryside and the hills and down to the coast, on roads that wound through Toulon and along the deep cobalt blue Mediterranean, sparkling with sunlight from a cloudless azure sky. We were on the Cote d'Azur. Vic wanted to see Saint-Tropez, so we cruised around the town that sat on a peninsula, searching for a spot to park. The harbor was filled with yachts and sailboats, and traffic crawled and sprawled along the streets. Pedestrians decked out in sunhats and sunglasses, sandals and shorts and striped shirts, milled about everywhere, choking the sidewalks and crosswalks, and burned either red or tan by the sun.

"Let's find the topless beach with all the nudie cuties," Vic said leeringly.

"Let's not," said Star, and Annie backed her up

"Let's just find some place to busk, and then blow this town," I said.

So we did just that. I was able to pull into a spot on a street that ran along the waterfront as a Mercedes pulled out. We set out on foot with our instruments, and found a couple of sidewalk cafes and a bar to play in. Then we hit the road again, winding along the coastline until we reached Saint-Raphael, where Star suggested we stop for dinner, and we all agreed to that. The hangovers were now gone, and our appetites had returned. We found an outdoor café to busk, and after finishing up there, wandered around until we found what looked to be an affordable bistro, where we had a dinner, which while not as grand as the one we'd had at the truck stop in central France, was still delicious and filling. Afterward, we walked around the waterfront area for a while before deciding to go back to a wide, sandy beach we had spotted between Saint-Raphael and Frejus.

When we once again found the beach, the sun was setting, evening shadows were lengthening, and most of the beachgoers had fled for the lights of town, or their homes and hotel rooms. So we pretty much had the place to ourselves. The moon had risen early, huge and full and golden, and as the sun disappeared it grew brighter and shone down over the water, making a rippling sparkling glow, giving the lazy waves a phosphorescent glow to them as they rolled in and lapped the shoreline. We brought out towels and stripped down to our shorts and swimsuits, and went swimming, which also served the dual purpose of bathing. We dried off and lay on our towels, watched the moon turn silver and the sky turn indigo in a sea of stars. The town was to our backs, and its lights shone as well. Traffic died down along the road that passed by the beach, so now we were in our own world, lost in a perfect Mediterranean night, hanging out together with a feeling of camaraderie, while planning our future as a band. Then Vic ruined the moment by reminding me that I was still in the group on a probationary status.

We had parked the bus on the street right alongside the beach, and that's where Vic and Star spent the night. Alice and Paddy laid their sleeping bags on the sand against the seawall where the bus was parked, and where they couldn't be spotted from the road. I found a spot for my bag near a rock outcropping, which also was fairly well hidden from prying eyes. We saw no other people on the beach that night, nor did the police notice us. So I fell asleep to the sound of the waves, and the occasional car passing by.

The road to Cannes twisted along a winding coastline, where rugged mountains, steep hillsides, and sharp ochre cliffs marched down to meet the Mediterranean in the hot summer sun, the sea a deep blue, with cottony clouds hanging in patches above us in the bright blue sky. Plane trees, oaks, cypress, and scrub brush dotted the rocky landscape, and the smell of lavender fields and of the sea perfumed the air that blew in through our rolled-down windows. Occasional mansions resembled wedding cakes of white, with red-tiled roofs, and the grand villas of the wealthy and privileged looked down their noses at us from hilltops and promontories.

Golden sandy beaches and pebbly coves marked the way to the glitzy port of Cannes, its wide boulevard lined on the beach side with palm trees and flower gardens, and on the north with stately hotels, expensive boutiques, and posh restaurants and cafes.

Uncle Zeke's Band was vacationing on the French Riviera, and we felt as out of place as the Beverly Hillbillies. The yachts in the harbor and the private beach clubs gave us that feeling, if nothing else did. But as we drove past the Hotel Carlton, I remembered it from Alfred Hitchcock's *It Takes A Thief*, and it occurred to me that one of the film's stars, Grace Kelly, was now Princess Grace, and taking up residence in nearby Monaco, just down the road from Nice. Vic decided we'd better get some busking in before the local denizens found us out and sent for the cops. Police is spelled the same in French as it is in English, and we imagined we'd be as welcomed by them as pariahs.

But it was a little too early in the day to busk, it seemed, as café owners frostily turned us down. So we looked the town and the beach over a little bit more, and decided to cruise on down the bay to its sister city of Nice, a wealthier and dowdier sister to be sure. The boulevard that ran through Nice was wider, as was the palm-lined promenade. The hotels were statelier, the yachts grander, the boutiques classier, and the bistros snobbier. The beach was pebbly, and mostly privately owned. However, there was a nice flower market in Nice, and after some snooping around and pavement pounding, we set up, with the manager's permission, on the sidewalk outside a swank restaurant, which had an outdoor area of tables and chairs attached. Inside the open front was an eating area, and at the end of that room was a long bar, behind which an overdressed bartender mixed drinks and wiped glasses.

We had no sooner finished playing the first song and launched into the second, when Vic suddenly jerked, with a look of surprise and pain, as if he'd just been stung by a bee. He looked furtively around and continued singing. Then Paddy jumped, with a startled look of annoyance. We were facing the inside of the building, and just then I caught a glimpse of the bartender pointing a pellet pistol at us. Immediately, Annie let out a little yelp, as the bartender ducked out of sight. When he popped up again, I pointed in his direction and said, "Hey, that asshole is shooting at us!" He fired another BB, and this time Vic stepped aside and yelled, "Hey, cut it out frog face!" Then Paddy jerked again, and we immediately packed up and moved down the street. Vic wanted to go back and have some words with the bartender, but I remembered our scene with the French in Lyon, and talked him out of it.

We all decided that Nice wasn't very nice, and definitely not our niche, and we should head on down the line, which we did without delay. At different times in its history, Nice had been under the thumb of the Greeks, the Romans, and the Italians, all of whom had subsequently left. Now we were joining that exodus. We came, we saw, we left. We conquered nothing.

We pulled out of the snarled traffic of Nice, and ventured further down the coast, while appreciating the beauty of the sea and the sky and the beaches, and the snow-capped Alps to the north. The road hugged the mountains and limestone cliffs that crowded into the sea, twisting and turning, narrow in spots with breathtaking views. As we rounded one curve, we were able to look down on the Principality of Monaco, not much more than a small city, crammed into a peninsula-like spit of land about a mile square. Yachts were moored in its tiny harbor, and bright white buildings clustered together, gleaming in the sun. A road branched off and led down into the storybook kingdom, complete with a palace and a prince and princess, and at Vic and Star's urging, I pointed the nose of the bus downward into its bowels.

I navigated slowly through crowded narrow streets of tall villas and hotels and shops and other clean buildings that smelled of wealth. We drove near the Royal Palace perched atop Le Rochen with its princely trappings and palace guards all decked out in spotless blue and white, with gleaming brass and silver accoutrements, and continued on to the Monte Carlo district, with its Italian rococo design in the square overlooking the Mediterranean harbor. More uniformed guards clustered about the Casino as well, and there was an abundance of smartly uniformed police, seemingly everywhere. We didn't merely feel like fish out of water, as we had in Cannes and Nice, but rather as fish in a bowl, on the inside looking out. We decided to leave Monaco before we got into any trouble.

Back on the cliff-hugging main road again, we continued on towards the Italian border. But just about a mile before reaching it, we came into the little town of Menton, in a bay sheltered by the mountains, and looking more Italian than French. The main part of town lined the waterfront, while the rest of Menton perched itself on steep hillsides, alongside fragrant citrus trees and flower gardens. People strolled along a promenade, which ran along the waterfront, next to the avenue we were driving. The pastel-colored hotels and vistas we drove past seemed older and more subdued than their counterparts in Nice. Ladies sipped afternoon tea in seaside salons, while cafes, an open-air market, and flower stalls lined our route, and stately trees surrounded an arcaded square with a fountain and statue.

"This looks like our kind of joint," said Vic, who then told me to find a place to park. We grabbed our instruments and wandered on over to a little outdoor café, where a smiling woman greeted us in French, and after Star explained our mission, welcomed us as if we were a famous string quartet come to entertain. We performed our customary material, passed the hat, and then the woman—who was generous of spirit as well as girth—invited us to sit at a table, clapped her hands, and instructed the waiter to bring us glasses of wine on the house. We asked for menus, and finding simple and affordable fare listed, enjoyed a leisurely final meal in France.

An hour later, we were waved over the border into Italy.

CHAPTER NINETEEN

La Dolce Vita

We drove into a long, dark tunnel, and when we emerged into the light, we were on the Italian Riviera. The road was still narrow and winding, hugging the side of a mountain, and offering dizzying views of the Mediterranean, but we were relaxed, knowing we were now among the friendly Italians. Even the little cities and towns we passed through seemed more inviting in the bright summer sun. They had Italian names, filled with vowels; names like San Remo, Alassio, and Savona. But then we hit rush hour traffic in the smoggy industrial sprawl of Genoa, and some of the glitter rubbed off. Still, it was exciting to be driving through the place where Christopher Columbus hailed from. We saw a sign proclaiming the "*Casa di Cristobal Colombo*" was nearby, but when we stopped for gas and inquired, the man who took our money told us in English that nobody knew for sure where Columbus was born or lived, and so the Christopher Columbus House was mainly a tourist scam. So we drove on through Genoa's old center seaport area, and continued along the scenic coast of Italy's Riviera.

We ambled through Camogli and Portofino, two little fishing ports with brightly painted houses and narrow streets, and on along cliffs overlooking the Mediterranean, and dotted with pines, heathers, junipers and other vegetation, and through many more quaint little towns until we reached the larger and more promising city of La Spezia.

"Let's check this place out, Steve," said Vic. So we cruised along the waterfront area, with its inviting little beach and flowery gardens, until Vic spied an ice cream parlor with an outdoor café, where people were sitting around leisurely, eating Italian ices and drinking sodas and socializing. We parked in front, and Vic and I headed inside to find the person in charge. I'd taken one semester of Italian when I was at Santa Rosa J.C., and I was eager to find out how much I'd remembered.

A large man with graying black curly hair and a generous mustache stood smiling behind the counter, wearing a white shirt open at the collar. I stepped up to the counter, smiled and addressed him in badly mangled Italian.

"Buon giorno, signore. Com'e sta?

"Bene, grazie," he replied, still smiling.

"Noi siamo—uh, musicians." I made the motion of strumming an air guitar to make him understand. *"E possible siamo a cantare?"*

Before I could butcher the language any further, the man erupted in a laugh and said, "What is it you boys want, eh? You wanna play some music here, sing a some songs? Well, it's okay by me."

We stood in stunned silence for a moment before Vic stated the obvious.

"You speak English!"

"You betcha I speak English. I lived in Brooklyn for many years. Where you boys from?"

"California," I said. Then I added, "What are you doing here?"

"Well, I'm-a from Italy. After I retired from my job in the States I come back here an open up dis business. Now whad kinda stuff you boys play?"

"Folk and country," said Vic. "We'd like to set up outside and play for tips."

"You knock-a youselves out," said the man. "Have a good time. Then maybe you like a some ice-a cream, huh?"

"Yeah, that would be great", I said. "And thanks."

We played some songs, passed the hat, and hung around the ice cream parlor for a while, visiting with our new friend from Brooklyn, who went by the name of Joe. And then, because there was still light in the sky, we pushed on to Viareggio, also on the coast, but now in the region of Tuscany. Vic spotted a large outdoor café. We parked the bus, and asked around for the boss, who as it turned out also spoke good English.

"Mind if we play some songs here?" Asked Vic.

The man hesitated before replying, and then said apologetically, "No, I don't think so. I no think my customers like it so much."

This got an immediate reaction from Vic. I don't remember the exact exchange, but I do recall Vic giving the Fascist salute and comparing him to Mussolini. The man blushed red in the face and shouted, "Mussolini? No one ever call me Mussolini. No one ever give me such an insult. You get out now, crazy Americans! You no come back here."

We left, Vic grumbling about what a Fascist the guy was, and me feeling very embarrassed. I tried explaining to Vic that wasn't the way to talk to people when you're in a different culture, or even in your own for that matter. But he would have none of my reasoning, and reminded me I was still on probation, so I shut up and drove us around town, looking for another place to play. We finally found a restaurant with both outdoor and indoor seating areas that looked like our kind of joint. When the owners discovered we were American, they burst into smiles and bent over backwards for us, making us feel welcome, and were not only enthusiastic about the music, but afterwards provided us a meal of pasta and vegetables and wine at no charge. Vic took it all in stride, remarking that this was the way we should be treated everywhere we went.

After sundown, we found a bar to busk, and when we'd milked the place for all it was worth, searched out a spot to crash for the night. The waterfront area had a long promenade, and a wide sandy beach. We parked the bus on the street facing the beach, Paddy and Annie slept inside, while Vic and Star camped on the sand. I found a small spot on the beach, hidden from view, and rolled out my sleeping bag, then fell asleep to the rushing of waves against sand. In the morning, after breakfast and cleaning up in the restroom of a café, we pushed on again.

The road now wound east, along the Arno River and through the Arno valley, with it's sun dappled hills and quiet countryside. We followed the signs that were marked *Firenze*, which my map of Italy identified as being the name for Florence, the cradle city of the Renaissance. We soon reached Tuscany, which had been sitting in the shadow of the Apennines since its founding by Julius Caesar. During the Renaissance, Florence had been ruled by the Medici, and was synonymous with names like Michelangelo, Donatelli, Dante, and Da Vinci, and the sinister Machiavelli. We crossed over one of the bridges on the Arno that led into the old city center. Over to our left, we could see the Ponte Vecchio, the old medieval bridge with its overhanging load of shops and buildings. Once inside the center, we were surrounded by old buildings with red-tiled roofs, as well as plazas with statues and sidewalk cafes, but were hard-pressed to find anywhere to park. We finally found a spot on a narrow side street that didn't have a sign posted to prohibit parking, and we gathered our instruments together and set about exploring.

It was while we were busking in the Piazza Santa Maria Novella that a young Italian hippie stepped out of the crowd of tourists, flashed us a toothy grin, and dropped a handful of *lire* coins into Vic's guitar case. He stayed there for the rest of our set, moving rhythmically to the music, his long black hair tossing about, and applauding loudly, shouting "Bravo, bravo!" after each number. Then, as we began packing up our instruments, and Vic scooped the coins and paper notes out of his case and into his pocket, the slight and slender kid, looking to be still in his teens, stepped forward and made his introduction.

"I am called Tony. You are Americans, yes? Your music is very good. I like very much."

"Nice to meet you, man", said Vic. "We're Uncle Zeke's Band. I'm Vic, and this is Star."

Star said hello, smiling graciously, and then she introduced the rest of us to Tony, who as it turned out to be, was a student at the University of Florence.

"Do you have a place to say?" asked Tony.

"No, man, we don't. We just hit town," Vic answered. "Know of any place we can crash?"

"But you must stay with me, of course," said Tony. "I live very close, on the Via degli Avelli, on the top floor. It is small, but there is room for everyone."

"Thanks, man," said Vic. "That's righteous of you."

"I'll sleep in the bus," I said.

"*Buono, bene*. But first you must let me show you around. I know some good places for musicians to play."

And so Tony became our guide, showing us some of the famous statues and buildings, like the Medici Chapel, and tagging along with us as we busked outdoor cafes, bars, and restaurants. We stayed with him three nights, cooking in his small kitchen, and using his shower and bathroom. I spent each night in the VW, the curtains drawn tightly. The flat was on a street wide enough to park on, and fairly quiet, so I slept undisturbed. Tony was a generous spirit who loved music, and as far as we could tell, the only Italian hippie in Florence. The morning of our fourth day, with our gas tank full and bread in our pockets, as well as traveling money in Star's bag, we said goodbye to Tony and headed out of the city and back on the road, this time driving northeast toward Bologna.

We made a wide circle through Bologna, Parma, Milan, and the little towns and villages in between. Everywhere we found a good reception, especially with the curious small town locals, who for the most part did not speak English, and so I employed my rudimentary Italian. We did enough busking to keep the gas tank and our stomachs filled, before turning due south to the coast again, where the road intersected Genoa. From there we retraced our path along the coast toward France, stopping a couple of times to eat and busk, and to spend the night in San Remo, near the border. Vic was against stopping in Nice again, but he relented with Cannes, where we had the good luck of being well-received.

There was only one hitch with our return trip along the Cote d'Azure, and that came after we had pulled out of Saint-Raphael, heading toward Frejus. It was late, and we drove aimlessly through the hilly countryside looking for a place to camp. We finally settled on a small, semi-flat area between the road and the railroad tracks, with just enough space to park the bus, and for me to roll out my bag on the ground. But between the trains that roared past us, and the ants that crawled over my body on the way to their nest, I got nothing but fitful moments of rest. Too tired to push on come morning, and not finding another willing driver, I insisted we stay in Saint-Raphael another day, while I caught up on my sleep. So the rest of our little rag tag band hung out on the beach, swimming and tanning, while I took some power naps in the sweltering heat inside the VW. We pushed on that afternoon to Aix.

Back in Aix, while busking, we met two Americans of French descent named Yvette and Jeanette, who gave us the use of their shower and let us sleep on their floor and couch. Yvette was attending the American School, and her sister Jeanette was visiting from Berkeley, California. Both girls were attractive blonds, and Jeanette was just shy of 21, with noticeably clear blue eyes. Yvette had a French boyfriend, but Jeanette was single, so I latched on to her right away.

Yvette's apartment, modern by Aix standards, was located on the Rue du Puits Neuf, a narrow street not far from the Cours Mirabeau. Jeanette and I took a stroll down to the market to buy some food to fix for dinner, and by the time we walked back, we were holding hands. Yvette knew of a party happening at a Chateau in the countryside the next day, so she made a phone call and got us a job playing music there. It was a birthday party for one of her French friends. We busked that night on the Cours, and the next day took a drive out to the Chateau, which was just to the north of town, in a peaceful country setting. Before the party got started, Jeanette and I took a long walk, and kissed under a tree in the warm afternoon, with the smell of full summer earth and greenery in the air.

The celebration began with food and drink and socializing in the tranquil, soft light that was common to Aix evenings. Then as the sun set, our band set up inside the barn, and the party ramped up, with dancing to the accompaniment of bluegrass and folk music. Vic and Paddy were pretty well sloshed by the time we had packed up our instruments, and Star had had a row with Vic for getting too friendly with a cute French girl. But all in all, the party was a great success, and Vic made arrangements for us to sleep at the Chateau that night. Yvette drove on back to her place, but Jeanette stayed with me, and we slept up in the hayloft and made love in the fresh hay, and slept until the sun filtered into our hiding place in the morning. We stayed in Aix-en-Provence through the weekend, and after I failed to persuade Jeanette to come along with us to Amsterdam, we hit the road again in an early afternoon of late July.

We camped out that night, in the countryside north of Valence, and I went to sleep inside the bus to the sound of crickets, with my thoughts switching back and forth between Jeanette and Monika, who I imagined being in the arms of her new lover. And because I was allowed to sleep in the VW on this night, I missed out on all the excitement that Vic clued me in on the next morning, while we were breaking camp.

"Man, you shoulda seen it, Dupree. UFOs, I swear to God! The sky was full of them."

"UFOs? What are you talking about?" I said.

"There were these lights up in the sky," said Vic. "They looked like stars, only they were doing maneuvers, shooting all over the place. No airplane could go at those speeds or make sudden sharp turns like they did."

"They even stopped in mid-air," continued Star, "before shooting off again."

"Why didn't you wake me up?"

"Didn't think of it. Besides, it all happened so fast. I think they were putting on a show because the French are setting off an atomic bomb in the Pacific."

"Then why weren't they flying over the Pacific?"

"Who says they weren't there too? Maybe they're keeping their eyes on the Frogs, or maybe they were just making a point. Anyway, it blew our minds."

"Great," I said. "The one night I sleep inside, I miss out on the action. Next time, wake me up."

"I doubt we'll ever see that again," said Annie. "It's a whole new experience for me. I never believed in UFOs before, but now I do."

We got in the wind again, stopping in the next town for coffee and croissants, and soon we were back in Antwerp, playing in the pub we'd first visited a few weeks before. Taking the back door through Belgium, we rolled back into Holland on the last day of July. Our sweet life on the road, our working vacation as Vic called it, was over. The dog days of August were staring at us, and my future was about to take a radical turn.

CHAPTER TWENTY

The Big Split

Upon our return, it seemed as if tourists had descended on Amsterdam like locusts. The Vondelpark was overrun with hippies, camping in their sleeping bags. They covered the steps of the Dam monument like pigeons on a statue. With the hordes came the heat. And because Holland was wet with rain all year round, the humidity hung in the air like clothes dripping on a line.

Our first gigs, which would kick off with a four-night stand at the Octopus, were still a week away. So if we wanted to eat in the meantime, we'd have to go out busking again. This did not suit Vic, for although we'd been on the road for nearly a month, it seemed nothing had changed, especially with our immediate fortunes. That, coupled with the heat and humidity, darkened his mood, and I had to step lightly around him. We argued often, mostly about little things, but I felt as if he were acting like a petty tyrant grabbing after power, and trying to hold on too tightly. When I questioned an arrangement of a new song, or asked to have one of my own considered for inclusion, he took it as a threat to his authority. I was torn between my desire to stay with the band, and be a part of the music we were making, and the desire to punch him in the face.

Since Vic was burnt out on busking in Amsterdam, we headed off to Haarlem and Utrecht, pounding the cobblestones and breezing through the bars and restaurants. One night, at a bistro in Utrecht, I caught Vic admiring himself in a mirror as we performed, reminding me of a line in the recent Carly Simon song, "You're So Vain." He saw me out of the corner of his eye, shot me a dark look, and turned back to the audience. That little unguarded moment widened the rift between us.

We had been expecting the record label to release our single in early September, which we hoped would change our fortunes overnight. But the company announced they were pushing the release back to October, so Big House Pete continued to book us mostly into the same old places, although he had a well-paying private party gig lined up for us following our run at the Octopus. After I had a spat with Vic at the party, the hostess, a pleasant young Dutch woman, took me aside and said, "What's the matter? You look like you've just lost your best friend." There was some truth in that statement.

With Monika and me no longer in a relationship, and feeling more estranged from the band, I spent much of my time alone now, trying to write songs in my flat, or wandering about the city on my own. I checked for mail at American Express on a regular basis, and one day a letter arrived from my old Santa Rosa J.C. buddy, Randy Bleu. He and his girlfriend, Joyce, were on their way to Europe, and would be landing in Luxemborg soon. Maybe we could get together? That's about all he had to say, but I thought it would be great to see him again, as I seemed to be running short on friends at the moment.

After finishing up those first gigs that Pete had booked for us, Vic and I made an effort to get along, but it was a fragile truce. Next, we returned to Haarlem to play at the Ship Pub, and then back to Amsterdam for a night at the Melkweg, where there was no doubt whose band it was, nor who was the star. Vic made a big show of introducing Annie to do one fiddle solo, and Paddy to do one Irish song. The rest was all Vic. I complained to him as we packed up our instruments, about my lack of representation, and that I thought we had performed sloppily. Vic's eyes narrowed.

"You're pushing your luck, Dupree. If you don't like the way things are, you should just quit and go back to California."

I said nothing further, but clenched my jaw, picked up my bass and amp, carried them out to the VW and locked them inside. Then I gave the key to Paddy, and told him he would have to drive, because I felt like walking home. But I did not walk directly back to my flat on Govert Flinckstraat. Instead, I detoured to the nearby

Vondelpark, where Monika was working her overnight shift at the Crisis Center. She was surprised to see me, but she was gracious about my unannounced visit, and I could see concern in her expression.

"What's wrong," she asked sympathetically. "You seem depressed."

"Yes," I admitted, "depressed and angry."

"Is it about Vic and the band?"

"You know me too well."

"What's the problem now? Vic still treating you like shit?"

"What else?"

"So what are you going to do about it?"

"Nothing, I guess. I still want to be in the band."

"Then you'll get no sympathy from me," she said, her mood changing to impatience. "You either need to assert yourself or quit."

"And do what?" I said.

"Go off on your own. You're the best singer in the band. You don't need Vic."

"I don't know how," I complained. "Where do I start?"

"You start by going around to the places where you've played before and asking for a chance to play solo."

"I don't want to do that," I complained.

"Well then maybe you just like to suffer. Anyway, stop complaining to me about Vic. I'm tired of hearing about it."

"Okay," I said dejectedly. Then I changed the subject. We made small talk for a little while, mostly about her work and her studies, and the weather, and such. I didn't ask her about her new boyfriend, and he didn't offer any information about him, which suited me fine. Finally I said goodnight, and walked back to my flat in the early morning hours, feeling lonely and low.

Our next gig was at Boddy's Music Inn, where we finally wore out our welcome. Vic and Paddy got annoyingly drunk, played badly, and Vic and I got into an argument onstage. An audience member shouted out, "Hey, man, music is supposed to be fun. Take your bad vibes somewhere else." Ted Boddy fired us for being unprofessional and having bad attitudes, and this time I didn't feel like going back and apologizing and begging for another chance.

Instead, I quietly seethed with resentment, making the effort to keep my mouth shut about it. But I wasn't able to keep the lid on for long.

The breaking point came at De Kosmos on a Wednesday night in the third week of August. I don't remember what led up to it, but right after the gig was over I went off on Vic about something, and he lashed back at me.

"I've had it with you, Dupree. I just can't work with you anymore."

"I can't work with you either."

"I don't know what your problem is. I've always treated you as an equal, in fact I've treated you like a brother, and all you ever do is complain. Well I've had a belly full. You're out of the band. You're fired."

I looked around for backup from my band mates, but all Annie could say was, "I'm sorry, Steve."

I turned to Paddy, who stood shoulder to shoulder with Annie and he said, "Well, you know how it is, Steve. Me and Vic go way back."

I looked at Star. She looked away.

"Fuck you," I said in Vic's direction. "You can't fire me, because I quit."

And with that, I grabbed up my equipment and stormed out to the bus, tossed the bass and amp inside, started the engine, and drove straight to Govert Flinckstraat, where I parked down at the end of the block, and walked back to my flat. The rest of the band would have to walk home.

I lay awake for hours, thinking about all the years I'd known Vic, and all the things we'd been through together. I reminisced about our surf band, and the early times together on the road, when I had looked up to him and wanted to be like him. What had happened to all the camaraderie between us, and to all my dreams? I felt lower than a snake's belly.

I kept the bus for three days, mostly hanging out at my flat, wondering what to do about my future. Fortunately, I'd been paid for the gig at De Kosmos before it had all blown up, so I had money to buy food. But now what? I was no longer in a band. How would I support myself? After all, I wasn't like Vic. I didn't have his confidence and aggressiveness in hustling gigs. I began making plans to go back to California and start all over.

After a few days, Big House Pete showed up and shouted up at me from the street below. And since my window was open, and I could hear his shouts, I leaned my head out and answered back.

"What do you want?"

"We need to talk. Let me in."

"No. I'll come down."

I met him on the street shortly.

"We want the Volkswagen back."

"Then you can pay me my share for it."

"We plan to do that, and to pay you your share for the equipment as well. We're having a band meeting at the office this afternoon, where we'll settle up and sign some papers to that effect."

"What time?" I asked.

"Around three o'clock. Bring the bus and your gear."

"Okay, Pete. There's never been any bad blood between us."

"I know. It's just the music business. I wish you could have stayed on. I think you're a good musician, but maybe this is best for everyone."

I felt like a real loser just then, but I couldn't argue with Pete. He had always treated me fairly. We all came to an agreement that afternoon. I was a few hundred guilders richer, and now traveling lighter, with only a guitar, my backpack, and a sleeping bag. But I didn't have enough money for a plane ticket home. There was only one solution, one thing to do, and I had been avoiding it for too long. I would have to go out on my own and busk. I'd have to make the rounds of the clubs and places I'd played at with the band, and ask for solo work.

I had been dreading doing this, but I steeled my will, and went out that night, stopping by familiar places, playing and singing and passing the hat. The experience gave me a little money, but more importantly, it boosted my self-confidence enough that I began making the rounds each night. I would explain that I had quit the band, and was working solo now, and was able to land a few gigs. Ted Boddy said he'd be happy to have me back at Boddy's Music Inn, mainly because I had been the best singer in the group and had

had the most professional attitude. Those were his words, and they gave me great satisfaction. But it was still hard at first to present my songs to audiences, without the strength of a band to hide behind. And I was woefully short of material. I had to learn some new songs in a hurry. But learn them I did, and as my fortunes improved, I began thinking less of returning to California and more of how to support myself in this manner.

I went to work every night. It took no time at all to line up some gigs—Boddy's, Ahknaton, The Doubledecker, Kosmos, Folk Fairport, De Waag, and the Melkweg. I felt very intimidated the night I stood alone on the stage at the Melkweg, and stared out past the lights into the crowded room. But when I began receiving warm applause after every song, I loosened up and had a good time. Soon my calendar was filled with gigs through the middle of September. On the nights I wasn't gigging, I was out busking around Amsterdam, and some nights I took the train to Haarlem or Utrecht. I found new spots to busk, that the band had overlooked, like the quiet little bar just around the corner of one of the canal streets. When I first approached the bartender about busking, she gave me some encouragement.

"If you'll come back at 9:30," she said, "a tour bus makes a stop here for a drink. We're on their list as a typical Dutch bar. Then you'll have a good crowd."

I took her advice, and she was right. I did have a good crowd, many of whom were Americans, and most of whom were happy to put money in my hat. Whenever I was out busking around town, I would try and time it to be at this little Dutch bar around 9:30. The tourists would have their drink and push on, and so would I.

I made some new friends in those first days on my own, including two British folk singers, Reg and Davey. I met Reg while out busking. He was new in town, so I gave him some good leads on places to play. I met Davey Brown at Folk Fairport, where he was playing one night. We hit it off right away, and from then on, I would try to make it to his gigs, and he to mine. Then one night, while I was playing at Boddy's Music Inn, I took a break after my first set, and a young hippie-looking guy with long blond hair, clear blue eyes, and a neatly trimmed beard called me over to his table and offered to buy me a beer. We introduced ourselves.

"I'm from Texas," he said. "Name's Michael Murphy. I'm a singer and songwriter too. Just dropped off a copy of my record to the bartender there."

"What brings you in here?" I asked.

"Well, I went over to England to try and get some gigs. My wife is from there. But I couldn't get working papers, so I thought I'd stop by Amsterdam and see what was going on. But it doesn't look like I can get the right papers here, either, so I'm fixin' to go back to Austin."

We talked a while longer. I finished my beer, shook his hand, and went back onstage. He left during my second set, but when I was finished for the night, and enjoying a Heineken at the bar, the bartender put his record on the player and dropped the needle. It sounded pretty good. I looked at the album cover, a close up of Michael Murphy's face, and noticed a reference about him being a "cosmic cowboy" on the back cover. I never ran into him again, but I did find out much later that he was a leader in the "outlaw country" scene in Austin, along with Willie Nelson, Waylon Jennings, and others.

Summer was on the wane now. It had been just about a year since I had first come to Amsterdam, and almost a year since I'd settled in. Before long, 1973 would be finished as well, and I knew I didn't want to spend another winter in this city. I could vividly recall how cold and wet it had been the previous winter, and how I had looked longingly at those posters of Greece and Spain in the travel bureau windows. But going south in that direction would cost money, and lots of it. I didn't think the plan was a realistic one, but was I no longer in a hurry to get back to the States. So for the time being, I would stay put, continue playing solo at least through the fall, and worry about the winter when it drew closer. However, a change was in the air, subtle but definite.

One day my friend Willem, who had loaned me the use of the cracked house on Govert Flinckstraat, suddenly appeared and told me he needed the flat back. He was moving back to Amsterdam from Haarlem, and I had to find a new place by the middle of September. At first I panicked, and then began putting out the word to everyone I knew, including Monika, that I was looking for new lodgings. She didn't know of anything offhand, but sympathized with my plight, and invited me to dinner for Tuesday night.

The very next day, though, I was given a lead on a houseboat for rent. I met the woman who owned it, and we walked on over to the canal where it was moored. It was a tiny little boat, but the price was right, and I was desperate, so we shook hands on the deal. In the morning, I packed up my belongings and moved on over to where I had last seen the little boat, and to my amazement only the bow and part of the cabin showed above water, with a rope still tethered to a cleat. The rest of the boat was submerged in the dark green canal. I stood in silence for a few moments, not believing my eyes, then hefted my backpack and slunk back to Govert Flinckstraat. Once I had unpacked, I brought out the letter I'd received from Randy, and reread it.

"Hello, Steve. Joyce and I are in Paris, house-sitting a great apartment on Avenue de Clichy for a friend of ours. You should come down here and visit. Or maybe I can get up your way for a visit."

There was more, but that was the paragraph that grabbed my attention. I hurriedly wrote a reply to Randy to the effect that I was in a state of flux and didn't know what my address would be if he came to visit, but that he could look me up through Big House Pete, and I gave him Pete's address and phone number. Then I walked down to the post office and mailed it. That night I went out busking, and started putting the word out again about my living situation. But no other prospects turned up.

On the afternoon of the 25th, I walked along the Kalverstraat, the shopping street for pedestrians only. I wandered along, looking in shop windows, and stopped at an ice cream shop and bought a vanilla cone. Then, on an impulse, I decided to visit the Begijnhof, just off the Kalverstraat. It was a quiet little courtyard, enclosed by a church and three-story buildings that had once housed nuns. In the middle of the peaceful courtyard, there was a statue of Christ with a halo, which I found comforting. But as I was strolling into the courtyard, I had to stop in my tracks, because heading my way was a familiar smile, beaming out from a long, open face framed by long straight brown hair, a lanky body, and a confident long stride. The man was wearing hiking boots, sand-colored corduroy pants, and a wrinkled shirt with a notebook and pen peeking out of its front pocket. I found myself staring unbelievably at Randy Bleu!

"Steve!" he exclaimed. "You got here after all, but you're a little late. I was just about to give up and leave."

"Randy," I said, shaking his hand. "What are you doing here? What are you talking about?"

"Didn't you get my message? Isn't that why you're here?"

"No. What message?"

"I've been in Amsterdam since yesterday. I called your old manager, but he wasn't sure how to get hold of you. He suggested I visit the Folk Fairport, but I didn't have any luck there. So I left a message with him for you to meet me here at two o'clock today. Now it's almost three. If you didn't get my message, how did you find me?"

"I really don't know. For some reason, I was drawn here."

"Are you putting me on?"

"No. I had no idea you were here."

"Maybe you're clairvoyant. Anyway, am I glad to see you, and to be in this really groovy place! Who'd have ever thought we'd run into each other in Europe?"

"Where did you stay last night?"

"At a youth hostel. It was pretty crowded."

"Every place is crowded right now. But you can stay with me tonight. How long are you in town for?"

"A few days, a week at most. I'm just playing it by ear right now. Joyce is holding down the fort while I'm gone. What about you? You said you had to move. Have you found a new place yet?"

"No luck. Only had one lead, and it literally sunk."

"Hey—I've got a great idea," he said enthusiastically. "Why don't you come to Paris and stay with us? I've been doing some busking there and making a little bread. We could team up. It'll be fun."

"Sounds good," I said. "Let me show you around a little, then we'll go back to my pad. My ex-girlfriend invited me over for dinner tonight. I'll give her a call, and ask if you can come too."

And that's what I did, after we stopped at a herring stand and Randy bought some raw herring and rolls, and both of us had an

Amstel beer. Monika said she'd love to have us both over, so we picked up Randy's belongings, including his Gibson guitar, at the Central Station, and hauled it over to my place where we ran over a few songs together, visited Monika for a home cooked dinner of moussaka, and went out busking. We only made about fifteen guilders apiece, and had a pint of Guinness on the house at our last stop. But it was fun, and it felt good to be playing music with someone else again, without all the bad vibes that accompanied being in Uncle Zeke's Band.

We spent the next day learning and rehearsing a batch of songs, both at my flat and at the Vondelpark. As it turned out, Randy had a nice tenor voice to match my baritone, and he had a good feel for harmony singing as well as lead. He introduced me to some songs I hadn't heard and vice versa. I was all fired up about playing music again. It was rejuvenating.

We had dinner at an Indonesian restaurant, did some busking, smoked some hash at the Folk Fairport, and then dropped in on my friend Davey, who was playing at Boddy's. He invited us up to do a guest set. Due to the fact that we were stoned, we were pretty sloppy in our playing, but still, it was a good experience. While we were there we heard that Commander Cody and the Lost Planet Airmen would be hosting a press conference the next night at Boddy's. Since they were from our neck of the woods, Sonoma County, we decided to crash the affair, and found ourselves chatting up members of the band over Heinekens. We continued our routine for the next several days, taking the train to Utrecht one night to busk. During the day, we'd work on songs, and then Randy would go out exploring on his own. Our last night together was great, and we made over one hundred guilders. But as we were finishing up with the busking, we ran into Vic. Randy could feel the bad blood between us, as I introduced him to my former bandmate. After some tense moments passed, we went our separate ways.

"Man," said Randy, "I picked up some really bad vibes back there. What gives? You guys played together for a long time, didn't you?"

"Let's go get a drink, and I'll tell you all about it."

Since it was Randy's last night in town, we hung out at a pub over pints of Guinness until the early hours, before turning in. We talked about his plans after Paris, which included a trip to Greece, and then on to Israel. And we talked of Paris, and Randy made it sound very inviting.

"Yeah, Steve, you should really come down and join me for a while. We could have a groovy little duo. You don't have to worry about rent, and we could really clean up playing in the streets and the Metro."

Randy left on the second day of September. As I saw him off at the train station in the late morning, I promised to join him in Paris around the middle of the month—after I had finished up the gigs I was committed to, and had a little more traveling money stashed away.

The next two weeks passed in a blur of gigs and busking and saying my goodbyes to the city, to friends, and to Monika. I decided to take a little gift of marijuana to Randy, so I bought a tiny stash at the Lowlands Weed Company boat, and concealed it in the false bottom of a matchbox, smug in my belief that it would never be found, even if, God forbid, I were to be searched at the border.

I hung out in front of the American Express office on the Damrak, where all the deals and transactions among young travelers were casually made, and found a French guy holding up a sign announcing that he was looking for riders to Paris.

"When are you leaving?" I asked.

"As soon as I get one more rider," he said.

"How much are you charging?"

"Nothing, really. Just share the cost of petrol."

"Then count me in," I said.

"Meet me back here tomorrow morning around ten," he said.

In the morning I packed my belongings, left the key for Willem above the doorway to the second floor flat that I had called home these past few months, and with an air of expectancy, headed out onto the street with my pack, sleeping bag, and guitar. I had the pot for Randy concealed in the matchbox that was inside a pouch of tobacco, along with my pipe, in a pocket of my fringed jacket, which hung over my backpack. I met up with the French driver and three other young guys in front of the American Express; we loaded up the van, and headed out of Amsterdam and into the open countryside of southern Holland, toward the Belgian border. My happiness of getting on the road again and hooking up with Randy was tempered by a feeling of nostalgia for Amsterdam and a sense of leaving home. The sun shone through thick clouds, the tires hummed on the highway, and I closed my eyes and settled back for a long ride.

CHAPTER TWENTY-ONE

Tales of Two Cities

It was late in the day when we crossed the French border on the highway to Paris and came to a stop at the checkpoint. We were in the third vehicle in line, and the two before us were waved across in quick order without fanfare. But when our turn came, and we handed our passports to the guard at the post, he took a keen interest in us, as did the second guard who approached the van and inspected us all with beady eyes. I got the impression that this was because we were suspicious-looking hippies. A third border patrolman, in blue uniform and cake-pan cap, now approached us and addressed the driver in very officious tones.

"He wants us to empty out our pockets," said the driver. We all emptied out the contents of our pockets for inspection—wallets, combs, loose change, car keys, and the like. One border guard became fixated on my tobacco pouch. He took it from me, opened it, and inspected first the pipe, sniffing it for hash residue, then the tobacco, poking around in it, looking for anything hidden in its texture. Then, almost as an afterthought, he shook the matchbox, opened it, and dumped out the matches. He looked carefully inside, tapped the box upside down into the palm of his hand, and the false bottom fell out, and with it the stash of marijuana. His face lit up in surprise, and then triumph as he called the other two guards over to view his great detective work. He had caught me red-handed, and the other two were examining his find with great satisfaction, as if together they had just made the drug bust of the century. My heart skipped and I suddenly felt sick to my stomach.

Wound up now, and full of self-importance, the guard barked some orders to the driver, who pulled over to a parking lot next to the border patrol building, and killed the engine. He swore at me in French and English for being stupid enough to try and smuggle drugs across the border. We would all have to suffer now for my mistake. But after having rifled through everyone's baggage, and giving the van a thorough shakedown, there were no more discoveries of contraband. Passports were handed back to everyone but me. I was ordered to take my belongings out and place them on the ground. The van took off, the driver still swearing at me in French, while I hoisted up my backpack and guitar and followed two guards into the building, where I was seated in a waiting room, an official hovering ominously over me. I took out my guitar and began playing and singing a little to break the tension in the air. Then I was led into the inspector's office, and seated across from his desk while the arresting officer showed him the evidence—my matchbox and the pot. He glared at me haughtily as if I had just committed a vile heinous act, and for all I knew, maybe I had.

The inspector stood up and slowly stepped over to me, evidence in hand and began grilling me in French. I smiled, shrugged, and said *"Non parle pa francais."*

He repeated the question, this time more forcefully. I smiled and shrugged again. Now he stood over me, waved the matchbox in front of my face, and spoke menacingly, but this time added "Amsterdam?"

Suddenly, it became clear to me that he was asking where I had got the pot. I nodded my head, and said "*Oui.*"

Now came another question that I did not understand, and I stared blankly at him, and said *"Non comprends."*

He pushed his irate face close to mine and repeated the accusation, this time ending his sentence with "Club Paradiso?" He had decided that I had bought the pot at the Paradiso in Amsterdam. And although I had copped it at the Lowlands Weed Company, I nodded and answered in the affirmative, and again he appeared pleased. Next he seemed to be asking me how much I had paid for it, and when I shrugged he prompted me with the answer he wanted to hear, which was ten guilders. I nodded.

Now his investigation seemed to be complete, so he went back to his desk, studied my passport, put a sheet of paper in his typewriter, and gave an order to the man who had been guarding me, who saluted, and left the room. I stared at the world map on the wall while the inspector typed up something.

Shortly the man who had left the room returned with another uniformed man, who could speak a little English. He and the inspector had a short conversation, after which the inspector motioned me over to the desk, rolled the sheet of paper out of the typewriter and placed it on the desk facing me. He handed me a pen, and motioned for me to sign. I stared at it blankly. It was written in French.

"What is this?" I said.

"Confession," said the English-speaker. "Sign."

"But I can't read it. I can't sign something I can't read."

The inspector reached across the desk, grabbed hold of my shirt with one hand, and raised his other hand palm out as if to strike me. He said something loudly in French.

"Sign," said the other one.

I forced a smile, the inspector let go of me and put down his hand, and I wrote my name at the bottom.

"Now what?" I said in as friendly a way as I could, given my highly tense state of mind.

"You pay the . . ." he reached into his memory for the next word, "fine."

"How much?" I asked, bringing out my wallet, which contained a little over two hundred guilders.

He took the wallet from me, pulled out all the bills, and then handed it back empty. I still had about seven guilders in coins remaining in my jeans pocket. He gave the bills to the inspector, who counted them out, then put them into an envelope and placed it on top of the desk. The two men held a short conference after which the English-speaking one addressed me.

"Now we send you home. We deport you."

The inspector turned to the world map that hung on the wall behind him and pointed to New York, saying something in French.

"No," I said. "Deport me to Amsterdam."

He pointed to New York on the map again. I walked over to the map and pointed to Holland. "Amsterdam." The inspector looked over to the other cop, who nodded.

"Amsterdam," said the inspector. He spoke some words to the other man, who left the room. He sat back in his swivel chair, picked up the confession and began reading it. I took out my guitar and began playing and singing quietly. The inspector looked over his paper at me curiously, then relaxed and went back to his reading and counting out the money again. Then he began filling out a report. The English-speaking cop returned, spoke to the man who had been guarding me, and then said to me, "Come with us, please."

They led me outside to a waiting car, where they placed me with my belongings in the back seat. Then one of the men got in the front with the driver, and we went a short distance to the Belgian border, where the car stopped next to the guard post. The guard who was riding shotgun helped me out as one of the Belgian border guards walked over and began inquiring in French as to what the hell was going on. An argument ensued, with the French guard pointing at me, and the Belgian guard shaking his head no. They argued some more, and then the Belgian guard called me over.

"You cannot enter Belgium," he said pointedly. "You must go back to France."

The French guard argued again with him, apparently saying that I couldn't go back to France either.

"You must go back to America," he said.

"I will," I agreed. "But first I must go to Amsterdam to have money sent to me so I can fly back home."

"How much money have you now?"

"None. These men took it all from me."

He spoke to the French guard again, and then to the other Belgian guard, and after they conferred, he returned to me.

"How do you plan to get to Amsterdam?"

"By hitching," I said, pointing my thumb in the air to illustrate.

"Very well, but you must not stop in Belgium. You must keep going. You are not allowed, and you must go straight to Amsterdam."

I told him that nothing would please me more. The border guards had one last huddle, the car sped off, and the Belgians pointed me down the road, away from their post.

I soon got a ride to the outskirts of Ghent, a few miles into Belgium, and was dropped off beside the road, while the driver headed over a bridge that spanned a small stream, and disappeared into the countryside. The sun was going down, and there seemed to be very little traffic, so I dropped my gear on the ground, and ducked under the bridge to take a quick leak, and then returned and sat next to my backpack and watched the sun fade away. I began looking around for a place to bed down for the night, should I need to, when I saw a figure walking along the road toward me. As he got closer I noticed he was a young man, around my age, with long hair, a slender build, and wearing glasses. When he was close enough, I waved and smiled, and he waved back. He stopped beside me, and greeted me in Flemish. I answered back in English.

"Oh, you are American? Where are you going?"

"I'm trying to get to Amsterdam."

"Oh, yes, a very nice city, Amsterdam. I have been there myself. Where are you coming from now, Paris?"

"No, I was going there, but I got stopped at the border, and now they've sent me back. I have no money, so I have to get back to Amsterdam."

"Have you been to Paris before?"

"No, but I've been in France before."

Then I told him of how I had traveled with Uncle Zeke's Band in France and Italy and he seemed very interested.

"Have you been to *Firenze*?" He asked.

"Florence? Yes, we stayed there a few days."

"Firenze is also a very nice city. I have a friend there, a guy named Tony."

"Tony?" I said, surprised. "We stayed with a guy named Tony. He put us up for several days in his apartment. He was young and thin, with long black hair, and very friendly. He lived near the university."

"Yes," said the Belgian, smiling broadly now. "He must be the same one. I don't imagine there could be another Tony like that in *Firenze*. It is a small world, no? My name is Theo," he said, holding out his hand, which I shook.

"I'm Steve. Well, Theo, it looks like I might be stuck here for the night. Do you know of a good place where I could camp out in my sleeping bag?"

"You can stay with me, of course. You're a friend of Tony's, and he is my friend also. I live about one and a half kilometers down this road," he said, pointing toward the little bridge. "Come along, it will be a pleasure to have you stay the night."

He lived in a little farmhouse, rustic and cozy, and after a long conversation over a bottle of wine, he turned in and I slept on the floor. In the morning he fixed me coffee and bread with butter and jam, and I walked down to the road again, and caught a ride into Ghent. I spent the rest of the day hitching through Belgium and Holland, and arrived in Amsterdam in the early evening, with two guilders left in my pocket. I entered the cracked house on Govert Flinckstraat, and found the key to my flat where I had left it, above the door. I went out busking that night, as a matter of survival. I spent the next several nights busking from early evening until after the bars shut down, and then hit the after hours clubs. Some nights I would start out in Amsterdam, then take the train to Haarlem or Utrecht, and then catch the last train back.

I spent nearly a week in Amsterdam, hustling for traveling money, and during that time Willem did not move back to the flat, nor did I hear from him. I considered myself fortunate to have this extension, but was worried about crossing into France again. I could not afford to get stopped at another border crossing. Then I heard from a friend that there was a train to Paris that left at midnight from the Central Station, making no border stops. I thought it sounded too good to be true, but I was willing to give it a try. I had enough money now for the train fare, and a little left over to live on for a few days, so I decided to chance it.

After some early busking on my last night in town, I went through the same routine as the week before, packing up my belongings and placing the key above the door. I walked along Amsterdam's busy streets, and caught a tram down to the Central Station, where I bought a ticket and waited. The train left Amsterdam at midnight, as scheduled, and I took a seat by the window, where I watched the changing scenery for signs that we'd crossed the border into Belgium. I stole glances at my watch and tried to relax, but the closer we came to the French border, the more keyed up I got, worrying about being caught and deported again. But then we were actually inside France, and there was no border stop, nor did any officials board the train to check passports. Only the conductor came by from time to time, checking and punching tickets. I almost felt safe enough now to let out a great sigh, but I didn't lest I jinx things. Finally, we rolled into the outskirts of Paris, and then into the center of the City Of Lights and came to a halt at the Gare Saint-Lazare.

I stepped off the train and into the station, and as I headed toward the exit that led to the street, I spied two plainclothes Parisian cops intently watching the comings and goings of suspicious persons. They were both wearing trench coats. I tried not to appear obvious or nervous, as I moved nonchalantly but quickly out of their view. Then I found a telephone box, and called Randy for directions. The sun was up, and I hoped he would be as well, which he was.

"Steve," he said excitedly. "Where are you?"

"At a train station in the middle of Paris."

"What kept you? We've been expecting you for days."

"It's a long story. I'll tell you all the details later. How about some directions."

"Which station are you at?"

I told him.

"Great! You're just a few blocks away."

He gave me directions, which I jotted down in my pocket notebook. I hung up the phone and headed out into the Paris sunlight and down crowded sidewalks that shared space with canopied shops of produce and flowers and meats. Soon I was at the address given me, on Avenue de Clichy, a busy street of buildings that mixed old architecture with the modern, lined with trees whose leaves were already turning in early autumn. The apartment building stood next to a *boulangerie* filled with the smells of fresh pastries and baguettes. I pushed the outside buzzer, and momentarily Randy was down on the street level, letting me in.

He helped me with my guitar, and upstairs in the comfortable two-bedroom apartment, Randy and Joyce and I had a reunion, and I was introduced to their friend Sam. He was a small but charismatic character with thick red hair and beard, and wearing what turned out to be his regular mode of dress, a long white robe tied with a sash. His change of clothes turned out to be a long brown robe. He looked like a wandering monk from Medieval times.

I caught Randy up on the misadventures that had delayed me. He said the gift of pot I had planned for him was thoughtful, but not worth getting arrested for. Besides, he said, there was plenty of hash to be had in Paris. Just the other day, when he had been busking in the Metro, someone had thrown a chunk into his guitar case, and he still had a little left over, which he then broke out, and we smoked in a chillum. Then he told me of his adventures in Paris, and about the couple at whose mother's apartment he and Joyce were crashing.

Sonia was a friend of Joyce's from the States. She had married a Frenchman, Willie, and they had a house on the outskirts of Paris. Willie's mother, who was spending some time in Israel, owned the apartment which Randy and Joyce were more or less caretaking.

Sam was crashing on the couch while he waited on a money order to arrive, so he could fly back to New York. In the meantime, he was a man with no visible means of support. However that was nothing new for him. Being from New York, he was a natural hustler with street smarts that he had finely honed after years of bumming around Europe and India, where he had learned how to make chapatis and other Indian dishes. Somehow the universe took care of him, that's what he said anyway. But the truth is he was a human sponge, and had a way of charming anyone out of anything, so that he was never without food, clothing, or shelter. As a matter of fact, he had conned Sonia out of the material for his robe and talked Joyce into sewing it together for him. As Randy remarked to me, "He is a beggar who keeps his sense of dignity intact."

Randy knew his way around Paris like I knew my way around Amsterdam, and so every day we worked on songs, learning new ones and polishing others, before heading out to busk, him leading the way. It felt great to be making music again with a partner, one

I got along with easily. Playing and singing together was a joy for both of us, and to be doing it while exploring this exciting vibrant city filled with history and culture was an added bonus. Like Vic, Randy was outgoing, and brimming over with energy. As far as he was concerned, we were having ourselves a grand adventure, and we were all having it together, he and I and Joyce. He had a singing voice that was reminiscent of Neil Young, high and lonesome sounding. I liked how it cut through the noise of the crowds and the underground Metro. My voice carried as well, but I had been busking for well over a year, while Randy had only been at this for a few weeks. He was not yet a songwriter, but the songs he chose for our repertoire complemented my choices and worked well for our playing and singing styles. He introduced me to songs like the Grateful Dead's "Friend of the Devil" and old folk and country chestnuts like "Sitting On Top Of The World", and "I Live One Day At A Time."

After a breakfast of coffee and baguettes, and maybe some fruit, we'd work on songs, and then he'd say, "Hey, Steve, let's go out and make some bread!" So we would head out someplace, like maybe nearby Montmartre, the highest hill in Paris, where we found a great view of the city, spread out to the horizon. We would set up shop in the Place du Tertre, where dozens of artists were at work on easels, mostly painting portraits for the crowds of tourists mingling all about. Randy would place his cap on the ground at our feet, to catch change, and we'd take out our guitars and play and sing until we'd had enough. Then we'd move on to another part of the area, and set up in front of a café or restaurant. Or we might go sing down in the noisy underground Metro, where the crowds were the best around the noon hour, and we'd really rake in the dough. We'd sing until either our throats were raw, or the police moved us on. If they were in uniform, we'd usually see them coming, and quickly pack up and split before they could accost us. But sometimes a plainclothes cop, obvious in trench coat and Inspector Clousseau hat, would sneak up on us, flash a badge, demand our passports, which he would eye carefully, and then run us off.

When that happened, we'd catch a subway train to another part of town, like the Latin Quarter on the Left Bank, and set up on a cobbled side street or in a square, like the Place Saint-Michel, where there stood a beautiful fountain and a bronze statue of St. Michael slaying a dragon. On our first outing there, we found a French street person, a real character, who would dance around, clown like, flicking a lit cigarette in and out of his mouth, while passing the hat for us. For his troubles, we'd cut him in on the take. He'd also warn us when the cops were coming, so we could pack up and disappear into the crowd. One time a chunk of hash was tossed into the hat, and became hidden in the lining when Randy scooped it up as we ran from the cops. It wasn't until we were back at the apartment that he discovered it and we smoked it. Sam had a habit of bringing hash back to the pad as well. We never knew how he had come by it. We just chalked it up to his hustling skills, but he always shared it with us.

One day, when we were over on the Left Bank, we decided to go see the Eiffel Tower, a stunning piece of iron architecture that rose over one thousand feet into the sky. We stood underneath it looking up, while Randy told me the story of a Parisian tailor, "Birdman" Reicheldt, who made himself a modified cape with wings that he could flap with his arms. In 1912, almost a decade after the Wright brothers had flown at Kill Devil Hills, he ascended to the highest platform and leapt into the air, flapping his arms madly. A large crowd of onlookers watched in fascination as he plummeted straight to the ground, flapping all the way. I felt dizzy as I looked up, thinking of the Birdman's first and final flight, and then I came up with a great idea.

"Hey," I said, "let's busk right here for the tourists, just for the hell of it."

Randy thought it was a great idea too, so we got out our guitars and started playing and singing with gusto. A small crowd gathered around us, but about halfway through the third song, someone warned us the cops were coming, so we lit out of there. We headed down the left bank of the Seine, stopping to admire the huge Notre Dame cathedral sitting on an island in the middle of the river, and the boats and barges as they drifted along. We came to the next subway station and took a train to the Orleans station, where Randy said there was a great neighborhood to play in. There we found little bistros and bars, and cafes and bookstores. Randy talked to the owner of one bookstore, who let us busk on the sidewalk in front of his shop. We did well there, and in some of the little bars and bistros, where after playing a few songs we'd have a glass of cheap wine or a light meal, or even just snacks to tide us over. Randy picked up a couple of books at a used shop, but I was hanging on to as much money as I could, as winter was not that far off, and I did not know yet where I would be after Paris.

One day, we took the Metro to the outskirts to busk at a huge flea market. We'd find a spot, do a few songs, scoop up the hat, and move on to another location. We did well there, and in many other places. But now autumn had settled in, and we noticed the change. There was a chill in the air, the skies were increasingly gray, and at night we had to bundle up in jackets and warm clothing. With each day, there seemed to be fewer tourists in town, while the cops were catching us more often, and demanding to see our passports, looking for evidence of expired visas. Randy and I discussed the matter of how much longer we'd hang around Paris, and we decided to head south soon. He and Joyce wanted to see Greece and the Middle East, and head over to Israel for the winter, and besides, he said, he and Joyce were beginning to tire of the scene. They had, after all, been in the apartment many weeks now.

One night we all went out to visit Willie and Sonia at their house. We took the Metro to a distant stop, and walked the rest of the way. We had a nice dinner together, I was introduced as a friend from California, and we ended the evening over wine and small talk, before walking back to the Metro station. When we got there, we discovered that we had just missed the last train for the night. Sam suggested we hitchhike back home, but I was dubious, as there was hardly any traffic at that late hour. "The universe will provide," he said optimistically, so we stood on a street corner with our thumbs out. In only a short while, a sedan pulled over, and Joyce spoke some French words with the driver, who invited us to pile in, which we did, practically sitting on each other. As it turned out, he was going to the Avenue de Clichy, and let us off right in front of our building. I was thinking I had just witnessed a miracle, but Sam just grinned and said, "See? I told you the universe would provide."

It rained the next day, and the wind blew leaves off the trees that lined the avenue while Randy and I watched out the window.

There would be no busking today, and we agreed the time to leave was now. The next night we had a great feast together in the apartment, Sam fixing Indian food with chapatis, Joyce fixing a salad, and Randy and me providing the wine. Sam's money order had finally arrived a couple of days earlier, so he would be leaving the next morning, taking the train to the airport. We waved to him as he walked off down the street, bag slung over his shoulder, and clothed in a long brown robe. Then Randy and Joyce and I headed down to the Metro, where we caught a train to the end of the line, and walked out onto the sidewalk on a cold cloudy day. We hiked down to the freeway entrance, where a long line of hippies stood, all hitching south, as we were.

Randy and Joyce got a ride within an hour, and as we said our goodbyes, we promised to meet up in Athens. I spent another four hours by the side of the road, watching other people get rides by ones and twos, until finally in the evening, with the smell of rain hanging heavy in the air, a Peugeot pulled over. A nicely-dressed and well-groomed man opened the passenger door, and invited me in. I tossed my gear in the back, and settled into the front seat. He introduced himself, asked me where I was headed, and said that he could take me to a town I'd never heard of, but I gathered that it would be a long ride, which sounded good to me. I remarked that he spoke English quite well, and he told me he was a doctor and had learned it for his profession. He said that since I was in France I should learn to speak French, and offered to teach me some basic expressions. So as we sped down the highway, and Paris faded away, I began learning some rudimentary French.

CHAPTER TWENTY-TWO

Chasing the Sun

The rain pattered down steadily in the post-midnight hours as I huddled beneath an overpass, just north of Orange, my collar turned up against my neck, and my gear sitting on a fairly dry spot on the ground. There was very little traffic at this hour, and I was resigned to the possibility of spending the night there. Before the driver had let me out, and turned off to go to his home, I had learned to say a few things in badly mangled French, such as "Good day," "Good night," "Please" and "Thank you"—those sorts of basic necessities. But I was a stranger in a strange land, and feeling terribly alone and lost. Then from seemingly out of nowhere, a stranger approached, walking purposefully toward me. He was stocky and swarthy and wearing something that passed for a raincoat. He stopped before me and greeted me in a language I did not understand, but I reciprocated with a, "*Bonsoir.*" He then said something to me in French. I shrugged my shoulders and said, "*Je ne comprends.* I'm American."

"Ah," he said, smiling, "American." He touched his finger to his chest. "Turk. Turkey."

"Yes," I said, "you're a Turk." I shook his hand and then he asked me something in Turkish, to which I just shrugged. He asked again, this time gesturing for sleep by putting his head against his folded hands and closing his eyes. I shook my head no. He said something else, pointing down the street and gesturing that I should come with him. I got it that he was offering to put me up for the night, but I hesitated. What if he was planning to rob me? But when he pantomimed sleep again, and his smile seemed so genuine, his eyes so trusting, I nodded my head. "*Oui. Merci*. Thank you."

I followed him a few short blocks in the rain through narrow streets between tall tenement buildings until we came to his building, which he pointed to and said something to let me know we'd arrived. I followed him up narrow stairs into a small room. He smiled and waved his arm about, showing a bleak apartment with a tiny kitchen and bathroom, then pointed to the floor next to his bed, and made the sleep gesture again. I thanked him and rolled out my bag on the floor and climbed in. He crawled into his own bed and shut out the light.

In the morning, I awoke to sunlight streaming in through a tattered curtain on a small window, and looked about the room, not remembering for a moment where I was. My Turk friend was already up, and cheerfully wished me a good morning in his language. Soon I was also up and dressed and drinking a strong cup of Turkish coffee out of a worn mug. It was easy to see that my benefactor lived in poverty, but out of the goodness of his heart, he had shared what he had with a stranger who appeared to be in need. I felt very grateful, and wished I could have told him so in Turkish, or at least in fluent French. I tried to offer him money, but he shook his head no. So I just smiled and shook his hand again before heading back out to the highway to continue my journey.

Just after noon, I hiked past the large fountain in the Place de la Rotonde at the foot of the Cours Mirabeau, elated to be back in familiar Aix-en-Provence. I strolled down the broad leafy avenue, past cafes and bistros and onto a side street where I picked up a baguette at a bakery, and salami and cheese and a bottle of wine at a small market. Then I found a bench to sit on, made a sandwich, and washed it down with some of the wine. I stuck the unfinished bottle in my backpack, and took a long look around. The sun was shining, and the air felt comfortably warm on this autumn day. People strolled lazily by, shops were closed for the long lunch siesta, seagulls spun lazy circles in the clear blue sky, and all seemed right in my world. Later I stopped by Yvette and Jeanette's place on the Rue du Paits Neuf. Yvette gave me a warm welcome but mentioned that Jeanette had returned to the States, and that her boyfriend had moved in with her, so I knew not even to ask if they could put me up. Instead I asked her to send her sister my regards, before I sauntered off.

That night, after busking up and down the Cours, my pocket full of French francs, I had a reunion with Chris in his flat on Rue Fontaine D'Argent. I retrieved my old spot on the floor in his cramped art room, and we caught each other up on our lives over the past couple of months. I told him of my split with Vic, and my travel plans, which largely consisted of chasing the sun south, and making as much traveling money as I could in the next few days. He told me of his art projects and of a book he was reading about an artist and his gay lover, and when I looked into his face as he spoke, I realized he identified with the artist. But I didn't care about Chris' sexual orientation—that was his business. As far as I was concerned, he was a great guy and a generous spirit.

After he had gone to bed, I sat at the window a long time looking at the soft sky and the moonlight playing on the red-tiled roofs of the buildings below, and felt myself transported back in time, as if I had lived in this part of France during the years that some of these buildings were erected, or maybe even centuries earlier. Maybe I had been a troubadour here in another life. There was just that kind of magical quality in the air of Aix in the stillness of the night.

Late in the morning, after having a *cafe au lait* and croissant at a bistro, I set out busking, and met two other young musicians, a long-haired bearded American banjo player wearing a denim western shirt and jeans named Michael, and a slender young black Frenchman, dressed in a loose-fitting black silk shirt and carrying a leather bag over his shoulder. He was playing guitar and singing in English, and together they sounded so great I wanted to join them. I introduced myself to the black kid, who said his name was Jimi Guyard, and it was spelled like Jimi Hendrix, but pronounced "Zheemee." I asked if I could tag along and blow some harmonica with them, and Jimi said in excellent English, "Of course. I think it better that way. Usually when we run into other street musicians, they want to fight over the territory. But instead you want to join with us, so you're welcome."

I made the rounds with Jimi a couple more times in the next few days and he gave me his parents' address in Saint-Jacques de

Grasse, near Cannes, and told me I should look him up on my way back from Greece in the spring.

As I was walking down the Cours one afternoon, a wiry, ragged French hippie hit me up for spare change. "I haven't eaten in three days," he whined. I gave him a five francs note, and less than an hour later, ran into him in a dimly-lit bar, on a side street where I had gone to busk. He was sitting on a stool, drinking wine and smoking *Gitanes* from a freshly opened pack. When he spotted me his face lit up and he said, "Hey, *mon ami*, let me buy you a drink." I told him no thanks, seeing as it would be my own money he was buying me that drink with. I decided that from now on, I wouldn't give any spare change to hippies who hadn't eaten for three days. Maybe if they said they hadn't eaten for one day, as that would be more believable, but probably not even then.

That evening, while I was singing at an outdoor café, a young guy wearing tight-fitting slacks and a violet colored shirt, open at the collar with the top two buttons unfastened and a gold chain around his neck, approached and asked if I were an American. Then he wanted to know how long I'd be in town.

"I don't know," I said. "A few more days maybe. Why?"

"My name is Daniel. I own a nightclub, *Le Sideral*, not far from here, and I'd like to hire you to perform there on Monday night. I'll pay you seventy-five francs."

"Sure," I said. "What kind of music do you want to hear?"

"Just what you're playing, American folk music. What is your name?"

I told him, he gave me his card, explained where the nightclub was, and told me to show up around nine-thirty to set up. Soon I began seeing handbills all around town.

> *"Daniel Touati annonce la reprise des soirees TROUBADOUR, au SIDERAL, tous les lundi soir a 22 h., a partir du lundi 8 octobre. AU PROGRAMME: Chanson—Folk Music—Atelier de recherché—apres le spectacle, DANCE PARTY. Au programme aussi: STEVE et un super boeuf."*

I understood just enough to know that it was supposed to be a dance party followed by the troubadour Steve, but folk music and dancing seemed to be at odds with each other, as it proved to be when I showed up for the gig on Monday night. The small crowd listened and applauded politely, but they had really only been there to dance and socialize, and I was merely an object of curiosity. I did get paid, though, and it capped off the good run I'd had the past week in Aix. I decided it was time to hit the road, and said goodbye to Chris in the morning, each of us wishing the other well, and promising to meet up again in the spring.

I caught the bus to Marseille, and then walked around asking, "*Ou est le gare*?" until someone corrected my pronunciation and pointed me to the train station just around the corner. Inside, I bought a ticket to Venice, and tried to keep out of sight of the trench coat clad *gendarmerie*. Being illegally in the country, I needed to keep a low profile. Finally the train arrived, and I climbed aboard and found a seat, and stashed my gear in the rack above. I had worn my nicest, cleanest shirt and pair of unpatched jeans for the border crossing, tied my hair back in a ponytail, and hoped to appear inconspicuous.

We crossed into Italy without incident. The smartly-uniformed border guards walked briskly through the compartment, glanced briefly at my passport and moved on. I let out my breath and relaxed into my seat, trying to catch catnaps as we rolled across northern Italy through the long night, the monotony broken whenever we'd make a stop in a city like Torino or Milano, or when the conductor would wake me up to punch my ticket. But when the early morning rain ended and the sun shone in rays of gold through the parting clouds, the well-dressed and attractive young Indian couple in the compartment with me announced cheerfully that we were approaching Venice. The train clattered over a long causeway across a lagoon, and through the open compartment window I glimpsed the city of Casanova, built on canals, and we came to a stop with a jerking and a grinding of brakes at the end of the line—the Santa Lucia station.

I stepped out of the noisy station and into the cool of the morning, down some wide steps still wet from rain, to the Grand Canal. There was a waterbus, a *vaporetto*, waiting at an adjacent dock, its motor idling as it took on passengers. I almost stepped aboard, but then realized I didn't know where I was going. So instead, I ducked back into the station, stored my backpack in a locker, and set out walking. There was a small bridge near the station that crossed over the Grand Canal, and I took it.

On the other side, I found myself in a maze of narrow streets, tall buildings that housed shops and apartments, and occasional small tiled squares complete with statues and covered wells. There were no cars to be seen anywhere, as the only modes of transportation were by foot or by water. I strode along, guitar in hand, taking in the wonder of this Renaissance city of elegant decay, looking as if it was sinking slowly into the lagoon (which it was), with plaster flaking off some of the buildings, until I was completely lost. And then I came to the majestic sixteenth-century Rialto Bridge, which spanned a narrow part of the Grand Canal, and crossed over, noting the row of decaying but still regal looking *palacios* that lined the canal, and the water taxis and gondolas that passed underneath the bridge.

After much meandering, I entered the Piazza San Marco, or St. Mark's Square, named after the saint whose bones were supposedly housed in the Basilica, or church, which anchored one end of the square. The Basilica was Gothic in size, but a crazy mix of architecture, with Roman-style arches, French Gothic roofline, onion-shaped domes, golden Byzantine mosaics, and built of marble and brick and wood. In short, it was ostentatiously grand in a schizophrenic way. Next to it was the exotic looking Doge's Palace. The rest of the immense square contained a clock tower, a tall *campanile* (bell tower), and buildings housing offices, shops, and a museum. Outdoor cafes were everywhere, their tables and chairs spread out into the plaza, and the whole place teemed with tourists and pigeons. "This," I said to myself, "looks like a good place to busk."

I had no sooner taken out my guitar, and placed the opened case on the ground, when a concerned local rushed over to me and said, "You are not allowed this. You must go *pronto* before the *polizia* come."

I thanked him, and had just packed up and began to leave when I saw two policemen with their distinctive pointed hats hurry my way through the crowd. But I got away clean, and headed out of St. Mark's Square, along the lagoon to a small canal, and set up shop next to the bridge. I was able to run through a few songs before two plainclothes cops stepped up to me, shoved their badges in my face, and asked to see my passport. After thumbing through it, one cop handed it back and told me in so many words to move along. No singing in the streets here. So I wandered again, and ended up at a little piazza where there were some sidewalk cafes. I asked permission to sing, it was granted, and I began strolling around with my guitar. Then I made the mistake of approaching a table where an uptight middle-aged American couple sat perusing menus.

"Goddamn it!" hissed the pudgy red-faced man. "We didn't come all the way to Venice to hear this shit!" Then he snapped his fingers for the waiter, probably to have me tossed out. But I was one step ahead of him, picking up my case and moving on to the next cafe, where I had a better reception.

I pocketed the few *lire* I had made, and went off to find a cheap place to have lunch. I ordered pizza at a small stand, but it turned out to be tough as cardboard and about as tasty, so I bought a cheap glass of Chianti to help wash it down. I decided maybe I'd better just find a cheap place to crash for the night, and strolled along until I ran across a small pension, in an area removed from tourists, met the nice elderly lady who ran it, and paid for two nights in advance. Then I returned to the station by way of *vaporetti* for my backpack, and settled into the small but comfortable room at the pension.

In the evening, I went out busking again, and this time, I hit the jackpot. At my third stop, a busy sidewalk café, I met three Italian teenagers who requested Bob Dylan's "Blowing in the Wind." Then they asked me to sit with them.

"Buon giorno," I said.

"Good evening," replied the pretty girl in the middle with the long black hair and open smile. "You are from America?"

"Yes."

"I am Gloria, and these are my friends, Laura and Massimo."

I said hello to the other girl, a shy brunette with soft brown eyes, and the smiling well-dressed boy.

"I'm Steve," I said, shaking all their hands. Gloria told me she and Massimo were sixteen, and Laura fourteen. "You speak very good English."

"Thank you," said Gloria. "We study it in school. We like to practice it, so now we have the pleasure to practice on you."

We sat together a long time and talked about ourselves and about politics and the state of the world, and I spoke of my travels and plans, which they thought were wonderful. They all were intelligent, very well informed, socially conscious, and fans of music, especially folk music. Gloria asked me for the words to one of the songs I had written, and I scribbled them out for her, feeling very flattered. After they settled their bill, they invited me to join them for a stroll. They would show me around Venice a little, and we would find an ice cream stand. We all felt very simpatico together, as Gloria put it, and I agreed to meet the two girls the following afternoon at this same spot. As I walked back to my pension much later, I stopped to watch a street vendor roast chestnuts on a charcoal brazier, and then bought a bag. The night air was crisp and the chestnuts were warm, and I drank in the sights and sounds of a quiet part of the city as I walked.

When I met up with the girls the next day, they said I must come with them to see a Communist Party parade through the streets of Venice, so I could be exposed to a part of their culture most tourists are ignorant of, namely, their complicated politics. We watched from the sidelines as a group of young communists marched by, wearing red bandanas, carrying signs and red flags and singing a song about the "*bandera rosa.*"

Before parting, Gloria gave me a little card. Inside was written: "Be your life happy and free, Steve. We'd like to tell you and give you much more, but we think our friendship can be enough. Ciao!" It was signed "Laura e Gloria." We promised to stay in touch and write each other, and I headed off for another night of busking. I had done well that day with the lunch crowds, and that night, I did even better, playing inside a couple of nice restaurants as well as the cafes, and ran into no more grumpy American tourists.

In the morning, I bought a ticket to Trieste, and took the train to the Italian border town on the Adriatic. I purchased a ticket for Athens when we arrived at Trieste, and walked outside to kill time before the train arrived. I sat on a bench, staring at the ticket and fixating on the price it cost. I would arrive in Athens with just enough money to get by for a very short time. I debated returning the ticket and hitching, but Yugoslavia was a big country, and hitchhiking prospects seemed slim to none. I closed my eyes and meditated, hoping to clear my mind enough to make the right decision. After a few minutes of this I felt calm and rested and opened my eyes to bright sunlight. Then I noticed right across the street some young people loading bags into a blue Ford Transit Van. I was immediately drawn to them. I stood up, grabbed my gear, and hurried expectantly over to the van.

"Hi!" I said. "Where are you heading?"

"We're off to India," replied a dark haired bearded guy wearing a blue denim shirt and jeans. He had a heavy British accent, pronouncing India, "Inja".

"I'm off to Greece myself," I offered. "Just bought my train ticket. My name is Steve."

"Roger here." I shook his hand. He introduced me to his mates—two other guys and a woman with dark hair, pulled into a knot on her head. All appeared to be in their twenties.

"You'll be going through Greece won't you?" I asked.

"Right. Have to go through there, it's on the way."

"Have you got room for one more? I've got my ticket, but it's expensive and I'm low on cash. Could I ride along as far as Greece?"

"Well, I don't know. What do you all think?" he said, addressing the group.

"It's alright with me", said the girl, whose name was Kate.

"Long as you're willing to chip in on food and petrol," said George.

"I've no problem with the idea," said the third guy, Ian. "We've enough room, just."

I thanked them profusely, loaded my pack into the van, and hurried off to cash in my train ticket. By the time I returned, they were ready to go and we hit the road, and crossed easily into communist Yugoslavia. We hit the Adriatic coast at Rijeka, where we bought groceries at a bare-bones little market with few choices and many empty shelves, then headed south along the winding rocky coastal highway, overlooking a deep cobalt blue sea. All day, we followed the Adriatic coast, with the eight-track player providing the soundtrack for our journey.

"Who's that band?" I asked of the country-rock group harmonizing through the speakers.

"That's the Eagles," said the driver. "Don't tell me you've never heard of them?"

"Never."

"They're a big new American group. This is their second album. I'll put on the first one later."

And so it went, until late in the day, when we pulled over on a wide spot between the road and the cliff for a break. The guys pulled out the cooking gear, the girl the food, and she cooked it up over a portable camping stove. Then we drove on again until almost nightfall, when the driver found a nice spot to camp on a bluff covered in trees, the lights of a nearby restaurant shining in the twilight. We all piled out and walked over to the cliff where we watched the sun set. Then George brought out a bottle of scotch, which he passed around while we talked and relaxed. The sky darkened ominously with clouds, and a cold breeze blew up over the ocean, promising rain.

"Looks like rain," said Roger. "We'd better turn in. You're welcome to sleep in the van with us, Steve."

But I had drunk a little too much whiskey, and had a warm buzz on. I felt like camping outside in my sleeping bag, and said so.

"You might get wet," said Kate. "You're better off inside."

I had a little plastic ground cloth with me, not much bigger than my sleeping bag, and felt if I set up under a tree and pulled it over me, I'd be perfectly fine.

"Suit yourself," said Roger.

I laid out my bag, placed the ground cloth on top, put my shoes on the ground next to the tree trunk, and crawled inside, snug as a bug in a rug. As I was dozing off, the rain began. But filled with whiskey contentment and my own sense of invincibility, I just burrowed deeper into my bag. The ground cloth was working just fine to keep the rain off. But as it came down faster and harder, the ground soaked up the rain, and it quickly ran off and began soaking my bag from underneath. My fool's paradise came to sudden and disastrous ruin as I slipped on my wet shoes, grabbed my soaked bag, and knocked at the door of the van. It opened and I sheepishly climbed in, found a narrow spot next to a warm body, and spent the night shivering in a clammy bag.

In the morning we left in a light drizzle, and drove through the day. The rain lifted, but the sky stayed overcast, and when we took a lunch break, I laid my bag on the roof of the van, hoping it would dry out a little. However, that night when we camped out again, it was still damp, and I slept fitfully. But the next day was clear, and we stopped off at the walled and fortified old city of Dubrovnik, where we took in the sights and snapped photos of the place. We went along the coast a bit further, then a little beyond Kotor turned onto a small road that pointed northeast, and intersected another small road that led to Skopje. We drove all night, and along a fifty mile portion of bumpy, unpaved road, through Skopje, and south toward Greece. In the morning, we crossed the border and had our passports stamped, and by mid-morning we were in the Macedonian Greek city of Thessaloniki.

My British friends let me off on the outskirts of town, and where the road forked they would continue eastward, while I would head south. I thanked them again for the long ride, and we wished each other safe journeys. With my pack and guitar sitting by the side of the road, I watched the van disappear out of sight, and then a feeling of fatigue and loneliness swept over me. The sun shone dimly through an industrial haze, and my senses were assaulted by the stale city smells of smog and dust and petrol and diesel fumes, and the high pitched whine of motorized bikes and low rumble of cars and trucks. The buildings were square and plain and painted in whites and drab colors, and the part of the city that I could see seemed drab as well, with a couple of smokestacks in the distance adding a little variety to the landscape.

After a while, I hefted up my gear and shuffled over to a nondescript café and took a seat at a small, worn table with a stained tablecloth, and ordered up a coffee and rolls. The coffee was Turkish—strong, bittersweet and served in a small clear glass. It contained enough caffeine to give my weary mind and body the jolt it needed to get back out on the highway. Before leaving, I used the Men's room, and the toilet turned out to be just a small hole in the floor. I walked down to the fork in the road, where a sign printed in both Greek and English pointed south to Athens. I dropped my gear again, and impatiently waited for a ride—which, as it turned out, was a long time in coming.

In the afternoon, as a newer model Volkswagen microbus slowly approached, I jumped to my feet and stuck out my thumb, and it pulled over for me. Inside a gay black couple from Berkeley, George and Harold, welcomed me aboard, offered me some figs, which I gladly accepted, and we were off along a highway that skirted the Aegean Sea. The guys told me they were driving around Europe on an extended vacation, and were in no hurry. As if to underscore that statement, they soon pulled over at Mount Olympus, and George said they were going to spend the night at a campground there, and that I was welcome to join them. But there was still plenty of light left in the sky, and I was impatient to get to Athens, which with a little luck, I figured I could make this same day. So we waved goodbye, as they motored off toward the mountain and campground, while I deposited my gear on the ground again and waited. I studied Mount Olympus, mythical home of the Greek gods, looking ominous and mysterious and dramatic. Dense forests covered its lower slopes and the rest of the mountain rose sharp and stark and naked.

As I stood there by the side of the road, I could feel the history of Greece creep over me, the feeling of an ancient land whose earth was trod by countless generations and whose soil had been tilled since time immemorial. The sun dipped lower in the sky, and after a while, a Greek farmer in simple dress, with stubble on his face, pulled over and offered me a ride in the bed of his Toyota truck. He let me off near Larissa, a broad agricultural plain, sparsely populated. I found out just how sparsely as I waited in vain for a ride until long after the sun had disappeared and the night closed in. I was tired and hungry and felt like kicking myself for not taking George and Harold up on their offer of camping. A meal cooked over a warm campfire sounded nice at the moment.

While I waited, I thought about Vic and the band, and imagined them playing great paying gigs and touring behind the record that must have been released by now. Maybe I had been a fool to let myself be tossed out of the band. I certainly didn't seem to be faring any better on the road alone.

Then I thought about Monika, and I could see her clearly in my mind when I closed my eyes. She stood before me in tight-fitting jeans with her long, fine blond hair spilling over her shoulders, her eyes a limpid blue, and her bright smile melting my heart. I could hear her sexy voice with the cute Dutch accent, and almost feel the warmth and fullness of her mouth on mine. Then my reverie was shattered, as I thought of her with her new lover, imagining him as tall, strong, and handsome. My lonely solitude came clearly into focus, as I surrendered to the darkness and emptiness around me, and I felt like crying. But maybe that was just because I was hungry and exhausted from the road.

I wandered off to a nearby cornfield, spread my bag on the ground, and crawled inside. The ground was hard and lumpy, but it made no difference after a while, as I nodded off to sleep. I awoke to a chill in the air, and dew on the ground and on the cornstalks. It was also on my bag, but that was to be expected, as it was now the middle of October, and there was a change of seasons in the air.

Around mid-morning, I caught a ride along the quiet stretch of road, with an older Brit in a bright red sports car, and we flew on down to Athens. He asked me about my plans. I told him I figured on holing up in Greece through the winter, but when I told him how much money I had, he seemed skeptical.

"That won't last long," he said discouragingly. "You'd better plan on wiring home for more money or else finding a job." He succeeded in bringing me down for a while, but not for long, because soon we were roaring into Athens at top speed, and I was let out in the heart of the city. With the sea on one side of the city, the mountains on the other, and sprawl and smog in between, I couldn't help but make a comparison to my hometown of Los Angeles. But the smell in the air was not that of L.A., but of Greece, and I couldn't describe it to anyone then or now, except to say that it was at once familiar and exotic. The city teemed with people and activity and noise, and the traffic rivaled that of Los Angeles, except for the fact that there were many more whiny motorcycles and Mopeds, and pedestrians choked the sidewalks. The buildings were of all sizes, but mostly tall, and cramped together.

First thing I did was to find a place to eat, then set out looking for a cheap place to crash for the night. I asked every hippie and young person I ran into until I was directed to a hostel near Syntagma Square. It turned out to be not really a hostel, but a fleabag hotel that crammed as many young travelers into a room as possible, for the equivalent in drachmas of about a dollar apiece. The toilets and showers were shared, of course. For those who were on a really tight budget, the roof of the building was available for half the price of a room. I chose the latter, both to save money and to have a nice view of the city.

I left my pack and bag on the roof, feeling there was nothing there worth stealing, and set out into the city on foot, guitar in hand. I found the American Express office in nearby Syntagma Square, and checked for forwarded mail. I was hoping to find a letter from Randy, telling me he'd arrived, and where he was staying, but there was none. There was, however, a letter from my brother Mark. I pocketed it, and went out exploring, ending up at the Acropolis, which had a commanding view of the city on one side, and of the port and the Aegean on the other side. A couple of post-middle-aged women tourists approached and asked me to snap a photo of them, with the Parthenon in the background.

"We should have done this while we were still young," one of them complained. I felt I should be glad just to be young and on the road.

After they left, I sat down among the ancient ruins in the warm sunshine and opened the letter from my brother. Among other things, he spoke of his girlfriend, and how insecure he felt in the relationship. "Sometimes I feel like I don't deserve her, like I'm not good enough for her." He also talked about how he was having trouble controlling his emotions, and how he felt very depressed at times. At one point he said, "Sometimes I feel like I just don't fit in." Then he said he wished he could be on the road with me, or at least see me, before closing with love from everyone.

I put the letter back in my pocket and sat for a long while, looking out on the city, my thoughts of Mark, and also of Monika. Then I headed on back to the hostel, as I remembered Scarlett O'Hara's words. "Tomorrow is another day."

CHAPTER TWENTY-THREE

Grecian Odyssey

At night on the roof of the hotel, I took out my guitar and played a few songs for the other young travelers, including The Drifters' "Up On The Roof," which became a singalong, since all of us were drifters and up on a roof. We hung out, smoking a joint that was passed around as the discussions rambled between road stories, rock music, the Watergate scandal, and of course home. Most of the folks at the hotel were on some sort of vacation, and heading back to the States or their home country eventually, but not me. The road was now my home, and I wanted only two things: a warm clime to spend the winter, and a place to gig. In the morning after breakfast, I set out to look for the latter.

I found a large flea market to busk, but didn't make enough drachmas to buy a decent meal, so I gave it up. In the evening I made my way to Plaka, at the foot of the Acropolis. It was a bustling pedestrian area of narrow lanes and stepped alleys filled with cafes, tavernas, restaurants, and tourist shops. I asked at a couple of places if I could play, but was turned down. As I approached one restaurant, I heard music coming from inside, so I entered a dim but spacious room where an attractive woman was singing what sounded like either Greek pop tunes or folk music, accompanying herself on the bouzouki. I was captivated, so I sat at a small table, and ordered a glass of retsina wine while I listened. She had light-colored hair and big beautiful brown eyes, and she exuded natural charisma. She seemed to be about my age, perhaps a little older. When she finished her set and packed up, I asked her to join me at my table.

"Hi! My name is Steve. I loved your music. You have a great voice."

"Thank you. I'm Elly." She offered me her hand, which I shook. "I see you have a guitar. Are you a musician too?"

"Yes, and a singer. I've just come to Athens and I'm looking for some gigs, some places to play."

"That might be difficult. Even I have trouble finding steady work. And I think you being an American, would need a work permit."

"I loved that last song you did. What was it, a folk song?"

"No," she laughed. "It's something I wrote." She told me the name of the song, which had a Greek title. "It means, 'I Complain to the North Wind.' Are you a songwriter too?"

"I try to be," I said, "but I don't have much to show for it."

"My ex-husband is a composer," she said matter-of-factly. "His name is Mikis Theodorakis. He's in exile now, an enemy of the people, so the government says, because he writes patriotic songs and songs of freedom. We are living in a bad time now. Since I am the ex-wife of Theodorakis, the secret police follow me around. But they are so obvious."

We talked a while longer, and then she invited me back to her apartment to play some songs together. She lived nearby, on Mesimias, in the Ambelokipi section. It was within walking distance, but we took a cab, which she paid for. Her apartment was on the ground floor, simple but comfortable. We exchanged songs for about an hour, and when I left, we wished each other good fortune with the music business.

Her parting words were, "Watch out for the secret police. They might follow you because you know me." I snuck looks all around on my way back to the hotel, but saw nothing suspicious. Maybe she was acting just a little paranoid. Months later, I found out her fears were justified.

The next day I was busking at the Agora, an open-air market, when a tall black man strode deliberately toward me. He tossed a bill into my case, and when my song was finished, struck up a conversation. He was from the States, and said his name was Walter. He offered to buy me a beer at a local taverna, so we walked on down to the nearest one and ordered a couple of bottles of Ajax. Walter was not only tall, but also broad-shouldered, and a commanding presence. He was in his thirties, and exuded a powerful energy, especially from his eyes and his voice. He told me later he was an Aries, so he was by nature of fiery temperament. He said he was waiting for his wife to arrive from the States. He was expecting her to show up in the next two or three weeks. Then they would perhaps travel on to Turkey. I told him I'd planned to meet some friends in Athens, a couple from California, but so far hadn't connected.

"I picked up a couple from California," he said, "and gave them a ride all the way across Yugoslavia and Greece and dropped them off in Piraeus. They were going on to Crete."

"What were their names?"

"Randy and Joyce."

"Far out! Was Randy a lanky, talkative guy, and Joyce a quiet green eyed brunette, about medium height?"

"Sounds just like them."

"They're my friends! Did they say anything about meeting up with me?"

"Yeah. They said they were supposed to meet a friend in Athens, but had forgotten to arrange a rendezvous. They didn't know when you'd get here or where you'd be staying."

"Man, what a small world! I guess I'll have to catch the ferry to Crete and go look for them."

"There's one leaves every night from the docks. It's an overnight trip. I'll give you a lift down there. Where's the rest of your stuff?"

I told him, and we headed off. He drove a Metro step van outfitted for living in, complete with a bed and a stove, shelves, and storage areas. We picked up my gear from the hostel and tossed it into the van. Then Walter made an announcement.

"You know, I've been thinking it over, and I've decided to go with you. After all, I'm just killing time waiting for Marsha. I may as well be traveling around Crete, seeing the sights. We could drive around the whole island. We'll start at the farthest end, work our way along the coast to the other end, drive over the mountains to the south side of the island, and go the length of the southern coast.

We're bound to run into them somewhere along the way. There can't be that many Americans on Crete."

The port at Piraeus was large and bustling, with ferries coming and going to the many Greek islands from various docks day and night. There were two ferries to Crete; one went to Hania, the other to Iraklion. We bought tickets for the latter, since it carried vehicles as well as passengers. We hung around the terminal killing time, nursing ouzo and beer at a nearby taverna, until it was time to board the large diesel-powered boat. It would be an overnight trip, so Walter planned on sleeping in the van. I climbed the stairway to the main deck, and rolled out my sleeping bag in a quiet area where no one would step on me. The ferry got underway after dark, backing out into the busy harbor and then into the calm Aegean Sea, and our odyssey was underway. I went to sleep with the rolling of the ship on the water beneath me, a moonless sky unimaginably filled with stars above, and the smell of the sea in my nostrils, and the humming of engines and the sound of the boat chopping through waves in my ears. I slept peacefully and emerged in the early morning to a bright crisp day, filled with promise.

Walter and I had strong Turkish coffee, served with glasses of water, and sticky sweet baklava in the lounge, and then went out on deck to watch as the island of Crete came into view. Crete was the largest and southernmost of the Greek Islands, sitting in the Mediterranean halfway to Africa. It was also the most recent island to become part of Greece, in 1921.

We made our way down to the vehicle deck, and after we had docked at the ferry terminal in Iraklion, on the central coast, Walter started the engine and we waited our turn to drive away and into the busy city, which was the capital of Crete. Although the city itself was very old, it's history going all the way back to Minoan times, many of the buildings were new, having replaced the ones shelled during the Battle of Crete in World War II. After a short drive around the harbor, and a stop at a souvlaki stand for a quick meal, we drove over to the nearby ruins of Knossos, the mythical palace of King Minos. The site itself was a current archaeological dig, was quite large, and in the process of being restored. A few tourists wandered around the site, but at this time of the year, it was relatively quiet. Considering Knossos was the center of the Minoan civilization, and had preceded Classical Greece by a thousand years, I not only understood the historical importance of this place, but I could feel the antiquity all around me, as if ghosts from the past still resided here. A slight breeze whisked through the ancient palace, and the dust of the ages swirled around momentarily, as the thought hit me that eventually we're all just dust in the wind.

Since Walter wanted to start at one end of the island and work our way in a circle, we headed west toward Hania. The road wound around a steep rocky coastline, along the deep blue Sea of Crete, with foothills and mountains to the south, until we reached the city of Rethymnon, as old as Iraklion, only smaller in size. As we approached, buildings crowded in together showed both new development and the rebuilding from the war. Then we came to the harbor, which held Venetian buildings and a lighthouse, left over from when Venice ruled Crete. Inside the old city were mosques and minarets left from when the Turks occupied the island. Past the harbor and lighthouse, on a point that jutted out into the sea, stood a large old fortress, also a legacy from the Venetians, built to repel Turks and pirates. We hung around the harbor area and had lunch and Henninger beers at a small waterfront café, and talked.

"The Greeks are a handsome people," said Walter. "They're also very friendly, but they can be brutal, especially the Cretans. They've been occupied so many times, from the Romans to the Venetians to the Turks to the Germans that they've become fierce fighters. Besides that, they've had a blood feud going with the Turks for centuries. Both sides have committed atrocities and given no quarter. If you treat them right, they can be very hospitable. But if you fuck with them, then watch out."

I decided to take his words under advisement.

We took the road out of town again, west along the coast, winding through low hills and beside steep bluffs, and as we neared Hania, we overtook a red and white Volkswagen bus traveling slowly in the same direction. Walter pulled around it, and as we glanced over while passing, we saw the driver, another black man. Walter honked and waved, pulled in front of him, motioned for him to pull over, and steered the step van to a wide spot overlooking the sea. We all got out and walked toward each other, Walter and the other driver smiling broadly.

"Hey brother, where you from?"

"San Francisco," said the friendly, slightly chubby man with close-cropped hair.

"I'm from New York, bro. Name's Walter."

"Obie."

The two exchanged elaborate handshakes, and then hugged.

"Man, you don't see too many of us around here," said Obie.

"You ain't bullshittin', brother."

"Whatcha doin' in Crete?"

"Killing time, and cruising around with my man Steve, checking out the sights."

"Hey, Steve! Good to know ya.""

"Hi."

"I'm supposed to meet up with my wife and maybe go on to Turkey. What about you?"

"I live here man."

"You jivin' me?"

"No. My wife and I've been here six months. We'll have to move on eventually, but we got a kid and we want to raise him in Europe for a while, so he gets a taste of something else besides the discrimination back home."

"I dig you brother. I'm on the road myself indefinitely. Where's your place?"

"We live in Hania, not far from here. If you're in no hurry, why don't you follow me home, I'll introduce you to Sharon, and we can hang out. You're both welcome to stay for dinner, and we'll even put you up."

So we headed on over to Obie's little house, painted white and blue, simple and plain and cozy, and met his wife Gloria, who was a redhead with freckles. Then we met little Amani, who was not quite two. Gloria said they were trying to get away from the racism back home, but that sometimes it reared its ugly little head on Crete as well. Inter-racial couples stood out here. Nonetheless, they were enjoying a different lifestyle in Greece, and appreciated the friendliness of the Cretans. Of course we stayed for dinner, talked long, and spent the night, me on the floor and Walt in the van. Next morning we headed into Hania, drove around a little, then parked and walked around the harbor with its Venetian lighthouse and

Venetian buildings that lined the waterfront. On the road again, we turned east this time, retracing our route.

I had no clue as to where to look for Randy and Joyce, so I could only ask the few hippies we ran into in Rethymnon and Iraklion if they'd seen them, which they hadn't. That night we camped on the beach outside of the town of Sitia, situated on Sitia Bay on the northeast coast. The following afternoon we continued along the coast until the road turned slightly inland, and we crossed over the eastern tip of the island to Vai, a palm-lined sandy beach in a small lagoon-like bay. The date palms had been there for maybe thousands of years. Whether they were planted there, or had traveled as seeds across the Mediterranean from North Africa, was anyone's guess. There was a taverna at Vai, as well as showers and toilets. Just a little north was a small village where we could buy provisions. Walt decided we'd camp there for a while.

Walter liked to drink, and he did not like to drink alone. Sitting around the campfire we'd built, he brought out a bottle of krassi, a cheap red Greek wine, uncorked it, and began his nightly ritual of taking a slug and passing it to me. The wine was strong, bitter, and burned going down. I tried to wave the bottle off several times, but as I said, Walter did not like to drink alone, and so I became his unwilling drinking buddy. He would sit next to the fire, mesmerized, poking the firewood around with a stick, keeping the flames alive, and nipping off the bottle. As he drank, Walt underwent a personality change, becoming animated and talkative. Later on he'd either get morose, or confrontational, or if I was lucky, just sleepy. But in the early stages of his drinking he could be quite sociable and loquacious, and so I learned a lot about him and his background. He told me about his alcoholic father, how he had to grow up at an early age, how he'd gotten his girlfriend pregnant when they were still kids in high school, and that's how she had become his first wife. I heard about his drug smuggling days, and how he'd been caught at the Spanish border with a large stash of opium, and had gone to prison for it. Then he told of how Marsha had broken him out of that seemingly impregnable fortress.

"Marsha was great. She smuggled me in a file, which I used to cut through the bars. Then on the night of the planned escape, she had a car waiting just outside the walls of the prison, with a change of clothing and a fake passport. I made a rope out of sheets, and climbed out the narrow window. The rope didn't reach the ground, so I had to fall the last few feet. As soon as I hit the ground, I made for the car, which had its engine running, and we raced for the border. There was a very tense moment at the border before we crossed into France, when I thought the guards would challenge the passport, but they waved us across. After everything Marsha did for me, I felt obligated to her, enough to marry her. I still feel obligated. Without her help, I'd be rotting inside a Spanish prison right now. Of course, I have to be real cool now, and keep a low profile, in case Interpol is still looking for me."

Later I found out that Marsha was Jewish, and also from New York.

The second night at Vai, a Volkswagen camper van pulled alongside us. It's occupants were two young American women, probably college students, who were traveling around. Walt invited them over to the campfire, and we all chatted for a while. They politely refused the bottle when it came around though. When it got late, and they decided to turn in, Walt said, "If either of you ladies get lonely tonight, just come on over and climb in bed with me. I'll leave the door unlocked."

The girls laughed nervously, and said, "No thanks," but Walter pushed the point.

"I'm serious," he said. "No need to sleep alone. I'm here for you."

After they retired to the van, he said, "You got to ask for what you want. Most women like the direct approach. Besides, if you don't ask, you'll never know if the answer will be yes. It's worked for me before, on more than one occasion"

Every night for three nights I got drunk with Walter, and every morning I'd wake up sick and hung over. I didn't know how long I could keep up with him. But something that happened on the third night convinced me it was time to strike out on my own.

We'd run out of wine, but Walter bought some raki at the little village. Raki is like moonshine, a strong clear distilled spirit. It burns much more going down than krassi, and it can knock you on your ass. We were about three sheets to the wind when Walter started going off on pacifists, and saying they were just pussies who were afraid to fight. I quoted Jesus' line about turning the other cheek, a big mistake on my part. But then, my judgment was impaired by raki, and I was about to make another serious miscalculation.

"Bullshit! Nobody turns the other cheek. Nobody's like Christ, and you can't convince me otherwise. It's a dog eat dog world! Next thing I know, you'll be telling me you're a pacifist."

"I am."

"You mean you wouldn't fight if someone attacked you? You would turn the other cheek?"

"Yeah, I would."

"Bullshit! I don't believe you. Prove it right now. Stand up!"

Recklessly, I obliged him by standing up and facing him, arms at my side. He towered over me, his intense brown eyes were swimming in red, and his face was screwed up in a drunken rage. He made a fist and before I knew what was happening, my reflexes slowed by the raki, I felt a terrific punch to my face, saw stars, and landed on my back on the sand. Being as drunk as I was, I didn't feel the full effect of the pain yet, but I was dazed.

"Get up and fight back, you pussy!"

I stood and faced him again.

"Let's see if you turn the other cheek this time!"

He hit me again. I saw stars, ate some sand, and rose a second time. Now he un-balled his fist and stared at me curiously.

"You did turn the other cheek. Goddamn! I never saw a Jesus Christ before. I never saw anyone turn the other cheek. Goddamn."

He passed the bottle, but I waved it off.

"I'm sorry man, I'm sorry. You're a goddamn Jesus Christ. I'm sorry. Here—have a drink."

He shoved the bottle at me, and again I refused it.

"You refusing to drink with me?"

He was getting angry again. I took a drink and almost threw it up. But then, Walter did not like to drink alone. In the morning my whole body hurt, my head pounded, my stomach churned, and it seemed nothing short of death would cure me. I resolved to get away from Walter, because if I didn't my health was in serious jeopardy. Fortunately, Walter had run out of both food and booze, and he decided to drive back to Sitia, a town large enough to have a good supply of both. When we got to town, Walt went into a shop, while I walked across the street to mail a letter. As I reached the post office, the door swung open and out stepped Randy Bleu and Joyce Rosen. My mouth dropped open, but I couldn't speak. They were equally surprised.

Almost immediately we were enjoined in reunion. We caught each other up on our travels, and I learned that the night I had been dropped off by the side of the road at Mount Olympus by George and Harold, the couple had camped at the site next to Walter, Randall and Joyce. If I hadn't been so goddamn impatient to get on down the road, I could have been hanging out with my friends instead of shivering alone in a cornfield, and we could have all gone on to Crete together. As it turned out, our chance meeting in Sitia was even more of a coincidence, as Randy and Joyce weren't staying there, but in a small village on the southern coast. They had hitched a ride over the mountains in order to do some shopping and get some mail off

"I'll give you a ride back," offered Walt.

"You're welcome to spend the night," said Joyce. "We'll all have a party."

"Yeah, and there's a place for rent right next door to us," enthused Randy. "Wait till you see it, it's a groovy little place right on the beach, simple and laid back."

Simple turned out to be an understatement, for after we took the narrow winding road over the mountains, and emerged in the tiny village of Makrigialos, we stepped back in time, away from most of the modern conveniences, and into a community which was living pretty much the way it had lived a hundred or more years ago. The little fishing village, which faced south on the Sea of Libya, was mostly confined within the small bay that enclosed it. To the west, a rocky point jutted out from the end of the pebbly beach. To the east, another mass of rocks stepped out into the bay to close the crescent, creating a natural, if small and shallow harbor. On this east side of the village there was a taverna, called Galiopies, and it was the community gathering place—mainly because it was the only building that had electricity, which was provided by a diesel-powered generator. At night, it was lit up inside with fluorescent lights, and outside by a string of bright bulbs that ringed the entrance. A black-and-white television blared inside, and the villagers gathered around the magic box watching reruns of American sitcoms like "I Dream of Jeannie," with dubbed voices. The taverna served beer, retsina, ouzo, and the vile krassi wine, and provided free snacks to eat with your drinks. They also served meals of octopus, squid, anchovies, and other dishes. The other business establishments were a bakery, which made fresh loaves of bread each morning, and a small market that offered only the barest of essentials.

The villagers dressed in peasant garb, the women in black with their heads covered, and the men in mostly brown or black, often with knee-length boots. Most of the men fished, some in boats so small that they would pull them up onto the beach at night. Others worked the fields and greenhouses above the village. There were also itinerant shepherds who drove their flocks along the roadside and sometimes camped in the hills out of town.

A string of small, whitewashed cottages lined the pebbly beach, and Randy and Joyce rented one of these. It had two rooms, and a little kitchen, where Joyce prepared meals on a Coleman stove. There was a small bathroom with shower and toilet and sink, but no running water. A well just down the road and up from the beach provided their water. In order to wash, or flush the toilet, they would toss a bucket down the well, pull it up by a rope, dump the water into a container, and haul it back to the cottage. The well water had a salty taste to it, so it was difficult to drink. But Randy solved that problem by adding some krassi to the water, from a big jug he kept on hand, and the bite of the wine overpowered the saltiness. (Later, just before we left the village, Randy discovered another well up the hill that provided sweet drinking water).

The cottage next door to them was vacant, and after Joyce sweet-talked the landlady about me, I was able to rent it for the equivalent of thirty dollars a month. It was smaller than their place, only one room and a tiny bathroom, but it had a bed and a table and chair. The floor was tiled, and the walls whitewashed. There was a window next to the doorway, which faced the sea, only twenty yards away. There was no glass in the window, so a fresh breeze blew in freely. But at night I could draw the wooden shutters across the window and close it up. An oil lamp provided light.

Walter left after the first night, heading out to Ierapetra, about twenty-five kilometers down the road, and I moved into my new home. Counting out my traveler's checks, (which I had changed into bills of fifty deutschmarks while in Athens), I figured that if I could live on one dollar a day rent, and one dollar a day food, I had enough to last until the end of the year. As it was now late October, that meant a little over two months if I was careful with my spending.

But what else did I need besides food and shelter? My friends lived next door, and Randy and I settled into a daily routine of learning, practicing, and writing songs. Often, we would climb up on the roof of his cottage and play music, gazing out on the water. We also had books to read, and long walks to take, and at night we could drop by the taverna, or hang out with the young German guy, Joachim, who stayed in the last cottage on the beach. He had long blond hair and blue eyes, and was spending his time translating a book from English into German. He was happy for our company, as the villagers would have little to do with him. They had made him a scapegoat for the German occupation during World War Two. There was a family in the village that was similarly ostracized, because they had collaborated with the Nazis. Although the war had ended decades ago, these Cretans neither forgot nor forgave. At first, the villagers were indifferent to Randy and Joyce and I, treating us as outsiders but after a while they warmed up to us, and would greet us with a hearty *"Yasoo!"*

The days unfolded lazily in a stream of timelessness, and after a while we didn't know what day of the week it was until Sunday arrived, when the villagers would dress in their finest dark colors and go off to the Greek Orthodox Church to worship. We were able to buy condensed milk and instant coffee at the little store, so we would start our mornings off with coffee and fresh baked bread with tahini butter at a little table set up outside Randy and Joyce's cottage, while we warmed ourselves in the sun and watched the fishing boats on the sea before us. Days passed into weeks, and though the days were warm and pleasant, the nights became cooler. I would often walk down to the rocky point, and climb to a spot where I could survey the whole village, and the bright blue sea, and would write or meditate or think.

October became November, and then Thanksgiving was upon us, although we ended up celebrating a week later, when Walt blew back into town, this time with his wife Marsha. Also with him, in their Volkswagen bus, were George and Harold, who I had last seen at the turnoff to Mount Olympus. They were living down the coast now in Ierapetra, as were Walter and Marsha. We invited Joachim, and the eight of us had a starch-laden meal—mashed potatoes, stuffed cabbage, and bread—with plenty of krassi to wash it down with. Then our visitors moved on, and December moved in.

The days were cooler now, and the nights cold. We had no way to heat our cottages, but my sleeping bag kept me warm. However, I was running low on money, and I needed to find some work. As if in answer to my plight, one night at Galiopies, a farmer named Nikos offered work to Randy and Joyce and me. He didn't speak enough English to explain what it was, but we were to meet him at half past six in the morning. "*Dulya avrio.*" Work tomorrow.

None of us had alarm clocks, so I offered to be the alarm clock, as I usually woke up early, I planted the seed in my mind to wake up at six, just before I dropped off. But I awoke at four, and awakened the others, and we ended up waiting around a couple of hours, drinking coffee, and getting wired.

"Look," I'd assure them, "there's light in the east. The sun's coming up." Eventually it did, and Nikos met us at the appropriate time, we climbed into his little truck, Randy and me in the bed, Joyce in the cab, and he took us out into the fields where he motioned for us to pick weeds. Then he pulled up a clump of them and said, "*Manergia*," making the sign of eating.

"Maybe that's supposed to be our lunch," said Randy sarcastically.

"Or maybe he's going to pay us with weeds," said Joyce.

Joyce lasted till our lunch break, and called it quits, walking back to the village alone. Randy and I toughed it out until the end of the day, when we both threw in the towel.

"*Dulya avrio*?"

"*Ochi dulya*," said Randy, making a clicking sound with his tongue against his teeth and jerking his head slightly upward, the Greek way of saying "no". Nikos was disappointed, but he paid us a few drachmas, which we used to get drunk on down at Galiopies.

In the morning, a great storm blew up from the south, coming from the direction of North Africa. The waves rolled up onto the beach, and came very close to the little unpaved path that ran alongside the cottages. Fishermen brought in their boats, and the ostracized family asked us to help them drag their boat ashore, as no one else in the village would lend a hand. They didn't ask Joachim, for although they had collaborated with the Nazis, he was a German, and they blamed the Germans for their predicament.

The storm cleared overnight, and in the morning Nikos came by asking if I'd work for him again. Randy had already turned him down flat. This time, Nikos assured me, the work would be much easier, and inside a greenhouse. "*Dulya simera. O kipos. Poli kalo.*" (Work today in the garden. Very pleasant.) As it turned out, though, it wasn't at all pleasant. It was a long day of repetitious stringing of wire in a humid greenhouse, standing on a stool. And every time I would fall off, Nikos—who was sitting comfortably in a chair, watching me—would laugh and tell me how worthless I was.

At the end of the day, he invited me over to his house for a meal with his family. Most of the villagers had gone in together to buy a freshly slaughtered pig. Each family received a different portion. Nikos got the liver. I hated liver. But I had to sit and eat it and pretend I liked it. Before the meal, he brought out a bottle of raki, poured us each a glass, and made a toast. We downed the strong liquid in one long gulp. If someone had lit a match near me, I would have breathed fire. There came a second toast. Then his wife served the liver. Fortunately, my taste buds were partially burned off. Nevertheless, I meekly asked for another glass of raki. Any liver that went down after that bypassed my taste buds altogether. I drug myself home, and skipped the part where I would get a bucket of water from the well, pour half of it over me, soap up, and then rinse off with the rest. Instead I went directly to bed and shivered inside my bag until I passed out.

I gave up on the idea of working for Nikos, but now it was well into December, and I was about broke, as was Joachim. He was supposed to have gone back to Germany in September, but the thought of the brutal winter back home, compared to the mild and pleasant weather in Crete, kept him on. We both needed to find work. It was at this time that a construction company came to town and started building a hotel down the road for the tourist trade that would soon be coming to Makrigialos, and Joachim and I hired on as laborers. The job paid top wages—five dollars a day. We lasted almost three days.

The first day, we spent mostly pulling nails out of boards, gathering materials, and cleaning up the site. All the time Joachim would complain, "No milk today." The second day, we mixed concrete and ran wheelbarrows of the stuff up a ramp and poured it into forms. Joachim spent the second day grousing. "No milk today." The third day, the boss figured we just couldn't cut it, so he laid us off. I was actually happy. I wasn't cut out for this kind of work. I needed to move to a larger town where I could play music.

I hadn't had a proper shower or bath with hot water in two months, so I decided to go to Ierapetra, rent a hotel room for the night, and take a long hot bath. There was a bus that went to Ierapetra once a day, leaving Makrigialos early in the morning. Randy and Joyce would take it once a week to buy groceries, and would stay overnight with Walt and Marsha. I planned on catching it first thing in the morning, but overslept. I was determined to have my hot bath, though, so I started walking, hitching as I went. It was a very pleasant day for walking, warm and sunny. But there was just no traffic. Every now and then a moped or a three-wheeled cart would putter by, but no offers. So I just walked along, taking in the scenery until the sun had crossed the halfway point and was heading toward the horizon. I figured I had walked ten or twelve miles before I finally caught a ride in the bed of a small pickup, which deposited me in the center of Ierapetra.

I checked into the nearest hotel, and found out the bathroom was down the hall and was shared. I also was told that to get hot water I had to build a fire in the boiler room, and was shown how to do it. I took small pieces of wood from a pile, made a fire under the boiler, and then had to wait forty-five minutes for the water to get hot. Then I was free to bathe. But when the forty-five minute waiting period was up, I walked to the bathroom and found the door locked. I knocked, and a male voice told me to go away, he was taking a bath. Taking a bath with my hot water! There was nothing to do but wait until he was finished, build another fire, and wait another forty-five minutes.

This time, I waited in the bathroom behind a locked door. I filled the tub past it's halfway mark and stepped in. It was the most sensual experience I had ever known. I sat there immersed in water, and soaked and scrubbed until the water was tepid before rinsing off and changing into clean clothing. Then I went out exploring the town.

Ierapetra still showed signs of the Turkish occupation, with its minarets and domed mosques. There was also the obligatory Venetian fortress. But unlike Makrigialos, parts of Ierapetra had wandered into the twentieth century, including it's modern cafes and "discos." I also noticed a lot of young tourists in town, many of them Australians. I saw the busking possibilities here, and decided it was time to take the Steve and Randy show on the road. We had worked up a couple dozen songs, and hadn't yet had the opportunity to try them out in public. I was seeing the opportunity now, in the brightly colored lights of Ierapetra after dark. When I got back to Makrigialos the next day, I brought the idea up with Randy, and he agreed, as did Joyce. It was time to move on.

A few days before Christmas, while it was still dark outside, Randy and Joyce and I sat alongside the road that led out of Makrigialos with all of our belongings, and waited for the rickety old local bus to arrive. When it did, we climbed aboard, found seats, and rumbled off eastbound along the southern coast of Crete, heading for the twentieth century and what we called modern civilization.

CHAPTER TWENTY-FOUR

Land Of The Minotaur

In the months that we had been in Makrigialos, we had been isolated from the rest of the world. We read no newspapers, and saw no news on the television. Therefore when we arrived in Ierapetra, we were stunned to learn that a coup had taken place in Greece, and now the country was under the rule of a military dictatorship. While we had quietly reposed in the nineteenth century, without benefit of modern conveniences, tanks had rolled through the streets of Athens, and even in Ierapetra, far removed from the mainland of Greece, soldiers had paraded through the town and had confiscated weapons from everyone, even if they were only little .22 caliber bird rifles. So although we might be able to do a little busking around the center of town, where the tourists were, we needed to tread lightly. Walter was especially wary, because of his criminal record and fugitive-at-large status. He was highly nervous when I accompanied him to the police station so he could get his visa extended. However, it went off without a hitch.

I secured a bed at a cheap hostel, while Randy and Joyce crashed alternately with Walt and Marsha, and with George and Harold. My hostel was very basic, and loosely run. My first night there, an American who was crashing in the same room as me, brought in a young woman he'd picked up at a disco, and had sex with her in the bed next to mine, while I tried to ignore them and get some sleep. Finally it quieted down, there was a pause, and I heard the guy, who was obviously drunk, say, "That was great. Wanna do it again?" The girl mumbled something, pushed him off her, and rolled over to sleep.

We began meeting other travelers and expatriates who had settled into Ierapetra, like Rod and Doris, a couple with two children, from Edmonton, Alberta. When Walter would drop by their place, he was usually drunk and overbearing, and would carry on passionate political monologues, including his views on the Israeli-Palestinean problem (he was pro-Arab), with the overwhelmed Canadians, who were too polite to tell him to fuck off. There was another couple in town that was seeing as much of the world as they could with the limited time they had. The husband, Joey, had multiple sclerosis, and was confined to a wheel chair. This would be his last journey before he would become completely incapacitated. Randy and I learned the song "Joey, Joey" from the musical *Most Happy Fella.* The lyrics were about a guy named Joey, who is a free spirit, and whenever he gets tired of his surroundings, hits the road and moves on. We sang it for Joey, and he was visibly moved by our gesture.

Randy and I did a bit of busking around some of the tourist bars, but were cautioned not to play in the streets, or draw too much attention our way. The police in town were a little uptight. I watched as one cop accosted a young couple holding hands. He told them public displays of affection weren't allowed, except in the discos.

We made a few drachmas from busking, and it was certainly easier and more profitable than pulling weeds or mixing cement. Then a rumor began circulating around, probably started by a drunken Australian, that there was to be a big outdoor concert, something along the lines of Woodstock, only smaller, the following weekend in the hills above Ierapetra. It was rumored that Joni Mitchell would be there, as well as James Taylor, just to name a few acts. The rumor persisted and became embellished, and after a while was excepted as fact. And so Randy, Joyce, and myself, as well as others from Ierapetra made a pilgrimage to the spot out in the countryside where the concert was supposed to take place. When we arrived, all we found was a vacant field with scores of hippies milling around, but no stage, no bands, and no party. This looked like an opportunity for the Steve and Randy Show, so we found a spot to set up, took out our guitars, and played the two-dozen songs we had practiced, before passing the hat.

We ended up with a hat full of change, a big chunk of hash, and a note that said, "Have you heard Joni Mitchell's song about playing for free?" That really rankled me, as if we were taking advantage of the situation by being mercenary. We were, of course, but I didn't want to see it that way. I figured since we were the only musicians to show up for the supposed rock concert, and we were the only ones that had performed, we should be rewarded for our effort. Months later, on a kibbutz in Israel, Joyce and Randy would meet and become friends with the guy who had written the note, and misunderstandings would be sorted out.

On Christmas Eve, Rod and Doris had a party at their house, and all of us in our little community stopped by. Randy and I played a few songs, and after a couple shots of Greek brandy, decided to go busking. We played in the streets and at the sidewalk cafes, and in the tourist bars. We made some good money, and with revelers buying us drinks along the way, got pretty wasted. I ended up passing out on a couch at Rod and Doris' place.

A new year was about to unfold, and Randy and I discussed our musical future together. He and Joyce wanted to go to Israel in the spring, but also wanted to stick around Crete a while longer. We decided that we'd soon run out of opportunities in a town the size of Ierapetra, so we should find a larger city to work out of. A Brit had told me that Hania would be a good place for us, as it was not only a larger town, but also there were a lot of Americans around, mainly because of the Naval base at Souda Bay. Randy and Joyce wanted to hang around Ierapetra a little longer, but I was all for moving on. We decided I would go on to Hania, Randy would follow a day or two later, and Joyce would stay behind for a few more days.

Of course I'd been to Hania before, but had only blown through, and not really studied it fully. Now I walked along the little harbor and took in the old Venetian houses and buildings that lined the waterfront, and all the little outdoor cafes, with their white awnings and tables and chairs along the sidewalk. At the end of the breakwater, as I entered the harbor area, there stood a tall lighthouse which had been built by either the Venetians or the Turks. A Turkish mosque also survived in the harbor area. Beyond the Venetian fortress, which stood across from the lighthouse, there was a beach, nice for strolling along. The water was a brilliant blue, and so clear you could see the bottom, and spot little fish darting about.

Through word of mouth, I found my way to a so-called "hostel"—in reality, just a crash pad—at 49 Zampeliou, just off the waterfront. It was on the ground floor and was nothing more than a large room with concrete floor, an adjoining bathroom with cold water for showers, and a long, narrow kitchen, where dirty pots and pans and plates and cups were stacked up, both in and next to the sink. The place was filthy. It looked as if the floor had never been swept. The main room was also a study in squalor, with beds and mattresses strewn around, and no privacy. The walls were covered with graffiti. On one wall the lyrics of "Stairway To Heaven" were written out and illustrated by some unknown artist. On another wall was enscribed the lyrics to Bob Dylan's "The Days Of '49." The hippies who crashed here just called the place "Forty-nine." I had second thoughts about staying, but the price was right for my miserly budget—less than a dollar a night.

During the first few days I was at Forty-nine, I tried to initiate a general cleanup. I single-handedly washed all the pots and pans, plates and utensils, swept and scrubbed the floors and made the pathetic little bathroom presentable. The place stayed clean for one day, and then reverted back to its natural state of squalor.

The uniformed police stopped by on a regular basis, checking passports and searching for illegal drugs. A visa was good for three months, after which it had to either by renewed, or the holder would have to leave the country. The police made a note of when a person's visa was about to expire, and would show up on that date to deport them. People who wanted to stay on in Crete would usually leave town just before their visa expired, go over the border to Turkey or Yugoslavia for a month, and then re-enter Greece. My passport was scrutinized, and I knew as well as the cops did that my visa was only good for a couple more weeks. I would have to do something about it soon.

On New Year's Eve around six o'clock, I was hanging out at Forty-nine, when in strolled Randy, guitar in hand and pack on his back. We broke out our guitars and played and sang for the denizens of the place, who whooped and hollered and applauded, and then we went out busking. We hit the cafes on the waterfront, then walked over to the heart of the city and played in the streets, the market plaza, and tavernas. The streets and bars were crowded with revelers who were running around with plastic horns and whistles, blowing them incessantly. We got a good taste of Greek friendliness and hospitality. We not only made some bread, but in addition, the locals offered us drinks and cigarettes. I politely passed on the cigarettes ("*Ego then kapniso, parakalo"*—I don't smoke, thank you), but drank toasts with ouzo and brandy until I could hardly see straight.

The highlight of our night took place at a bar where an Australian girl danced on a table, while we faked some flamenco music on our guitars. Somehow Randy and I stumbled back to Forty-nine, where we entertained the group there until midnight, when a chillum was passed around to welcome in 1974. Then everyone began drifting off to sleep, save for a few who continued smoking hash, drinking, and talking in loud slurred speech. One guy was trying to sing the Jimmie Rodgers song "When It's Peach Picking Time In Georgia," but he was too drunk. He just kept repeating, "When it's peach picking time in Georgia, when it's peach picking time in Georgia, when it's peach picking time in Georgia, it's peach picking time in Georgia," ad nauseam. 1974 had arrived in a hedonistic stupor.

As my visa reached it's expiration date, I began to get anxious. So one day I walked out of town, along the road that ran beside the sea, until I came to the small village of Platanias. There I found a room to rent at a pension, owned by a friendly and gracious widow who dressed in black. It was, in fact, a tiny one-room attached cottage, complete with a bed, a chair, and a sink. The toilet and shower were in another building. After settling in, I walked to the nearest police station, just outside the village, and applied for an extension to my visa.

"How much money have you?" asked the cop in charge.

"Two hundred and fifty dollars," I lied. First I showed the official a hand full of drachmas, then my traveler's checks, which were made out in bills of fifty deutschmarks each, and flipped through them, so that only the number showed on the ends. I was hoping he would assume these were dollars, since I was an American. In actuality I had less than a hundred bucks.

"Why are you in Kriti?"

"I'm a university student, and I'm doing research for a thesis on the influence of the Venetian occupation on Cretan architecture."

"I see. Have you a return ticket to America?"

"Yes." Another lie.

"Where is it?"

"At the pension where I'm staying."

"And where is that?"

I told him, and also the name of my landlady, and that seemed to satisfy him, because he looked up from the passport on his desk, smiled at me, and with a great flourish, stamped a new visa, good for another three months.

"Enjoy your stay."

Afterward, I continued west along the road to Maleme, where a war memorial had been erected by the Germans in honor of their fallen soldiers, who had been killed trying to take the airfield there during the Battle of Crete. An entire parachute battalion had been wiped out as they fell from the sky, and tried to organize on the ground. They had met with unexpectedly fierce resistance, not only from the allied soldiers, but also from Cretan farmers and peasants, who had joined in the fight with clubs and pitchforks and ancient rifles.

Walter's words came back to me. "Don't fuck with the Cretans."

It was very cold that night, and the only thing I had to warm the cottage with was a charcoal brazier, and a bag of olive pits that had been turned into charcoal. I filled the brazier with the pits, lit them, and watched them burn down to a nice warm glow. Then I bundled up and climbed into bed. I had closed the door and window tightly, and as the room gradually warmed up, I drifted off to sleep. I awoke suddenly with a buzzing in my ears, and a pulsating green ring before my eyes. My throat was parched completely dry, I was dizzy, and could hardly breathe, being starved for oxygen. I dragged myself to the edge of the bed, stood up, and started for the door, but fell flat on my face. The door handle was within reach, and from my position on the floor I grabbed for it, and pulled the door open. Fresh air suddenly filled my lungs and I breathed in deeply. My heart began racing as the air reached my bloodstream. I crawled outside and lay on the ground, heart pumping, sucking in air, and regaining consciousness. I had come within seconds of dying by asphyxiation. I was so unnerved by the experience that I spent the next two days staying at Obie and Gloria's, recovering my wits, before returning to Forty-nine and my partnership with Randy.

Randy and Joyce had no problem renewing their visas, since they had moved into a respectable pension, they had sufficient traveling money, and return tickets for home. But the police soon came sniffing around at Forty-nine again, and singled me out for attention. Deportation day had arrived.

"Passport!"

I handed it over, and watched the smug look on the cop's face change to a frown. He said something to his partner, who looked at the passport in disbelief, before handing it back in disgust and leaving.

Later that week, we ran into two Greeks who had seen us out busking on New Year's Eve and recognized us. The tall one with blue eyes and wavy blond hair was named Socrates. He was dressed in what looked like the latest hip fashion. He wore a silk shirt with long, pointed collars, open to the second button, and a gold chain around his neck. The shorter, darker man, who wore a suit, was his business partner. But he wasn't a silent partner, because while Socrates did all the talking, his partner did all the translating, and his English was more than passable. They told us they were opening a nightclub soon, and were interested in hiring us as performers. Socrates was very animated in his enthusiasm, and drew us in. We wanted to know more. He told us to meet him in the plaza tomorrow at noon and he would take us there so we could formally audition.

We swung by the plaza at noon the next day and found Socrates and his partner ordering souvlakis at a stand, so we joined them. Then they whisked us out to their club in a taxi, and showed us around. The building was on the beach, outside of town, on the road that ran to the western tip of the island. They said it wasn't quite ready, there were still some finishing touches to be made, but the club would open soon. And while they sat watching us from a table, we stood on the stage and played our best songs, after which they applauded, then asked if we had any good stage clothes. We said we were wearing the best we had, but we could buy some new threads if he wished. Then they whisked us back to town in the same cab, bought us dinner, and Socrates gave us fifty drachmas each, with which to buy some nicer clothes. Socrates then admonished us to refrain from any more street singing, as it would damage the reputation of his business. He wanted high class performers, not street buskers.

We met with Socrates a couple of days later at a restaurant in town, to discuss the details of a performance contract, and he said the nightclub still wasn't ready to open, just a few more details, check back again the following week. Randy decided not to wait around any longer. He and Joyce were now staying with Obie and Gloria, and were feeling the pull of the road. They wanted to go back to Ierapetra, and then on to Israel. Randy said he was tired of busking, and of waiting around for Socrates to make up his mind. He needed a change of scenery. So we agreed that it had been fun playing together, and that we would catch up again in Israel or in California, and relaunch the duo. And then one day Randy and Joyce were gone, and I was once again alone.

But I wasn't really alone, for I had made friends at Forty-nine, and also befriended a couple that ran a small bar on the east side of the harbor, with a nice view of the sea. They were a young Greek named Stellios, and his American wife Sharon. Both were hippies, Stellios being the only Greek hippie on the island that I knew of. He was slender and had long black hair and a neatly trimmed beard. Sharon was a typical-looking American hippie who wore either peasant dresses or jeans, and had an aversion to makeup. Their place was warm and pleasant, as were they, and I used to drop by and play a few songs. Not to busk really, but just to hang out. Sometimes I would smoke a joint with them, or Stellios would treat me to a Henninger beer.

I made one more effort to get in touch with Socrates. One day, I walked down the road that led to his nightclub on the beach, strolled up to it, and peered through the window. There were four men inside, dressed in business suits, looking the place over and talking in serious tones. I stepped through the doorway, and their attention turned immediately to me. One of them said something in Greek, which I didn't understand. I asked for Socrates. One who did speak a little English asked me why I wanted to see Socrates. I told him I worked for him.

"You work for Socrates?" I had his full attention now, as the room went silent and all eyes were on me.

"Yes. I'm a musician." I pantomimed playing a guitar. "I'm supposed to sing here when the place opens."

"Socrates is not here."

Two of the other men began talking now in hushed tones, but I couldn't understand them.

"When will Socrates be back?"

"Socrates will not be back."

"Okay, thanks. I guess I'll leave then."

I walked away wondering what had happened to Socrates. Maybe these men were from the government, and had decided he didn't have the right permits, or hadn't paid the right bribes, and so had put the brakes on his plans to open the place in the foreseeable future.

But when one door closes, another opens. The next day, I heard about another club that was opening in town, and approached the owner about performing. I auditioned, and he thought it would be a great idea to have American music in his new club, as he was trying to attract the American sailors stationed at Souda Bay as customers. He would be opening in a few days and he wanted me to sing every Thursday, Friday, and Saturday night. He would pay me ten dollars a night. Considering I was living on about a dollar or two a day, that sounded like a good deal. He had me walk with him over to a place that sold records, and help him pick out a half dozen LPs of popular American groups, so he would have some background music to play in the club when I wasn't singing. I obliged him, and with a handshake we sealed the deal. I was to start the following week.

There was a group of us at Forty-nine who were getting tired of the dump and wanted to find a better place. Among the group was an eighteen-year-old American girl named Mary, who I was attracted to. She had lived on a commune back in the States, and now was traveling and living on her own in Europe. I admired her independent nature. She was a brunette with long hair, brown eyes, and a nice sense of humor. She was also very earthy and open. Two other guys at Forty-nine were also hot for her: Barry, a long, tall blond Texan, and Bruno, a slightly built French guy with long, curly brown hair and an infectious smile. He also had a powerful, outgoing personality and great sense of humor.

One day the four of us decided to take a walk out into the country. We ended up about twelve kilometers inland at a village named Alikianos, where there was a fourteenth-century Greek Orthodox Church and a small olive oil factory, as well as the small whitewashed houses of the village, and the obligatory taverna. On the outskirts of the village, we had a view of lush orange orchards, olive orchards, fields of sheep and goats, and snow-covered mountains in the distance. We also met a hippie couple in the village, Canadian Dave and Baku, a German girl, both of whom worked in the orange groves. They told us there was work to be had in Alikianos picking oranges or working in the olive oil factory. They invited us to come stay with them in their little house until we found work and a place of our own.

By the time we had returned to Hania that evening, Bruno and Mary had hooked up, and Barry and I had offered condolences to each other. We all decided to move to Alikianos the very next day. Another couple threw in with us as well. Manfred was a tall and muscular German with long brown hair and beard, and was wise and kind. He had traveled all over the world, and gained a lot of insight for his years. Carol was a tall slender blond from the States with blue eyes, long hair and an easy-going personality.

Baku and Canadian Dave's house was white with blue trim (the national colors of Greece), and had only one room. There was no electricity, but a spigot outside the house provided fresh water, and there was an outhouse with just a hole in the floor to squat over. At night it was wintry cold, so we all laid out our sleeping bags on the floor and huddled together for warmth. It gave new meaning to the expression "three dog night," for we had what amounted to a big puppy pile. After a couple of days, I hiked back to Hania to start my job at the Kriti Bar.

In the Minoan culture, there was a mythical being called the Minotaur—half man and half bull. In a way, the concept was not unlike the Cretans. They were close to the earth-working the fields and orchards, herding sheep and goats, fishing the sea; and living into ripe old age. They could also be like the bull if you tried to invade their land, or rule them through suppression. Just outside Alikianos, I passed a monument dedicated to the martyred freedom fighters of the village. Most of the Cretans had not completely surrendered to the Germans during the war, but had fought on using guerrilla tactics. According to the plaque on the monument, most of the men and boys of the village had been slaughtered by the Germans in reprisal for their resistance. A little further on down the road, there was a prison. During the war it had housed enemies of the Third Reich. Now, according to Barry, it housed felons, many of them hippies who had been busted for drugs, including pot and hash. It was a sobering thought, since all of us smoked a little hash now and then.

The Kriti Bar opened on a street near the plaza and open-air market to little fanfare. But word of mouth soon began bringing in business—first the local hippies, then the American sailors. They were required to wear civilian clothes off-base, so as to not intimidate the locals. As one local explained to me, "Crete has been occupied many times. First the Romans, then the Venetians, Turks, and Germans." He paused and added very deliberately, "And now the Americans."

Among the sailors who would hang out in the Kriti Bar on weekends were members of a Navy SEAL team. During the week, they would sometimes pull up into the harbor in their two power boats painted Navy grey, and tie up alongside the wharf. Then they'd go over to a café for a meal or a drink before heading out to Souda Bay again. They always wore their civvies.

The Kriti looked like a typical American tavern, with the bar itself in the center of the room in a horseshoe shape, tables and chairs around the rest of the room, and booths along the side. The restrooms were in the back. I sang from a barstool in a little corner, and on my breaks I would socialize with everyone, making new friends at the same time. One of the guys I met, Wayne, became my good buddy. He was twenty-two, of medium height and build, and had dark hair that was grown as long as Navy regulations would allow. He also pushed the envelope with his beard, which although neatly trimmed, was a little on the long side as well. He asked me where I was staying, and I told him Alikianos, but tonight I would be crashing at Forty-nine. He said there was no need for that. The Navy paid him a stipend to live off-base, and he had a two-room apartment in town. His roommate had just been transferred to the States, and had shipped out earlier in the week. I was welcome to stay in his spare room any time I liked. I gladly took him up on his offer. He also told me I didn't have to walk all the way to Alikianos, as there was a daily local bus that went to Omalos, and stopped just outside my village.

When I returned to Alikianos, I found things had changed. My friends had moved into a larger house, this one with two rooms. The rent was seven dollars a month, so with seven of us, my share would be one dollar a month. The house was just on the outskirts of the village, and like every other place, whitewashed. It had one large room, which we used for sleeping and hanging out, and a smaller adjoining room with an earthen floor and a fire pit in the middle, and a chimney in the ceiling for the smoke to vent. This was the kitchen, and the women built many a fire and cooked many a meal over the fire pit. There was a single light bulb hanging from the ceiling of the main room, and a water spigot outside in the yard, which was fenced in with a hand-built stonewall. A trellis of thatched tree limbs covered part of the yard, and a little garden grew there as well. A couple of trees shaded the yard, and the outhouse was out back, of course. There was a baby goat that belonged to our neighbor, which began wandering into our yard, so we more or less adopted it. Manfred and Carol took turns bottle-feeding it milk.

Barry had found work in the olive oil factory, and he kept us supplied with bottles of fresh virgin olive oil, which we dipped our bread into during our meals. We picked up fresh loaves daily from the local baker. The rest of the folks worked in the orange groves, so we always had fresh oranges to eat. With a job in Hania, I hung around during the day, playing my guitar, writing songs, reading, and going for long walks in the countryside. Thursdays I would catch the bus to Hania, play at the Kriti Bar, and stay at Wayne's apartment. It was an idyllic life. Wayne had a record player, and he bought records at the Navy Exchange on base. Through him,

I discovered John Stewart and Jim Croce, and managed to learn songs off their albums to add to my repertoire.

One day, Bruno brought home a French hippie he had met in Hania, and informed us he would be spending the night. The new guy turned out to be overbearing and had no intention of leaving. The following night he showed up with a lady friend, who he had invited to stay, and the next day brought another friend. The three newcomers took no part in the chores around the place, but just took up space, and had decided to stay on indefinitely rent-free. Resentment began building with the rest of us, but no one took initiative to evict the freeloaders. Then Bruno, the guy who had opened the door to these deadbeats in the first place, left town because his visa had expired. He expected to stay gone for at least a month. I had a few confrontational words with the lazy newcomers, but it was a waste of my breath. So I decided to spend more time in Hania at Wayne's. Henceforth, I would only visit Alikianos two days a week.

Now I had a couple of extra days to spend in town, when I wasn't working. If it was raining, which it did frequently in January and February, I would hole up at the apartment, listening to records, learning new songs. But if the sky was clear, I would go exploring Hania. I would see the Greek Orthodox priests in their beards, and black robes and funny hats, sitting at cafes drinking coffee and looking serious. At other tables, old men in peasant garb would sit with coffees or ouzos and finger worry beads. The open-air market, which had lamb and goat carcasses hanging from hooks, and octopus and squid and fish on ice, and everywhere fresh fruits and vegetables and olives, and all manner of goods, was usually crowded. At night I would often hang out at Stellios and Sharon's bar, and it was from Stellios I learned the fate of my almost-employer Socrates. He was in prison, perhaps the prison we passed on the road to Alikianos. He'd been busted for smuggling pot and hashish, after a long investigation involving authorities from Athens and Hania. Now I understood who the men in his nightclub had been—plainclothes police. When I had told them I worked for Socrates, they probably thought I was a drug runner for him. It had been a close call for me. However, I hadn't seen the last of the Greek police, or the secret police in particular.

One night Wayne and I went over to a club we'd heard about on Nea Chora Beach, down the road to the west of the harbor. Inside we met a couple of young ladies, Doreen from the States and Jennifer from Scotland, and we chatted them up. It turned out they were bar girls, paid to socialize with the lonely sailors that hung out there, and encourage them to buy drinks. If we wanted to sit with the girls, we'd have to order something, so Wayne sprung for a couple of Ajax beers.

"It's not like we're whores," said Doreen. "We just talk to the guys. The owner, Stephanos, thinks it's good for business to have a couple of single girls in here to provide atmosphere."

"We don't get paid a lot," said Jennifer, "but it helps with the rent and spending money, and it's a pretty easy job. We get asked out a lot, but we always turn the guys down. It would ruin the point of the job, that we're supposedly unattached."

"We're sort of fantasy girls," added Doreen.

I was quite attracted to Jennifer, who was a cute, trim young brunette of medium height, with long hair parted in the middle that cascaded over her shoulders. She had beautiful blue eyes, and a warm smile, and was dressed in a peasant blouse and a skirt. She wore a handmade hippie necklace and silver bracelets, and rings covered most of her fingers. None of them looked like engagement rings, though, so I asked her what time she got off.

"Usually around midnight."

"Good, I'll pick you up and we can go for a walk."

"Stephanos wouldn't like that."

"Then meet me outside. I'll walk you home."

She agreed, and Doreen agreed to go with Wayne. We walked them back to their apartment, which was in town. I loved listening to Jennifer, because her voice was lilting and musical, with only a trace of Scottish accent, and she was the type of person who was sociable by nature, which suited her well for her bar girl job. But when I asked her if she had a boyfriend, her mood turned dark, as did her voice.

"I was with a guy until recently."

"What happened?"

"He went off and joined the Israeli army."

"Is he Jewish?"

"No, just macho. He thinks fighting in a war will prove his manhood or something. It's all so stupid. So now I have to worry about him getting killed."

I changed the subject, and we talked about how long she'd been here, what her plans were, what living in Scotland was like, that sort of thing. I didn't kiss her that night, but when I finally did, I found that her lips were soft and full and her body was warm and fit snugly in mine. I started visiting her regularly, stopping by her bar for a beer now and then, and seeing her on her night off, if I wasn't in Alikianos at the time. The word got around that we were hanging out together, and some of the SEAL team guys began seeing me in a new light and congratulating me on my success. One of them confided he wished he were in my shoes.

Winter was still hanging around with the accompanying cold nights, so Jennifer made me a poncho out of a wool Navy issue blanket one of the sailors had given her. She was creative, not only with a needle and thread, but in other ways as well. She liked to draw, and she liked to write poetry and other things, and had the most beautiful handwriting, very artistic. We got on well, and enjoyed each other's company, and I would sing songs for her. We finally had sex impulsively in an olive orchard in the middle of the afternoon. We had been out for a walk, and took a break in the shade of the orchard. We sat on the cool ground with new spring grasses carpeting the field, and began kissing and caressing each other.

"You want to make love?" I asked.

"Uh-huh," she said breathlessly, and pulled up her peasant skirt. Right in the middle of our act, an old grizzled farmer came riding by on his donkey, caught sight of us, and began yelling in Greek and waving around the donkey whip he held in his hand.

"We better go," I said, zipping up.

"Olive orchards aren't what they're cracked up to be," she laughed nervously.

We finished our expression of intimacy back at her place.

Spring eased itself in quietly throughout March, and life was good. In Alikianos, things continued at an easy pace, with most everyone working in the warm sunshine. Vegetables and herbs began sprouting up in the garden, and we had been accepted by the villagers as a part of their community. I think this had to do with the fact that everyone was gainfully employed, including me. The Greeks valued hard work, and didn't think much of the hippies who laid about on the beach at Matala and lived in the caves there. Sometimes our neighbors would bring by offerings of food, or include us in a celebration. During Easter week, someone slaughtered a lamb, and the neighbors invited us over for a feast. I declined on the grounds that I had to go into Hania, but I thanked them for their graciousness. There was a young Greek guy who began hanging around with us. He would bring his bouzouki over and play it, and I would play guitar. I met an American guy at the Kriti Bar named Dave, but to distinguish him from Canadian Dave, we called him Cherokee Dave. He would drop by our place from time to time and visit and play his guitar. So once we finally kicked the French freeloaders out, we were a big, happy, extended family.

In Hania, life unfolded casually as well, with me singing three nights a week, hanging out with Wayne and smoking hash with him now and then, and spending time with Jennifer. Then Stellios disappeared. I went down to his bar one night, and only Sharon was there. What she had to say unnerved me.

"The police picked him up last week. They searched our place and found some hash. He told them I knew nothing about it—it was his alone, and that's why I'm not in jail. They'd been watching our place ever since Socrates got busted. I guess they thought we were part of a drug ring or something. You know we weren't dealing drugs, just smoking a little with our friends. I don't know what to do. They won't give him bail, and they won't let me see him. I'm trying to get a lawyer, but they cost money, and I'm having a hard time raising it."

I offered my condolences, and now felt the repression of the military dictatorship that ran the country like a shadowy evil force. One night I was walking around the plaza after my gig at the Kriti, looking in shop windows, and just thinking, when I noticed two men following me. When I looked over my shoulder to check them out, they suddenly turned and pretended to be window-shopping. One of them was tall and wore a trench coat.

I remembered Elly's words in Athens. "The secret police follow me around, but they are so obvious." In the week that followed, I began noticing these two shadowy figures were keeping an eye on me, and they were obvious about it.

It was now April, and Jennifer's visa was about to expire. Doreen decided it was time to leave the island as well, so the two made plans to go to London. They bought ferry tickets to Athens, and since Wayne had the next two days off, we offered to accompany them on the overnight trip. Jennifer and I huddled together on a deck bench, talking intimately, getting closer than we'd ever been, and knowing we'd soon be missing each other. Then it got late and the girls went below and found bunks. Wayne and I stayed topside, sitting on top of a cabin. I took one of his cigarettes, emptied a little tobacco out, crumbled some hash and stuffed it into the end of the cig, twisted the end, and lit it up. Just then, a couple of men in long coats marched by us, looking straight ahead, and disappeared into the lounge. After we had finished smoking, they walked stiffly past us again. Then Wayne and I found a spot to roll out our bags, and we went to sleep on the deck.

After docking in Piraeus, we caught a bus to the center of Athens and had breakfast at an outdoor café, before heading off to Syntagma Square so the girls could buy their plane tickets. Then we did some sightseeing and went to a park, and Jennifer and I tried to make the time together as meaningful as possible. Too soon it was time for them to catch their bus for the airport, and Jennifer and I had one last long kiss before she stepped aboard, found her seat, and waved to me from the window. We promised to keep in touch. Wayne and I killed some time, and then headed back to Piraeus to catch the night ferry to Hania.

On the night crossing, there was a group of Greek soldiers aboard. After we had gotten underway, some of them made a circle on the deck, and while one soldier played the bouzouki and another a tambourine, they sang and performed folk dances with their arms across each other's shoulders. It was fun to watch as the bouzouki player stumbled around trying to stay on his feet, and the circle of dancers weaved to and fro with the rocking of the boat on the water. The stars filled the night sky, and as we got into deeper water, the boat rocked and rolled more, and so the soldiers finally went below deck. Wayne and I walked into the lounge and had a seat at the bar. In the reflection of the mirror we noticed two figures watching us intently, and at the same time pretending not to.

"Wayne, don't turn your head, but you see those two guys standing in the corner watching us?"

"Yeah."

"You recognize them?"

"I think I saw them in Athens earlier, when we were in Syntagma Square."

"I saw them on the boat last night. They kept walking past us."

"They look really familiar." There was a pause as recognition finally hit. "Yeah, now I know where I've seen them before. They're Hania police. I wonder what they're doing here."

"Those are the same guys that have been following me around Hania lately," I observed. "They followed us all the way to Athens and now back again. They're probably the same cops who arrested Stellios—the secret police. I think they've got it in mind that I'm a drug dealer."

"Shit! What are we going to do? If they follow us back to the apartment, we're screwed. I've got a big stash of hash back there."

"We've got to give them the slip," I said. "Let's ignore them, finish our drink, and then take a stroll around the deck. As soon as they're out of sight, we'll duck down below."

We gave them the slip and ended up in a compartment with the soldiers. I took out my guitar and sang songs while they whooped it up, and kept passing a bottle of retsina our way. Then they invited us to take a couple of empty bunks for the night, which we did. In the morning we waited until the ferry was pulling into Souda Bay before appearing on deck.

As we made our way to the railing where the gangway was, we spotted the police in the lounge, and they soon made their way out on deck and took up positions behind us. But we had worked out a plan. We would ignore them, pretending we hadn't spotted them, and walk casually down the gangway. They would be expecting us to take the bus into town again, so we slowly and nonchalantly strolled toward it. But as we came to a line of taxis, we suddenly ducked into the back seat of the nearest one, whose engine was idling, and told the driver to take off as fast as he could. We hurried down backstreets, taking a circuitous way back to the apartment, all the while shouting instructions to the driver and looking out the back window to see if we were being followed. We weren't. As soon as we reached the apartment, I paid off the driver and we rushed inside.

Wayne got his stash of hash and flushed it down the toilet. I hurriedly packed all my things, and tried to think of where I could hide out for a while. Then it came to me. One of my casual friends was a career Navy petty officer named Roy. He was in his thirties, homely and socially inept, but a really nice guy. He frequented the Kriti Bar because he was in love with the bartender, a divorced American woman who had a great smile and a killer body. He had once invited me to a party at his apartment, along with the regulars at the Kriti Bar, as an excuse to get this bartender he was crazy about over to his place. I knew where Roy lived, which was nearby, I knew he had a spare room, and I knew he was just cool enough to let me lie low there for a while.

I snuck down alleyways and crooked streets, all the time looking over my shoulder until I reached Roy's place. He wasn't home yet, but the door was unlocked, so I let myself in. When he showed up late in the afternoon, he was surprised to see me, but after I explained I needed a place to stay for a few days, he very graciously offered me his spare room. My visa was almost up, and I would have to leave town soon. But in the meantime I would keep a low profile, make plans, and play a few more nights at the Kriti Bar to get some more traveling money together.

Time moved very slowly for the next few days, as I tried to shake off a growing feeling of paranoia.

CHAPTER TWENTY-FIVE

On The Run

I had been in Greece six months now, and with spring in the air, I began feeling the tug of wanderlust. My visa was about to expire, and I didn't see any point in renewing it again. After all, Randy and Joyce had left town, and so had Jennifer. And the secret police would be happy if I left town as well. Constantly looking over my shoulder was getting tiresome. I had enough traveling money saved up to last a while, and more than one vagabond who had blown through Hania had mentioned a town in Spain where I might do very well. It was Sitges, just south of Barcelona, and it was supposed to be a happening place.

I had been in touch with Laura and Gloria in Venice, and when I sent Laura a letter telling her of my plans to return her way, she was insistent that I stop and visit. And Monika, my former Dutch girlfriend, wrote to tell me her job at the Crisis Center had ended, and so had her relationship with her boyfriend. She said that she was going to the south of France at the end of April and that she missed me. Well, it was the middle of April now, so I decided to get in the wind again, and wrote to her that we could meet up in France. Then I came out of hiding to say goodbye to some of my friends.

I dropped by Sharon's place. She was still trying to get a lawyer for Stellios. We wished each other luck. I dropped by the Kriti Bar and Jennifer's old club, Giorgio's, and told everyone, "*yasoo*," which meant both "hello" and "goodbye." I ran into the Navy SEALs as they were tying up their boats, and they wished me luck on my travels. Then I began strolling around the harbor, where the sunlight was shimmering on the clear water. I spotted an English hippie couple I knew, sitting at an outdoor table in the sunshine, and I wandered on over.

The woman, Rosemary, reminded me of Star, with her long light brown hair and cheery smile and peasant dress, and her partner, Geoff, looked a little like Vic—slender, long hair and beard, wearing a Hindu shirt. But his facial features weren't as sharp, nor were his eyes as intense, but soft and bright. I sat with them, Geoff offered me a beer, and I brought out my guitar and played a few songs. Then after farewell handshakes, I continued along the waterfront until I came to a café where a couple of Greeks motioned me over, one pantomiming playing the guitar, and the other clapping his hands and yelling "*Opa! Opa!*" I understood them to mean they wanted me to play, so I took out my guitar again and obliged them. Then one of them shoved a chair over to me, the other pushed over a glass of krassi, and they invited me to sit. As I did so, I glanced over my shoulder and spotted the secret police walking by, watching me out of the corners of their eyes. But I didn't worry. I wasn't doing anything suspicious, and besides, they weren't about to make a scene in a public place like this. I was wrong.

One krassi and two songs later, a uniformed cop strode up to me, said something in Greek, and motioned me to follow him. I shrugged my shoulders, put up my guitar, and left with him to the protest of the men at the table. As we walked I asked where are we going, what's this all about, but he would only reply, "Come. Tourist police." I gathered we were going to the office of the Tourist Police, someone who could speak English, and then I'd find out what was going on.

The office of the Tourist Police, which was located on Gianari, in the heart of Hania, was in a small building that I had not noticed before. I was led inside and made to sit in a chair across the desk from the officer in charge, who then dismissed the regular cop with some words in Greek and a wave of his hand. Then he turned his attention to me.

"Passport, please."

The official had close-cropped black hair and a neatly trimmed mustache, and was wearing a dark suit. He spoke perfect English without much accent. At the moment his face was as stern as his voice.

"Your visa is about to expire."

"Yes, I know. I was planning to leave Crete tomorrow."

"I am afraid that is not possible. You are under arrest."

"For what?"

"Playing music without a license."

"But I was just singing some songs for some men who requested I play."

"No matter, it is against the law to make music in public without a license, especially for money. I am certain is also illegal in your country, no?"

"No. I do this all the time in my country. Besides, I have been singing at the Kriti Bar for quite a while now, and no one there seems to think it is illegal."

"This I did not know about. You have been in Hania for some months now?"

"Yes," I said, opening my guitar case and taking out my guitar, "and I have been enjoying my stay very much." I began strumming some chords while smiling. The officer now visibly relaxed, his expression softening. He sat back, thinking, and drumming his fingers on the desk.

"I have many American friends in Hania, from the naval base. Do you know James Pierson?"

"Yes, he's a friend of mine. He hangs out at the Kriti Bar." In truth, I barely knew the guy.

"Yes, he is a very nice man. We have been friends for some time. He tells very funny jokes. Do you know Roy Hanley?"

"Roy? Yeah, he and I are very good friends. In fact, I live with him at his apartment."

"Truly? Well, it seems we have much in common."

He thought for a moment, picked up my passport and studied it, then became absorbed in reading the complaint on his desk. Meanwhile, I had begun singing an upbeat song, quietly, smiling all the while. The officer looked up at me and said, "You sing very nicely. I would like to just forget this whole incident and give you another chance. However, there is a problem. The two men who made the arrest warrant are my superior officers and there is nothing I can do. I must keep you here tonight, and tomorrow morning we will go to court at ten o'clock. I am sorry."

"What do you think the punishment will be?" I asked, still strumming the guitar.

"Oh, I do not think it will be so bad. You will probably pay a fine and go to prison for thirty days and then be deported."

I thought about the prison on the road to Alikianos, where all the foreigners were rotting away. If the secret police were running this show I would more likely do thirty years.

"Couldn't you just let me go? I could be on a boat to Athens tonight, and then I'll just stay gone."

"I am sorry. My hands are tied in this matter."

"Do you have to lock me up tonight? I'd like to take my guitar to Roy's and have him watch it, along with my belongings. And I would like to make myself presentable for court with a change of clothes and a shower."

Now the man leaned back in his chair, clasped his hands on the desk, thumbs together, and gave me a long studied look.

"If I release you, do you promise to return here to my office by nine o'clock in the morning so I can escort you to court?"

"Yes, I give you my word."

Now he unfolded his hands, while I put up my guitar, and the beginning of a smile played below his mustache. He gave me a long thoughtful gaze before saying, "You know, it's too bad you didn't take the ferry to Athens yesterday, the one that leaves from Souda each night at half past eight. Then you could have left Crete before these troubles came. And once gone, of course, you would have preferred to not return."

"Yes," I agreed, catching his drift. "I would have never returned."

Now his smile became more obvious, as he stood and walked to the door, opening it for me. "I think we understand each other. I will see you here in my office at nine. And say hello to Roy for me."

I walked out of the office knowing I'd just been given a reprieve. The Tourist Police had a soft heart and he was giving me a way out. I hurried over to Wayne's and told him I had to get out of town. He had always admired my fringed leather jacket, so I handed it to him. I wouldn't need it now that summer was on the way. Besides, I had the poncho that Jennifer had made me. Then I rushed over to Roy's apartment, packed my belongings, and said goodbye, thanking him once again for having me as his guest. I snuck over to a taverna near the bus stop, where I could wait until it arrived to take me to Souda Bay. I stayed out of view of the street and nursed a Henninger. When the bus arrived, I walked over to it nonchalantly and took a seat. So far so good. Once at the ferry dock I bought my ticket and laid low until it was time to board. After boarding, I went below deck until we had set sail and were outside the harbor, and only then began to relax a bit. Back on deck, the fresh salty breeze smelled like freedom.

In the morning, I made a beeline for Syntagma Square and the American Express building. Perhaps I could find a ride out of the country. I didn't have to wait long, for I ran into a young German who was driving to Venice, and looking for passengers to share expenses. He had a VW Variant station wagon, like the one I had driven around Germany with Vic and the band, and he could take four people. I signed on, and he told me to meet him back here at four in the afternoon. I killed time with buying and mailing postcards, having lunch, and taking a long walk, down to the Acropolis and back. When I returned to the American Express, the German had his quota of riders, two Canadians and two Americans, myself included. We piled our backpacks and sleeping bags in the back, and all squeezed in, and drove out of the crowded polluted bustle of the big city, headed north. We were over the Yugoslavian border before midnight, and now I completely relaxed. I was beyond the reach of the Greek authorities, a free man once again.

We barreled through Serbia in the south, and took turns driving. At one point, the German pulled over for a rest stop and said he was too tired to drive any further, and wanted to sack out in the back. We folded down the back seat and arranged the gear for sleeping space. I suggested we just stop for the night and carry on in the morning light, but one of the guys, a fast-talking character from New York City, would have none of that. He was in a hurry to get to Venice. He offered to drive if I would sit next to him to help keep him awake, and I agreed. Now the rain started and it began pounding steadily. The sound of the rain and the swishing of the wipers made me drowsy and there came a time in the predawn when I could no longer keep my eyes open, and I asked him to pull over and let us all sleep for a while.

"It's okay, man," he said. "Just go ahead and nod out, and I'll keep driving. I'm wide-awake. I can drive all night long. No problem. I'll crash later."

That last statement turned out to be prophetic. I don't know how long I slept there in the front seat, but I was suddenly jarred into consciousness by the skidding of the tires on the gravel shoulder, and opened my eyes just in time to watch the car fly off the road and over an embankment. There was a violent crashing sound as the car rolled over and over and I tumbled upside down and back again, and the thought came to me in fearful clarity that this is what it felt like to die a violent death. This was literally the end of the road. Then everything went black.

When I came to, it was still raining, but lightly. The light of dawn was just bright enough to see by, and at first I thought I was dead, but then I realized that the car was sitting upright in a soggy field, and I was indeed still alive. I could hear someone moaning, and I noticed that the impact of the crash had popped the windshield out. My door was jammed, but I climbed out the passenger window, and limped around to the back of the car. I saw that the driver, the guy from New York, was walking around in the muddy field, swearing, and complaining that he would be late to Venice. What an asshole, I thought to myself, as I pried open the back door and began checking on everyone. The Canadians crawled out of the tangled mess of baggage, and seemed to be uninjured, but the German was in bad shape. He had been the one I'd heard moaning. We pulled him out, and laid him on the ground. He was in severe back pain and didn't think he could move. It was about this time the shock of the crash wore off, and I noticed a sharp pain in my right hand, and saw a bump protruding upward. I thought a bone might be broken. The Canadians were both okay. All those packs and sleeping bags had cushioned them as the car rolled over and over down the embankment. But it hadn't protected the car's owner, who lay on his back in the mud, moaning and swearing in German.

It was getting lighter now, and through the misty drizzle I could see a Yugoslav farmer hurrying our way, dressed in baggy pants and rubber boots, and wearing a ragged coat. It seems we had landed in a pasture of his farm. He came over and inspected us with a look of concern and words of consolation. Then his wife appeared, he shouted some orders to her, and she headed quickly back to the house. He tried to help the German to his feet, but he couldn't walk without excruciating pain, so we carried him to the farmhouse. There we laid him on the kitchen floor until an ambulance arrived. The attendants loaded him onto a stretcher and into the back, and we all climbed in, except for one of the Canadians, who decided to stay behind to watch our belongings.

As it turned out, the farmhouse was just outside the town of Leskovac, and so we were soon at the hospital, where the German was x-rayed. It was determined that he had not broken any bones, but had wretched his back badly, and would be admitted to a bed in a shared room. I showed the emergency room attendant my hand. He turned it over, squeezed it, and when I screamed, he just laughed. He squeezed it a second time, and I gritted my teeth to not scream, but tears filled my eyes. He laughed and dismissed any idea of an x-ray, but wrapped my hand up to the wrist with an elastic bandage and sent me on my way. I discussed what we should do with the other two guys, and Gordon and I decided to stay in town a day or two to make sure the German was going to be okay. The New Yorker, who had caused the accident in the first place by falling asleep at the wheel, said he would get his belongings and hitchhike on to Venice. He was in a hurry.

We hiked on back to the farmhouse and the wreck, got our gear, and climbed back up to the road. The New Yorker set out hitching, while the rest of us walked down to a bus stop and waited for a ride into town. Once there, we checked into a hotel, seemingly the only one in town. We had to surrender our passports at the desk, and we opted to all share a room. There were only two beds, but I volunteered to sleep on the floor, as I was used to it. That night, after changing some money, we had a meal in a restaurant, and set out exploring Leskovac. At a park, a local who spoke a little English stopped to chat with us. We were having a happy little conversation when a policeman in a green military-like uniform marched up to us, slapped the guy across the face, and told him in so many words to get lost. He slapped him again for emphasis, and the poor guy didn't need any more prompting, slinking away angrily. Then the Communist policeman turned his attention to us.

"Passports!"

"Sorry, pal," I said. "We don't have them. They're at the hotel."

"Passports!"

"Hotel Tito," I said pointing to the downtown area.

He gave up on this line of attack and told us in a language we couldn't speak, but the intent we guessed, to also get lost. So we went back to the hotel.

In the morning we checked on the German, who was feeling better, but was very distressed about his car being totaled. We sympathized with him, but there was nothing we could do, except to agree that the guy who had been driving, and was now conspicuously absent, was an asshole. We wished the poor German a speedy recovery, and decided to take the train on to Venice. There was a local that went to Belgrade, and from there we could catch the Orient Express, bound for Trieste and then Venice. The train didn't depart until late afternoon, so I decided to visit the farm couple that had helped us, and took the bus out there.

When I knocked on the door, the wife was startled to see me, but when she realized who I was, invited me in with a big smile. Her husband sat at the kitchen table, the plates from the mid-day meal awaiting removal, which the wife took care of while the husband stood to greet me with a big smile and a gripping handshake. He told me his name was Tomic, and I introduced myself. Then he invited me to sit, and the wife joined us.

"England?" He asked, pointing to me.

"America," I said.

"Ah, America! *Dobro*."

I soon found out that *dobro* was the expression for "good".

He smiled broadly, stood up and walked over to a shelf, which contained a meager supply of canned and dried goods, and took a package down. He brought it over, and pointed to it. It was a box of Uncle Ben's Converted Rice, with a smiling Uncle Ben on the cover. He set it down on the table.

"America," he said, pointing again to the box. "America. *Dobro. Dobro*."

We talked awkwardly for a while in two different languages, but I was able to thank him for helping us, and he was able to convey to me that he liked America, that America had helped the Yugoslavs during the war, but that the communists had taken over, and he did not like communism. It occurred to me that the policeman in town was trying to keep locals from speaking with us, as it might undermine Marshal Tito's grip on the country. We finished our conversation, and I left these two friendly, hardworking peasants, with handshakes and smiles all around, and went on my way, wondering what would become of the wreckage in their pasture.

We caught the train to Belgrade later in the day, and then had a few hours layover before the Orient Express would arrive. The Canadians went off exploring, but I stuck close to the station, killing time in the station pub, where local musicians were setting up to play. They had an accordion, a guitar, a mandolin, a violin, and a tambourine and hand drum. The group started out slow and ragged, but after a round of slivovitz, began playing faster, louder, and tighter. And as time passed, the more they drank, the better they sounded. By the time my train arrived, they'd had several rounds of the strong liquid and were tearing up the place. They had the patrons clapping and singing along, and really whooping it up. Although some of the musicians swayed on the stage and stumbled around, the music sounded fine.

The Orient Express raced through the night, with stops along the way, as I sat in a compartment, trying to catch naps, waking up for the conductor to punch my ticket, or to glance at the platform of a station we'd stop at. Eventually, in the light of day, we were over the border to Italy, and we made a stop at Trieste, before continuing on to Venice.

It was raining in Trieste, and seemed to blanket all of northeast Italy, for when I walked out of the Venice station and stood before the Grand Canal, it was still coming down lightly. Everyone seemed to be clad in raincoats or carrying umbrellas but me. All I had to keep the rain off was Jennifer's poncho and a Greek fisherman's cap I had picked up in Hania. I was tired, of course, from the overnight trip, but crossed over the bridge and started walking. I had Laura's address, but wanted to kill some time before seeing her, as she was probably in school at the moment. She was only fifteen, after all.

So I hoofed it on over to Piazza San Marco, through ankle deep water that became deeper in the square, which was nearly empty of tourists. A gondola poled its way across the square ferrying people, and planks had been laid over chairs and stretched across the square for people to walk on. I decided not to bother, and found an indoor café in another *piazza* to hang out in over a cappuccino. In the mid-afternoon, the rain cleared to a mist, I put on a pair of dry socks, and walked on over to Laura's place on San Polo, not far from the Grand Canal.

I rang the bell by the door of the high-walled pastel colored house, and when a woman opened it and looked at me with wide eyes filled with questioning surprise, I said "*Buon giorno! Sono Steve, un Americano, amico di Laura.*"

Well, Laura must have told her all about me, for suddenly she was all smiles, inviting me in, and calling for Laura, who appeared from upstairs, bounding toward me, blushing and smiling broadly. She had grown some in the six months since I'd last seen her, and I was so happy to see such a sweet and familiar face that I couldn't help but return her smile with interest. She had on a blue and white sweater, black skirt and a colorful scarf around her neck. Her long brown hair was parted in the middle, and it spilled down around her face, framing it like a picture. He eyes were a soft brown and her facial features were soft and oval, and the youthful exuberance she radiated was contagious. I asked about Gloria and she said, oh yes, she must phone her immediately, and to excuse her *uno momento*. So while she phoned Gloria I tried to carry on a conversation with her mother, who spoke just a little English, as I spoke just a little Italian, and she asked me about my travels and about my family, and then Laura was back saying that we could meet Gloria in a nearby café in twenty minutes.

Over Italian sodas at the café I heard about the falling out with Massimo, and about what the girls had been up to. Then they asked about my travels, and the first thing Gloria asked, as had Laura, was what was wrong with my hand. So I told her about my brush with death and the broken hand and how I couldn't play my guitar for a while, and they both agreed it was a shame. Then they explained to me about the flooded streets and squares in Venice.

"We call it *Acqua Alta*, the high water," said Gloria "It happens with rain and high tides. Venice is sinking, you know, so when *acqua alta* comes, we have to make bridges—Is that the right word?—across some of the squares. The tourists do not like it, but neither do we. It's the price you pay for living in such a beautiful city."

Then Gloria had to hurry home for dinner and to do homework, and I walked Laura back to her house. She had already invited me to dinner, and her mother had given the okay, so I wound up meeting her father and her brother and her grandmother, all of whom were warm and friendly and wanted to know everything about me and the places I'd been. I apologized for not being able to play my guitar for them, but I sang an a cappella version of "Return To Sorrento," which endeared me to all. After a wonderful dinner, Laura asked permission to take a walk with me. She was given the okay, provided we returned by half past ten.

So Laura took me out on the town, so to speak, showing me around the parts of Venice most tourists miss. The rain was gone now, as were most of the clouds, and the stars and moon shone brightly down on the canals, rippling the waters with light, and at times I thought I could see them reflected in her eyes. Gondoliers poled under bridges, some of them singing wonderful Italian songs, and it was all just so romantic, that I forgot all about Laura's age, and took her hand in my uninjured left one.

"I wish I could play some songs for you, Laura."

"That would be very nice, but I wish more that your hand would be healed. I can remember your songs in my heart, and I have the words to some that you sent and I will always keep. I hope we will continue to write when you get to Spain."

"I promise I will."

"Do you know where you'll be?"

"I'm planning on going to Sitges. I've heard there are some good places to play there. But for now you can write me in care of *Poste Restante* in Barcelona. I know I'll be stopping there on the way."

"I will do that."

Then we walked some more, and talked more, and on my way to taking her home, we stopped along the Grand Canal and I took her in my arms and kissed her tenderly. She put her head on my shoulder for a few precious moments before returning my kiss, and the time seemed to stand still. But then we walked on, I got her home before her curfew, said goodbye to her parents, and then she said, "Go with God, and write many songs for the peoples and the countries you will visit."

"I will do that. *Arrivederci mi buon amica.*"

"No *arrivederci*," she replied, "but only *ciao*. We will meet again."

"I hope so. *Ciao, ciao*."

And then I walked through quiet narrow Venice streets and over small bridges, and found my way to the pension where I had stayed before. Next day I caught the train to Nice, from where I planned to hitchhike back to Aix.

CHAPTER TWENTY-SIX

Reunions in France

The traffic was thick in Nice in the afternoon, as I stood on the curb of the traffic island in the center of the main road through town. There, at a light, I was listening to the idling of engines and then the shift into gear as Renaults and Opals and Peugeots and other classy rides crawled to the next traffic light, all the while breathing in their exhaust fumes. In my tired-from-traveling state, I was running out of patience from hoisting my thumb in the air and receiving only blank stares in reply.

Then, I spotted a middle-class American family waiting at the light in what was probably a rented Volkswagen van—dad driving, mom in the passenger seat and brother and sis in the back taking in the scenery—including me, who was a curious oddity to inspect. With guitar and pack parked on the narrow island, I trotted back a couple of car lengths and said to the driver through the open window in my friendliest manner, "Hi there! Would you have room to give a fellow American a lift down the road?"

The driver in starched sport shirt and sun-visor who had been doing his best to ignore me, now turned a nervous glance my way and said in an agitated voice with not a little impatience, "No, I'm sorry. We're full."

"I won't take up much space, I promise. I've been standing here for hours."

I was feeling desperate, and I realized I sounded like a beggar.

Now, while the light was still red and he had his chance to prove he was a Good Samaritan and a generous American, he glanced into the back where the kids were also eagerly awaiting the outcome of this meeting and turned to me with an expression of underlying horror and said, “No. I can’t do it. There are . . . children in the car.”

And as the light changed he let out the clutch and hit the accelerator, in a hurry to get away from a menacing, degenerate hippie, and I was left breathing his exhaust, with horns beeping and honking and everyone impatient to get somewhere pronto. Well, I had someplace to get to as well, but there had to be a better way to do it. I remembered Jimi, my folksinger friend from Aix who had given me his home address, and I decided to take him up on his offer to visit.

I found Jimi’s address but no phone number in my book and decided to take a chance by just dropping in, since he lived near Cannes, just the other side of the bay. So I walked until I found a local bus to Cannes, and then changed to Grasse, where I wandered around in a very upscale neighborhood, asking all around for his street, which I finally found after dark. But then I could not find his address, though I walked back and forth and all around. Judging from the stares I got from the people in the neighborhood, I decided it would not be wise to go knocking on strange doors this time of night asking in English for the address of a guy named Jimi. Instead I walked on out of Grasse and into some wooded hills, where I found a secluded spot to sleep on the ground. Being back in France was beginning to suck.

In the morning, I caught the train into Marseilles, and tried to avoid the stares of the trench coat cops as they quickly scanned the faces of all the people getting off the train, looking no doubt for escaped convicts, drug smugglers, suspicious foreigners, and the dregs of humanity. But I passed inspection without a second glance and was soon on the bus to Aix, rolling out of the port city and up into the foothills, passing little communities and farms and red-roofed houses, the smoky-blue hills in the background overlooking my favorite French city. I was deposited in the middle of town, and with guitar in hand, I began walking, filling my senses with the sights and smells and sounds of Aix-en-Provence, now bursting with the joy and fullness of mid-spring. I strolled on up the wide sidewalk of the Cours Mirabeau, its tall plane trees with bright green foliage arching over the boulevard and meeting at the top to create a tunnel that led up to the fountain at the end, where I turned up the little cobbled side street to Chris' flat and buzzed the door. Soon, we were having another happy reunion over a bottle of cheap French wine.

Since the broken bone in my hand had had a week in which to heal, I took the bandage off and inspected it. The bone had never been set right, so there was still a bump there. But the hand and fingers worked just fine. When I tried playing my guitar, I could play for just a little while before my hand would cramp up, but I decided I'd go out busking the next day anyway. For now I would just take a walk around town, see if I could find some new places that looked ripe for the picking, and later hang out with Chris at the apartment while I tried playing some songs as he worked or read. In the evening, we had a meal together, which he lovingly prepared, and it was simple and tasty and nourishing. Then I took another walk down the Cours, all lit up nicely and the sky a soft blue and people all out strolling around or sitting outside at tables and under awnings and chatting happily over meals and glasses of wine at bistros and cafes. The night air mixed the sweetness of the trees with the scents wafting out of kitchens, and the sound of the cars cruising around the Rotonde and the fountains bubbling filled my senses and made me smile. I felt like I'd come home again.

The next days passed peacefully, in the brightness and cheerfulness of late April, while I went about my routine, adding new places to play: on side streets and in the outdoor marketplace by the old cathedral and the large square at the Hotel de Ville, with it's fountain and outdoor cafes, and a bistro on a quiet street where the maitre d' asked me to come back again. And I was meeting new people, artists and students mostly, some of them friends with Chris. But in a way I felt I was killing time until I could rendezvous with Monika, and also meet up with Randy and Joyce, who were wending their way back from Israel by way of Turkey and expected to be in Aix any day now. So there was a sense of expectancy in the air, along with the sweet smells of spring, like the bouquets in the flower market, or the sounds of happy chirping of birds as they mated and made nests and otherwise worried for naught.

I received a letter from Monika, and a postcard from Randy on the same day. Monika had decided to push her vacation back, so she would meet me in Sete on the coast near Montpellier in about a week. Randy should be in Aix at any moment, and that moment came the very next afternoon, when I ran into him and Joyce walking up the Cours carrying backpacks and a guitar. After a carafe of wine at a small café at the end of the street, we went over to Chris' place, where introductions were made and I asked him if any of his friends could put the couple up.

"Well, we're all friends around here in this part of the world, us ex-pats, so your friends are my friends, and you all can just stay here if you like for a few days."

"Won't it be a little cramped?" I asked.

"Not at all, because I'll just go on over to the Chateau Noir for a few days. It's an artists' cooperative, and I've got some work I can do over there and there's a room for me to stay in. Another artist and I are working on some lithographs, so I'll actually be able to get a lot done there. I'll leave you the keys. Just make yourself at home."

We couldn't begin to thank him for his generosity, although we tried. But that was just the kind of guy Chris was.

So Randy and Joyce and I had our reunion, and we caught each other up on our travels and adventures, and then, of course, we went out busking that night. Then Randy decided we needed a gimmick, so he bought us matching pairs of disguises, Groucho Marx masks—glasses, big nose and mustache, which we slipped on the next time we went out on the town. The maitre d' at the bistro I had frequented welcomed us and we ended up playing there every other night, and we discovered the Rue Riffle Raffle, an underground street where we could stand in our Groucho Marx masks with a guitar case open on the ground, and sing our hearts out, and there were no police to chase us away. In fact, at no time when I was in Aix did a cop ever run me off or even give me the stink eye.

One night, we were invited by someone from the American School to a meeting of their guitar club, in a house near the campus. We showed up, and there were a half-dozen others with their guitars and varying degrees of talent, and we went around in a circle taking turns playing, some singing as well. When our turn came, we blew their minds, and our own as well, because by now, we'd gotten tight together. Besides, to play in an intimate setting like this, instead of in the streets, where we had play and sing at full volume, was a very pleasant experience. I also made a new friend at this gathering: Janet, a small and serious brunette from Oregon, with whom I soon hooked up. The next night, Randy and Joyce had the apartment to themselves, because I was sleeping at Janet's place in the Moroccan section, where laundry hung from open windows and balconies overlooking the narrow cobbled streets, and the air smelled of curry and couscous, and at night we made love in her narrow bed to the sound of middle eastern music coming from somewhere in the old stucco building.

And then April became May, and one day Randy and Joyce walked down to the main highway out of Aix and stuck out their thumbs to northbound traffic on a return trip to Paris, before flying out of Luxembourg on Icelandic Airlines back to the States. I likewise got in the wind, boarding the bus to Marseilles, where I would catch the train to Sete.

I watched out the open compartment window as landscapes passed by, like pictures on a screen, of white and ochre cliffs, yellow spring flowers and cypress trees from Van Gogh and Cezanne's brushes, and vineyards and orchards, and the greens and browns of the spring earth, and the little whitewashed red-tiled farmhouses, as we headed north to Avignon, then through Nimes and south into Montpellier, where I changed to a local. It was a short ride into Sete, a little enclosed seaport on the Mediterranean, part fishing village and part tourist town, and I had the name and address of the hotel where Monika had registered us, and after looking at the town map at the station, I figured out I'd have to catch a downtown-bound bus. Fortunately, the French are very accommodating about having the bus station located right next to the train station, so it was only a short while later that I was deposited near the Canal Royale. By asking passers by in my butchered French, I was able to locate the hotel, which was on a nearby side street.

I walked into the lobby of the quaint older hotel, dropped my pack and guitar, and tapped the little bell. The owner spoke some English, I showed her my passport, and she led me upstairs and unlocked the door to a cozy little room, handed me the keys, and left me with a smile and a cheerful "*Bonjour.*" I set down my gear, then opened the window, which looked out from the second floor to the building next door. On past it, Mediterranean-style houses stepped up a hillside, and finally at the top of the hill, in the background, a cluster of trees. This was the Mont Saint-Clair, and later on, from the street, I would be able to see the great white cross atop it. But for now, I put away my things, stretched out on the soft bed and lay there looking at the ceiling and trying to remember in detail the features of Monika's face.

Then, I washed my face at the sink and used the toilet, and I went out for a little stroll. When I returned, Monika was in the room, unpacking. She must have been on the train right after mine. She was dressed in a long-sleeved light blue cotton blouse with a tan print vest over it and a long skirt and leather sandals. Her blond hair, parted at the side, fell down straight past her shoulders toward her waist, and there was a hint of eye shadow accentuating her limpid blue eyes and a touch of lipstick that made the teeth in her broad smile look even brighter than I'd remembered them.

And then we stepped into each other's arms and embraced and kissed as if no time had ever passed between us.

"You look good and you smell good and you feel good," I said, as her head rested on my shoulder.

"You look good too," she said shyly, pulling back so as to look into my eyes, her cheeks blushing pink.

"How was your trip?"

"Very nice. We passed through Paris. Now I'm here and so are you and I have some weeks free for holiday."

"What happened to your boyfriend?"

"Oh, that," she said, pulling away and walking toward the window, where she spoke with her head turned away from me. "That's quite over. He was too dominating and played too many head games." Then turning to face me, "But you never played games. You were always good to me. I'm sorry I treated you so shitty."

"Forget it. It's all in the past. We're here now, so let's just enjoy it."

"Yes," she agreed, and stepped up to kiss me again. Then we lay on the bed, close together, holding each other, exploring each other again, and talking intimately about what we remembered about each other, and what had transpired in our lives since I'd left Amsterdam, and it all felt so familiar and so right. Later we cleaned up a little and went out exploring Sete. We had dinner at an outdoor table of a restaurant that faced the Canal Royale, and then went strolling arm in arm, without a care in the world, and made passionate love that night in the cozy little hotel room.

In the morning we walked over to the Place Aristide Briand, a large plaza lined with rows of tall, stately trees and benches for sitting, and boxed in by shops and cafes and bistros, where we sat at an outdoor table eating croissants and sipping café au laits in the cool morning sunshine. When the sun was high in the sky, we walked down to the port harbor, past small fishing boats tied up to the quay, where fishermen sat mending their nets, and to the breakwater with its tall slender lighthouse at the end, where the boats sailed in and out of the harbor. On the other side of the breakwater was a narrow spit of sand strewn with boulders, but it served our needs as a private beach. We climbed down to it and found a spot to spread out beach towels. Monika slipped off her dress to reveal a brown two-piece bathing suit, and after I slathered her with lotion, she lay back on her towel soaking up rays while I sat on a rock and played my guitar. And in the later afternoon we read books and talked and strolled down along the water, and in the evening I went out busking at the restaurants along the canal and around the plaza, and when I had made enough money, Monika and I dressed up and went out to a nice restaurant and ate good food and sipped good wine and had good conversation, and I felt like a man of means. Later on, we stopped by the little crepes stand in the Place Aristide Briande, and back at the hotel we made love again in quiet, tender intimacy.

This became the pattern of our days in Sete, and then Monika explained that we would go next to Lodeve, a small village northeast of Montpellier, where we would stay with her Dutch friend Rick, an old lover. We talked things over and it was decided I'd go back to Aix for a couple of days while she went off to Lodeve and set things up with Rick. We took the train together to Montpellier, had lunch at a café, and I saw her off on the bus to

Lodeve, then headed back by train to Aix where I had unfinished business.

The unfinished business of course was Janet, but when I arrived at her apartment, she was cool toward me, and I soon discovered why. Her French girlfriend had returned from Paris and was now living with her, and the relationship was quite close. So I excused myself and went on my way, knowing my perceived problem had found a resolution that was good for all concerned. The other bit of unfinished business I had was to express once again my gratitude to Chris for all his hospitality and friendship, and to say a proper goodbye to Aix-en-Provence, because I sensed I would never return again. So I gave back to Aix some of what it had given me, by spreading around my busking francs on food and coffee and wine in the cafes and bistros and bars, and buying postcards and little souvenirs to send home. And then *adieu* to Aix, and I was back in Montpellier and on board the diesel-powered bus that headed off on a small road through the countryside and dropped me off in the town square of the quiet village of Lodeve, looking as if time and history had passed it by.

I had Rick's address, and after asking around, I was pointed in the direction of a small road that led out into the countryside, and I started walking. I walked along past little farms and vineyards and past trees whose branches were full with new growth and new leaf, and past fields and ponds. I walked until my feet hurt and the pack on my back cut into my shoulders, and the guitar, which I kept switching from hand to hand, felt heavier with every step. I walked until the sun sank low on the horizon, and still I walked, occasional cars or motorbikes passing with a honk, and never did I see an address on any house or building. Finally, when there was hardly enough light to see by and all I could hear was the sound of the evening birds, I sat down on the ground by the side of the road, defeated, and lay on my back on the pack, unable to find the strength to remove it. After a minute or so on the ground, I sat up and looked across the road to a small, whitewashed stone farmhouse set back from the road, with a small vineyard behind it and a light glowing in the window. I summoned enough strength to rise to my feet and cross the road to it, intending to ask if the occupants knew the address or whereabouts of Rick Van der Vleet.

There was a blue painted wooden door in the back, partly open, and just inside stood a broad-shouldered long haired bearded man, about thirty and of medium height, wearing a blue work shirt and blue denim coveralls, Behind him, sitting in a chair by the light of an oil lamp, was a very familiar face, and before I could ask the man anything, I heard Monika's voice say, "Hello, Steve, is that you?"

Then Rick took my hand in his firm, calloused working man's hand, shook it, and said, "Hello, Steve, nice to meet you," in a thick Dutch accent, and then "Please come inside."

It was a small room. It contained, besides table and chairs, some shelves filled with books and odds and ends. An adjoining room was the tiny kitchen, consisting of a stove and sink. Through a door that was ajar, I could see a dimly lit room, which I took to be the bedroom. As soon as I had unfastened my pack and dropped my guitar, Monika stood to embrace me, giving me a quick kiss on the lips, and then stepped over to the table to lift a bottle of wine, pour some into a glass, and offer it to me.

"Did you walk all the way from town? It's five kilometers. You must be very tired."

"Please sit," said Rick, offering me a chair at the table.

I sensed a certain distant coolness from Monika toward me, and an unspoken connection between her and Rick. I was puzzled and annoyed.

"So you got here okay, I see." Monika, dressed in a white blouse, jeans, and boots, with an unbuttoned black sweater, and maybe a little tipsy from the wine, seemed to be making small talk. Something was wrong with this picture.

"Rick has set it up for you to play in the town square in Lodeve on Saturday. There has been much publicity about it."

"De whole town should turn out for you," said Rick. "You're de famous troubadour from America. You can pass your hat around and make some money."

That sounded good to me, and took my mind off the uneasiness that emanated from Monika. So we sat around talking a little longer, while the darkness crept in from outside, and I was made aware that there was no electricity in the house, and no toilet either. I was shown the shovel outside the door, and pointed in the direction of the vineyard, and told if I needed to have a bowel movement, to go dig a hole. I also found out that Rick supplemented his grape growing with a job in town, and he had to get up early. He told me I could sleep on the floor, bade me goodnight, and he and Monika retired to the bedroom.

So that was it! Never lovers ever friends, as they say. Well, it seemed to be true. I could no more be just friends with Monika than it appeared Rick could. Stung by the pain of jealousy and loss, I stomped outside and slept in my bag on the ground, vowing to leave the next morning and head on to Spain. Never mind that I had been banging another woman in Aix behind Monika's back, this current situation was an affront to my ego, a slap in the face. I felt cuckolded.

I tossed and turned on the hard ground, and in the morning dug a hole and filled it in, and then went inside to say goodbye to Monika. But when I saw her beautiful smiling face my tongue wouldn't work, and she said, "Good morning. I've fixed you some breakfast—coffee and bread and cheese. How did you sleep?"

"I didn't. And I didn't know about you and Rick. I'll be leaving right after breakfast, and I won't see you again."

"Please don't go. I want you to stay. I'm just very confused. Rick and I have a history, just like you and I do. Don't make me choose between the two of you. I love you both."

"It would never work out. You should have told me."

"I didn't know how. But please don't leave. You have your concert in the square, and Rick wants to meet with you for lunch at the café in the square. He's left you his bike to ride. He says he wants to talk."

"Well, I guess I owe him that, since he's putting me up, and he set up the concert for me, and you probably didn't even tell him about us. So I guess I'm not angry with him. I'm just pissed off about the way things are."

"I am so sorry. I don't blame you for feeling this way." Then changing the subject, "Here, drink your coffee." After setting it on the table, she put her arms around me and hugged me, and some of the anger dissipated.

I took Rick's bike and rode along the sun-dappled road, taking in the fullness of spring and the freshness of the country air, sometimes smelling of cows, then of vineyards and of grass and hay. What had been a long tortuous walk the night before, now was a breeze as I whizzed past the trees and the ponds and the farmhouses, and then I arrived in Lodeve and found Rick at an open air café, smoking a cigarette at a table, and I parked the bike and joined him.

"Hello, Steve, I'm glad you came. What will you have? I am treating you."

I ordered onion soup and bread, as I wasn't really hungry, and a glass of wine. Then we got down to business.

"I think we should talk about Monika. We both like her, and she likes both of us. So dat is our problem."

"What can we do about it? It's your place, so I'll just leave."

"No need of dat. Here is what I propose—we both sleep wid Monika. Since I was wid her last night, you should be wid her tonight. Dere is no udder way to be fair. What do you say?"

"What does Monika think?"

"I will talk wid her tonight. She doesn't want to choose, dis way she won't have to."

We all hashed it out over dinner, and Monika agreed it would be the fair thing to do. That night I slept with her in Rick's room while he slept on the floor in the other room. Then we settled into a routine for a few days. We would all have breakfast together, Rick would go off to work, and Monika and I would spend the day with each other, and sometimes I would go off on the bicycle for a long ride through the countryside, and other times I would play my guitar while she read. Sometimes we would take walks together, or just sit and talk. When Rick would come home in the evening, we would all sit down to a meal together, and later drink wine and talk, and then Monika would either go off with me or with Rick, but somehow it all worked out, and I was able to keep my jealousy in check. But there were moments when I could see the hurt in Rick's eyes because he knew he couldn't really have her any more than I could and the day would soon come when we would all go our separate ways. So there was only whatever love any of us could grab from the moment.

On Saturday we all went to town in Rick's Citroen, and I set up in the cobbled square of the centuries old village, the mayor introduced me with some flowery French words, and I played and sang, and as Rick had promised, it seemed the whole village had turned out, and they were an enthusiastic audience as they gathered around me in a wide circle. Someone passed the hat, which came back overflowing with francs, and the man who handed it to me said in very good English, "I hope this helps you with your travels. We enjoyed the music very much."

"Thank you. I appreciate it very much."

And then a woman who knew Rick invited the three of us to a party, so after I had said all my *merci beaucoups*, and pocketed all that money, we got back in Rick's car and followed her over to the house where the party was to be. Everyone mingled out in the patio area and back yard of the host's home, eating *hors d'oeuvres* and sipping wine and champagne, and conversing happily. Monika and Rick both spoke French fluently, but I was left in the dark. Occasionally someone would speak a few words to me, and if they knew any English, they would inquire about my travels and my music, but mostly I stayed close to Monika, so she could translate for me. Rick stuck close to her too, so it would be hard for a passing stranger to tell which one of us she was with.

Monika looked radiant, with the late afternoon sun reflecting in her eyes and shining on her golden hair. She really came alive and animated when she was around people, happy to be at the center of the socializing and sharing. Then she spied two children playing, and her whole face lit up as she watched them, the motherly tenderness in her face and voice so obvious when she smiled and said, "Oh, look, see the children? Aren't they sweet?"

I could tell her biological clock was ticking, and my heart almost broke, it ached for her so badly. As if sensing this, she took my hand in hers and squeezed it, then gave me a tender kiss on the cheek, and then the lips. Now my heart swelled, and I knew that she loved me. But in another moment, she went over to Rick, saying something to him in Dutch that I couldn't understand, and squeezed his hand as well.

After dark, we returned to the farmhouse and renewed our nightly routine, and I could feel the time slipping away from the three of us, as I lay alone in my sleeping bag on the floor. And one day, which came too soon, Monika's holidays were all used up, and it was time to leave. Rick drove us into town, and when the bus for Montpellier arrived, he said goodbye, kissed Monika for the final time, and as we pulled out of the square, I looked out of the window and saw the pain and sorrow etched clearly on his face as he waved.

In Montpellier, we boarded the train to Avignon, where we checked into the Hotel Boquier, a cozy older hotel close to the train station. Our room was on the second floor, and the only view we had was of the narrow street below. But that didn't matter to me. Nothing did. I was alone with Monika again, and whatever jealousy I had been trying to suppress the past week now lifted away from me like a balloon set free. We were together, and we were in the City of the Popes, where I had once been with Vic and the band. Today, though, there would be no busking, only precious moments together roaming the streets and squares of the walled-in city, savoring the view of the Rhone valley from the ramparts behind the palace, and taking the little ferry across the river to a café on the other side where we sipped wine and gazed out on the Pont D'Avignon, which ended abruptly in the middle of the river, and then lying on the cool grass by the river bank, holding each other close and kissing and caressing hungrily. Later, we had a meal in a fine restaurant on the Rue de la Republique before strolling back to the hotel through pedestrian-friendly streets, and in the humble room we made love in sweet abandonment, holding each other closely, quietly, until she drifted off to sleep. I lay awake a little longer and listened to the sound of a train pulling out of the station, heading into the unknown night.

In the morning we had coffee and rolls in the station café while we waited for her train.

"I had a wonderful time being with you," I said.

"Even in Lodeve?"

"Yes."

"Your really should hate me."

"I love you."

"I love you too." Then after a short pause, "But it can never work out, can it? We can never really be together."

"No. But that doesn't change the way I feel."

"Please write to me," she said. "Let me know where you are and how you are."

"We'll keep in touch."

And then her train arrived, and she kissed me just before stepping aboard.

"I'll see you in Amsterdam," I said.

"When?"

"Someday."

And then she was gone on a moving train, and I felt a part of me leave with her. I sat silently on a platform bench until my own train arrived, going in the opposite direction, and watched through the window as we rolled through the countryside and past the estuary and the inlet where Sete went about its everyday routines without us. We clicked and clacked along the coast, and over the border into Spain and after the customs men had left, and we were underway again, I stood in the vestibule between cars and watched the Spanish landscape pass by and felt the freshness of the May air, and my heart, which had been empty since Avignon, began to fill once again with a feeling of freedom and unexplored futures.

There is a season for sowing, and a season for reaping. But there is also a season for waiting. I waited in expectation of something new and unknown and inexplicable.

CHAPTER TWENTY-SEVEN

One More Season In The Sun

I stepped off the train and onto the platform and walked along the platform and into the little station that was marked SITGES above the door. Out the other side of the station building, there was much activity of people walking on sidewalks, and little cars navigating narrow streets, and busses idling their diesel engines next to the station in the brilliant sun of the Spanish Costa Dorada. I stood in a plaza, and not knowing exactly where to go, I started walking downhill, as that is where the street that ran beside the supermarket led. I followed the second street on the left, which also led downhill, the narrow Isla de Cuba, where the buildings on either side of the crowded pedestrian street sprang sharply upward, until I reached nearly to the end of the two-block stretch, which dead-ended into another street. I noticed, on the left, a sign that read "Kentucky Bar" over the opened door. I walked out of the bright sunlight into the dim room and approached the bartender about a singing job. He called out to the owner, a stout, blond haired older man whose name was Hans.

"No, I am sorry," he said with a German accent, "ve don't need any music here. Ve haf coming an Irish folk singer who vas here last summer. He should arrive any day now. In fact, he should haf already been here."

So I thanked him and stepped across the street to an Irish pub, The Dubliner, and went through a similar routine. In this case the owner was a tall, thin American with a pencil-thin mustache, standing about six foot four, with black hair, and penetrating brown eyes. He was introduced to me as Lindy, by the bartender. Lindy was loud and high-strung and a larger than life character.

"We already have a musician," he said, "an English guy named Willie who does a lot of Irish songs. He'll be here for the whole season. You can ask around at some other places in town, but I think it's a little late. By mid-May every bar is booked."

"Well, thanks anyway. What time does the music start here?"

"Willie's here from ten to midnight."

"Thanks. I'll drop by later and catch the show."

So I wandered onward, making a right where the street dead-ended, and asking at a couple more bars, then hooked a left at the Calle San Pablo, and on the right was a pub with a sign hanging out front which read "The Spotted Dog", with a painting of a Dalmatian in the center. I stepped inside the spacious room with tables and chairs and booths in the center and along the wall, and a long bar on the right side.

"No, can't help you there, mate," said the English bartender as he drew a pint of Watney's for a customer at the bar. "We've got a regular here already. He's an yank like yourself, name of Peter."

Again, I said thanks, and dejectedly worked my way on down to the bottom of the hill, where the narrow street emptied onto a wide beach of golden sand on the other side of a car-friendly street and a long promenade. To the right, the beach stretched a long way down to a bluff where it ended. To the left, the beach continued on a short way to a rocky outcropping, atop which stood a magnificent church from the thirteenth century, and which overlooked all the beaches, including the one beyond the point. All along the promenade, the beach was lined with palm trees, and the calm azure blue Mediterranean lapped gentle waves onto the shore, and the sinking sun caused the waves to wink and sparkle. All along the waterfront, on the opposite side of the street, were hotels and restaurants and shops and sidewalk cafes, and everywhere tourists and townspeople alike crowded the scene.

As it was getting late in the day, I wandered and asked around until I found a cheap room for the night, and after cleaning up and having some food, I went out walking again, ending up at The Dubliner just before ten. Willie took his place on a barstool in a corner near the front window, and played a long set of Irish drinking songs and ballads, English folk songs, and American country-western, stopping between tunes sometimes to sip on his pint of Guinness. When he took a break, I joined him at the bar, complimented him on his singing, and told him of my dilemma in finding a place to gig.

"Yep," he said, "every bar in town's got a singer by now. You ought to try elsewhere. There's a place just north of Barcelona, Arenys de Mar on the Costa Brava. It's a resort town like Sitges, only smaller. I hear there's some clubs there where you might land a job."

I thanked him, finished my beer a few songs into his second set, and then went out wandering again. I stopped by The Spotted Dog and listened to Peter, the slight curly-haired American with a dark mustache who dressed in jeans and a sport shirt and wore a fisherman's cap, like the one I'd picked up on Crete. I chatted him up on his break, and found out he was from Sonoma County, California, where I had lived before my European sojourn.

"Far out!" he said. "What a small world! It's too bad you're not sticking around. We could do some guitar pickin' and hang out together."

"Yeah, too bad. I don't know where I'll end up. I'm just living day to day."

"Yeah, brother, aren't we all."

I left town the next morning, and in Barcelona, where Vic and Star had once lived, checked at the main post office for mail, which yielded a letter from Randy, one from Laura, and a third from Jennifer. I tore hers open first, while sitting on a bench in the train station. She said she was back home in Scotland, listening to Joni Mitchell on the stereo,

"I enjoyed that night ride very much," she continued. "We got closer then. I was afraid I'd become attached to emotions and feelings I had for you—still am. Difficult to explain here and now, this way, but I believe you understand what I mean. So many things begin and end so quickly—like butterflies. Butterflies make me sad. I think of you traveling with your sleeping bag, pack, and of course guitar, passing through people's lives and your own. Travel on and keep on giving the joy to people—I have some here in my heart, walking with me. Take care, Steve, and give my love to Spain." Then she signed it, "Much love, Jennifer."

I had to savor that for a while, closing my eyes and remembering her face and smile, before I could open Laura's letter. Inside the envelope there was a long letter from Gloria, who was fluent in English, and a shorter one from Laura. Gloria spoke of school ending and how she and Laura were looking forward to going away on holiday, and all about the political situation in Italy, and then closed by asking me to continue writing to them. Laura wrote that it was, "raining cats and dogs at Venice, and there's *Acqua Alta*! Do you know? Try to see the best you can around you, and stop many people in your heart and in your mind. Please write to me and Gloria as soon as possible. Everyone here remembers you. Keep smiling! *Con amore*, Laura."

Randy was brief. He said he was back home and it was hard to adjust to routine after all that traveling, which meant so much to him as an experience, and he hoped to run into me again back in California, and maybe put a band together. I returned the letter to it's envelope and put all three of them in the leather pouch that Jennifer had made for me on Crete, which was fastened to my belt, and waited until my train arrived. After a short ride, I stepped off onto the platform at Arenys de Mar, and started walking. After getting turned down at three different bars, I came across one run by Americans for Americans, and the boss asked me to audition. I sang a few songs, mostly up-tempo peppy ones, and then asked if I was hired.

"No, I'm afraid not. You're good, but not what we're looking for." But as a consolation, I suppose, he bought me a beer.

In the twilight I walked down to the beach, and gazed out onto the sea, wondering what to do next. There was a carnival set up nearby, with a huge Ferris wheel, and a carousel, and other rides, and the people walking along the promenade seemed to be in a festive mood. It wasn't yet summer, still the end of May, but this far south it felt like summer, and after watching the sea and the wheel and the strollers for a while, I decided to spend the night in Arenys, and went looking for a place to crash. I found a cheap hostel nearby, paid my money, and picked out a bunk, which I set my pack on. Then I put my guitar away in a locked storage room, and wandered into the common room, where young people from all over were hanging out.

I soon made friends with a Dutch girl from Amsterdam named Lizbeth, and her friend, a petite brunette from California named Karen. After sharing a communal meal together around a dining room table, the three of us, plus a guy from British Columbia, decided to take a walk down to the beach. Lizbeth warned me that curfew for the hostel was ten o'clock, at which point they locked the doors. If you missed the curfew, you'd have to sleep on the beach. We strolled down to the beach, and now the sun had set and colored lights lit up the carnival, and the Ferris wheel spun slowly all lit up, and a few stars were winking on in the night sky. We walked and talked and had glasses of Sangria wine at a tapas bar, and then it was almost curfew, and time to head out. But the Canadian had hooked up with Karen, and they decided to take their chances sleeping on the beach, so Lizbeth and I walked back alone, and she started crying softly.

"What's wrong?"

"Karen was supposed to be my friend, and she knew I liked Tom, but she took him right away from me anyway," she said with quiet anger. "You see how it is."

"I'm sorry. I didn't know. If I had known, I would have hit on Karen, swept her away, and you could have been alone with Tom."

Now she laughed a little. "That would not have been necessary, I think. But thank you for trying to cheer me up."

"*Als U belieft.*" You're welcome."

We walked back to the hostel in silence, beating the curfew by five minutes, and before lights-out, Lizbeth gave me her address and phone number in Amsterdam and told me to look her up next time I was there.

I took the train back to Barcelona in the morning, and unable to decide where to head next, I tossed a Spanish coin in the air and caught it in my palm. If it landed heads I would go north to Amsterdam, tails I would head south along the Spanish coast. It came up tails. At the ticket window I had a sudden urge to return to Sitges and give the place another try. While I was walking out of the Sitges station and across the plaza, I spotted Willie coming my way, pack on back and guitar in hand.

"Hey man, where are you going?"

"I'm leaving town. I got a lead on a club in Dusseldorf, Germany. It's called Danny's Pan."

"Danny's Pan? I've played there. You don't want to give up a steady job to go there. You better rethink this idea."

"My mind's made up. I'm tired of this place. Danny's Pan is supposed to be a good-paying gig."

"Does Lindy know you're leaving?"

"No. I didn't tell him. I guess you can have my job there."

"Well, thanks. Best of luck to you, man."

"You too, mate."

I rushed on over to Calle Isla de Cuba 3, and told the bartender, a Brit named Tony, that I had just seen Willie get on a train headed out of town, and wanted to know if they had found a replacement for him yet.

"Are you sure he left?"

"I waved him goodbye at the station."

"I'll go ask Lindy."

He walked through a door at the back of the pub, which led to a private apartment, and returned moments later.

"He doesn't believe you, but I do. Come round a little before ten and bring your guitar, and we'll see how good you are."

At the appointed time I showed up, Willie did not, so Lindy agreed to try me out. I played every song I knew, including my repertoire of half a dozen Irish songs.

"You can have the job," said Lindy. "You'll play for tips and beer every night, from ten till midnight. You'll have to learn more Irish songs, though, especially the drinking songs and songs of rebellion. I have a Dubliners record and another by The Clancy Brothers. I'll put them on cassette tape and let you borrow a player so you can listen."

I thanked him, and before heading out Tony asked if I had a place to stay.

"I was planning on crashing at the hostel."

"I've a cheap hotel room nearby. There are two beds. You can move in with me and we'll share the rent."

"Okay. Sounds good to me."

After closing time, I followed Tony out and moved into his room. This became my new home for a while, and The Dubliner my steady gig. I soon found out that the clientele for The Dubliner were mostly Brits and Americans who didn't particularly care for songs of Irish rebellion, and that the American who ran the Irish pub had a German wife and a two-year-old son. I began getting the impression that Lindy was a little off, when I found out that even though he didn't speak German himself, and his wife spoke fluent English, he wanted his son to speak only German. Most Spaniards didn't speak German, although many of them understood English. It just didn't jibe. I heard from Tony that Lindy had spent twenty years in the army, and then had been a soldier of fortune in Africa, he was an alcoholic, and his brains were a little scrambled. This turned out to be an understatement.

Lindy had a longstanding feud going with Hans, and would try to disrupt his business by placing a speaker outside, facing the Kentucky Bar across the narrow street, and blasting up the volume of my singing, hoping to lure away customers. One night he lobbed some cherry bombs over toward the Kentucky Bar, and when the Guardia Civil rushed over a few minutes later in their cornered hats and submachine guns, asking who had fired weapons, Lindy said in a highly agitated voice, "Quick! They just ran down the street. They had guns. Go catch them," whereupon the soldiers of Franco's private guard took off running. Hans stuck his head out of the doorway of the Kentucky Bar and shouted German obscenities at Lindy.

Another time, Lindy went on a three day bender, wearing out his welcome in every tapas bar and pub in Sitges. At one point he ran into The Spotted Dog near closing time, wearing a World War Two flyer's hat and goggles, and yelling, "There's been a plane crash on the beach! Someone go help the survivors, but first, give me a drink!" The bartender phoned Lindy's wife, who soon showed up and dragged him away by his collar, all the while nagging him in German and English until they were out of sight.

The narrow streets of Sitges were teeming day and night with tourists—Germans, Dutch, Americans, Brits, Canadians, Aussies, French, Belgians, and just about any nationality imaginable. Someone mentioned to me that Sitges boasted over six hundred hotels and bars, and it hardly seemed possible, although it was true. But Sitges was a small town, really, and I soon ran into Peter on the street.

"Hey, it's great you're here for the summer and got a gig at The Dubliner," he said, and after asking me where I was staying, said, "Let's get your guitar and mosey on over to my place and do some jamming."

Peter introduced me to his girlfriend, Valerie, who was a slender, longhaired brunette with a quick smile and an even temperament, and soon the three of us were close friends. He started playing at The Spotted Dog at ten, and often went well past midnight, so after I'd finish up at The Dubliner, sometimes I'd go over to his pub and hang out a while. Toward the end of my first week in Sitges, I saw a couple of guys pounding the pavement with their guitars, and struck up a conversation with them.

"Where're you guys from?"

"Jersey," said the tall one with curly dark hair and short beard. "I'm Andy. This here's my partner, Rich."

Rich, the shorter one with long thick brown hair and a mustache, and wearing sunglasses, set his guitar down and shook my hand. "How's it goin'?"

"Good. Been here long?"

"Nah," said Andy, "we just blew in. This looks like one big party town. I guess you noticed the guitars. We got a duo, 'Rich and Famous.' He's Rich and I'm famous. If not now, I soon will be. Know of any place we could get a gig?"

"Not really. Things are pretty well sewn up. What kinda stuff you guys do?"

"We do some of my originals, kind of pop rock stuff, and some Jim Croce."

"And a lot of blues," Rich added. I found out later he was an excellent blues lead guitarist, having taken lessons from one of the best blues players in New York City. Andy was more the rock and roll star wannabe, but they both had that rock swagger and attitude, and were from the same Italian neighborhood in Paterson.

"Jim Croce?" I said. "Maybe you could teach me a couple of his songs. I really dig him, but only got turned on to him after he died. I never got to see him play."

"We did, and man, he was incredible! Me and Rich sat right up front, and I could see all the chords he was playing. What a performer! He told great stories, and had the audience in the palm of his hand. And it was just him, a guitarist, and a bass player."

"Yeah, Steve, you shoulda been there. Shit, that guy Maury could really play the guitar. Then they all got killed in a plane crash. What a drag."

"Yeah," added Andy, "we try to be like those guys. So do you know anywhere we could find a gig?"

"Well, if you're willing to learn some Irish songs, I know a place you might land a gig at."

"Cool," said Andy. "Where do we go?"

"It's an English pub called the Kentucky Bar, run by a German, who has his mind set on getting an Irish folksinger in there. But the guy's about a month overdue, so he's obviously not coming. Let's go someplace and I'll teach you a couple of Irish drinking songs you can audition with, then I'll take you over there. He'll insist he's already got someone hired, but just tell him you'll fill in till the guy shows up. Once you've got the gig, you can sing whatever you want."

Rich and Andy got hired at the Kentucky Bar, and they soon dropped the Irish songs and did their own thing, and developed a following of regulars, which pleased Hans. They stayed on all summer, and we all became friends, Rich and Andy and Peter and me. Sometimes we'd hang out somewhere on afternoons and jam. One place in particular was in the hills just outside of the main part of town, under the shade of a pair of trees that overlooked the valley below. We'd bring a blanket and some wine and our guitars, and maybe a couple more pickers would join us. Then one day, when I was sitting under one of the trees alone, a farmer from down in the valley raised a rifle in my direction and fired. I heard the report and felt something go whizzing by my head, something that sounded like an angry hornet. I got the message, and we didn't go back there again.

The Spaniards loved fiestas, and in Sitges they were abundant. It seemed that every week, there was some sort of religious holiday to celebrate, with parades and ringing of bells from the church atop the point, and fireworks that lit up the night and reflected off the calm Mediterranean. In general, the nightlife really didn't begin in Spain until nine or ten, when the restaurants and bars became crowded, and the boisterous throngs pressed along the meandering Sitges streets. Since I didn't go to work until ten, I was often out walking the streets earlier on, checking out the crowds and watching the fireworks, and it was on just such a night that I literally ran into a young woman who I assumed was an American, and struck up a conversation.

"Oh, excuse me."

"Keep your eyes on the road you big lug," she said jokingly. "Did you fail the test for your walking license?"

I quickly scanned her face, and was knocked out by her warm smile and big brown eyes. He brown hair was long and straight and fine, her face broad and tanned, and she filled out blouse and jeans with just the right curves.

"My problem is I can't walk and chew gum at the same time."

"Not a good excuse. You're not chewing gum. I'm Julie," she said, offering me her hand. "And this is my friend Joanne."

I hadn't noticed Joanne until now, but said, "It's nice to meet you. I'm Steve."

Joanne was a slender brunette with dark curly hair and an open smile.

"Are you an American?" Asked Joanne.

"Yeah, I'm from California."

"We're from Ontario," said Julie.

"Ontario, California? Small world!"

"No, Ontario as in Canada, dummy. Toronto, as a matter of fact."

"How'd you end up over here?"

"We wanted to see Spain after our first year of college. We landed in Barcelona, came on down to Sitges, and both of us landed summer jobs. I work as a waitress at a restaurant, and Joanne is a maid at a hotel. We share a room together. What about you?"

"I've been traveling around Europe for a couple of years. I'm a musician. I sing at The Dubliner on Isla de Cuba, from ten till midnight, seven nights a week."

She glanced at the large watch on her wrist and said, "You'd better get going. Looks like it's almost time to go to work. Where's Isla de Cuba?"

I gave her directions, and she promised they'd drop by later. And that's how it began for us. Being on the road, and far from home, a vagabond would instinctively reach out to strangers and form temporary relationships and live in the moment, because the moments were all so brief and the future uncertain. The shift from being strangers to becoming intimate happened in a compressed time frame, and without following the accepted dating customs of home. So it was only a matter of days before Julie and I were hooked up and sharing a one-room apartment together, overlooking the broad San Sebastian Beach, to the north of the point where the old landmark church of the same name stood. Joanne soon hooked up with another American and then they too were sharing a place together.

Julie and I worked nights and spent our days together. She also had two nights a week free to hang out with me, as I didn't go to work until late. Our apartment was on the second floor, above a noisy bar. We could sometimes hear the jukebox blasting out songs that were new to me, since I didn't have a radio to listen to; songs like "It Never Rains in Southern California" by Albert Hammond, and "Ventura Highway" by America, and "Daniel" by Elton John. During the hot and humid days we spent together, we would walk across the street to the beach, or sometimes take a taxi up to a nearby country club where we would use the swimming pool for a small fee, and Joanne and her boyfriend, or Peter and Valerie would accompany us. We would sit around the pool under big umbrellas, drinking sangrias and feeling like millionaires.

Once, on Julie's day off, she and I took the train to Barcelona along with Peter and Valerie, and we rambled along Las Ramblas, the wide boulevard of shops and stalls and bars and a large marketplace, and at the end was the waterfront. We visited the Picasso Museum, and saw one of the architect Gaudi's buildings before rushing to catch the train back to Sitges in time for our pub gigs. Other times, I would visit Julie at her restaurant, where she worked outside in the patio area, and if things were slow, we could hang out over a glass of wine together before she had to wait on customers.

From ten to midnight every night, I would sit on a high-backed barstool next to the front window and sing into a microphone for the Brits and Scots and Irish and American and German and Canadian tourists who would wander in off the street for a pint of Guinness stout or Harp lager. I would take requests if I knew them, but mostly I would sing a variety of Irish songs, American folk and country songs, and songs I had written. At first, crazy Lindy had tried to pass me off as an Irishman named Davy Byrne, but of course no one bought it, so he gave up on that gimmick.

The Dubliner filled a long narrow room, with one side taken up by the bar, and beyond it a couple of tables. Along the other side were booths for people to sit in. There was one table by the front door, and I squeezed into a space between the window and the bar. Alongside me on the wall was a Pong machine, where you could drop coins and play a game of ping-pong on a video screen. There was no jukebox, but when the live music was absent, Tony would play records on the stereo.

There was a Spanish photographer in Sitges, who made his living going from bar to bar and snapping photos of couples, then taking orders for the finished product. Rich and Andy began calling him "El Presidente," because his jowly face resembled Richard Nixon's. Soon all of us knew him by that moniker. It seems that almost everyone in Sitges, but especially the Americans, hated Nixon, and were following the Watergate scandal with great interest. On the day Nixon resigned, there were great celebrations in the streets and the bars. I imagined it must have resembled VJ Day, at the end of World War Two.

Julie and I had to move out of our apartment in mid-July, as the high tourist season had arrived, and the landlady decided to triple the rent. But we soon found a new place to live in a spacious house in the hills above town, beyond the railroad line. We moved in with a group of hippies from all over, including Germany and Holland and Mexico. Peter had fixed us up, as he and Valerie had been living there, and after we arrived, we totaled nine in number.

Julie and I squeezed into a tiny room that contained a large bed and not much else. But we had the use of the rest of the place, including the kitchen, something we hadn't had in our apartment, (which in retrospect hadn't been more than a glorified hotel room without maid service). At our house on the hill we had a washer to use, and a clothesline on the roof to dry our laundry in the blazing summer sun. We lost our great ocean view in the process, surrendering it for a view of houses and apartments all squeezed in tightly, but we gained the companionship of others of our approximate ages and inclinations. We all shared the kind of family spirit I'd known with my friends in Alikianos, when I was in Crete. The days in Sitges were long and full and packed with life and love and companionship, but my time at The Dubliner was running short.

One day I made the mistake of swimming at San Sebastian Beach, and went out beyond the bluff, where raw sewage floated in the water, spilling out from the large pipe that protruded from the bottom of the bluff. I hurriedly swam back to shore, and went home and showered. But later, I began feeling ill, and for two days and nights I lay immobile at the house, suffering from fever, headaches, and dysentery. When I finally returned to my job at the pub, Lindy informed me I'd been fired. He had replaced me with a burly, tattooed Brit who favored American country-western, and specialized in doing Johnny Cash numbers. I wondered if Lindy was planning on naming him Davy Byrne as well.

It was time to find another job. I started hustling around, and found a bar where I could busk early in the evening. It wasn't very busy at that hour, but the gig was better than nothing. Then I wandered into the DOK Bar, on a side street near the beach just south of the point, run by a tall, gregarious Belgian named Joost. Joost was from Antwerp and spoke with a Flemish accent. He had long, wavy blond hair, blue eyes, and a wide toothy grin that lit up his long face. He seemed to always be smiling and joking around, and went out of his way to make his customers feel at home and happy. Before I could even ask about a job, he noticed my guitar and said, "Ja, man, come on in! Let's hear some music. Let's liven things up."

There were few customers and the room was quiet, but as soon as I got my guitar out and slung it around my neck, he poured me a glass of Belgian ale and said, "Ja, man, let's all have a party!" After I had played a few songs, he applauded and said, "Take a break and have another drink. What's your name?"

I introduced myself and sat at the bar, and then he said, "That's what this place needs, is live music. Are you staying in Sitges for some time?"

"Yes, and as a matter of fact . . ."

"Good. I think I want to hire you. Can you sing here every night, let's say from nine to midnight?"

"I'd love to."

"How much do you charge?"

"How much can you pay?"

"Well, we are not very busy here, but maybe music will bring more people in. I'll start you off at a hundred pesetas a night plus tips."

"I'll take it."

"When can you begin?"

"How about now?"

"Good," he said, shaking my hand vigorously. "We have a deal. Let's toast on that."

Then he poured himself a beer, lifted it up to me and said, "Prost! To our mutual success."

The DOK Bar was well lit, with red wallpaper and décor, and red curtains in the window, small tables with red upholstered chairs, and other, more plush chairs; the effect of which was to promote conversation and make the customers feel at home. Every night I stood in a corner and sang, and sometimes sat on a barstool. There were a few regulars each night, including two Spanish girls of college age, and they became fans. Immediately, Joost took me into his confidence and said, "Better not fool around with those two, or there could be trouble. They're under twenty-one, so the police could arrest you."

"Don't worry," I assured him, "I'm not interested. I have a girlfriend."

"Why haven't I seen her?"

"She works nights, but I'll have her drop by tomorrow."

"Good. Tell her to bring a friend."

Julie showed up the next night with Joanne, and Joost immediately began working his charm on them, buying them drinks, and treating them as if we'd all been friends for years. The girls were hooked, and came round to visit whenever they could. Although the place was initially slower than The Dubliner, gradually and by word-of-mouth, it began filling up with regulars.

Now that I was no longer working at The Dubliner, I had to change my mailing address to the house on the hill. One day, a letter arrived from my old friend and former band mate, Marty Power. He got my address from Annie, with whom I'd also stayed in touch. He wrote that he was being discharged from the Army in September, and planned to move back to Sonoma County. He said he wished we could get another band together. Randy had said the same thing to me, but here in Sitges, California seemed a million miles and a lifetime away, and I had no plans of returning Stateside anytime soon. The hot August days just seemed to roll along in a kind of rhythm, like the waves washing in on the sands of the Sitges beaches, slow and regular and eternal.

At the end of August, Julie and I decided to take a weekend trip to Andorra, a tiny country in the Pyrenees, between Spain and France. Julie's boss gave the okay, and Joost said I could take the time off if I would bring him back some record albums for his bar, because he could get them cheaper and tax free in Andorra. He gave me a shopping list and some money, and told me to have a great time, and he'd see me when we returned.

We packed our bags and took the train to Barcelona, then transferred to a bus that took us through the Catalonia area of Spain and up into the mountains to Andorra, where we arrived in the Principality's capital city of Andorra la Vella. At over three thousand feet above sea level, the city of old stone houses and narrow streets crammed tightly into a deep valley surrounded by mountains. Stepping off the bus and into the center of the old city we noticed the pleasantly cool weather, a relief from the hot humidity of the coast. The people of Andorra spoke Catalan, Spanish, or French, or a combination of the three. Of course, being mainly a tourist destination, many spoke English as well. So not foreseeing any problems with the language, we set off to find a place to stay.

It hadn't occurred to me to make hotel reservations beforehand, nor had I even considered the remotest possibility that every hotel room in town might be booked, a fact that we discovered only after walking for hours and checking every hotel in town. After midnight we came to the end of the line, and were told by the owner that there was nothing available. We collapsed on the front steps of the place, weary, defeated, and miserable. We sat there for a long period, not saying anything, and then Julie began sobbing.

"Why don't you say something?" she pleaded. "You haven't spoken to me in hours."

"I don't want to talk. I'm too pissed off. I'm afraid if I start talking I'll swear a blue streak."

"I don't mind. I'm angry too, and tired and cold and hungry. But I feel like you're completely ignoring me, and that's what hurts the most."

"I'm sorry," I said, putting my arm around her and comforting her. "I feel like this whole thing is my fault."

"No it's not. You didn't know there would be so many tourists in town."

"It was a weekend. It should have been obvious."

"What will we do now?"

"I think we ought to get in out of the cold."

I rose, and opened the door to the entryway for her, and we sat underneath the stairwell. "Let's try to get some sleep here."

Of course we didn't sleep a wink, and when the hotel owner spotted us there early in the morning, she was compassionate.

"You should have told me you had absolutely no place to stay. We have a little storage room with a rollaway bed for just such emergencies. I can show it to you now. You probably want to sleep all morning. Have you had anything to eat?"

"Nothing since yesterday."

"Come to the kitchen, I'll fix you something."

So we had breakfast in the owner's kitchen, and then she showed us to our bed in the tiny room, and after showering we fell asleep until the early afternoon. We spent a short time sightseeing, and then had to catch the bus to Barcelona, so we could make the last train to Sitges for the night. Back home in Sitges, we slept like the dead.

The next day I discovered a letter that had arrived while we were gone. I looked at the return address and the handwriting, and was suddenly filled with dread. It was from my father, who had never before written to me for any reason, including birthdays and at Christmas. I sat down in a chair and forced myself to open it.

"*Dear Steve,*

Bad news doesn't always travel fast. Mark just couldn't make it, and he is at peace now. We laid him to rest last Thursday, after many months of suffering."

My father went on to say that I should call home collect, and should plan on returning to California soon, as there was now a gap in the family, and my presence could help fill it and ease some of the grief. I was stunned. I had suspected my younger brother was bipolar, but since I hadn't seen him in years, I had no idea how depressed he had been—enough to take his own life.

Julie saw the look of sorrow on my face, asked what was wrong, and then tried to comfort me, but I told her I needed to be alone for a while, and went for a walk in the hills. I reminisced on all the things I had loved about my brother, and all the great times we had had together growing up. I knew I would have to go into town and make the phone call, maybe from the DOK Bar, and I knew I'd have to start thinking about getting a plane ticket back to the States, but for now I just wanted to be alone with my thoughts and my tears, and I didn't want anyone to see them. Tomorrow, I would start saying my goodbyes, as I had done in every place I had lingered in the past year. But for the moment, I only wanted to grieve quietly.

CHAPTER TWENTY-EIGHT

Homecoming

The summer season was still going strong in Sitges, hotel rooms and bars filled, streets and shops and beaches jammed with tourists, and still money to be made by business owners and barkeepers and musicians and summer workers. But the season had come crashing down on me, like the falling of a stage curtain.

I gave my notice to Joost at the DOK Bar, and began saying goodbye to another place and another season. I wandered around Sitges alone while Julie was at work, visiting places like The Dubliner and The Spotted Dog and the Kentucky Bar, making my way along the crowded streets and promenades. When Julie got off, we went for a stroll along the beach and ended up beside the church on the point, overlooking the Mediterranean with the moonlight shining a wide silvery path on it's rippled waters.

She held me tight, while we sat on a bench, and did her best to comfort me, and to encourage me to open up to her. But I kept my feelings to myself, not wanting to be intimate. I was moving on, and I knew I'd never see her again. Just another temporary relationship of the road whose time had run out, although it had been great while it lasted. Life is not a series of snapshots you can hold and study and savor indefinitely, but an ongoing movie with a constantly changing cast and crew and locations and subplots. The time had come to exit this scene gracefully. And yet we would have one more night of lovemaking, and it was to be passionate, and consumed with a hunger that could not be satisfied.

I had decided to return to Amsterdam, where I could find a cheap charter flight home, and was planning on taking the train to

Holland by way of Barcelona. But word got around that there was a driver with a Volkswagen van who was collecting passengers for a trip all the way to Amsterdam, and that seemed a custom fit for me, so I signed on. We gathered the next morning by the bus stop on the palm-lined road out of town, the Passeig de Vilafranca. Besides the Dutch driver and myself, there was a young German guy, a French girl, and in an improbable coincidence, Lizbeth, the blond Dutch girl from Amsterdam who I had met in Arenys de Mar. She had been in Sitges for a couple of weeks, but this was the first time we'd run into each other since Arenys. I kissed Julie goodbye, the driver loaded all the gear and then us into the van, and we drove off. I waved to Julie from the side window as she stood there by the bus stop crying, the Volkswagen made a u-turn and rolled up the hill and around a bend, and Sitges disappeared from sight as we pulled onto the main highway to Barcelona and just kept on going.

I was apprehensive when we crossed the French border just south of Perpignan, but the border guard seemed more interested in the driver's papers than our passports, which he gave the cursory once over. Finding the driver's registration and insurance in order, he waved us across and I relaxed.

We were inside France now, and I had no further worries. So I watched out the window as the scenery flashed by, containing familiar scenes from the past. I thought about Monika and our doomed love affair as we drove past Sete and through Montpellier and Avignon. Then we turned north to Orange, along the route I had taken more than a year before with Vic and Star and Paddy and Annie, and I reminisced on our time together, and wondered if they had a gig tonight, or were out busking again.

Having stayed in touch, I knew that they were still living in the same rooms in Amsterdam, that the record had fizzled, and their recording contract lapsed, which had predictably pissed off Vic, especially toward what he saw as a conspiracy to keep him from finding his rightful place among the stars in the musical galaxy. I took turns behind the wheel with the Dutchman and the German as we retraced the previous summer's route, driving ever onward through Lyon, Dijon, Reims, and finally to the border crossing into Belgium outside of Lille. Here we were pulled over not by the Belgians, but by the French border control, who collected all our passports and took them inside a building while we waited in a parking area and I held my breath.

Some time later, the official returned, and handed back passports to everyone but me. My heart sank. The guard motioned for me to come with him. I asked the driver to wait for me, and turned in my seat to the French girl.

"Please," I said, "come with me and translate. I don't speak any French, and I know you speak good English."

She followed me out of the van and into the building, where I was ushered into a room. The guard tried to keep the girl out, but she spoke up saying she was my translator and insisted on going with me, so he relented. I was made to stand in front of the desk where the officer in charge held my passport in his hand while he glowered at me. I felt a sense of déjà vu creeping in. He said something harsh in French. The girl translated.

"He says you are in France illegally. You have been deported, and are not allowed to be in this country. You are subject to arrest."

"Tell him I knew that I was not supposed to be in France, but I did not know that applied to just passing through on my way to another country. Tell him I am going from Spain to Amsterdam, where I am supposed to fly back home to the States."

She translated.

"He says that is no excuse. You are an undesirable and not allowed to be in France."

"Tell him I understand and am sorry, I did not know I was breaking the law, and as he can see I'm on my way out of France right now. And if I'm allowed to leave the country I'll never return."

Again she translated.

"He says that is a good idea, because if you ever do return, you will be arrested and sent to prison."

"*Oui, monsieur, je comprend,*" I answered.

He gave me a long, contemptible look, then handed my passport back.

"He says you may go, leave immediately, and never return."

"Merci," I answered, and we beat it on out of France, the Belgians lazily waving us across after looking at the driver's

papers. I felt so happy I could kiss the French girl, which I didn't, but thanked her profusely.

It was late in the second day of our journey when we drove into Amsterdam, and the driver deposited us in front of the American Express office on the Damrak. Lizbeth asked me if I had a place to stay, and when I said no, offered to put me up for the night at her parents' home. We caught a tram and rode on out to the outskirts of the city, and after introductions and the customary pleasantries of conversation and of making a guest comfortable, the parents retired. Lizbeth and I talked a while longer, and then I unpacked in the tiny guest room, showered, and immediately fell into an overdue sleep, untroubled by border guards or an uncertain future. When I awoke refreshed in the morning, the world took on a bright and happy new look. I thanked Lizbeth, said, "*Tot ziens,*" and caught the tram to the Centrum, getting off at the Dam, across from the Queen's Palace, where the hippies and young travelers hung out on the steps of the monument like they were a permanent part of it.

There was a familiar feeling in the air of homecoming, and I set out walking through familiar streets and neighborhoods and along canals that sparkled in rippled light from the late summer sun of September. Soon the autumn would return to Amsterdam and with it the yellowing of leaves, and then the rains and the strong winds from the North Sea that would tear the dead leaves from the trees and send them sprawling into streets and canals. But on this fine day, the gingerbread brownstone buildings stood in long rows tall and proud against the cloud-spotted sky, seagulls sailed on the breeze, and ducks nestled peacefully on houseboats and bobbed on the waters like boats at anchor. I phoned Monika's student apartment building, but she was out, so I headed on over to the Damrak, where some travel bureaus were located, and found a cheap charter flight out of Brussels, leaving for New York the following week. From New York I would catch an American Airlines flight back to California. So I had nearly a week to kill, but I was home again, and filling my days in Amsterdam would be easy and pleasurable.

This bit of business concluded, I continued on to Annie and Paddy's cramped room on the Haarlemmerstraat. They were at home, practicing an Irish tune.

"So you made it back to Amsterdam? Long time, no see," said Annie.

"Hey, Steve, welcome back. Nothing's changed, as you can see."

"How are Vic and Star?"

"About the same," said Annie. "You haven't missed much, except Vic is working an angle with another record label to maybe do an album. Oh, and we have a new bass player, and you won't believe who it is."

"Rene Kaak?" I offered.

"Not even close. Remember Derek, the friend of R.J.'s who went with us to the airport when we saw you off to London? He's our bass player now."

"Are you kidding me? That's unbelievable. How long has he been over here?"

"I'm not really sure, but he's been playing with us a couple of months. I forgot to tell you that the last time I wrote."

"Where's he staying?"

"Got something to write on? I'll give you his address."

I pulled out the pen and little notebook I always carried in my front shirt pocket or in the leather bag on my belt, and copied the address down. I made a long trek past the Central Station and the harbor, along the Prins Hendrikkade to the Zeeburgerdijk, which ran beside the Singelgracht, found Derek's building, and let myself in, inquired about, and found him living in a tiny loft with a window that looked straight down on the street and canal below.

"Hey, Steve, good to see you again. What brings you back this way? I thought you were in Spain."

"I was, but now I'm here." Then I told him about my brother, and my plans to fly back home, and he listened sympathetically, sitting cross-legged Yoga style on the mattress on the floor. Derek reminded me of a Hindu yogi, with his thin frame and wispy beard and long thin blond hair. There was also tranquility about him, and his eyes were clear and focused. We talked of our friend R.J. back in California, and we talked of the circumstances of his being in Europe and of his travels and adventures before hooking up with Uncle Zeke's Band, and then the conversation turned to the band itself.

"I'm playing your old bass and using your old amp," he said. "It belongs to the band, but they let me use it for gigs. You see I'm not really a band member, just a hired hand. They only use me for paying gigs, but not for busking, so I go out on my own sometimes with my guitar and do a little busking myself. Vic says if this recording contract comes through and they do an album, he'll use me as a sideman. But he really just wants to keep the band a trio, so they'll only have to split the take four ways."

"Four ways?"

"Yes, don't forget about Star. I heard about your getting fired from the band. What happened?"

"I wasn't fired, I quit."

"Is there still bad blood between you and Vic? I know you guys used to be close."

"I can't speak for Vic, but there are no more hard feelings on my part. In fact, leaving the band was the best thing that could have happened to me. It opened up new vistas, new opportunities and new adventures. I met great people, and I made many new friends. And I gained a lot of confidence about my abilities, musical and otherwise. I discovered I could make it on my own, without Vic's help or anyone else's for that matter. It taught me self-sufficiency. I was able to go solo, although I would prefer to be in a band again. But that might just happen. Marty Power is getting out of the Army this month, and Randy Bleu is back in Sonoma County and wants to start a band. So maybe that's my next venture. My being back in Amsterdam like this is good for tying up loose ends. And now, running into you again is a real trip, especially since you're my replacement in the band."

"A temporary replacement only. But it's not coincidence. I don't believe in coincidence. Everything happens for a reason."

"I'm starting to believe that myself."

"Do you have a place to stay tonight? You're welcome here any time. It's a little cramped, but we can make room."

"Thanks, I may take you up on that offer. First, though, I have some unfinished business with someone. In fact, I should find a phone box and give her a call. Maybe I'll see you later."

"Okay, brother. Drop by later and we'll do some jamming."

"Mind if I leave my stuff here for a while?"

"Not at all. It'll be safe here, and you can take a load off your back."

I headed back toward the Central Station, as I knew there were telephones there, but found one along the way, and dialed Monika's number. This time she was at home. She asked if I would like to come over, and I said yes; so I caught a tram, and then walked the rest of the way, rang her bell, and was buzzed in. She met me at her door. Seeing her standing there in the doorway dressed smartly in a light brown blouse, tight-fitting jeans, and brown boots, it was as if we'd turned back the clock and I was dating her again, calling on her like this. She smiled, gave me a hug, and asked me to come in and make myself at home and then said, "What a surprise to see you! I didn't expect this at all. Why are you in Amsterdam?"

"I told you I'd see you here again."

"Yes, but I didn't really believe it."

"Actually, I'm on my way back to the States. I've got a charter flight out of Belgium next week. My brother died, and it's best I visit my family now. I haven't seen them in over two years."

"I'm sorry to hear that. Were you close?"

"I think so. I know I'm going to miss him a lot."

"Would you like a glass of wine?" Without waiting for a reply, she poured me a glass of white wine, and then one for herself.

"Could I stay here tonight?"

"That would not be good. I've been seeing someone new."

"Is it serious?"

"No, but I don't feel good about you staying here. We would end up making love, and then I would get attached to you again, and that's just not healthy for me. My emotions are too fragile right now."

"I understand. Would you like to go out to dinner tonight?"

"I don't know. I am supposed to see Franz."

"Cancel it. Tell him you're busy. We'll go have a *rijsttafel* in the Indonesian restaurant, just like the old days."

"The old days are not that old. Remember Sete?"

"I'll never forget those beautiful days. So shall we have dinner together?"

"Why not," she said, leaning over and giving me a peck on the cheek. "We'll pretend we're starting over like when we first met. But I still won't sleep with you."

And so we had our night on the town, first the Indonesian meal, Dutch treat of course, just like the old days. Then we went to a quiet brown café in the Jordaan, where we talked over glasses of wine, and fought back the urge to get intimate again. But when I walked her back to her place, I grabbed her close to me and kissed her, and for just a moment I thought the old magic would return, but the moment slipped by, and she broke free and called out goodnight to me as she closed the door behind her. I walked on back to Derek's tiny room, and since it was a weeknight and Uncle Zeke had no gigs, he was at home. We smoked some hash and played a little music together, and then I crashed on the floor in my bag.

The next day I ran into Vic at Annie and Paddy's place, where they were having a rehearsal. Vic looked up at me with guarded eyes, and then said, "Hey, Dupree! I heard you were back. I was also sorry to hear about your brother." Then he put his guitar down, rose, and shook my hand. "I mean it, I'm really sorry, man."

"Thanks. I appreciate it."

I took a good look at Vic now, standing before me, and it was almost like the old days when we were still friends, and he was my mentor, and I could feel no ill will toward him for anything.

"I had a brother who died," he said sincerely, "so I know how you must feel."

"I didn't know that, Vic. I'm sorry."

"It was a long time ago. He was my older brother. He was fifteen at the time. He was hit by a car."

There was a moment where we might have bonded again, but Vic quickly changed the subject.

"We never made any money off that single. Those cheap bastards probably cooked the books so they wouldn't have to give us our share. But we saved a couple of records for you to take home. Star has them. I'll make sure you get them before you leave town. Anyway, we got another label interested in us now. Looks like we're going to do a whole album this time. Derek might play bass on it. It'll be mostly my songs, of course, but Paddy's doing one of his songs, and Annie's got an instrumental we might cut. So it looks like we're finally in the Big Time."

"Congratulations. I wish you a lot of success."

"Thanks, man."

"Well, I won't keep you from your practice. Just wanted to say, 'Hi.' Maybe I'll come back tomorrow, and we can jam some."

"You're always welcome, Steve," Annie said just before I left.

I popped in at Boddy's Music Inn later and Ted was there. He was happy to see me, told me Uncle Zeke had been burning their bridges all over town, but that I could stop by tomorrow night and sing for beer and tips if I wanted to. I told him I'd love to. He bought me a Heineken, and then I headed out again to visit some more of my old haunts. For the next several days I saw Amsterdam as the tourists do, something I'd had neither the money nor inclination to do when I had lived here.

I took the canal tour on one of the ubiquitous little boats that ply the waterways of Amsterdam, the tour guide pointing out all the interesting sights and their histories in both English and French. I visited the Rijksmuseum, the neo-Gothic building that housed works of Rembrandt and other Dutch masters. I also went through the modern Van Gogh Museum, which contained over 500 paintings and 600 drawings by the brilliant but troubled artist, and wondered why I hadn't visited these places before. And I went back to the Melkweg for a drink, and to reminisce about the night Monika and I had hooked up there.

I spent the rest of my days in Amsterdam like mad money I had been given to splurge with. During the daylight hours, I took long walks along the canals and through the Vondelpark and down to the Lowlands Weed Company for marijuana tea, and went browsing through the Waterlooplein flea market. Nights I would do a bit of busking, dine at cheap eating spots, and hear live music at the Folk Fairport or Boddy's Music Inn. I also looked up old friends, or hung out with Derek, smoking hash and discussing the meaning of life. Each day and night unfolded into the next with a seeming timelessness, like the waves I had watched washing ashore every day in Makrigialos. But unlike the permanence of waves, my time in Amsterdam was soon used up, and the final day arrived. Monika invited me over for dinner.

"How's your new boyfriend?" I asked after we had taken our places at her little table and the food was served.

"I don't see him anymore."

"Why not?"

"Oh, I think he's not my type. Too conservative, and too controlling, I think."

"I'm sorry."

"I'm not. You can sleep here tonight, if you like." She gave me that wonderful sexy smile that lit up her eyes, and I could see a slight blush coming to her cheeks.

"I want to, more than you know, but I can't, because if I did I'd fall in love with you again. And then I would miss the train because I would want to stay here in Amsterdam with you, and I just can't do that. I have to go back to the States."

"I know," she said regretfully. Then she added, "Maybe I'll come to the States too, and visit you in California."

"That would be nice, but I don't think it'll ever work out. We're just star-crossed, that's all."

"Star-crossed," she said cocking her head a bit and wrinkling her brow. "What does that mean?"

"It's an American expression. It means fate is against us. It means our relationship will never work. It was doomed from the beginning."

"Don't be so dramatic," she said. "It's not as bad as all that."

"Can you see any way to make it work? I can't live in Holland and you can't live in California, and that's where I have to go now."

"Yes, you're right of course. It's quite impossible. But it's been nice."

"Yes, it has. I wouldn't trade our time together for anything."

Later I kissed her goodnight, and walked back to Annie and Paddy's place through the cobbled Amsterdam streets and across canal bridges in the cool of a perfect late summer night, remembering all the times I had walked these very streets with guitar in hand, struggling to make a living as a musician, and how it had never really seemed a struggle, but a blessing.

Monika saw me off at the station in the morning, just before the train left, and she waved to me one last time.

"I'll see you in America," she shouted from the platform.

We pulled out of the station, and I strained my neck to watch out the window as Amsterdam slowly disappeared from sight. I wanted to hold it in my sight and my memory as long as I could, like a postcard or a snapshot, because I didn't know if I would ever see this beautiful vibrant place again, which held so many memories for me.

However, life is neither a postcard nor a snapshot, but only a movie. So as we rolled along out of the suburbs and into the countryside, I shut my eyes and tried to imagine a movie on the screen of my imagination. It was a little out of focus at first, but then it became clearer as I concentrated.

A couple is walking along on a rain-washed cobbled street under a cloudy night sky. The camera pans in to reveal an American hippie in a fringed jacket and jeans, and close beside him a slender blond Dutch girl, wearing jeans and a sweater, her arm linked with his. She is pointing out a tower along the canal.

"This is called the Weepers Tower," she is explaining in a warm voice with a feminine Dutch accent. "This is where the wives and lovers watched when their men went out fishing. They would watch until the boats were out of sight."

"Why is it called the Weepers Tower?"

"Because each woman knew that they might never see their man again, and so they wept."

Then the couple embraces and kisses as the camera pans up and away.

The train moved onward as I wept silently with eyes closed.